Indiana authors

FC17 10/02

W9-BZV-358

# IN THE RIVER SWEET

ALSO BY PATRICIA HENLEY

Fiction

*Worship of the Common Heart: New and Selected Stories*

*Hummingbird House*

*The Secret of Cartwheels*

*Friday Night at Silver Star*

Poetry

*Back Roads*

*Learning to Die*

# IN THE
# RIVER SWEET

## PATRICIA HENLEY

*Pantheon Books  New York*

Copyright © 2002 by Patricia Henley

All rights reserved under International and Pan-American Copyright Conventions. Published in the United States by Pantheon Books, a division of Random House, Inc., New York, and simultaneously in Canada by Random House of Canada Limited, Toronto.

Pantheon Books and colophon are registered trademarks of Random House, Inc.

Grateful acknowledgment is made to Yale University Press for permission to reprint an excerpt from *The Tale of Kiều,* by Nguyễn Du, translated and annotated by Huỳnh Sanh Thông. Copyright © 1983 by Yale University. Reprinted by permission of Yale University Press.

Library of Congress Cataloging-in-Publication Data

Henley, Patricia.
In the river sweet / Patricia Henley.
p. cm.
ISBN 0-375-42127-0
1. Vietnamese Conflict, 1961–1975—Children—Fiction.
2. Lesbians—Family relationships—Fiction.   3. Americans—Vietnam—Fiction.   4. New Orleans (La.)—Fiction.
5. Catholic women—Fiction.   6. Married women—Fiction.
7. Orphans—Fiction.   8. Indiana—Fiction.   I. Title.
PS3558.E49633 I5 2002      813'.54—dc21      2002022018

www.pantheonbooks.com

Book design by M. Kristen Bearse

Printed in the United States of America
First Edition
2 4 6 8 9 7 5 3 1

FOR KATHLEEN AND CHARLEY

Do not fear to put thy feet
Naked in the river sweet.
Think not leech, or newt, or toad
Will bite thy foot, when thou hast trod.
Nor let the water rising high
As thou wad'st in, make thee cry
And sob, but ever live with me
And not a wave shall trouble thee.

*—John Fletcher*

# IN THE RIVER SWEET

# 1

Jesus would not say fag, she knew that much.

Father Carroll said it. Limbo had laughed but Limbo did not know any better. His job was to make sure the johns were clean before Mass. He carried the cleaning supplies in a wooden box like a toolbox and whenever Ruth Anne walked by she could smell the disinfectant—waxy, nearly toxic—the same odor there had been in her church growing up. It was a comfort to her.

The boys and the girls from the college had come to Father Carroll and they wanted to put a sticker—a decal—on the church door. The decal was a symbol of them. They wanted to put the decal on the door and it would let everyone know—all of them—that they were welcome at St. Joan's. They wanted a decal on every church and every restaurant and every public space in Tarkington but that was quite a bit to hope for. She tried to tell Laurel that.

Father Carroll had said no. We can't do that. I understand your cause, he said, but the bishop would not approve. He foisted it off on the bishop. He wanted to be liked, even by them.

In the lunchroom, where they counted the Sunday collection, Ruth Anne wiped up a few granules of instant coffee Limbo had spilled. She gripped a sour sponge in her hand. A jackhammer vibrated outside the narrow window. Orange cones surrounded the jackhammer and the few cars dipped around the man who operated it. Finals were over; most of the students had left for the summer, and the streets and restaurants and dance clubs and parks were empty without them. Limbo hunched at the table, poking at the numbers on his cell phone with the eraser end of a pencil, waiting for his mother to pick him up. Once in a while he would hiss *Yesss* to the game he played against himself. She was sure Father Carroll said it; he shook his head. It was the same way Limbo said Bless their little hearts when he heard gossip. Bless their hearts. It can't be helped.

Laurel had said it can't be helped when she told Ruth Anne and Johnny. They called it coming out. She came out. Laurel was their only child and she came out. Their baby. They still called her our baby the way you do. Joking. But meaning it too. Laurel had said, I'm twenty-four years old and I want what you have. Love and affection. She and Oceana were together every day. Johnny had introduced Oceana to Laurel when Oceana worked at Brambles the summer before. He hired her to work beside him in the kitchen, deboning chicken or chopping scallions, so that he could devote himself to the finer points. Hard sauces and marinades. Roasted garlic. Laurel had gone up the hill to borrow a cup of dried cherries. They called it borrowing when they took a half-dozen eggs or fruit from Brambles' big kitchen but they never gave back what they borrowed. That was last July. Not quite a year. July, when the night sky would be green-blue like handblown glass until nearly ten o'clock. On break Oceana in her whites would smoke a cigarette on the brick patio behind the kitchen and Laurel would sit beside her in a metal chair that left a pink grid on the backs of her thighs and Ruth Anne would know she'd been up there again when she saw the pink grid. They would talk. Johnny had said he saw Laurel patting Oceana's cheek.

It was all right to want a decal on every church, but you had to be realistic. We start with a fag decal and where will it end, Father Carroll said. Where?

She did not tell Johnny.

If she told him, they would go off on it and they would talk about it for hours. If Laurel only knew the way they whispered. They wanted to understand the coming out and they talked about how they had brought her up and the boys she had skateboarded with and whether being a tomboy had anything to do with it even though they knew it didn't. Ruth Anne had done the research at the public library. The books were stacked beside their bed.

Johnny's truck shimmied at high speeds. They took the back roads to get to River County where the round barns were. Johnny felt at peace among them. No matter how many times they went out there he always said that the Shakers were the first to build barns round to keep the evil spirits from accumulating in the corners. River County was the round barn capital of the world.

At his favorite place beside a red barn surrounded by wild rye, he sprayed a halo of repellent to kill the chiggers and mosquitoes. The river lazed beyond the barn and if it were early spring they could hear the high river, but not now, in June. In June the river was flat and if they walked all the way down to it the unending whine of the insects would make Ruth Anne anxious. Johnny would not make her stay on the river-bank long. He never wanted her to be anxious or unhappy. He only wanted to see the green river to know it was there.

He spread the old quilt on the ground. There was a certain pleasure in seeing what he had packed for them to eat. He lifted everything out of a basket and set it down in a way she could tell he had imagined as he packed. Two cheeses and a loaf of herb bread with cuts across the crust that had split and blistered as it baked. Red wine with real wineglasses. Radishes trimmed like rosettes. A dessert to knock your socks off, he said. A miniature lemon tart.

They sat down on the quilt in the rye—the new green and the nod-ding dry stalks from last year. No one would see them and Johnny liked that about this particular place. He had inquired at the round barn mu-seum and found out that the owner lived in Minneapolis. The night was held at bay by the sunset on the taller gone-to-seed rye and they were in a bowl of it: dusky, romantic. She was happy he had brought the big quilt, for the big quilt would keep her from touching the rye which looked lovely but felt like wire brushes if you came in contact with it. She saw Johnny as he had been when they were young. This was not imagination; on the contrary, as Johnny talked, the decades would peel away; she hoped he saw her in the same light. At first they would talk about domestic issues. Was Laurel at home and was Oceana's orange Nova parked in the driveway? Had Moxie been walked? But after two scant glasses of merlot Johnny could get her to take off her blouse and she had known they were going to the round barns when she dressed that morning and she wore a blouse that would encourage him to ask her. She wore a blouse she knew looked good on her: red, with her red hair. And beneath that, a camisole. Johnny loved a camisole and this one was cream-colored stretch lace and he pretended to count the freckles below her collarbone before he slipped the straps down.

They fooled around on the old quilt. Johnny brought two pillows from the lockbox of his truck and they fooled around in what felt like the first night of summer in River County. The round barn did not disappear into the dark but became more substantial, blackish red, with the full moon above, its light shining down like a gossamer top hat.

She did not exactly forget to tell him about her bones but she let that news dwindle when Johnny slipped her straps down. What the doctor had said dwindled and what Father Carroll had said dwindled. What was good about sex was the forgetting of all her cares and woes. Johnny fed her wine and brought her into the married moment: he had his ways.

Let's do a loop, he said when they had packed up the truck. They swerved in the gravel and took a drive along the river to a T that meant they were going the long way back. They rolled their windows down. Johnny sang an Irish song he had learned from his mother, "Peg o' My Heart." Was he thinking about her or was he simply singing the song? Johnny could get stuck in time if he brooded about his mother; she had left when he was ten years old and she had become just another part of history he did not want to know about. If anyone asked about his mother he would make that clear in no uncertain terms. But he was in good spirits and Ruth Anne did not think he was about to brood. He was only flinging his voice to the barns and the barn swallows and the bats.

They stopped at the frozen custard near Delphi. The digital thermometer at the bank across the street read 83 degrees. Blue lights zapped the insects that swarmed around the frozen custard. Kids who were still too young to drive loitered on the concrete tables, eating boatsful of ice cream. Johnny got out and brought them cones and they sat in the cab of the truck eating them in the blue insect light. The news about her bones picked at her and finally she told him.

Her old doctor—a woman with horses and property—had fallen in love at the age of sixty-three and closed her practice and moved to the Upper Peninsula.

That morning she had missed the old doctor from the vantage point of an examination table in the new doctor's office. Goose pimples crept over her legs and arms under the thin cotton gown. A poster of a koala bear had been tacked above the table with the stirrups where the new doctor would make her press her heels: Hang in there, baby. She had always gone to the old doctor and the old doctor had been there for her when Laurel was born and she had been there when Ruth Anne was sick afterward from the IUD and she had been there during the surgery even though a specialist had performed the surgery. Her old doctor had held her hand as the sedative took effect before they wheeled her into the operating room for the surgery that meant she could not have any more babies. She had been only thirty years old. A priest long gone had told them it was all right to use birth control and they had believed him. She paid the price for that. The old doctor knew all about Ruth Anne's body; she had been a patient with a three-inch file; no one had asked about her reproductive history since before Laurel was born in 1974.

A chubby, blue-eyed nurse entered the examination room. How're we doing? she said. And, Let's check your height to see if you're shrinking. She giggled. Ruth Anne wanted to say, spitefully, Didn't they teach you not to say such things? She stood tall, stretching her spine as if an invisible cord tugged at her from the heavens, and she measured as she thought she always had, around five feet six inches. The snappy nurse stood with Ruth Anne's chart on a clipboard pressed against her belly and the questions began. Later, Ruth Anne felt certain the nurse never dreamed she would provoke a lie.

Number of live births?

Adrenaline irrigated Ruth Anne's body, the urge to bolt, to slip into the pink paper flip-flops the nurse had given her and walk right out the door.

One, she said.

Her voice sounded meek and true. It was a lie she had not told in a long time. Only one baby had made its wet and malleable way down that birth canal, she lied. Only one baby had pawed at her breasts, rooted there, red-faced.

That was the part she kept to herself when she got around to telling

Johnny at the frozen custard what the doctor said about her bones. She always had and always would keep that to herself.

For a long time Ruth Anne thought that God had punished her for using birth control, but Laurel had patiently talked her out of that.

Laurel taught composition at the college for a pittance and she still lived at home. After dinner she and Ruth Anne would sometimes sit on the deck that looked away toward the golf course and they would talk into the night while Johnny closed. The lights of Brambles up the hill were cozy yellow squares in a long row. They might have the telephone beside them on a redwood table and Johnny might call after he counted out what was in the register and he might call again while he waited for the boy or girl who mopped to finish. Johnny was owner and chef and manager and always close to home. He was up the hill, not far, but he would call to say hello to them, his girls. Moxie might be lying there beside them, in dog dreams. Late in the summer, fireflies would curlicue among the burning bushes. And Laurel would explain to her what God could mean if people were not so dead set on the stories in the Bible. Hominids walked the earth 3.6 million years ago. Their footprints were found in Tanzania in the 1970s. If you believe that, how can you believe the literal Bible stories? Thinking that the Holy Spirit only worked through the people who wrote the Bible is just another form of idolatry, Laurel said. Don't you think the Holy Spirit could work through someone now? Don't you think new books could be written and added to the Bible? Don't you think the Holy Spirit works through people of other religions? These were ideas she brought home from free lectures given by professors from out-of-state.

If she believed what Laurel said, Ruth Anne might lose her part-time job at the church and what mattered to her—receiving Jesus on her tongue and marking the seasons with the liturgy. Laurel said that whatever is out there in the sky is also within us. Or we are in it. Our sinews, bones, blood, and hair. That's eternal life. Her bones were already part of the cosmos, but that was no consolation.

Ruth Anne would imagine telling other truths she might be forgiven for. The photograph was in a cinnabar basket, the smoky red lacquer carved with dragons. She could picture it; she knew just where it was in the attic closet: hidden on a shelf behind Laurel's girlhood dresses. A christening gown, a first communion dress, a confirmation dress. *Tell* her, *tell* her, a voice would insist from within and that voice had been there since Laurel was thirteen or fourteen, a long time to be tormented during the talks on the deck. She imagined saying, There's something I have to tell you. Or, There's something you need to know. But she never did. She could not bear the unpredictability of telling the truth. After Laurel had gone to bed or after Laurel had gone indoors to grade freshman essays, Ruth Anne might have a spell.

He was a man now.

Whenever she told the lie or whenever she did not tell the truth that kept insisting to be told, a blank-faced boy or a blank-faced teenager or now a blank-faced man rose before her like a bad dream. His features would be erased. Her throat would tighten when she remembered him. Her arms would feel again the giving away to his grandmother and her breasts would feel the glut of milk she had to stop with the long muslin bandages. Her nipples prickled in memory. She might bring a box of tissues to the deck and cry her way through the box and later Johnny would saunter down the hill, whistling contentedly, and when he saw her in the light that dimly lit the deck he would know from the look on her face that she was having a spell. Johnny had stopped asking why a long time ago. They reserved hard liquor for grief or emergencies and Johnny might make her a strong drink and sit beside her until the spell was over. He would hold her hand. Not speaking until she stopped crying. Then he might whisper words of love that sounded like a foreign tongue for all she felt them at that moment.

The sign loomed ahead at the edge of the airstrip, lit by a floodlight shining from the ground up. VIETNAM VETS GATHERING. OCTOBER 10–12.

The airstrip was a long, weedy field with broken tarmac and a limp wind sock. In a corrugated metal hangar a droplight cast a white skirt over the engine of a plane that had been set up on a plywood table. A lone man in a blue mechanic's jumpsuit leaned over the engine. Johnny hoped that Ruth Anne would not notice the sign and he hoped that they would not have to talk about it.

He turned on the radio. Music he thought of as hard-edged blurted from the radio and he pushed the button to scan the stations until he found what he thought they both would enjoy: the blues hour.

He had heard her out about what the doctor said.

Before you get worked up, see what the bone test says. Wait and see.

He wants me to stop cycling. He wants me to walk instead. He wants me to jump off the deck over and over. For the impact.

So many times he had watched her push her bicycle out to the flat section of the driveway beyond the copse of birches. She would swing one leg over the bicycle seat and look both ways on the county road before settling into her ride to work. He could see in the dart of her body that she left her worries behind. She felt like a kid again. Now the doctor had scared her with the story of a woman who was bedridden. He said that when the bedridden woman reached around and gripped her spine it felt like sand.

That woman's thirty years older than you are, hon.

But still.

I know, he said, taking her hand. By then they had passed the VIET-NAM VETS sign and he knew she would not bring it up.

He could not get the old doctor out of his mind. He kept forgetting that Ruth Anne had a new doctor. The old doctor knew all about them and their troubles. It was some relief that she was gone, though he would never say that. When she was sick from the IUD the old doctor had looked at him as if it were his fault that she had chosen the IUD. Johnny had not had an opinion about the method. He had left that up to Ruth Anne when she went to the birth control clinic downtown.

Having sex did not feel the same when he thought there was not the possibility of making a baby. It was not better or worse; it was just different. When they had first been married and wanted babies he had been shocked at the way it felt inside her when he thought she might get pregnant. He thought of destiny as female and he was in her grasp. He could not get over how their life might change irrevocably as a result of that one urge that one night. He had wanted babies. He and Ruth Anne had been only children and they wanted what they did not have growing up: the many voices clamoring, children on a bed in pastel PJs, smelling clean, waiting to have their hair brushed and a story told, the winter sledding parties, the sand castles.

Johnny's family line was sparse; the men had died young on both sides. His great-grandfather from Galway had died building the Brooklyn Bridge; he fell into the river and his body was never recovered. That was the story that stayed with him as a boy. You could die working. Johnny had always worked in kitchens and he thought of them as safe havens.

Except in the rangers. In the rangers he had been trained to whisper without being heard and he had been trained to use a compass and he had been trained to operate a radio and send the worst messages life had to offer. That was so long ago that what he remembered were patches, nothing continuous, nothing like a newsreel. A field of opium poppies in the valley below. Fish nibbling infected flesh from his back.

Before that he had thought, You will live to have babies and grandbabies.

But grandbabies were not in the cards for him. He knew that now. Out of the blue he said to Ruth Anne, I guess we'll never have grandchildren.

She looked at him sharply, as if she'd been drifting someplace faraway, and her face shone coppery in the mercury lights from a new mall on the east edge of town. They were almost home. The radio played Bonnie Raitt, a song she sang before she quit drinking, a song about love gone wrong. Ruth Anne said, Some of them do have babies.

The miracle of modern medicine, Johnny said, and they laughed. He was grateful they could manage a laugh about it.


At the house Laurel and Oceana were cooking Chinese.

Ruth Anne could smell the prickly ash—a little like pepper or bergamot—before she stepped into the kitchen. There was a hullabaloo upon their arrival, with Moxie on his stiff-from-sleep arthritic legs limping over to greet them and be greeted and Oceana and Laurel in a hug at the stove that looked to Ruth Anne too intimate as they extricated from it, blushing. The window A/Cs belched like the sound a tuba emits; the fans whirred and clicked. Johnny excused himself to trudge up the hill and check on all that might have gone wrong in the big kitchen without him there to oversee. Was he excusing himself, Ruth Anne wondered, because the kitchen at the house felt too cramped to contain them and their daughter and her girlfriend? That's what they would say: girl-friend. Oceana willowy in shorts and a tank top. Laurel in a once white apron with CHAT and a blue cat on the bodice.

We've been to meditation, Laurel said, by way of explaining why they were cooking late.

Oh?

A Buddhist nun's visiting, Oceana said. She licked her fingers and wiped them on a tea towel she had slung over one shoulder. Here, look, she said, handing Ruth Anne a photograph of the nun who smiled radiantly, her face nut-brown, her black hair nearly not there, a buzz cut. Her voluminous maroon robe the color of dried blood.

Ruth Anne sat down at the table and Laurel said, Your button.

Hmm?

Laurel grinned and said, Your blouse is buttoned wrong.

Ruth Anne looked down and redid the top three pearly buttons on the red blouse. She felt the wine now. She was a little sorry she had drunk two glasses. Her paperback book was upstairs and she wanted to be already in bed with her book and no one keeping her from reading until she fell asleep. She asked for aspirin and water and Oceana, ever solicitous, brought them to her at the table. A wheel of lemon floated in the refrigerated water.

Are you all right, Laurel said, fingering tofu cubes into a skillet of smoking oil.

It's hot is all.

We heard what Father Carroll said about the decal.

Ruth Anne fanned her face with a catalog. That couldn't have come as a big surprise to you.

No, but still. We hoped against hope.

I'm awful tired, Ruth Anne said.

We can talk tomorrow, Oceana offered. It can wait.

Ruth Anne went upstairs to her bedroom. Laurel followed her. An ancient window unit struggled against the gathering heat on the second floor. The skylight was moist with humidity but the colors were cool. Pale grassy walls and a gray cotton counterpane. Sisal rugs. Out the casement window waved heart-shaped catalpa leaves lit by the porch light.

What's up? Ruth Anne said.

Can Oceana spend the night?

Don't ask.

We could sleep downstairs on the sofa bed.

Ruth Anne placed her hands gently on Laurel's cheeks. She was close enough to smell the herbal soap Laurel used. Sweetie—

Laurel jerked away. Never mind. She turned with a dismissive shrug and clattered down the stairs.

She would be mad and she would swell up like a toad, Aunt Teensy would've said. You'll get glad again. You will. Ruth Anne saw no point in going after her and she turned off the A/C and opened a window and undressed. Her heavy hair felt damp, irritating, one more irritating thing, and she braided it to keep it off her neck and shoulders. She lay in the dark, listening. A breeze came up and shook the catalpa hearts. She felt her own heartbeat and she thought about her bones growing porous and what the doctor had said. Johnny would call it a day of Critical Mass if he had been privy to all that she mulled over. By Critical Mass he meant one worry piggybacks on another. They had gone to meditation. Would Laurel still be Catholic if she went to meditation? The lie she had told at the doctor's office came back like a slap in the face. She pushed away the thought of him and the cinnabar basket carved with dragons. She wanted to sleep. She wanted Johnny in the bed ASAP. Johnny's touch and his chest a place to lay her head could keep her from a spell if he came to bed in time.

In a while she heard the Nova sputtering to life and the crunch of the Nova's tires over cinders. The girls were smart with their degrees and Ruth Anne had never finished hers and it had always bothered her. On Saturdays she worked in reserves at the public library and she had first dibs on every single book acquired by the library. That did not make up for not finishing her degree. Once she had known French, enough to read Flaubert aloud. The girls were smart and yet they hadn't figured out that Father Carroll's attitude was the prevalent attitude. Safety was not an option for them, decal or no. If you heard fag from a man like Father Carroll, who wouldn't you hear it from? You could not avoid those words in Tarkington but ten years ago they were a rarity. Gay. Queer. Dyke. Limbo would repeat it; Father Carroll should have thought of that. He repeated whatever he heard like a two-year-old. Father Carroll said it one way and Laurel and Oceana said it another way. She was no longer taken aback by their queer jokes. It had been almost a year. She had grown accustomed to them. They would laugh at the pamphlet put out by fundamentalists and she would wonder where the pamphlet came from, but they never said. Oceana would read aloud, If you are one of those fools who goes around parroting that God loves everyone, this world's condition is your fault. They laughed. Don't be one of those fools who thinks that God loves everyone. Yellow, red, black, or white. Straight or dyke. On the refrigerator they had taped a postcard of a protester at a lesbian wedding. A heavy-set woman in a sharkskin cape carried a picket sign: BRIDES OF SATAN. The woman had been on a treadmill of fury forever. You could see it in her face.

She thought about getting up again. She thought about cleaning. She had become the kind of woman who might get up in the middle of the night and scour the stovetop with cleanser. There was satisfaction in it.

Johnny slipping down her camisole straps in the sunlit rye by the round barn seemed a million miles away.

# 2

Limbo's given name was Henry.

When he was five years old he danced the limbo at a wedding and ever after would not answer to Henry. In warm weather he would wait at the library's back door for Ruth Anne to open up, his headphones slightly askew, his CDs in a silvery pile on the concrete step. The young women who worked out at the Y would be getting out of their cars in tight pink leotards or running shorts and jogging bras and Limbo would furtively watch them and bop to his music, toes tapping, until he heard Ruth Anne's bicycle clicking as she wheeled it up the ramp the people in wheelchairs used. He would close his eyes to slits and pretend he had not noticed the women going in. Ruth Anne felt an urgency to get there, knowing he would be waiting. Limbo had been ten years old when he started waiting there every Saturday and now he was seventeen.

She pedaled across the river bridge and through the placid streets. Monday she would start to follow the doctor's orders. Monday would be soon enough to walk. When she thought about it her body felt molasseslike, as if she might sit right down on the road or sidewalk and melt. She knew those fast walkers in their sweat suits, chattering away, their gray hair rinsed with colors called Champagne or Sunset, and she had smugly rolled her bicycle past them and now the doctor said she must be among them. The bone-density test was a week hence. The doctor had not said how it worked and she hoped it would not hurt or be humiliating. It would not be so bad as a mammogram, surely, where the technician never smiles and treats your breasts and all the muscles surrounding them like meat, pressing them into a plastic vise while you hold your breath, never crying out, although you feel like it. She hoped she would not have to answer questions she did not want to answer.

Humidity had clung like a soft rind to the land all night before. At two o'clock and five o'clock she had gotten up and looked out the bedroom window, willing Laurel to come home, but Laurel had not come home. Ruth Anne did not want to ride past Oceana's apartment on Nebraska Street but she could feel a tug in that direction. Her heart sped up thinking about it. She would be prying and she did not want to pry when she thought about it in the abstract but she felt the tug nonetheless toward the tumbledown house on Nebraska. Oceana was still a student and she had not settled down. She studied horticulture and she would get a job somewhere else and she would leave town. Leave Laurel. For safety's sake Ruth Anne could justify riding by the house to see what she could see. If the Nova were there she would breathe a sigh of relief. Oceana's apartment was on the second floor, with a magnolia tree—its leaves dark and durable—just below the long Italianate window. One morning in April, Ruth Anne had seen them locked in each other's arms at the window. They could not get close enough.

She ran a red light and cut behind a charity store down an alley to Nebraska. Even though Limbo would be waiting she did not have to open until almost eight-thirty. She would manage by herself until half-past nine when the clerk named Daisy would come just in time for the Saturday morning rush. Daisy would move like a mountain in her beaded sweater set and settle behind the circulation desk, where she would try to avoid getting up again until lunchtime. Her bosom resting on the counter; her rings and glassy fingernails sparkling in the fluorescent light. She would have smoked a cigarette on the back steps right before her shift began and then she would smell ashy all morning. Daisy's stolid presence always came as a surprise to Ruth Anne; she never saw her anywhere but at the library. Daisy lived with her father in a suburb east of town past a superstore. Sometimes she brought flowers from her garden in a Mason jar: daffs or California poppies or zinnias. Limbo made her nervous, even after all these years. It was always Ruth Anne and Daisy on Saturday; the librarian never came in; he trusted Ruth Anne to be accountable. If she rode by the house on Nebraska, the muffin she carried in her rucksack for Limbo would be cool by the time she saw him but he would not mind. She almost always brought Limbo a bit of whatever they had for breakfast, a muffin or Danish or a slice of homemade bread dripping with butter and jam. She would first wrap it in a paper towel printed with flowerpots and then tuck it inside a sandwich bag. Limbo would eat the breakfast treat and then he would find a quiet nook somewhere in the library, near the newspaper racks or at a microfiche machine not in use, and there he would clip his fingernails and wrap the clippings in the paper towel. A tight little packet. This he would present to Ruth Anne when he asked her to check out his CDs and books. He would say, Your fingernails keep right on growing after you die. He read children's books about dinosaurs and baseball. Ruth Anne always said thank you and she never acted as if there were anything the least bit strange about receiving his fingernail clippings. There was something wrong with Limbo. He had been hard to adopt and the woman who was his mother now had picked him from a picture book of hard-to-adopt children in Indianapolis. Limbo's mother worked in a greenhouse on the east side not far from the library and her ex trimmed trees out in the county. Ruth Anne imagined that once they had shared a dream about family to go to the trouble to adopt Limbo but now it was Father Carroll who took Limbo to baseball games in Chicago twice a summer.

Whenever she thought *hard to adopt,* a feeling like the fear of dying would work its evil all over her body. Her son would not have been hard to adopt but the words brought him to mind. He had been a beautiful baby. She would sometimes wonder why Limbo had become attached to her and she could not help but think that Limbo had been put in her life to remind her of him. He would be older than Limbo. He would be older than Laurel. Lately, young men reminded her of him. She could not stop thinking, Would he be like you? Would he be like the man who checked out travel books for Argentina last Saturday? Would he be like the man who delivers artichokes and lettuce to the restaurant? She had no right to think of him as kind or smart or curious or ethical. She had relinquished all rights.

I'm coming, Limbo.

A block from Oceana's building was the wild house. Boys lived there. A pair of Converse sneakers had been flung up to the electric wires and dangled where starlings twittered. Yellow extension cords lay tangled on the porch. She had seen them on the porch playing their guitars and keyboards, with the menacing black speakers set up in the yard. Their amplified music like trucks crashing. The day they moved in she had come out of the library after work into blinding evening sunlight and when she swung her leg over the frame and cast her body and bicycle homeward a boy at the wild house had shouted, Show us your tits. She had not told anyone and it never happened again. No one was about now. They were not morning people.

The library's neighborhood was in a poor fettle. Down the block she pedaled past a permanent yard sale, with doughy easy chairs left out in the weather and bicycle parts sorted in piles—hard black seats and tires without inner tubes. Dogs staked on short chrome chains would rise and bare their teeth when she rode by. Once ladies in straw gardening hats had invited Ruth Anne to step into their cottage gardens and view the delphiniums. Once Johnny would not have given a thought to her working until after dark. From October until May it would be dark when she traversed the cobblestone streets to head home where Johnny made her feel protected.

A Volkswagen bus was parked in front of Oceana's building, its rear end plastered with bumper stickers: FLUSH RUSH and WWF and IT TAKES A VILLAGE and FREE TIBET. But no Nova. She got off her bicycle and wheeled it around to the back of the house to peek into the garage, for they had a three-car garage, its metal doors dented and the short driveway to it overgrown with volunteer bluestem grass. You could still get in to park a car and she would peek inside and go.

A black cat with a white ring around one hind leg sat licking its paw on the sidewalk. The morning newspaper lay on the bottom step leading up to the back porch. No one was about but the cat. He meowed at her. She walked her bicycle alongside the garage windows that faced the side street and her eyes did not adjust at first to the grimy windows but then after a moment she was able to see inside: the Nova had been pulled into the garage beside a riding lawn mower she could not imagine they had any use for. Of course they were in the house, safe and sound. Sleeping or tenderly holding each other or doing whatever they did for sex. She did not want to think about that. She leaned her bicycle against the garage door and went over stealthily to the cat and petted him. This is where my daughter goes for love and affection. She sat down on the top concrete step and listened, almost holding her breath for someone to shuffle out for the newspaper, but no one was about. Somewhere a clothes-dryer tumbled; that might have been next door. She smelled the lemony fabric-softener. What she hoped is that the girls knew how to keep a secret. It took practice. She had not even told a priest at reconciliation. It used to be called confession and it did not feel the same. It did not feel cleansing. Her heart could never be cleansed. Whenever she went she had to find a way to live with it. Don't tell. Don't tell. The longtime lie was a callus growing over her heart. She had wanted Laurel to have a life that did not require keeping secrets but it was too late for that. She hoped they had not stood at the window last night in each other's arms for the world to see. With one hand she petted the cat and with the other she shook open the morning paper. A sheaf of grocery coupons slipped down to the crooked sidewalk.

There on the front page was a color photograph of the Unitarian Church with FAG CHURCH spray-painted on its brick wall. Once she had accidentally taken an overdose of vitamin B and in a panic she had felt the blood rush to her head and in the mirror her face and neck had been bathed in a rash like a birthmark and she had that feeling now, sitting on the quiet steps with the wild house down the block silent in sleep and only the cat meowing, unable to be comforted. She knew that brick wall and cycled past it often. Redbuds grew in a crescent beside the wall in spring and now geraniums bloomed forth in cement bins. The spray paint and the geraniums had become the exact same color on the front page of the newspaper: a cheap red. Bleeding around the edges if you looked real close. If you let the shapes recede and the sound the words made in your mind and what the words evoked—if all that faded and you knew nothing of fags—you might go on to the secondary articles, the news of a refurbished public pool or health department violations. You might think, That has nothing to do with me and my secrets.

Did you see it? Limbo said. Did you?

See what?

The paper, he said, grinning. Did you see the paper?

I did.

Mama said, See. I told you.

And what did she tell you?

Mama said, If a church put up the decal there'll be trouble. You know. Like Father Carroll said.

He knew he was not supposed to say fag. Someone had made that clear to him. With one hand he picked at the words WRIGLEY FIELD on his T-shirt and he put his other hand in his pants pocket so that he could touch himself without her seeing. When he was a boy he would grab his penis when he was excited or worried but his mother and Father Carroll and just about everyone who knew him had told him over and over that he could go to jail if he kept that up when he was grown. Limbo understood about jail. He read adventure comics and he understood jail and criminality.

It's a terrible thing, Ruth Anne said.

It's terrible.

No one has the right, she said, to paint words on the church.

It's not our church.

Nonetheless.

Nonetheless.

They will get in trouble. You understand that, don't you, Limbo?

Yes, ma'am, Ruth Anne.

She opened the library door and he took off his baseball cap and crammed it in his rear pocket. Ruth Anne walked through, flipping on light switches, and Limbo right behind her came along silently. He felt chastised, she thought, and that was all right. You had to be direct with Limbo.

After she had given him the muffin and watched him get settled in the magazine corner, after Daisy came in and clomped by leaving the smoky smell in her wake, Ruth Anne called Johnny in the big kitchen. He said he had his hands in bread dough; he would call her back.

Her eyes roamed fretfully over the blue reserve cards tightly packed in an oak card catalog drawer. She ran her fingers over them. Her breath caught in her throat. She made a cup of tea; she was allowed to have tea at her station. She was in charge on Saturdays. All the new books, wrapped in stiff cellophane, had been piled neatly beside her on a cart. *Oxygen Man*. A book about bees. *Exploring Bali*. A biography of Al Gore. Kids' books. Cookbooks. Science fiction novels that might be checked out once and never find their way back. Sunlight through the stained glass window dappled her station. It was an elegant and cramped Carnegie library from the early 1900s and once she had admired it nearly every time she went inside but now she was used to it and she knew its afflictions—the windows swollen shut with dampness and the crack in the basement where smelly water seeped in during the spring and the congested feel when schoolchildren crowded in to write their reports.

Laurel as a little girl kept floating through her mind. Her skateboard clacking to the floor of the utility room. Her rosy cheeks and the morning petals of breath on Ruth Anne's arm when she came into their bed to cuddle. Her love of Moxie—she would hug Moxie like family. The books they read aloud. Her vulnerabilities. Her schoolmates had called her Crybaby. She had wept for dead possums on the road.

The tea burnt her tongue. She watched the black telephone.

The computer screen was beige and soporific, like new luggage, like something neat and clean and never been scuffed. She idly tapped GET MESSAGES and there were requests from patrons. There was a message from an elementary school teacher insisting that her request for a book supersede all others. Jill had written. Sister Jill, though Ruth Anne never called her that, for she had been only Jill two years ahead of her in high school and a neighbor at Pier Cove. She had been only Jill when they had gone to Vietnam and only Jill when they came home. She had gone into the convent later. Ruth Anne saw her two or three times a year. She would drive to Michigan to see Jill in her monastery in a grove of cypress trees beside Lake Michigan. Our Lady of Holy Mysteries. Ruth Anne might take her bicycle and Laurel's bicycle and the two of them, Jill and Ruth Anne who had been girls together so long ago, might ride the bicycle path that curls like a giant wood shaving along the shore of Lake Michigan. They had done that three years ago and Jill wanted to do it again. Jill knew her secret and she never mentioned it. A half-formed knowledge visited her whenever she saw Jill's return address on an envelope or whenever she saw an e-mail pop up from Jill: she would have gone to the monastery more often if Jill had not known her secret. If only she did not know. It is work to be around people who know your secrets. It is work to keep a secret and when she saw the message from Jill, for a splinter of a moment, she thought only of the work of ignoring the secret when they were together. Jill's name on the innocuous computer screen brought all that back to her. But she loved Jill just the same. She was not a person you could stop seeing. There are some people you love so much that you will do the work of keeping secrets when you're in their company.

They still called themselves girls.

Ruth Anne Porter and her friends, Jill and Sue-Sue. She had not had friends like Jill and Sue-Sue since then. Sue-Sue was dead, and Jill worked in the monastery's nursing home as a social worker to the frail and the dying.

In the sixties they wore each other's clothes and shared their lipsticks and their combs. They slept over in the same featherbed. Sue-Sue's grave was up in Michigan and Ruth Anne was afraid to go there, afraid to go where memory took her. Her parents were buried there as well, on a pretty rise above the lake, drowned in a rafting accident. But it was Sue-Sue's grave she did not want to visit.

They still called themselves girls.

Early evening thunderheads pooled across the lake, north of Chicago. Greenery—Queen Anne's lace and fireweed and trees of heaven —seemed to vibrate with the storm's approach, seemed to tint the air and the beach green. Lake Michigan below the deck erupted in a grid of steely whitecaps.

Ruth Anne and Sue-Sue were nineteen years old. Jill, twenty-one. Drinking sloe gin straight from a contraband half-pint. Sue-Sue sat astride a hassock and cracked open pistachios with her teeth. Jill huddled under a quilt on the squeaking glider. Ruth Anne lay in the hammock, thinking about Johnny Bond. Now that Johnny himself had been gone for two months, the little-bigger-than-a-pinhead diamond did not feel so light on her ring finger.

Jill said, It's not a big country. If you went over you'd be able to see Johnny.

Just the two of you, Sue-Sue whispered slyly.

Ruth Anne said, I don't even know where Vietnam is.

They teach you all that, Jill said.

I'm not the Red Cross type.

We need a singer, Sue-Sue said. But you can't sing a lick.

Jill said, You have to be twenty-one for the Red Cross anyway.

I have to go back to school. Aunt Teensy would kill me.

Aunt Teensy doesn't give a hoot, Sue-Sue said.

Ruth Anne reared up in the hammock. You don't know that.

Patiently, Jill said, Ruthie. Look at any globe. You'll be thousands of miles from her.

In fact, now that Ruth Anne and Johnny were engaged, Aunt Teensy scrutinized her every move. More than ever. Making sure she did not stray. In their talk about college Aunt Teensy had said only once, Don't depend on a man to pay the bills. But their disputes about sex had been frequent for seven years, slaps and warnings and dire predictions and weeks she had been grounded for the slightest suspicion. It was simply what women said to girls, Ruth Anne thought: a false warning. For they all had done it eventually, given in, with or without benefit of wedlock, and she swore she would never say such things to her daughters, if she had daughters. What haunted her was Aunt Teensy saying, I'll disown you if you get in trouble. I went through that with your mother.

Went through what?

Never mind.

The word disown had a hollow sound, heartbreaking. Whenever Aunt Teensy said it Ruth Anne felt shut out of the house. Tears would rise like a fleshy lump in her chest.

You're smart, Jill said, her voice measured, sticking to the important question. You have to find a way to use the skills you have.

A headlong wind upset a wicker table. The bamboo chime next door went crazy. Sue-Sue said, Scoot over, and Jill rearranged the quilt to fit her under it. Jill looked as innocent as ever, with her hair in frayed plaits. She wore cat's-eye glasses with heavy black frames. Her brother was over there and she wanted to be near him. She had made it clear: she did not know if she supported the war but she wanted to support her brother and the boys like him. Sue-Sue had a daring look on her face, a mask of sex: blue eye shadow and kohl-darkened eyes, her weed brown hair teased into a rat's nest. At the strawberry festival her all-girl band played straight through a hailstorm and a man in a soiled seersucker suit had come up to them and said he wanted to send them to Vietnam to play for the troops. Sue-Sue would do anything. She had gone to a doctor in Grand Rapids wearing a wedding band from Woolworth's and he readily wrote her a prescription for birth control pills.

The night before, Ruth Anne had leaned against a flatbed of cantaloupes in a blue sundress. Last light had slanted across the lake and she knew her legs were visible through the full gauzy skirt. A boy offered her a cigarette. He in his apron stained with strawberries. He was a boy who had not been drafted. It was nearly dark. The boy and Ruth Anne listed toward each other. She had not intended to be there at closing time. Aunt Teensy had sent her down for a bag of yellow onions. She had not intended to stay, lollygagging around the fruit bins, saying, I haven't seen her and don't know where's she's gone, when he asked about a girl they had known years before. They were old enough to talk about a girl they had known years before and that did not seem right. She could picture him in grade school; once he had ringworm on his forehead and his mother had cut off a hank of his hair, just chopped it off, so that air would get to the ringworm and heal it. He had a small uneven scar the size of a grape at his hairline. He was just a boy she had known all her life. He liked to build fires on the beach and sit there poking a stick into the fire and talking. A clique of boys and girls did that now. It was a place to meet. It was a place to watch the moon rise in the sky and on the lake. She and Johnny had built their fires down shore away from everyone in a cove sheltered by weather-beaten white pines and the shadows of the white pines when the moon rose were hideous and she might think she saw hoodlums in the shadows but Johnny was there and Johnny would not let her down. She would burrow into him beside the fire he started with fat kindling he had carried from home. The boy's old man snugged down the rattling doors of the produce stand. Clicked shut a padlock. A quarter-mile away to the east the yellow neon lights of a service station flickered against a blue-black sky. She felt the grit of the engagement ring, its interference with the simplest pleasure: a cigarette with this boy from high school. She wanted to be held and to nudge shoulders and to kiss furtively beside a bonfire on the beach. She could not figure out how Johnny could be so far away and she with want like liquor in her veins could be standing there in the seductive night with a boy she did not care one whit for. Fireflies flashed and a truck went by, the radio spilling a song, brief cheer, across the barrow ditch.

The boy's mother rapped on the kitchen window.

His old man said, Supper. Suppertime, now. They heard the scrape of his shoes on the mat before he entered the house. It was that quiet.

The boy whispered, Will you be at the beach?

I have to work.

She was waiting tables for the summer at an Old English pub in Saugatuck. Aunt Teensy had said she could work in the candy shop but she needed the tips. She wore a uniform supposed to make her look like an English wench. A short apron over a sweltering brown skirt. A blouse with puffy sleeves and an eyelet-trimmed petticoat. She hated it but she needed money for fall term. She needed money to keep from borrowing sweaters and cigarettes.

What about later? He brushed a ladybug off her arm.

His old man opened the screen door. It's time now.

She remembered Johnny: his serious eyes, how much older he seemed in his army uniform, his long arms around her in the grocery store as they shopped for their last meal. Johnny Bond singing love songs the night they were engaged, Johnny Bond in church, letting her precede him up the aisle to communion like a gentleman opening a door, Johnny Bond's birthmark, a spot of white hair the shape of a peanut on the back of his head. That photo down at the dock in town, Johnny in white bucks, his hair still damp, grinning at her. One hundred morning glory seeds soaking in a yellow bowl. The steadfast way he had nicked every seed with a rasp the night before his father drove him to Fort Wayne. Sometimes Aunt Teensy would allow them an hour to themselves while she closed the shop or played a card or two of bingo in the church basement. They would lie in the hammock. That part—the jumble of clothes and Johnny's mouth, his whiskers against her skin— was difficult to recall. But the moon she remembered; the moon had been a flaxen sickle on Lake Michigan.

Sue-Sue would have said yes; she wanted experience and that might mean breaking rules you had made for yourself. Sue-Sue talked big: all rules are negotiable in the dark. Ruth Anne had dropped the cigarette butt and ground it out with the toe of her sandal. About the beach she said to the boy, I can't.

Jill passed her the bottle and said, So, what're you thinking?

Heat lightning flashed in the distance across the lake. The screen door clapped shut: Aunt Teensy coming in. Her lipstick greasy and seeping into the fine wrinkles above her lip, Aunt Teensy would come to the open window and say, without preamble, I never thought I'd end up selling fudge to tourists from Chicago. Or: It was a madhouse. The odor of the shop—sugar and cocoa and butter and vanilla—coated her hair, her skin. Ruth Anne would always think of her skin as buttery.

They saw her pale thin face through the screen door. A man asked me to go dancing. An *old* man— She shuddered. Do I look old enough for him? I guess I do. What business do I have at the Starlight? After I've stood on my feet the livelong day I've got no business there.

No one said anything.

Aunt Teensy felt a duty to Ruth Anne—the obligation to be home at a decent hour. It was a duty that still took her by surprise. She had reared her little sister when their parents passed away and that little sister had gotten pregnant and married a piano tuner and when the baby Ruth Anne had grown to be a girl of twelve, her parents went to Idaho for their first honest-to-God vacation. On the Salmon River they drowned. Aunt Teensy had taken her in. Her mother's room was almost as she had left it. Prom dresses hung in the closet and Ruth Anne had pushed them down the rod and never wanted to get rid of them. She would try the prom dresses on when Aunt Teensy was at work. She would press her nose against the scratchy nylon net to smell her mother.

Aunt Teensy liked her silence; she would want the girls to go home; their unpredictability—giggling or singing along to Motown on the radio—annoyed her.

It's late.

They knew what that meant: five minutes. Aunt Teensy turned and slipped through the darkened living room to the bathroom. Ruth Anne knew that she would absently stop and pick up the artifacts of her life— knickknacks or framed snapshots, beaded bags from the twenties she collected—and she would handle them in the frail light the outdoor lamp let in through the window. She would frown, puzzling over her possessions, as if they held some secret to her existence. The toilet lid banged against the tank.

Ruth Anne lunged from the hammock to the glider and got under the quilt. She passed the half-pint to Sue-Sue who stashed it in her purse. Aware of each other's body heat and the smell of baby oil, they stared out at the gathering storm. I'll do it, Ruth Anne whispered. I'll try to find a way to go.

Sue-Sue said, That's our girl.

Later that night a tornado touched down five miles inland, tearing the roofs from trailers perched above the Kalamazoo. A gas pump blew up and caught fire. Ruth Anne and Aunt Teensy felt the wind grow big, and they got out of bed and met in the living room and Aunt Teensy lit a fire and poured a glass of sherry. They waited out the storm. A kitchen window caved inward with the force, cracking like a shot.

Within the week Ruth Anne drafted a letter to her spiritual director at college. She wrote, Am I being called? Do you think it's the right thing to do? She did not mention Johnny or the engagement ring.

The letter from her spiritual director came late in the summer. The thick cotton paper it was written on had been watermarked with a crown of thorns. She wrote that a visiting French nun had mentioned the need for a volunteer at a convent library in Saigon. The convent had been given crates of books in English and French. The books needed to be bound and catalogued. You have your French, she wrote, and your library skills. It was just as Jill had said: she had skills. She had experience. Her freshman year she had worked at the college library fifteen hours a week for $1.25 an hour. The French nuns would put aside a certain sum for each month she stayed with them and that sum would be hers for college when she returned to the States. Meant to be, Jill said. Sue-Sue laughed and said, Those sisters'll go crazy when Johnny sneaks into the convent. They'll keep a tight rein on you, girl—

Jill's e-mail message was short: Call me. It's about Teensy.

Aunt Teensy was in the nursing home adjacent to Our Lady of Holy Mysteries. Whenever Ruth Anne drove to Michigan and signed in and walked the halls among the half-dead and failing residents, the orderly would tell Aunt Teensy she was there and sometimes Aunt Teensy would send word out: I don't want to see her. Other times she would invite her in and they would watch part of an old movie together. Aunt Teensy favored Gregory Peck and Judy Garland. The silence between them would swell like a fetid growth. Ruth Anne could not bring herself to stay for an entire movie.

Limbo stood at the circulation desk, craning his neck to indicate to Ruth Anne that she should come and check him out. Daisy sat smirking and Ruth Anne knew that Daisy managed her fear of Limbo by looking down her nose at him. She could see into Daisy's soul and she did not want Limbo's feelings to be hurt and she went out immediately to check out his books and to protect him. He handed her the nail clippings in the tiny white packet.

I know they keep on growing, Ruth Anne said.

They do.

What're you doing today?

Limbo said, Chores.

Good for you, Ruth Anne said. When he had gone she turned to Daisy and said, He wouldn't hurt a fly.

Daisy sniffed.

The telephone rang and Ruth Anne went to answer it and Johnny said, Don't worry about that, Ruthie. It was kids. No big deal.

I do worry. She watched the computer screen and wound the telephone cord around one finger.

The paper's hard up for news, you ask me.

What if she doesn't come home?

She lives here. She'll come home.

I went over there.

Don't stoop to that, Johnny said. Then, I have to go, Ruthie. Olive you.

It was what they said to lighten the moment: Olive you. Years before they'd read a string of puns in a magazine: Lettuce live together; I love your radish hair and turnip nose. The others had faded. Only Olive you stuck with them.

Three messages popped up on her computer screen. Me too, she said. Olive you.

She sat down and sipped her tea and the tea had turned cold and had a filmy scum over it and it was not appealing now. It tasted like dirt. Beneath a poster of Reggie Miller reading, Daisy checked out books for the patrons in line. Junior-high girls with their hair tied back in paisley kerchiefs circled the computer station, looking up Britney Spears. Ruth

Anne could keep an eye on them from where she sat. In the children's section a young mother in short shorts knelt down to read to her boy.

All was as it should be; they lived in a peaceful place. She could convince herself of that. It was kids, Johnny said. As if that made it not so bad.

She opened another message.

To: rabond@tarklib.in.gov
From: tt103068@dune.com

Dear Mrs. Ruth Anne,

I believe you are my mother. If you were Ruth Anne Porter in 1968. I am Tin Tran. I was born in Dalat on October 30, 1968. I live in Michigan now. My father and I have lived here since 1989. We are American citizens. My grandmother died in Dalat in 1985. I am Catholic and my father is Buddhist. He says that you know this about him. You are Catholic, he says. We have Catholics among our ancestors. It has taken me a long time to decide that I want to know you. Here is a stanza from a poem by Nguyen Quang Thieu, famous Vietnamese poet.

> *No one sees anyone clearly;*
> *I don't even see myself.*
> *Our voices rise like fish bubbles*
> *As someone casts a crescent along the horizon.*
> *It's the fishhook of dreams*
> *I've swallowed half my life.*

My father believes that you would enjoy these poems, but he does not know that I am contacting you. His heart fails him. I do not want to cause problems for you. But do you want to know me? Have you wondered?

Tin Tran

She reared back, as if the keys had singed her fingertips. Her heart drummed and the voices of the patrons churned around her, the girls giggling, the boy whining at the mother in short shorts. She glanced

around fearfully, although she knew no one but Daisy was allowed behind the circ desk. Her breath quickened and she shivered with cow-
ardice the way you shiver when you're sick. She would not be able to
speak if called upon to speak.

It was the message she had dreaded. It was the message she had
craved.

# 3

It's Saint Jude she prays to, Sister Jill said.

Ruth Anne said, Patron of desperate situations. Her voice was unreliable but Sister Jill did not notice. She wound the telephone cord around her crooked elbow. Her spells on the deck had felt like swimming underwater. Wanting to break the surface and breathe. Now she was allowed to come up and what was it filled her lungs? Breath of fright. Fateful air. The junior-high girls wandered out of the library: a gaggle of nymphs.

She hasn't asked for a priest. And I don't think she's ready for that.

What makes you think so?

She still watches the birds. She's still curious.

If I leave after work, I can be there by nine. She wanted to say, Johnny thinks it was only kids wrote FAG CHURCH on the wall. It was not the right thing to say. It was something to keep to yourself under the circumstances. Aunt Teensy thought she was about to die. All other concerns were supposed to be subsumed or ignored or postponed.

She thinks she's worse than she is. Sister Jill lowered her voice. The main thing is this, Ruthie. She's vulnerable. I think you could make up with her.

The mother in short shorts yanked her boy's arm. He shrieked and his shriek rang throughout the library. Daisy rose from her cushioned stool and leaned her bosom across the counter and reached down and handed the boy a penny sucker.

We'll see about that, Ruth Anne said. And then, Where do the Vietnamese live?

The Vietnamese?

They live in Michigan, don't they?

There's a parish in Cortland with a Vietnamese Mass every Sunday.

Every Sunday.

I think that's right. Why, Ruthie?

I just wondered. We'll have dinner, won't we? When I get there?

I get off right before Vespers. I'll sit and have dinner with the sisters.

Sit?

We meditate now after evening prayer.

Laurel meditates.

Oh?

They meditate with a Buddhist nun. She wished she could pull the words back into her mouth.

They?

Her friend. Oceana.

Oceana. A beautiful name.

It is.

We'll catch up. It's been too long. You could stay in Teensy's room—some family members do—

We're not ready for that.

I can reserve a room for you in the monastery.

Reserve a room for me. Please. We'll have a good visit, won't we?

A thread of joy wove through their talk. Unspoken. It was not necessary to speak of it. They would see each other, confide in each other. Jill was someone she could tell. The news was a visceral state: on her skin, inside her organs. She was different from everyone with this news inside of her.

We'll have a good visit, won't we? With that she remembered Sister Michelle at the convent in Saigon.

The nuns at the convent in Saigon in 1967 had worn brown habits and lace Breton caps and with their habits brushing the floor they had swept from room to decaying room. Sister Michelle had been from the States—the only one close to her age. The others were older and they were French. Sister Michelle had been a California girl before she became a nun and she knew the words to every Elvis Presley tune. Love me tender. That's when your heartaches begin. She read nurse novels. She had not thought of Sister Michelle in a long time and it must have been the thought of Jill coming to her monastery room that made her remember. The rooms at Our Lady of Holy Mysteries where Jill had lived for twenty years were narrow dorm cells with louvered windows you opened for a breeze, and the water from the basin faucets had deposited arrows of rust on the basins. The mattress would be lumpy. The sheets would be ironed. The easy chair would be orange and upholstered in plastic, not the least bit easy. The light would be harsh. They might turn off the light and talk in the dark. She had never told her about Sister Michelle. For a moment she felt the exhaustion of keeping straight what she had told and what she had not.

She said to Johnny, It's Aunt Teensy. She thinks she's dying.

She said to Father Carroll, I can't say for sure if I'll be back on Monday.

She said to Laurel, If she wants you, will you come?

Laurel said, Summer school starts Monday.

This might be it.

I don't like the way she's treated you.

We have to give up our grudges someday. Turn the other cheek was on the tip of her tongue but she did not say it.

Laurel said, She's the one with the grudge. What I feel is less than that.

When I die, I hope I'll be forgiven. She did not say, Forgive me for not letting you sleep over with her.

We have tickets for Bob Dylan. Dad's going with us.

She had forgotten that. In another family with no grudges Laurel would never say that. She would never think the Dylan concert more worthy of her time than her great-aunt dying. Ruth Anne did not blame her. How many times had they taken Laurel to see Aunt Teensy? Laurel was twenty-four years old and she had been taken to visit her aunt Teensy in Michigan every six years or so, like a cycle of nature. In some families decades could pass without true visits. In some families the true visits happen at the funeral parlor.

She wanted to tell Laurel. She wanted to say brother.

While Laurel at twelve sat bored in the cottage beside the lake in her Sunday best—a long shimmering shift and sandals—Ruth Anne and Johnny had stiffly built a conversation like a fence. Aunt Teensy had let them talk. She had been thin and she had taken up smoking. The cottage reeked of cigarette smoke. A patina of nicotine had soaked into the furniture. Ruth Anne all the while hoped that Teensy would not say nigger or slut in front of Laurel or that she would not rave about welfare cheats. She wondered where Aunt Teensy kept the letters she had written from Saigon. She wanted to ask about the prom dresses but she did not. Her hands itched to take up the photographs of her mother and father on the buffet. What she would have given to own one of those photographs. To search the eyes of her mother. Three snapshots had been placed in a row in one brass frame. Her mother on the hood of a car, laughing. In a one-piece bathing suit at the lake's edge. Pregnant, in a wool coat with square buttons, a scarf tied around her full head of hair. In front of the Mexican store in Fennville. Novena candles in the window behind her. Looking scolded. As if she were saying to someone, Don't take my picture. Don't keep a record of this. She was twenty in 1947: the war was over. They were living upstairs in one drafty room above the fudge shop, with a hot plate and a half-bath. Aunt Teensy let them bathe at the cottage. They could afford a nicer place or they could afford to buy a truck. The truck came first, for her father's business. An itinerant piano tuner, he ranged as far into Michigan's thumb as the Canadian border. Wanting those photographs: that was the visit Ruth Anne recalled but there had been other times.

She did not say to Laurel, When will you be home? That did not matter quite so much now. Johnny was right: Laurel would come back. Johnny had perspective and Ruth Anne did not. She was aware of that, always. Johnny took the long view. Johnny had been held prisoner and he knew how to take the long view.

Of course I'll come, if you need me, Laurel finally said. I wouldn't want you to go through that alone. We'll all come.

You saw the paper, didn't you?

We did.

Be careful, sweetheart.

We always are.

In the upstairs bedroom Ruth Anne packed a suitcase and waited for Johnny. He had left pecan pies baking in the oven at the big kitchen and he had said, Let me. Just let me do this one thing. At the cheapo station he would fill the Tercel's gas tank and wash the windows and check her oil. Moxie lay on the landing, his grizzled chin on his paws, sorry to see her suitcase on the bed. They aren't always careful. Laurel said that but they aren't always careful.

Johnny'll take care of you, Mox. Not to worry.

She packed for three days. Cortland would be right on her way and she would stop there and take a look around. It would be evening, but it would be safe. She would stop and find the church with the Vietnamese Mass. She would just look around.

She could not answer the e-mail. Not yet.

Maybe never. She whispered those words—maybe never—and thought, Have you wondered? But it was too big a door to open. Too weighty. Too treacherous. She wanted to think of what she would say and she repeated Dear Tin. Dear Tin. Dear Tin. tt103068@dune.com. October 30, 1968. Her water had broken while she held a brown egg in her hand, and she had almost dropped the egg. She could see for miles across the terraces beyond Dalat, the bright blue tin roofs of the farmers. A toothless man had sold her six eggs and she placed them in a plastic egg basket. It was morning, before the sun was up. The sun rose late in the mountains. You could see your breath in the mountains.

She might stop at any point in a library or a café or on a college campus. She might not be able to resist answering the e-mail. The secret felt like pregnancy. And would she show if she answered him? Would everyone have to know about it?

The bone-density test was Friday. She kept reminding herself of that, weighing being gone all week. She needed to be back in time for the bone-density test.

Teensy's vulnerable, Jill had said. She and Laurel shared a glance when they talked, a journey into each other, and it was that glance she could not remember sharing with Aunt Teensy, even though Aunt Teensy had been like a mother to her. She had bought her school clothes and Easter clothes and helped her with geometry and instituted a curfew and stocked the kitchen and Aunt Teensy had taken her to the emergency room the time she sliced open the ball of her foot on a piece of glass and Aunt Teensy had nursed her through bouts with the flu and she had given her a charm bracelet for her sweet sixteen birthday and she had taught her table manners, which fork to use first and which fork to use last, and she had taught her to drive a stick shift. Still, it was that soulful journey they had not made. Aunt Teensy knew about him and surely she had kept the Saigon letters. But the soulful journey they had not taken was about more than all Ruth Anne had written in the letters. It was a journey into how they had felt when Ruth Anne's mother drowned. The way they averted their eyes when they found themselves in the lonesome kitchen at the same time. It was acknowledgment of that and more the soulful journey would take them to and Ruth Anne had thought she was ready so many times and so many times Aunt Teensy had said, I don't want to see her. Could she look her in the eye?

If you had lived on the big lake, it would be with you always, a geographical feature you could conjure and feel even at a distance. Lake Michigan might be navy blue in summer. You might walk the shifting high sand dunes among the white pines and feel as if you rode—cruised—over the lake. In the winter on the dunes the claret cones of flower seeds somehow held fast and tipped determinedly to the gray-shell sky. An arctic wind would gale. Waves would freeze into fantastic barges and sleighs along the shore. Icy transport. With crews of queens and witches.

It was the lake she imagined exerting a tidelike pull on her heart. When she was a girl, it might as well have been the sea. Whatever was on the other side was not visible. Maupassant described the sea, the Mediterranean, as shining under the dusk's dying light, without a shiver, without a wrinkle. C'était l'heure du thé avant l'entrée des lampes. It was teatime, before the lamps were lit. It would be that time of day while she drove north. Past the blueberry farms and mint fields. She had read that story to Vo. He had been seventeen and she had been not quite twenty when she read the Maupassant story aloud in the corner of the tea shop while the men too old to go to war crouched on stools talking, their clothes rumpled, their voices indifferent. Smoke would rise and cling to the rafters. A wooden screen of lotus blossoms sheltered Ruth Anne and Vo from the men. Outside, a boy would wander down the street, tapping out a melodic announcement on a metal bar: noodles at the noodle stand were fresh. She might go and bring them noodles in the deep French crocks. A story that ended happily pleased them, but a sad story made them cry and there had been astonishment in the crying together. Until that last time. All other crying seemed to have been faint rehearsals when they cried the last time. And now the lake was laden like a sea with vessels of memory. Teensy. Vo and Tin. Her parents and Sue-Sue in the same cemetery under the syca-mores. The sycamore leaves would be the last to fall. They all beckoned her north.


Get that out of your hard head right now, Aunt Teensy said.

Ruth Anne thought, I'm nineteen and you can't tell me what to do.

Through the glossy evening light a waiter sashayed to their table and they ordered shrimp dinners and put on polite faces. Aunt Teensy shut up with the waiter right there. The polished mahogany hulls of yachts glimmered along the dock. People were having drinks on the yachts. Waving to each other. Being rich together, Ruth Anne thought.

September and Labor Day had come and gone and at the seafood house the maple leaves were red above the patio and lit by flicks of fire from the lanterns on the tables. When they first sat down Ruth Anne had said it: Vietnam. She used the unreal words she had been linking to-gether in her mind for weeks. Tucked in her straw purse were the letter on the heavy cotton paper with the crown of thorns and the letter from the French nuns, written in black script on thin blue airmail paper. The stamp on the blue envelope depicted the French opera house in Saigon. They were pleased that the Lord had spoken to her. The library books had been donated by a Vietnamese woman who could not afford to keep them. Ruth Anne gripped her purse latch and imagined the two letters, creased and torn from the times she had read them. Her passport and visa were hidden. She knew enough to hide what really mattered.

Tears sprang into her eyes, while the waiter with the mustache wrote down their orders. Battered shrimp and baked potatoes. Iced tea with lemon. She thought of the silver-plated hairbrush and Aunt Teensy's determination to paddle her with it. The flowery imprint the silver brush made on her skin. If Sue-Sue's mother had said what Aunt Teensy said, Sue-Sue would have cried, I hate you. I absolutely hate you.

Ruth Anne sat still. I can do what I want. You are not my boss any-more. Not really. Why had she gone to the trouble to tell? Why did she have to tell anyone? Tears gathered into a burning in her throat. She had no one else to tell and if she went to Vietnam right now without

Aunt Teensy's blessing she might never smell her mother again, in the taffeta and nylon of the prom dresses. Disowning meant that she could never touch again what her mother had touched. She sat still.

Aunt Teensy opened a compact and freshened her lipstick. She snapped the compact shut and whispered, Sue-Sue's a slut.

I'm not going for Sue-Sue.

You think I don't know why you're going?

The nuns're expecting me.

The waiter set their food before them on heavy platters ornamented with anchors and ropes. She could not eat but Aunt Teensy plowed through her shrimp and the steaming potato in its jacket. Ruth Anne watched her. She waited and sat still. She had chosen a public place to tell. At home there were locks on all the doors. In her lap she turned the engagement ring around and around on her finger. Aunt Teensy's mouth was slick with grease and she had managed to get a streak of sour cream in her hair and Ruth Anne would not say so. She would never say anything conciliatory or kind or helpful to Aunt Teensy again. She would never. She was through with that.

Aunt Teensy wiped her mouth with a big linen napkin like a nun's wimple.

I'll go back to school. This is only for a year.

You're *just* like your mother. All that talk about the war—

They paid the check inside and moved among the diners to the foyer of the restaurant and when her feet touched the wide steps leading out into the night Ruth Anne understood that all shelter had dissolved. She had the urge to go back in among the convivial diners. Aunt Teensy grabbed her arm, her fingernails digging in.

Girlie, you think I don't know what you're up to?

Ruth Anne jerked away. Nimbly she took the steps and hurried down a steel gangway to the dock. Cut loose. She ran into the windy night, alongside the festive boats and closed shops. She ran to the chain ferry, a gingerbread-trimmed barge, but a padlock clanked against the gate. Sue-Sue's mother lived down a gravel road on the other side of the river, around a bend from a shut-up motel with pink awning and plywood over the windows. Up and over the dunes lay the lake and the beach. She huddled trembling against a tree and she could see the motel awning and she could imagine walking down the winding road to Sue-

Sue's if she could get across the river. She knew the road. She knew all the roads around there and she was not afraid of the roads at night.

Aunt Teensy drove her sedan up onto the grass, headlights bouncing. She flung open the car door and charged Ruth Anne, swinging her square purse.

Get in the car.

She struck her with the purse. Get. Get. She dropped her purse and with her fist she struck Ruth Anne's temple. The night, a woozy darkness, cut into her head. She steadied herself with a hand out to the tree. Bark scraped her palm.

Get. Into. The car.

Ruth Anne squealed, I will, I will.

They thought that was the end of it. The silent ride home. The shove into her room. Aunt Teensy locked the doors to the cottage from the inside with keys only she possessed.

Ruth Anne cried in her room and in between the crying spells she would get up and look in the mirror at the bruise on her temple. She would gingerly pat the scrapes on her palm. Finally she stripped off her clothes and dug into the dark end of the closet and pulled out a lavender faille dress on a hanger padded with satin. She turned it inside out and sniffed along the seams until she detected the scent of White Shoulders near the bones of the midriff.

Aunt Teensy turned on the bathtub faucets to take her nightly soak. She put music on the hi-fi: Judy Garland.

Ruth Anne slipped the dress over her head and zipped it on the side. She whispered to Johnny, to his graduation photo in a silver frame on her dresser.

See me.

Remember me.

# 4

The French convent was a small villa on a prosperous street, shaded by trees with painted white trunks. Catty-corner to the convent, school had let out. Clutching drawings, swinging satchels, the children in blue and white uniforms were handed into cars and cyclos. The dark faces of the cyclo drivers glistened with sweat. Chicken wire covered the windows of the buses going by.

Nearby stood a temple with a sweeping tile roof and an ocher tiger painted on its façade. A woman hovered near the grillwork gate; six slaughtered geese had been slung on a wooden yoke she wore across her shoulders. Sister David said, Délicieux, mais non. She drew a long iron key from inside her habit and stuck it in the keyhole of the gate.

You will not need a key.

I won't?

There is always someone to open this door. Until curfew. And the doors inside—there are no locks.

She was a portly, pink-faced woman in the lace Breton cap and brown habit of her order. A plump Aunt Teensy. She cleared her throat every few minutes, a mucousy sound. An allergy, she explained. Around her waist, beads of a wooden rosary clicked with every step. You will not need a key echoed in Ruth Anne's mind: would they keep her there all the time? Her heart had hardened after the second day locked in the cottage. She imagined Aunt Teensy coming home to find the screen slit open with cooking shears.

Sister David chattered in French, testing her. She had met her at the airport and driven the Citroën with ease through the wide boulevards and the French had been fast. Ruth Anne had held her own.

She had not seen another woman with red hair and she had felt gawked at but exhilarated to be on the ground in her new life. Glad to get off the plane. To stretch her legs. A corpulent worm of hot moist air had entered the plane the minute the stewardesses unlatched the door.

They entered the convent. Shut tight the grille. Roses bloomed on either side of the brick walk. Ahead she saw the swish of brown skirts, the obedient sisters moving with decorum and efficiency—she thought of them as all alike and obedient. Not like her. A drove of bicycles leaned against one stucco wall.

In the kitchen, copper pots hung from racks. Fresh-baked baguettes lay cooling on a butcher block. A nun with her sleeves rolled high chopped celery with a stubby knife. Two Vietnamese women squatted nearby, shelling hardboiled eggs, their fingers working speedily, almost in rhythm. Peeled eggs shone in a blue crock on the tile floor.

Bonjour.

Chao em.

Ruth Anne said, Chao em, and one of the squatting women cackled, revealing a gold eyetooth like a charm. With a flick of her finger Sister David indicated that they were moving on and the others laughed in the kitchen, a filigree of French Ruth Anne could not make out. So the nuns were merry sometimes, not everyone as dour as Sister David.

Sister David said, Your room.

Ruth Anne slipped past her and she smelled the nun's odor. Not unpleasant, but sharp and exceptionally clean. Like a hard brown bar of soap an old woman might keep handy at her utility sink. She might have been thirty-five or she might have been fifty. Her cheeks were soft with down. Ruth Anne thought about splashing on cologne. The harsh soap smell made cologne the quintessence of luxury, nearly sinful. She set down her suitcase and dropped her purse and pulled off her rain jacket that had stuck to her arms in the humidity. Everyone had said to bring a rain jacket but so far it had been nothing but a nuisance. Her shoulders ached.

It was a plain room; the narrow bed made up with a thin coverlet. Suspended above the bed, a skirt of mosquito netting hung limply. Spiders had built webs in the slats of a chair. The casement window opened onto a garden where lavender grew willy-nilly. A picture of a woman saint hung above the bed. Ruth Anne did not recognize her. She had not been good at the saints but she did know her catechism and she had won prizes—gigantic Hershey bars and holy cards—for memorizing catechism. Why did God make me? To know, love, and serve Him. She wanted to hide the picture under the bed and maybe she would. The saint's tormented eyes brought to mind stories she had heard in elementary school: missionaries tortured with chopsticks. Stories she did not want to dwell on.

Sister David checked her watch. Dinner will be in two hours, after Evening Praise. You will, of course, attend Evening Praise. And morning Eucharist. Confessions are heard every Saturday morning.

She looked at her as if she might have plenty to confess.

Yes. Oui. Of course.

Your bathroom is through there—she gestured toward a blue door. You share with the sisters in the adjoining room. They have a system. For privacy. You slide the lacquered spoon under the door.

And there it was: a spoon like you would use to beat a pan of fudge, but lacquered with a forest: trees, monkeys, sunset. What it meant to have no locks on the doors came home to her.

The library is this way.

She led Ruth Anne through a tiled salon lit by chandeliers and down a long dim hall. They paused at a closet-sized room. A utilitarian stool had been placed beside a table on which there was a black dial telephone. A sister with pasty hands sat knitting behind a desk.

We have only one line. If you receive a call, someone will come for you.

She thought of all she said on the telephone, the giggles and love and heart-thumping silences and gossip. She did not think she would ever talk on that black telephone. But she would have to if she and Johnny were ever going to find each other; she would have to talk on the black telephone in front of the sister in charge of it. She would have to have a code. She and Johnny would make up a code and later they would laugh about the old nun and how they had fooled her.

Two doors down was the library, a square room, with high ceilings and French doors. A smell—old paper and moisture, tropical decay— rose up to meet them. Sister David pressed the light switch and four sconces lit up, one on each wall, flickering, yellowish. Lightbulbs in the sconces were held in the hands of art nouveau maidens, their robes in

brass tendrils. Clothbound books and leather-bound books and paperback books lay teetering on the shelves and on the tile floor.

We have been shorthanded. These boxes—

She gestured to the wooden crates, stenciled with TRAN in black
letters.

These are the books we've been given. By a generous donor. Madame Tran Thuong. The books you are to bind and catalog. These books
are not for the children. The school. In any case, our school is not as
large as it once was. Dependents are going home. For the time being.
The library is for the community and the people who come to Mass. An
equanimity comes from both—don't you agree?—attending Mass and
reading literature. It does not matter who you are in the world. You are
God's child at Mass. And if you like a good story, you like a good story.

Where did she get so many books?

Sister David lowered her voice and said, She went to Paris in the
fifties.

She raised the blinds and the garden lay beyond: roses and a palm
tree and a concrete bench. We are so very happy you have come. I hope
you will be content here. It's not very hospitable, is it? For a young
woman such as yourself.

The garden was hospitable. Familiar. It would be a place to sit in the
sun on a break, although, just then, a gray bank of clouds hung over the
garden and a spiral of bees droned above the flowers. I'll be fine, Ruth
Anne said.

Sister David turned around and pinned her with a frosty glance.
What had she done to offend her already?

I will.

Do you want to stay here and contemplate your work? Or do you
wish to go to your room? Would you like a pot of tea?

Some are merry and some are not, Ruth Anne thought. The nuns
could be divided thus: cheerful or mean-spirited. The entire world
could be divided thus. What she wanted was to pee and brush her hair,
but both might be considered vain. I'll stay here for a little while. But
tea sounds nice. Thank you.

I'll have the tea brought to your room. Sister David paused at the
door. Her pink face shone in the heat. Oh, yes, she said, you should
know—we are silent at meals. We listen to Scripture being read aloud.

You may eat in the kitchen if you do not wish to remain silent. In the evening we have a social hour from seven until eight o'clock. We gather in the salon. You have a clock?

Oui.

Oui, Soeur.

Oui, Soeur.

And skirts?

Ruth Anne glanced down at her mud-brown bell-bottom slacks. And then back to the nun. Oui, Soeur. Oui.

She left her there alone.

More alone than she had ever been; more alone, it felt, than she had been when her parents died, when she had brought her things in a plaid suitcase and cardboard boxes to live with Aunt Teensy at Pier Cove.

A knot of tears formed in her throat. Whenever she was alone Johnny made her feel better. They were connected, he had said, and he would be with her always. Think of me and I'll think of you. Every night when you are drifting off to sleep, think of me.

He was on a beach instead of where the red dust flew. Luck of the Irish. Only his mother had been Irish and half at that and she had run away to be an artist's model in Nashville, Indiana. His father did not appreciate mention of the Irish. Never mind what anyone thought at home. Johnny sometimes got to drive along the coastal road and sing his love songs. He had sent a snapshot of himself with a buddy and the other boy mugged for the camera, his teeth like a mule's. Ruth Anne wanted to cut the other boy right out of the snapshot. Johnny looked straight at her. You could trust him. On the back of the snapshot he had written, *2 dumb cherries, 1967.*

Thumbtacked to the wall behind him was her grainy graduation photo. She looked like someone she would never see again. She thought about Sue-Sue, behind concertina wire, without a decent shower, the walls of her room green with mildew. In her white patent-leather boots and miniskirt. Riding in a helicopter out to a makeshift plywood stage. And Jill in the Red Cross uniform she hated, the powder-blue sneakers, the powder-blue dress. She had been trained in Washington, D.C., for two weeks; it had been her first trip out of Michigan. One of her suitcases had been full of games to keep the troops distracted. At night Jill went to parties where she would drink a purple jesus—vodka and grape juice soldiers had mixed in a washtub. Although Jill would never say purple jesus out loud. That would be blasphemy; she could not stand the taste of that. But she was curious about the vodka. You get used to outgoing rounds, she wrote. A whine like tornado sirens. You'd be surprised what you can cook on an electric skillet. Letters had come from all of them before she left and their lives had seemed chancy but they had not confessed to fright. Giddiness glittered between the lines. While she would be going to Evening Praise and binding books. What choice she had she took: she decided to eat in the kitchen. She thought the word lassitude and she felt lassitude, her mind buffered by the heat, and she thought that the word did not sound the way it felt. It sounded almost pleasant. It sounded like something you would cherish. She picked up a book of French love stories and began reading. C'était l'heure du thé avant l'entrée des lampes. In this way she consoled herself, reading Maupassant with the doors open to the bees.

The trip from Pier Cove to Saigon had taken four days, a ride to Chicago by bus and then three different flights, first to Seattle, then to Okinawa. She had felt suspended from the rest of her life—a witness. Air Force officers were on the last flight and one of them liked her— he had offered her a cigarette, he had reached out and steadied her, touched her forearm, through turbulence. After that they talked. She thought, I am a grown woman now.

Johnny and she had not slept together but on her way to Saigon she knew they would. There would be a hotel where they would meet. Or a train station. There would be that frisson of pleasure in her abdomen, a feeling like speeding, against the law. That rising up to meet him. They had been taught it was wrong. Johnny lived in a trailer and you never knew when his father would come home and catch you. Aunt Teensy too was unpredictable—she kept the silver hairbrush in the drawer of an oak library table in the hallway. And Ruth Anne had been timidly modest. A shame like the feeling you have right before you vomit kept her from letting him see her breasts, her sex, in daylight, although Johnny knew her body in segments, what he had coaxed her to reveal in the dark. There was another reason they had not slept together: Johnny wanted her to know that he loved her aside from all that, for reasons he could not articulate and a few he could. She was capable of building a roaring bonfire on the beach; she knew where to look in the library to answer any question; and she had listened when he told her about the morning his mother left for good, her clothes packed in a red leather trunk. Johnny had given his secret self to Ruth Anne and she carried his secret self with her and he was willing to wait.

A yellow taxi had idled outside the cottage in a gray rain. The cooking shears she tossed into the flower bed. She had not even left a note. Aunt Teensy would send one letter to Saigon: You girls have got to learn the hard way.

She had gone to confession at O'Hare. Bless me, Father. She stumbled over the Act of Contrition. On the plane in the turbulence she prayed and she felt bad that she had stumbled over the Act of Contrition. She did not like to think about confessing what she and Johnny would do. The priest said, You'll be a breath of fresh air, my dear. She imagined it was what he said to any young person embarking on a new path.

Like a waiter in a French café, in the library she wore an apron on which she could wipe the glue from her hands. Sister Michelle taught her to bind the books. They wanted them to last. She was to reinforce the flyleaf with marbleized cardboard. She taped the corners and spine with buckram tape. Every book had a pocket glued to the front flyleaf, where the Due Date card would go. There was a system and she was to make the system work, to allow for no slippage. A small fee was paid by the library patrons; there was a tin tea box into which she was to place the money. The library had been closed for several months and Sister Michelle said embassy secretaries and officers at Mass were asking for books. People were hungry for reading matter. Hungry for another world, a poem, a romance set in Paris or New York.

Nearly a week went by.

She would sail past the telephone room and peek inside and she would feel the physical thrill of Johnny. She would anticipate it.

Her days began with a small baguette and green tea in the kitchen. Miss Cam and Mrs. Ha prepared the breakfast for the nuns and Ruth Anne would stay out of their way, glad to have fresh bread and tea, to be included in the morning. Joss sticks burned at the little altar in the room behind the kitchen where Miss Cam and Mrs. Ha slept. Once while they struggled to haul in a bag of rice from a storage room, Ruth Anne had glanced beyond their door. Two cats with meditative faces sat beneath the altar. She took in the photos and daguerreotypes in wooden frames. The smoking incense. One white carnation in an olive oil can. An offering of thumb-size bananas. They had taught her to use chopsticks and to say hello and goodbye in Vietnamese. They spoke French when it suited them, Vietnamese when they did not want her to understand.

Her love of routine nearly alarmed her. Binding books all morning. A lunch of steaming noodles. Time to read in her room. And then a final stint of work before Evening Praise. At the social hour she and Sister Michelle would play a word game—Guggenheim—while the others knitted or read or visited over tea in metal pots. The others did not matter so much. Intuition kept insisting: you won't be here long. She pressed that thought down each time it rose before her.

Sister Michelle was the oldest of six children. From Sacramento. She had gotten in trouble for having a special friend, a nun with whom she had grown too intimate, in the opinion of her superiors, and they had given her the opportunity to accompany certain educational materials to the sisters in Saigon. They called it an opportunity. Her brother was stationed at Phuoc Vinh and she had seen him twice. She taught an English class for Vietnamese secretaries. Ruth Anne had never before noticed this about a nun: she was exceptionally pretty, with baby blond hair she no longer had to cut, according to the new rules of her order. She wore it pinned in braided figure eights behind her ears. Her hands were small, with fingernails like minute pale seashells.

The fourth night, Sister Michelle knocked at her door after lights out. We could hang this, she whispered, displaying a small brass flashlight. We could share the light to read.

The beam cut across Ruth Anne's bed, a faint creamy light. Sister Michelle stood waiting. Her nightgown of thin cotton. Her shoulders exposed. Daisies had been embroidered along the neckline. She had the body of a swimmer, with broad muscular shoulders that still bore the freckles of a summer before she had become a nun.

We'll get in trouble.

The scent of her had entered the room: a lavender sachet. They won't care. They're my batteries. They don't want us using electricity. That's why we have lights out so early.

They rigged the flashlight. It dangled from a cord inside the mosquito netting. Sister Michelle settled in next to her. There they read, Ruth Anne her Victor Hugo and Sister Michelle her nurse novel. Once the lacquered spoon slipped under the door; water ran into the basin in the bathroom; she could feel Sister Michelle holding her breath and she held her own breath and finally let it come in feathery gasps and she was nervous, they were nervous together. Finally the spoon was pulled back under the door. They would get used to that. The wooden ceiling fan circled, squeaking. Insects beat against the windowpane even though they had left the window open. They lay on their stomachs, thigh to thigh, until they fell asleep.

On Sunday she finally went out. To Mass. There were officers in dress whites and diminutive Vietnamese women in silky ao dais and European women in summer dresses and broad-brimmed hats and nuns from different orders and children—boys in bow ties and girls in bouffant skirts, fiddling with sashes.

In the foyer Sister David said, You must meet Madame Thuong.

Madame Thuong in her ruby-red dress and high heels. A tall woman in glasses with rhinestone trim. Bonjour, Mademoiselle.

Madame Thuong is our benefactor. The books were given by Madame Thuong.

Bon jour, Madame.

This is my son, Vo.

Vo was tall and slim, with a finely squared chin. Sixteen or seventeen years old. His black hair lay in an unkempt wave across his forehead. His eyes were hidden behind dark glasses, although the foyer was cottony gray and dim. He wore a white rayon shirt, bright against his skin. He held out a hand to Ruth Anne. Slightly off-center, slightly unsure: he was blind. She held his hand and shook it firmly.

He squeezed her hand. Something like a match being struck.

In perfect English, Vo said, How do you like Saigon?

I haven't seen much of Saigon.

That will have to change.

Oui, Madame Thuong said. You must come to the tea shop and visit.

Sister David said, Oui, she will.

Ruth Anne was about to inquire further but the priest and the altar boys fussed into the foyer, ready for the procession down the aisle. She scurried along behind the nun. Slipping into a pew halfway to the altar. The priest and the boys passed by, an incense boat swinging. Sister David leaned over and whispered, Madame Thuong would like for you to read to the boy. He has a great love of literature.

Oh?

This is our part in the arrangement. We will own the books and you will read to the boy. At the altar the priest made the sign of the cross. I will lend you a bicycle. My three-speed. I have the only three-speed. Sister David opened a missal, ducked into it, making clear her intention to stop whispering. Her knuckles were raw, bluish, against the black missal.

No one had told her she would read to the boy. It would be pleasant to read aloud, a break in the routine. Such breaks ordered time: meals, Guggenheim, the chance to read in her room, Sister Michelle's American presence in her bed at night. She wanted to know what had happened to his eyes. And how he had learned English. The French Apostle's Creed startled her from questions.

Connie Mattingly stood on the steps after Mass, a bouncy woman from Kentucky who worked for a construction company. She introduced herself and invited Ruth Anne to a barbecue. She would fetch her.

Johnny might call. Johnny might call. She did not say what she thought, but Connie Mattingly saw, it seemed, the reluctance on her face, and said, You're here to see someone special, I'll bet. You can't count on that, honey. This'll be fun, you'll see.

She felt she had to ask permission but Sister David said, Enjoy the day.

Before leaving the convent she said to the sister in the telephone room, You'll write down my messages, won't you?

The sister's face wrinkled into a smile. And do you have a message for him?

I'm here. Anytime he wants to come.

Connie Mattingly waited outside the gate in a pickup truck. Ruth Anne hopped inside. They wove into a river of slow traffic.

You look terrific, Connie shouted.

Ruth Anne shrugged, grinning. She had worn her two-piece graduation dress, sleeveless, with an A-line skirt, made of shantung silk. In it she felt far from Michigan. She felt far from the convent but if she had turned around she might have seen Sister Michelle standing on the sidewalk.

So do you. Look terrific.

Her life was beginning in that moment with Connie Mattingly. Connie Mattingly affected an exotic style that suited her and the place and the time and Ruth Anne would always remember that day, the feeling of freedom. With Connie in her Indian-print skirt and a silk blouse and gold sandals. Long amber earrings. Everything gilt-edged. She was apple-shaped, with a ruddy complexion glowing under her makeup. A sliver of concern cut into Ruth Anne when she thought, Johnny wouldn't like her. Why was a mystery and she was fine with it remaining a mystery. There was no turning back.

It was a sunny day. The humidity high. She watched the women on bicycles, their long black hair swaying. On such a day at home she might have sat still in front of an electric fan.

They parked near a peach-colored villa. Run-down with paint peeling from the shutters. Connie and she toted a cooler of ice cream between them and up the broad steps. Connie said, All the men are married, honey. So watch out.

In the garden was an oil drum, cut in half, a makeshift barbecue, the charcoal briquets pulsing, afire. It smelled like home. A Chinese servant tended the coals and fanned flies from the chicken pieces soaking in a tin pan of whiskey-colored marinade on a table festooned with flowers. A bar had been set up; liquor bottles gleamed.

Connie pulled her along, introducing her. She was Connie's find. They were mostly men and they were cheered to meet her. She ate and drank and felt the headiness of Sunday afternoon cocktails with strangers who thought her good-looking.

After a while she found herself in a nook on a white iron bench near hibiscus the size of dinner plates, with a man. They had wandered into a cul-de-sac in the garden. Across the flagstone terrace and beyond the algae-flecked swimming pool, Connie laughed, spilling her drink a little. Everyone was laughing.

The man wore a blue dress shirt and white slacks. Sockless, in loafers. With a loose gold watch on his wrist. He said he was American, from a small town near St. Louis. She had drunk enough that she could not sort out his name from the other names. They had been talking—she had been listening—for a long time. He held her hand and ran his index finger over the engagement ring. His aftershave smelled unfamiliar. He must have been in his thirties; his hair had begun to gray near his temples. A cat had given birth to a litter not far from the bench, under a shrub, and human presence made her nervous and she paced between them and the kittens.

I don't feel well, Ruth Anne said.

I'll take you home.

She waved to Connie and they went out to the street. Hours had passed; it was dark. He hailed a cyclo. They tore through the streets, weaving in and out of traffic. A book was tucked in the cyclo driver's hip pocket and Ruth Anne wanted to know its title. But that would be impossible, she felt, to communicate with the cyclo driver. She could not concentrate. She perched between the man's legs on the edge of the seat, his arms around her. Her chignon coming undone. Her hair in strands plastered against her cheek. In spite of drinking too much too fast, she knew she was attractive to him and she enjoyed the moment. Sometimes that felt like the only reason to go somewhere: to see if you were desirable. She did not consider whether he was attractive to her. He petted her knee.

At the convent gate he sent the cyclo driver away. Lights lit up the convent windows, weak fires. He said, You haven't had much experience, have you?

She giggled. What do you mean?

The booze.

That's true.

I'd like to see you again.

Would you? She leaned against him, girlishly.

He slipped his arms around her waist and cinched her close. She noticed the spidery veins around his nose.

Are you married?

Does it matter?

He was around her father's age when he had drowned in Idaho. Do you have kids?

Let me kiss you goodbye. Let's keep it simple.

Kiss me goodbye.

He took her hand and pulled her away from the gate, under a pepper tree's long trailing branches. There was a bad smell under the tree, a decay. He gripped her arms above the elbows and kissed her eyelids, then her cheeks, her neck, a method he had, nothing to do with her. She waited to see what would happen. His face was clean-shaven, warm.

The lock in the gate rattled. They moved apart, reluctantly. Sister Michelle stood under the streetlamp, looking abject. Did you want to come in?

Yes, I want to come in. She turned to the man and said, Now you know where I live.

Smiling, he said, Yes, I see how it is.

She went to her room and changed into her pajamas. Her skin tingled with heat. She wished she could peel it away. She lay on the bed outside the mosquito netting, trying to lie still, trying not to feel a whir, the vertigo from lying down. She had not done anything she was sorry for. Almost, but not quite. She thought about the boys she had kissed—not many. She could not remember the first and that troubled her. The fan circling made her dizzy.

Telephone! Sister Michelle said.

Johnny would have said she was blitzed. I'll just tell him that. She said the word—blitzed, blitzed—under her breath. She slipped into her robe and went padding through the silent convent in flip-flops. Her heart beat fast—finally, finally. Sister Michelle followed her and took up her position at the desk in the telephone room. She picked up a well-thumbed deck of cards and feigned interest in a game of solitaire that lay half-finished before her.

It was Sue-Sue. She laughed at the other end. The line static-laced. She said she was working hard, a show every other day. These guys're so hungry for us. They're so grateful. And then later, she said, We went out in a helicopter—out to the ocean. We killed some sharks. With hand grenades. That's what they do for fun up here.

Ruth Anne felt sick to her stomach. She stopped listening.

But Sue-Sue kept on talking.

# 5

~~~~~~~

I WAS A STRANGER AND YOU WELCOMED ME.

At the church in Cortland a limestone pillar carved with wheat sheaves and Scripture gleamed under a floodlight. Matthew 25. Ruth Anne knew the verse but she had not thought of it in a long time. There were verses she kept close to her heart and verses that floated away even as Father Carroll proclaimed them. The doors were locked. She peered inside. The church might have been a public library or a town hall, its hardwood floors light and clean, the curving mosaic wall abstract.

Near the sidewalk she ran her fingers over the bronze plaque. Spanish Mass at 10 A.M. Vietnamese at 2 P.M. There were so many that they had a bronze plaque that might survive war or weather.

Across the street and for a block in either direction were the old bungalows, newly restored. Copper lamps glowed within. No one else was on the street. She saw herself as someone at a distance might: a woman wanting in the church. Wraithlike, not dressed for the cool. Someone might be unsure if he had seen her or not: Were his eyes playing tricks on him? Her son might walk up this sidewalk and go inside every Sunday.

Aunt Teensy's voice of years ago reminded her, Don't get your hopes up.

Michigan is a big state: the mitt and thumb, all the small towns where her father had tuned pianos: Charlevoix, Cadillac, Port Austin. She had liked the sound of the names when he spoke them. Her father was like someone she had read about in a story. His trousers steel gray. His crew cut stiff. A vein visible on his bicep. Something about it made her queasy. She would see the vein and try not to look at the vein when he would sit in his undershirt at the kitchen table in the heat of summer, smoking Lucky Strikes. He had started smoking Lucky Strikes during the war. They loved to talk about the war; it had been the central drama of their lives. They could tell you exactly where they were and what they were doing when they heard the news about Pearl Harbor, what the light was like, the radio, the people they were with, the meal about to be set on the table.

As if disturbed by wind, photographs fluttered in her mind's eye. Her father with a pack of cigarettes rolled into his T-shirt sleeve. The two of them dancing at the Starlight, a ball of mirrors blinking above them. She did not have the photographs and she did not know what Aunt Teensy had done with them. Laurel would have all the photographs she wanted when the time came. She had seen to that. Johnny and she had kept a record, however scanty it might seem without the other babies. Where had Aunt Teensy put those photographs? She had a few things in a storage unit provided by the nursing home. She had a closet. Ruth Anne feared that she had thrown them out, and what would that mean if she had? Would she have thrown them out for spite?

Did Vo have Saigon photographs that Tin had studied? She did not recall a camera but there must have been one. Tran Vo was a shadowy figure: a boy in French shirts that had worn thin; he could not cry tears because he was blind: she had made him shadowy. She wanted to be a good wife and she had not dwelt on Vo.

I'll disown you, Aunt Teensy had said. There was precious little to inherit and that was all right. She did not want Teensy's bric-a-brac, the beaded bags, or property. The cottage had been sold to a professor from Ann Arbor—a single woman who razed it and rebuilt it, keeping only the stone fireplace. The candy shop in Saugatuck and the recipes had been sold to a gay couple from Chicago. Jill kept track of Teensy's money and saw to it that bills were paid. She had enough to last another year in private care and after that she would be required to move. She did not want to move and Ruth Anne did not blame her. Jill said that she wanted to die before then.

A man in running shorts came whistling down the front steps of a house across the street. She could feel the lake, a mile or so to the west.

Johnny would not like her detouring to the church. He just wouldn't. He worried when she traveled alone. They did not like to be apart. When he brought the Tercel back, spiffed and ready to roll, he had said, You'll call me now, won't you?

Following her instinct, her memory of water, she got in the Tercel and drove to the state park; it was not hard to find even though she had not been there for years. The gate had not been closed but the sign said CLOSED AT DUSK. She parked the Tercel on the grassy shoulder and decided to walk to the lake. Johnny would not like it if he knew she was out wandering after dark, but Johnny would not know.

Aunt Teensy might be waiting and she would not take long. She did not want to make anyone wait.

Tin waited. She could feel it. Somewhere not far from the lake Tin opened his e-mail and waited. Casting the fishhook of dreams he had swallowed. The independence of her girlhood came back to her now that she neared the lake, like foreign phrases come back after years of disuse. Johnny would worry but what you do always feels more dangerous to the person at home worrying. Laurel would be all right. Laurel might even get over Oceana. Oceana might move away. It was only kids wrote that on the church wall. Johnny sounded sure of that. Their folks would set them straight.

The park road was well lit, with the dunes disappearing at the edge of the light. Grainy apparitions. Curvaceous. The wind was cold; the season would not begin until the Fourth of July. Until then, beachcombers bundled up in fleece blankets and windbreakers. She zipped her jacket and slung her purse strap over her head and across her chest so that her hands were free. Boardwalks switch-backed invitingly up and over the dunes. At the top she caught her breath. On the beach it was still dusk: the sky to the west a streak of green light below plum-colored clouds. What she was doing made a vibration in her body she could not control. Her jacket pocket was stuffed with old tissue and she uncrumpled the tissue and wiped her nose but the wind blew the tissue away and dried the tears on her face. She wanted to see him. She wanted to see him walk up to the church and open the door and go in and sing. She wanted to hear her voice next to his. But she did not want him to know. Not yet. All other feelings soaked up into shame, her familiar. Shame, the primary lesson.

➳

It's the morphine. But she might wake up around eleven.

Jill had been waiting inside the foyer at Our Lady of Holy Mysteries, keeping watch. Ruth Anne parked and crunched in her sandals over the river gravel toward Jill, the Virgin Mary an unyielding presence in the concrete circle between them. She was white marble, blue in the moonlight. Jill came out and they embraced and she said, It's the morphine.

It took me longer than I thought. The morphine had not been real to her until that moment. Teensy's pain had not been real. That felt like something she would have to pay for, not now, but later, when her own bones gave out. Teensy's pain had been only words—an idea: my aunt is in a nursing home. As if the nursing home could negate her pain.

She would not tell Jill about Tin. She did not know it until she saw her there in the river gravel with the Virgin in the circle and now secrets would separate them. She had thought she would tell but Jill was not the person to tell. The possibility for betrayal existed in that question— who would know first? It had to be Johnny but she could not begin the rehearsal, she could not find the words to say to Johnny: a terrible story would unfold. There was no end to what she might lose: the comfort of him never denying her what she wanted or needed, his bodily presence, the feel of him in the darkened bedroom when she would touch the scars on his back where he had let the fish eat the putrid flesh away to save himself and he would say, You heal me, Ruthie, you heal me, while the catalpa leaves like hearts waved and winked outside the bedroom where they had watched without even knowing they were watching the growth of the catalpa tree over decades, the times beside the round barn when he slipped her camisole straps down, the way he still took her out of herself when he slipped the camisole straps down. The future and the past. She was in danger of losing her past if this became a part of it. All the nearly forgettable touches and pats and hugs and pecks on the cheek that had kept her in a world separate from the girl she had been those fifteen months with Vo. If she told anyone, it would have to be Johnny. She felt her own death, hovering.

A brick breezeway connected the nursing home and the monastery so that the nuns could shuttle back and forth, taking care. Grapevines grew up and tangled above the pergola over the breezeway. The nuns made wine from the grapes and gave it to the priests who celebrated Mass for them. If Laurel were there she would say, Why is it the priests can have their Scotch and wine and the nuns cannot? Children do not know the way you hear their voices from a distance.

Jill took her suitcase and said, Let's get you settled and I'll take you over. It's only ten.

They passed the gold imperative SEEK GOD, yard-high wooden letters in the foyer. Down a sterile hallway and through double doors. Her room was as she had envisioned. The orange chair. The rust stains. Louvered windows let the lake breeze in.

They whispered, skimming through the darkened halls toward the dining room. Johnny and Brambles. Laurel. Laurel's teaching. Father Carroll and Limbo. The news of Jill's mother who had climbed mountains in Nepal. Her brother and his children. The new priest who served the monastery. A Dominican monk.

Jill hummed—not musically, but like a motor—a barely suppressed gladness. She wore loose, monochromatic clothes: gray pants, a white blouse and gray cotton cardigan, white socks, felt clogs. Her hair had grown gray and she wore it chopped off indifferently just below her ears. How much freedom there was in her indifference.

They paused before the photographs. Trappist monks mingling with Buddhist monks. The black and white robes against the burnt orange. A Buddhist monk laying a wreath on a grave.

Do you recognize the Dalai Lama?

I don't know that I do.

Jill pointed him out. In the act of teaching, one finger raised. Smiling patiently.

Why are these here?

It's part of the dialogue. One of our sisters is involved in the dialogue.

She felt as if she had leaped outside of time. The word dialogue brought up uncertainty, an irritation she could not pin down, galaxies forming, as yet unnamed. At home she had felt ashamed every time Laurel had mentioned the Buddhist nun and the meditation sessions. As if that deviation were a sin. A house that had been blessed by a priest had no room for the Buddha. But Laurel persisted. Laurel wanted to go to Mass when she pleased and sit meditation with the Buddhist nun whose head was shaved. She wanted both practices.

Are you all right?

I just didn't know.

Jill glanced at her watch. We have time. Let me show you our meditation space. She took Ruth Anne by the hand, her fingers cool.

The meditation space had been partitioned on three sides by rice paper screens. Black cushions—zafus—were laid at regular intervals on the floor. A poster of Thomas Merton hung on the back wall, commemorating the twenty-fifth anniversary of his death. THERE IS IN ALL THINGS AN INVISIBLE FECUNDITY, A DIMMED LIGHT, A MEEK NAMELESSNESS, A HIDDEN WHOLENESS.

Rife with contradiction. The quote made her crave a story, a story's concrete nouns, the names of cigarettes and roads and tools and clouds. A world to burrow into. She had a book of stories waiting in her room.

Do you like the feel of it?

I don't know.

Jill slipped off her clogs and entered the space and picked up a brass gong no bigger than a teacup. She smiled and with a tiny baton tapped the gong three times. Its sound oscillated toward Ruth Anne. She thought of organs, pianos, cellos, violins—how complicated, how like stained glass they seemed compared to this gong. She felt naked in its sound.

I'm tired suddenly, she sighed.

I'm sorry, Ruthie. Let's get you a cup of tea. Let's relax before we go to Teensy's room. She set the gong on a low table beside a vase of wildflowers.

It's called centering, she said, when they sat down in the dining hall, mugs of herbal tea in hand. Centering prayer. It's an ancient form of meditation.

Why do you do it?

The silence takes you to the divine. Beyond conceptualization.

Jill looked transparent in that moment, her cheeks flushed, her eyes bright. It seemed she had no hidden nooks and crannies to fortify.

I might want to try it, Ruth Anne said.

You have to take the training.

When?

At the end of the month.

I need a break, Ruth Anne said, grasping Jill's hand across the table. Or a change. I need something.

Jill smiled and squeezed her hand.

After the tea they went through the brick breezeway to the nursing home. The halls were two wheelchairs wide. Artificial spring bouquets had been hung on every door. Orderlies in blue cotton pants stood drinking coffee at the nurse's station. Jill introduced her to the nurses and the orderlies. She said that she would be around. Jill was optimistic. She was pushing for reconciliation and she told the nurses Ruth Anne would be around. Ruth Anne said, Yes, I'm her niece. How formal that relationship seemed when you put a word to it with strangers. The night was silent, for the most part. But someone cried out in a bad dream or pain from one of the rooms they passed and she could not tell if it was a man or a woman and she wondered: Is that what happens at this stage, gender disappears?

At Aunt Teensy's door they stopped and with one hand on the door handle, Jill said, How long since you saw her?

I'd have to think about it.

You know about her eating?

The doctor said she doesn't want to eat.

I didn't want it to be a shock.

She knocked briskly, lightly, and they slipped into the room, which was lit by a lamp Ruth Anne recognized from the cottage: a wooden bear sleeping. Aunt Teensy lay in a slight, crooked heap under a butter-yellow blanket.

Who's there?

It's Ruth Anne, she whispered.

Aunt Teensy stirred and opened her eyes. I can't see very well. Come closer.

Ruth Anne stepped to the bed and reached out and took her hand. Her hand was huge, the knuckles protruding, and Ruth Anne saw how shrunken she was. How her hipbones and backbone and femurs had diminished and left a residue of what she had been. Her collarbone seemed as if it had outgrown her.

Where's Johnny?

Johnny had to work.

They give me morphine. Did you know they give me morphine?

Jill said that.

I might be here one minute, gone the next.

That's true for all of us.

Aunt Teensy jerked her hand away. That's not what I mean. I mean. I mean I drift. So don't listen. If I drift.

All right.

Jill put her hand on Ruth Anne's shoulder. I'm going. You can find your way back, can't you?

I'll find my way.

A short, chipper woman in a flowered smock bustled in, her hair tucked up under a hairnet. In a Mexican accent she said, Missus Graham, you are awake. And with a visitor. She scooted around the bed, making adjustments here and there. She filled a tall plastic glass with water from a pitcher and she readjusted the built-in straw at a certain angle and set it on the tray that slid over the bed or away from the bed, the tray that contained all Aunt Teensy needed in her diminished state: water, reading glasses, tissues, a black-seed rosary.

This is Rosa, Aunt Teensy said. She feeds my songbirds.

Ruth Anne said hello.

Your aunt, she is a terror.

Rosa, don't be telling tales.

Rosa laughed and left the room.

I'm different now, Aunt Teensy said. She kept her eyes trained on the corner of the ceiling. Her face was cunning, shrewd beneath the net of wrinkles.

Ruth Anne said nothing. She was dependent upon Rosa and she would never say spic or nigger in front of Rosa. The times they had argued about that came rushing up to Ruth Anne, times she had forgotten. The way Aunt Teensy had made her skin crawl.

You can make wishes in these corners, Rosa says. You make a wish in every corner right before you go to sleep. When you wake up in the morning, whichever corner your eye spies first—that's the wish you get. I've made quite a few wishes since I've been here.

Ruth Anne wanted to reach out and take her hand again, but she thought it might be an intrusion or she thought it might hurt to have her jerk away again. The silver hairbrush appeared almost palpably before her eyes when she closed them. She kept her hands in her jacket pockets. In her pocket she had found a cellophane wrapper from a hard peppermint and she touched it gingerly and did not want to make the crinkly noise, but she felt it as a tenuous link to Johnny. Johnny had given her the candy on a walk through the golf course with Moxie: a spring day. She longed for Johnny.

None of them have come true. But Rosa says, Keep wishing.

# 6

I wouldn't say we reconciled. No.

They were in the big kitchen, after hours. Ruth Anne sipped her wine, the glass a delicate bell. Johnny peeled the label methodically from a bottle of stout. He had turned off the fluorescent overhead and it was nearly dark in the big kitchen; the patio lights filtered through the window screens, yellowy splashes against the kitchen's stainless steel. Insects whined beneath the liquid wind. Johnny still wore his whites, his apron smeared with dried salsa or blood around his thigh where he habitually wiped his left hand.

After a week?

It wasn't quite a week, sweetie.

He placed his hand over hers. A work week. It was a work week. I missed you.

I missed you too. How was your night?

Slow. It was slow. The rain—

The office door was open and in its darkness there was a recliner and on the recliner a quilt, the same quilt Johnny kept in his lockbox and laid out in the wild rye beside the round barn. She could see that he wanted her. It was not unusual for her to visit him after hours and allow him to seduce her. The night might end like that.

She got up and went to the back window and stared into the patio. Someone had left a baseball hat on the picnic table, turned upside down like a cup and filled with beer bottle caps. It was soaked from the rain. The roads had been slick, her visibility poor. Once she had pulled into a rest stop and with the other drivers watched the lightning cutting up the sky.

Limbo was here looking for you.

Ruth Anne turned around and smiled. He depends on me.

We all do. He put out his hand and then patted his thigh.

Ruth Anne set her wineglass down and went to sit on his lap. He smelled good; he smelled like Johnny, of spices and the woodsy aftershave he used. Olive you, he said.

Olive you too.

He kissed her tentatively. She opened her mouth a little and tried to feel the answer to his question. But she wasn't there. She could not come back and pretend that nothing had happened to her. They had read a book about marriage a long time ago and there was one rule in the book that had stuck with her even though she had not been able to obey the rule in its entirety; she had done the best she could. The therapist who wrote the book had written that you do not have to tell everything. But you have to tell everything that persists. A single thought that flits through your mind like electric current does not have to be revealed. But whatever persisted would come between you. Except for what had happened while Johnny was held prisoner, she tried to follow the rule.

She sorted out what she could tell. She slipped off his lap and picked up her wineglass and sat down across from him.

Listen. I did something that surprised me while I was up there.

What was that?

I meditated with the nuns.

I didn't know they meditated.

They do. It's called centering.

How was it?

It was hard. It was hard to sit still. With my thoughts.

So how was Jill?

Jill's fine. But listen. I want to go back there. I want to take the training session.

For the meditation?

Yes. She did not look at him but said, It'll give me another try. With Aunt Teensy. Being there'll give me time with her.

Whatever you want to do is fine. We'll miss you. We'll miss you every minute.

The sound of the girls—Laurel and Oceana talking, voice over voice—came buoyantly upon the evening. Ruth Anne looked up and saw them standing there outside the screen door. The screen mesh made a chiaroscuro effect over their pale summer clothes. Stopped in time at that moment. As if all of their lives would be thought of as before that moment and after.

May we come in?

By all means, Johnny said.

Mox hustled in with them and settled on the braid rug Johnny kept there just for him; his fur smelled damp.

Did you tell her yet? Laurel said. She had just gotten her hair cut; it stuck up in rosy spikes, and a tiny cutlass of it before her ears softened her look. She seemed elated, grinning.

I haven't had a chance, Johnny said.

Tell me what?

We—Oceana announced—are buying a house.

A house.

Yes, a house. She reached into the back pocket of her shorts and pulled out a creased and worn color photocopy of the house, which she held before her proudly: a small tan saltbox with a slightly out-of-kilter foundation. Mulch had been piled on a potential flower bed beside a flowering shrub, mock orange or bridal veil. It was hard to tell.

It's on Rhode Island. Your neighborhood, Mom. The library's. Laurel watched her closely, waiting.

They're asking seventy-five, but we think they'll take less.

Now it has some problems, Laurel said. But it's what we can afford.

I didn't even know you were thinking about buying a house.

Oceana said, It just came up. We walked by and saw the sign and it just felt like what we want to do. We can fix it up.

What kind of problems? Ruth Anne reached out and Oceana handed her the photocopy of the house.

Johnny said, shrugging, Nothing much. I don't know if it's anything to be concerned about. I think I can help them, Ruthie.

I'm surprised you didn't mention this. On the phone.

He shrugged again. The girls wanted to wait.

So, Mom—we'll have our own home.

I'm happy for you, sweetie. I am. And the soulful journey was up to her. She knew that. She was the one who must go where Laurel wanted to go. Laurel would not come back. She looked at her and saw the girl of the skateboard. The girl of the communion dress and the May queen with the wreath of rosebuds on her once curly crown. The girl who dated boys for a brief, brief time. She would come into the house after a date with a boy and Ruth Anne thought she could remember a dreaminess about her, a longing, after those dates. There had been a prom. Laurel dressed in a black georgette sheath and patent-leather pumps. Wearing a borrowed marcasite ring and necklace. Freckles across her upper back. The boy in a rented tux. They had consulted her about their clothes and the wrist corsage. Those photographs were tucked away in Laurel's room somewhere and now Laurel's room would be Oceana's room. Or would they keep up a pretense and have separate bedrooms?

Father Carroll won't give you communion, Ruth Anne said.

Oceana had taken Laurel's hand. You think I care about that?

You ought to.

Laurel pursed her lips: an exasperated squeak. She glanced sidelong at Oceana.

Ruthie. You're tired, Johnny said. He got up and carefully placed his empty stout bottle into a cardboard six-pack container, to be recycled.

Laurel shook her head and tears came into her eyes. You'll never understand.

I just know how hard your lives will be.

Time to go, Oceana said. She reached out for the photocopy of the house and Ruth Anne gave it back.

Don't go, Ruth Anne said.

No, I think we should.

Johnny said, We'll talk again. We will. He ushered them to the door. He had his arms around them and they let him lead them to the door. The screen door banged shut. Moxie whimpered and Ruth Anne said, Stop it, Mox. Just stop. She listened to them talking on the patio. Johnny saying, Let's get together tomorrow. I'll meet you at the house so long as it's before we open for dinner. Call the realtor again. He was walking them through it.

The hurt was a plaintive undertow in Laurel's voice: What is wrong with her?

He walked them a little farther away. His voice soothing, the peacemaker.

Ruth Anne could not remember the last time she had used the front door of Brambles, but she used it then. She dumped the last of her wine in the sink and set the glass upside down in a metal dish rack and she found her way through the darkened dining room, past the coffeemaker and the jewel-like tea bags in a wooden box, past the folded tray stands, past the buffet table. The odor of extinguished candles lingered in the air. The front door opened onto the grassy knoll with their house at the bottom and she dug her heels into the rain-soaked soil and she smelled the metallic rain still coming, not far off on the prairie, and she walked down to the house, leaving their voices behind on the patio and she did not think they saw her and she felt like a fool and a hypocrite and she saw the life she had lived as parsed. Never whole. Never had been.

The walk down was not a long one. Still, the lie of the trip came hounding her all the way down the knoll. She had sat with the nuns on the black zafus and her knees had knotted up and she had counted the seconds in a minute to get through the twenty-minute sits. Twenty minutes could go by in a heartbeat if she were reading a book of stories or playing with Mox or sitting on the deck with Laurel or riding her bicycle or having sex, but time expanded when she sat. It expanded and she filled it. She filled time with her thoughts. Jill had made clear that she should not try to stop her thoughts, but stopping her thoughts was a means to survival. On Sunday she had driven to the church with the limestone pillar and she—a stranger—had gone in to the Vietnamese Mass. She thought they hardly noticed her. Someone handed her a song sheet: Maria, Me Hang Cuu Giup! She followed the gentle singing and she sang beneath their voices quietly. She did not understand a word, but when it was time for the peace greeting they made their way to her, one after another, and they clasped her hand and said in English, Peace, Peace, Peace of Christ be with you. She watched for Tin but she felt certain he was not present. They looked into her eyes and their eyes were liquid, dark: familiar but not familiar enough. After Mass the Vietnamese priest said, May I help you? No. No, thank you. Every day that week she had driven to the small towns. She had found the restaurants with names like Little Saigon and Da Nang Diner, the spearmint and pork and rice smells. She had eaten noodles and springrolls. She had drunk café sua, the icy coffee over sweetened condensed milk. A watcher. Searching. And every day she had visited Aunt Teensy and every day Teensy had said, I keep wishing, and even though she did not really want to know, Ruth Anne finally said, What for? Teensy said, I'll never tell. I'll never tell you.

It's the morphine talking, Jill said. I'll bet she doesn't even remember her wishes.

All the lights were on in the house, bright solace. Ruth Anne stepped into the mudroom and without untying the laces she pried off her sneakers and slipped into sandals and went into the kitchen.

Limbo stood there, eating a chocolate bar.

What're you doing here?

Me and Father Carroll missed you.

I missed you too. But you can't just walk in, Limbo.

I'm sorry.

His yellow headphones rested on his neck; his backpack of CDs and comics were at his feet. He was damp and squished one shoe against the tile floor.

You know those guys? Across the street?

Yes.

They're musicians. His mouth was full of chocolate and he kept talking and wiping his hand on his jeans. They're real musicians. I'm going to play with them. I am. You'll see.

He had tried to convince someone else before this, it sounded like. That's good, Ruth Anne said. That'll keep you off the street. She laughed but Limbo did not laugh. Irony was lost on him.

Father Carroll said no.

Why did he say no?

He just says no.

Listen, I'll take you home.

I don't want to go home.

It's late, Limbo. For me, it is. I drove from Michigan tonight. I'll take you home and then I'll see you at the church in the morning. I have a doctor's appointment and then I'm going to see Father Carroll.

She could not tell him now that she was leaving for a while. The fatigue of having to tell washed over her. She gathered her purse and her keys and a bottle of water as she talked and with her voice alone she urged him out the door and into the Tercel.

The Nova was still there. The sky broke open with faint smoky clouds. Limbo finished the chocolate and she thought he had taken the chocolate from a cupboard but it did not seem worth it to try and make a lesson from that. He put his headphones on and slammed a CD into his player. The Tercel seemed almost too small to contain him now that he was older. His shoulders and arms were those of a man.

Across the river, she slowed for deep water in the street. The steely water splashed hard against the window, startling Limbo.

Take me to their house.

I'm taking you home.

I want to go to their house.

He meant the wild house and she knew what he meant, but she did not want to take him there.

Let me out.

Limbo, it's late. Your mother's going to wonder where you are.

Goddamn it—he pounded on the dash—let me out.

She swerved in rainwater. A horn bleated from the truck behind her.

She slowed and finally came to a stop in front of the library. The wild house was dark.

Get out.

I'm sorry.

Get out now. You can't talk to me that way.

I'm sorry. I'm sorry, Ruth Anne. Ma'am. I'm sorry. I'm sorry.

She said nothing. She wanted to withdraw her unfailing care for one minute more. She felt sick to her stomach. Being in the car with him on the empty darkened street made her sick to her stomach.

It doesn't look like anyone's home.

I'll be home. I'll be home. He opened the door and got out, stepping into a puddle. One of his CDs fell out of his pack to the street. He nervously tugged at the zipper of his pack. His mouth was streaked with chocolate. He shut the car door and stood there, a little unsteady, it seemed to Ruth Anne.

She rolled down the window and said, I'll see you tomorrow at the church.

Music boomed from the wild house. Led Zeppelin. People still listened to Led Zeppelin. She realized she had not asked about the Dylan concert and she thought she should ask. Life had gone on. Alliances had been formed: Johnny was helping them buy a house.

Thank you for the ride, Ruth Anne. Thank you. You're nice to me. You're always nice. Limbo said these things with his head partway inside the opened car window. He had begun to shave. She did not know when that had happened, but she saw it now. A red razor cut on his chin. He knew what to say to please you.

She pulled away from the curb, switching on the radio: a late-night jazz show. Just around the corner the neon lights of a tavern rippled in the rainwater that had not gone down the storm drains. She did not even glance at the library. The library looked like a place she was about to leave behind.

Father Carroll bobbed on the balls of his feet as they talked. He was in what he called his civvies—jeans and a pinstripe shirt—his belly soft above his belt. He pouted, vexed, and he could not conceal the tremor of his hands.

Ruth Anne folded dishtowels she had found in a heap on the counter. It was easier to tell with a chore in her hands. Out the window of the lunchroom, the road crew—men and women in hard hats—perched on the back edge of a flatbed, eating from fast-food bags.

What am I supposed to do without you?

I'm sure you can hire someone. A temp.

You won't be here to train that someone.

Father—

I think I understand. I want to understand.

The coffeemaker steamed and dripped, the little puffs the only sound. His mottled face twisted up with discontent, his eyes pinkish. The phone rang insistently.

Don't answer it.

All right. She folded her arms and waited for the coffee. The phone stopped ringing but the ring reverberated in the silence between them.

Those nuns—he waved a hand dismissively. That's not the way to God, Ruth Anne.

It's an ancient practice. She wanted to say what Jill said: Your mind comes home. He would scoff at that and the words stuck in her throat.

Ancient. Yes. That makes it right, I suppose. He sighed. Your family needs you right now. Laurel's keeping bad company.

You don't know the company she keeps.

I know what happens over there. He pointed a malicious finger toward the college.

Limbo came up the stairs, a rag in one hand and a spray bottle of window cleaner in the other. She sat him down at the cafeteria table and told him.

Who'll check out my books? He seemed like a boy again. Not at all like the person who had beat the dash with his fist and said goddamn it.

Daisy will.

Daisy doesn't like me. You like me.

I do like you, Limbo. But I have to do this. My aunt Teensy might be dying. She's old and she might be dying and I want to see if we can forgive each other. You know about forgiveness, I know you do.

With every person she told, different reasons seemed the best reasons. She did not tell Limbo about the meditation. He would not understand.

The night before, Johnny had come to bed and they had talked in whispers in the empty house. She had asked about the Dylan concert.

I just felt close to them, he said. All these young kids singing those songs.

So you decided to give them a down payment on a house.

It's not an exact equation.

I thought we had agreed to consult each other about spending anything over five hundred dollars?

I didn't spend it. I gave it to them.

The bedroom had been dark and rain pelted the skylight. Ruth Anne had hoped to tarry, to snuggle in, to be placated by his presence. She wore a shirt of his, a brown T-shirt with bowling pins embossed on the pocket. She had rubbed scented lotion into her skin, breasts to heels, and she thought they might return to the moment when she had sat on his lap in the big kitchen. But her agitation was a little like a tide in her mind; she sat up crossed-legged beside him, plucking at the tufts of thread on the counterpane.

I thought she might get over it. I thought Oceana might move away.

She has a job offer.

A real job?

She graduated. She's going to be the prairie director at the state park. Prairie director.

They're reclaiming the prairie.

Johnny had reached up then and touched her cheek. Don't be sad, Ruthie.

She had put her hand over his hand. She had kissed his palm and one thing led to another and they had both gotten what they wanted.

Johnny had passed the night in what seemed like a dreamless sleep, but she had twisted in the bedclothes, sighing with every what-if that danced before her in the dark. At last about dawn with the pinkish-golden light tipping the catalpas she fell into exhausted sleep. Moxie had been beside the bed slapping his tail when she woke up and Johnny had been gone, already at work. She rolled into the slight indentation his body had left and she had drunk in the smell of him and she had missed him already, but she knew she had to go. She canceled her bone-density test. It could wait another week or so. She did not think she would be gone more than another week.

Limbo said, My mother says, Don't wash that wall.

Father Carroll said, What wall?

You know.

Ruth Anne and Father Carroll made eye contact. Father Carroll shrugged slightly and she saw that he would not take it on.

What they wrote on the wall was wrong, Ruth Anne said.

My mother says, Don't wash it off.

Some people don't understand, but it's wrong.

You better get to work, Father Carroll said to Limbo. I'm not paying you to sit here with your feet up.

Later, she went to Oceana's house and knocked on the side door. The black cat with the ring around its hind leg was sitting there as if it hadn't budged since the week before. Birds pecked at new hard pears—like knuckles—on a dwarf tree in the back yard. A neglected yucca bloomed luxuriously, creamily. Tentacles of music from the wild house reached this far. The railroad track was a half-block east and a slight vibration from a train still miles away rocked under her.

Oceana answered the door in her robe and said, Come in. She'll be glad to see you. She led her through the halls, talking animatedly—of the sunshine and the ease of the day and that she did not have to work and that they might check out the farmer's market and that they might ride their bicycles out into the country to a cemetery where they liked to have lunch and make up stories about the dead. Oceana—this young woman who had become someone she needed to pay attention to—led her up the wide carpeted stairs, past a stained-glass window, diamond-shaped. She led her to her daughter. She could not be in the presence of her daughter without Oceana's help. Curiosity nearly took precedence over all her other emotions: they were letting her in.

Their kitchen was nothing out of the ordinary: yellow pasta bowls were stacked on an open shelf; a rista of garlic hung over the range. The other rooms she glanced into had a sparsely furnished, indifferent look. They had so few belongings that their voices echoed against the high tin ceilings.

Laurel measured loose tea into a tea ball. She turned and said, You're here, nodding self-consciously. Smiling. Her eyes were red and puffy.

Over tea she told them. There was no mention of the tan saltbox or the night before, but Ruth Anne did say to Oceana, Congratulations on your job. Johnny told me.

And, Sweetie, I know you'll look in on your father.

How long'll you be gone?

I can't say. Aunt Teensy needs me. She doesn't know it, but she does.

You're a good soul to forgive her.

I'm not so sure I have.

We'll come up there if you want us to.

I have your number.

Then the telling was over. The maneuvering was over. It seemed that every time in her life she had left, every time she had risen from some blind embeddedness, there had been lies to tell or sins of omission, at the very least. Later, on the road, she would remember the hugs. Laurel's tentative, with a kiss on the cheek. The smell of her like ginger. Some lotion she used. And Oceana—her strong arms speaking out: Yes, yes, we will embrace and accept each other, come on in and love us together. She would remember the way she said, Your number. The way she thought, Their apartment. How awful that felt.

# 7

An accident. Oui. Yes, merely a welding accident, Vo said. I was repairing my bicycle in my neighbor's shop. I was fourteen.

His mother was nearby and it was the first time they had spoken intimately. Ruth Anne whispered, Could nothing be done about it?

Some things can't be changed.

A servant girl—Mai—brought a tray to them behind the lotus blossom screen. On the tray, tea had been arranged. A metal pot with pale jade geometry inlaid around its belly. Steam rising. Two cups the size of votive candles. A packet of British biscuits from Hong Kong that had been offered the week before and the week before that, which had proven to be stale and tasteless. Flies lit on the yellow sugar scattered in a bowl. The cigarette smoke of old men wafted in the room. Behind the screen, she and Vo accepted—welcomed, although neither had said so—the illusion of privacy. Madame Thuong presided on the other side, her back to them. Once in a while she would turn, deliberately, and check to see what they were doing. Sampans with their red prows bobbed on the river in the distance. A child's record player scratched out music—the mornings she had come, Edith Piaf, but this afternoon, traditional laments. When Madame Thuong glanced over her shoulder, they were reading. It was the third time she had come to read to Vo. Just ask him, Sister Michelle had said. You don't know what she's like. She makes me feel like I shouldn't. He probably wants to talk to you, Sister Michelle said. Finally, Ruth Anne had whispered: What happened to your eyes?

I am lucky, Vo said. I read many books. I saw Paris and Hue. I was a daredevil on the monkey bridges. I had a girlfriend. He swiped the hair from his forehead nervously.

After the tea Ruth Anne said, Who was your girlfriend?

She wanted to say Johnny's name. She wanted to tell him about Johnny. They had read Maupassant's "Happiness." It was teatime, before the lamps were lit. Happiness, the simplicity of love, was on her mind. It takes you over. She felt feverish because of it and she wanted to say, Johnny will be here. I'm meeting him at Connie's apartment. Connie Mattingly has gone to Hawaii for two weeks and I have the key to her apartment on Nguyen Du Street. She had told no one, not even Sister Michelle. Particularly Sister Michelle, who came into her room every night and read under the mosquito netting. The next day we will meet Sue-Sue and Jill and the four of us will eat lunch together on a starched linen tablecloth. There will be proof for Sue-Sue that she could be bold. Sue-Sue will see it on her face, a smug carnality. For just that day it would be all right to be stuck on herself, stuck on what she and Johnny had managed. A woman will play torch songs on a piano. Johnny had called and described the Bamboo Forest and he had said he wanted it to be romantic, even if Jill and Sue-Sue were going to be there. The walls at Bamboo Forest were red and bamboo grew in enormous elephant pots and the woman at the piano wore a sequined dress. The gin would be Tanqueray. The prawns would be fresh from the sea. He had been breathless on the phone. I can't wait, Ruthie. I think about it all the time. You. I think about you. I don't want to have stories to tell. I don't want anyone to think I'm scary. Or weird. I just want to go home. I want us to make a life that doesn't have anything to do with this place. She had wanted to tell him what Sue-Sue said about the sharks but she didn't. She wanted to purge herself of the sharks bleeding into the sea. She did not want to think about it and she had hoped to tell Johnny and have Johnny absorb it. Johnny would absorb whatever bothered her; he would say, Not to worry, and he would pull her into his arms and therein lay a contentment not unlike the feel of being carried as a girl into the house by her father when he thought she'd fallen asleep in the truck across her mother's lap. They would drive up the lakeshore and back. A drive along the lakeshore to watch the sun set would be their entertainment. She would pretend to be asleep to feel her father's arms around her, lifting her into the starry night sky. Not to worry. But his call had been cut off. We will be at Connie's apartment together, with a view of the public gardens, the bonsai on a hillock. She had not been in the apartment on Nguyen Du long enough to notice the rusted ceiling fan inside a rusty cage. Connie had given her a tour of the three rooms and said, Help yourself to anything. Tabu. Liquor. Green dragon fruit in a milky-colored crock. Connie's clothes that hung in silky waves inside an armoire, skirts and blouses tailored at a shop on Nguyen Hue Street. For next to nothing, Connie said. When she said, Take a bath, if there's water, Ruth Anne thought, There will be water and there will be electricity and we will have one night when nothing spoils it. She and Johnny would lie down together under Connie's cool fig-green sheets. She had the key on a delicate chain around her neck under her clothes and when she felt the key between her breasts she thought of Johnny, Johnny's mouth. The rush of sex washed over her morning, noon, and night.

Vo said, She was a student. We were children. She stole cigarettes from her mother and we would smoke them under the Eiffel Tower. We would drink wine.

Madame Thuong appeared behind the lotus screen. She was still young, in a peacock-blue dress with a mandarin collar and sling-back heels. The style was dated; it was a look Ruth Anne associated with the clothes of a decade before, the fifties, what starlets might have worn. She drank in the details; other Vietnamese women dressed in loose pants and blouses or the graceful tunics. Madame Thuong's nails were polished and bright. Her rhinestone glasses were sharp at the temples and gave her a shrewd, disapproving look. Some women are completely at ease dressed up, their own works of art; it was work to be beautiful and Ruth Anne was young enough to think, I should work at it more than I do. Sister David made her feel the vanity of brushing her hair and Vo's mother made her feel she would always be somewhat slipshod; her hair would always come loose or fly away; buttons would go missing; the heels of her practical shoes would be worn down and not taken to the cobbler. She felt the censure of other women. Sister Michelle did not censure her; she needed her; she flushed to think of how they lay in the bed, reading, with the insects beating against the windowpane. Don't tell. Please don't tell.

Merci, Miss Ruth Anne, Vo's mother said.

That was the signal.

Merci, Vo said. She thought she detected a slight downward turn at his mouth, a disappointment. His lips were full. His hair fell across his forehead and he wiped it back. When you come again we will begin "A Simple Heart."

Others did not want to hear about your love. You felt it pressing from inside but telling would diminish it and be considered unkind. Like bragging. She did not want to be unkind to Vo. His voice leaped at her, in quiet animal urgency. Sister Michelle had been right: he wanted to talk.

Madame Thuong walked her through the smoky room, over the oiled wooden floor, among the old men, the domino players. At the door she said, Please read only stories. She nodded toward the din of the street, where sunshine burst upon the palm trees and the boys beneath, slinging a shoe along the sidewalk in a game of chance. This could end. He has been hurt enough. I want him to hear the complete stories.

Of course, Madame. I understand. She plotted immediately to read whatever Vo wanted. We'll pretend, we'll just pretend.

Later she would wonder why Madame Thuong did not read the stories to Vo. Later still, she would realize that Madame Thuong spoke a little French and English, but she did not have the patience or the skill to read aloud. The books had belonged to her paramour, a French officer. Pregnant with Vo, she had been a servant at a French garrison when they met. He had taken her to Paris and there she and Vo lived until several years after his death at Dien Bien Phu. The French took all their dead home, Vo would say. The stories would tumble from Vo very soon. His family stopped speaking to us the day he was buried. He is buried near Vence, above Nice. Nice is like your Hollywood. There are fast cars. A beautiful beach with beautiful women. My mother has been at the mercy of her beauty. Her father cast her out of the family when she became pregnant with me. My father was married to another woman. Her beauty has won her adoration and angels of death at her door. The next one, a French photographer, was killed at Pleiku, and it was then we were forced to return to Saigon.

Over the years in France, Madame had managed to secrete small sums away and she had her business to attend to. The tea shop. The garage next door where people parked their bicycles while they went to the market. She made a little money this way and that.

Outside, a man whose arms ended at his elbows painted pictures with his toes on small squares of fiberboard. A woman perched on a stool behind a zinc bucket full of bracelets made of jasmine threaded on twine. A GI in a T-shirt and boots leaned over the bucket and selected a bracelet for his Vietnamese girlfriend. The perfume of the jasmine rose in little clouds and dispersed before the patched awnings of the vendors. You buy me, the girlfriend said. You buy me.


It was twilight. Sister Michelle's shoes came brush-brushing down the hall and into the library. Ruth Anne had come to recognize the sound of her shoes. She switched on the sconces and a honey-colored light filled the room. She stood at the door, smiling. Why are you working now?

Ruth Anne wiped her gluey hands on the stained apron. I want to get ahead. I'm going to visit my friends for two days.

Where?

Here. They are taking a room at a hotel.

Ooh-la-la. The Continental?

Ruth Anne's heart went out to her. She was jealous and trying not to show it.

Nothing so fancy.

It's almost social hour.

I'm going to work through social hour.

Blushing, Sister Michelle shut the door and came closer. She surveyed the books Ruth Anne had finished binding, lovely stacks with stiff covers that would last a lifetime. Ruth Anne turned to her work table and pressed a Due Date pocket into a first edition of *Tender Is the Night*. The smell of the glue was the smell of elementary school, of scout meetings on craft night. While working in the library she often drifted involuntarily into memories of time before her mother died—the glue took her there. She thought of projects she had made for her mother: a stole of baby blue yarn and pincushions from Ball jar rings and lids.

She started, at Sister Michelle's hands kneading her shoulders. You shouldn't overdo it.

I'm not.

They guiltily, clumsily, spun toward the door at a feeble knock.

Come in.

Come in.

Mrs. Ha opened the door. She was a tiny woman in rayon clothes printed with jovial red airplanes. Her knees bowed out slightly. She peered up at them, frowning, from behind thick lenses spattered with the day's cooking residue. Sister Michelle, Miss Ruth Anne, bonsoir, bonsoir. She made a circular motion against one ear. Sister Michelle, you have a telephone call. Le bureau, le bureau. An emergency!

God in heaven. Sister Michelle dashed out the door.

Mrs. Ha stood aside, wringing her hands.

Ruth Anne instinctively crossed herself. Please, she prayed, nothing bad. Please. Keep. Johnny. Safe.

Come to the kitchen.

I am working.

We have le gâteau chocolat.

Merci, merci. I will wait for Sister Michelle, then I will come to the kitchen.

Mrs. Ha bowed slightly, backing out of the door. Ruth Anne wiped her hands again on the apron and untied its strings and laid it over a straight-back chair so that the glue she had wiped would dry. She went into the toilette and washed her hands. The mirror above the basin was fractured with age, a clouded silver. She had grown accustomed to getting ready for the day without looking in a mirror, for fear the lacquered spoon pushed under the door would not deter the nuns next door. She did not want to be caught by them and she rushed through her bathroom routine. When she did have occasion to see herself in private, it was an odd luxury. But now she saw worry and it was only at that moment she realized how much she cared for Sister Michelle. How much she did not want her to suffer. How much she depended on the feel of her thigh against hers, with only the flimsy cotton of their nightgowns between. She did not know what that meant. It was a feeling she had never had before with a girl. It was another threshold; she did not know what lay on the other side, if there was another side.

She went to her room and waited. She picked up a book and tried to read but she could not concentrate. What was Vo doing on such a night? What did he do with himself when she was not reading to him? She wanted to tell him Sister Michelle's story. She wanted to turn the evening into a story for him. The feeble knock at the library door. Le bureau, le bureau. Mrs. Ha wringing her hands. The chocolate cake. It had begun to rain, lightly at first, but as she waited, and as it grew dark, the rain fell dismally in the garden and salvos of thunder sounded in the distance. The lights flickered. She pulled a canvas suitcase from under the bed and opened it on the bed and began to pack. A few days before, she had purchased a nightgown and she had left it in the packet the shop girl had wrapped it in: a flat cellophane bag through which she could see the crumpled red silk peonies. Even as she waited for her friend, and to know what the emergency was about, she wondered if Connie had an iron and whether she could iron the gown without scorching it and she wanted everything to be perfect for the rendezvous with Johnny and she thought that such perfection could exist, was possible. She thought of the nights in the hammock on the deck at home. She placed the cellophane bag in the suitcase and covered it with a blouse and her bellbottoms. Hiding it.

She went to the door and looked down the hall. Sister Michelle came quietly, her pretty face in a bitter moue.

What is it?

My brother.

How bad is it?

Not so bad as it could be. He lost a hand. His elbow's crushed. He'll get to go home. She burst into tears.

Ruth Anne put her arms around her, held her. Later she would not be sure who had broken through the boundary first. Someone had moved the suitcase from the bed; the storm had abated, with the rain pattering gently on the roof tiles; someone had turned off the lamp; they lay under the mosquito netting in each other's arms. Once there were footsteps in the hall and they grew rigid, breathless. But whoever it was passed by. The crystal doorknob shined and for a moment Ruth Anne imagined it was turning, turning, and that they would be found out, but she shook away that feeling. Sister Michelle cried a little longer. Her baby blond braids had come undone. She kissed Ruth Anne's mouth. Each time she would say, afterward, Don't tell, please don't tell.

The next morning Ruth Anne assured herself, Those kisses are invisible; no one can tell. She won't tell.

Mrs. Ha had saved a slice of gâteau chocolat for Ruth Anne and she gulped it for breakfast, with a glass of coffee. Rain rang down again. There was a leak in the kitchen and a roasting pan had been set beneath it and the rain came ping-pinging into the speckled pan. Miss Cam slipped out of her room, sleepy-eyed.

Miss Ruth Anne, Where are you going?

To see my friends.

When will you return?

Day after tomorrow.

And how is Sister Michelle?

Sad. Very sad.

She did not want to talk about Sister Michelle. After the kisses Sister Michelle had gotten up, her clothes rumpled, not surefooted, sighing, a little drunk on what they had done. At the door she had said, I'll probably go home when he goes home.

I'll miss you.

Me too.

She did not want to think about the way kissing her felt like loving herself. Or loving all women. The kiss was the threshold across which she was surprised to see her mother; she thought of the odor of prom dresses at the dark end of the closet in the cottage at Pier Cove: White Shoulders. She only wanted to be held and I held her. There's nothing wrong with that.

She left them there, Miss Cam washing her face at a basin and Mrs. Ha measuring rice with a tin cup. It was early. The nuns were at Morning Praise in the chapel. It was a good time to leave. She had been eager for days; she had been eager all her life. She readied herself to leave, in spite of the rain. Sister David knew she was going and she knew when she would return. All of that had been arranged. It had not been hard to lie. She did not believe Sister David would want to know the truth. She did not think about Sister David's desires or the obstacles to chastity she might have overcome. This question never fully formed: Had she ever been wanted by someone the way Johnny wanted Ruth Anne? Sister David was only a power to escape. Sister Michelle was different. She was young. She had made a mistake becoming a nun. What they had done was invisible; no one could tell. She slipped into her rain jacket and took up her suitcase. She had piasters for the cyclo driver and she felt in the front pocket of her slacks for the wide worn bills she had folded in half and tucked there.

Mrs. Ha came into the hall where they could look out into the courtyard and the rain. Even the chickens took shelter beneath a bench, their heads beneath their wings. She handed Ruth Anne a pink vinyl rain poncho. Take this!

I don't need it.

You need it!

She stripped off the rain jacket and pulled the crinkly poncho on.

I'll keep this for you, Mrs. Ha said, clutching the jacket to her chest. Pull up the hood. She peered at the sky. Rainy season will be over soon. We will have mangos. The cay mai tree will bloom. You see. You see. Holidays will come. Christmas. Tet. I make coconut jam for Tet.

The convent was safe—she knew that now, in this particular moment with Mrs. Ha, but it was too late. That sort of safety would never be hers. She was engaged to be married. She would wait for Johnny in Connie Mattingly's bed. It would be like a marriage bed. That was the true threshold.

Sister Michelle's voice rang out in the kitchen. Bonjour! Shame and the sound of her voice thrust Ruth Anne into the courtyard and past the gate. The latch clapped shut behind her.

The rain had weight and force. People on bicycles, their ponchos stiffened by the wind, slowed in the street like one massive being. The cyclo drivers had pulled up under the shop awnings and they huddled under the leather hoods of the cyclos. Some slept. Some read. Only one noticed Ruth Anne emerging from the convent and he waved and staggered over and she did not even negotiate a fare. He wore a white shirt, soaked to the skin. Rain ran down his face. He tucked her suitcase under a plastic bag at her feet. Her face and hands were slick with rain. She did not care. She was going to Johnny and she would see Johnny within a few hours and that was all that mattered. She told herself not to think about the man who had escorted her home from the party. Riding in a cyclo brought him to mind. But he was not important. That had been foolish and you are allowed to be foolish now and again. Life allows

mistakes, without enduring consequences. If you are in another country and you are young, mistakes will fade into what you leave behind.
She told herself to think that way. Just don't do it again. Sue-Sue would
have wild stories to tell. But Sue-Sue was not engaged. She was a free
agent and she could kiss anyone or make out or sleep around. Aunt
Teensy called her a slut and slut was a word Ruth Anne did not like to
hear or think. Slut was a threshold you could not return from. Safety
lay with Johnny and marrying Johnny would protect her from such
foolishness. Johnny would save her from herself.

At Connie Mattingly's apartment building she paid the driver and he
wanted to come back for her but she said, No, it's not necessary, and she
climbed the concrete steps, past three women perched on the landing,
mending. Their needles and the scissors they shared glimmering. She
did not speak and neither did they. She unlocked Connie's door and,
with more relief than she had felt since coming to Saigon, she dropped
her suitcase and flung off the poncho, spraying rainwater in the foyer all
over the fake parquet floor. The lights had been left on, reading lamps
with dented brown shades. She opened the drapes and the public garden
was not visible; only a gray wall of rain. And within the rain, three military jeeps. And people in their rain gear, on bicycles, still traveling in
the blustery street. The conical hats. The police at the corners with billy
clubs. Connie had an eight-track tape player and Ruth Anne turned on
a tape, a woman singing some country song she associated with dirt
roads and one-pump gas stations south of the Mason-Dixon line—she
did not know where those images came from but it was all right, it was
emotionally arousing, to listen to the woman's sexy voice. There was a
mild stench in the bedroom she did not like—a mustiness like clothes
that had been dampened and rolled in a basket and left not ironed.

In the icebox—that's what Connie had called it—there was a carafe
of boiled water and a bottle of white wine and eggs and cheese. She
opened every cupboard, every closet. She wanted to know what was
available—books, food, clothes, drink. Connie had a stash of detective
novels. And confession magazines with lurid covers.

She had shown her how to light the hot water heater in the hallway.
She lit the heater and waited and she drew a not-quite hot tub of water.
She laid out her clothes and the silk nightgown on the bed. Johnny was
due by noon. After a bath she would read and when he arrived he would

find her in the silk nightgown with the red peonies. In the tub she went over all she could remember that Johnny had ever said about loving her.

When she stood up out of the bathwater she saw herself in the mirror. She raised her arms and turned and examined herself in the mirror: a young woman with pale freckled skin and red hair coiled in a loose chignon. One breast seemed puffy, slightly more round than the other. There was a scar above her right knee in the shape of a new moon, a sliver, from a cut she had gotten falling from her first, new bicycle. This freedom to view herself in the mirror had not been hers before; there was always someone who might catch her being immodest. She raised her arms and admired her breasts and her hips. She tried to see herself as Johnny would see her. What had happened with the man from the small town near St. Louis and what had happened with Sister Michelle had been relegated to a slim cranny. Johnny was coming. She would renew her engagement to Johnny and she would not stray again. She thought that when they slept together she would never want anyone else again; she would never fall prey to anyone else's desire for her. She had almost gotten in trouble and she vowed never to get near trouble again.

The warmth of the bath on her skin made her drowsy. She thought she would read but after the bath she fell into a deep sleep, wearing the silk peonies. She had turned off the country music. She had closed the drapes. It was a time of ease. A time when sleep could wrap her in its ease.

She slept until the middle of the afternoon, awakened by an old bad dream. Her father had used a tuning box with a needle that bobbed wildly and then settled—still—with the gradual coming into tune of every piano key. In the dream the needle never settled, the key rang out of tune, the needle tormented her.

Three o'clock. She picked up the alarm clock, unbelieving. She rose out of the bed in a stupor, thirsty. The rain had stopped. She could see the public garden. Vendors had opened their carts and people had stripped off the plastic ponchos. The waiting began.

Give up! At midnight she told herself, Give up. She had been through tears; tears would do no good.

An insight about her own vanity hovered just beyond her awareness. Years later she would understand; the humiliation she felt was knowledge of every vain and selfish thought she had indulged. But such insight must be invited. It has to be embraced. Instead she felt abandoned and afraid for Johnny.

She dressed in bell-bottoms and sandals. The nightgown she slung on the bed and, seeing it there later in the night, she thought it looked cheap, like a bit of trash. She put up her hair indifferently, pinning it with golden hairpins Connie kept in a tea tin. Her stomach growled and she had never felt so far from her own hunger. Finally she boiled an egg and ate it plain, with no salt or pepper. She opened the drapes to the nearly empty street. She would measure out the hours, waiting. Time would pass in cul-de-sacs of memory. Time would pass and then what would she do? If she were back in her own bed, with Sister Michelle stretched out beside her, she would be reading. That was the one reliable thing: reading. She tried to read "A Simple Heart." She would picture Félicité cooking and sewing and washing and ironing and bridling horses and fattening poultry and churning butter. She slowed and pictured each act and she wanted to know what Félicité looked like and she wanted to know why she would remain faithful for fifty years to a mistress who was hard to get on with. It was about choice. Félicité had no choice. Every choice made faithfulness less likely. She wanted to read the story to Vo. They would consider why. She got as far as the second paragraph. Her own life held the reins of her imagination. Scenarios were unfolding somewhere, scenarios affecting her: Johnny might have called the convent or Sue-Sue and Jill's hotel; Sue-Sue and Jill might be wondering when they would hear from her; Johnny might be in trouble—he might have had an accident or he might have hit a roadblock. There were worse possibilities. She would not think the worst. These were the channels she tooled in her mind. And, Why should Jill and Sue-Sue be free? Why should they be at the hotel, drinking gin-and-tonics? Why should Sue-Sue lack a conscience? She did not even know she was a slut and lived outside such judgments. Ruth Anne allowed her hatred of Aunt Teensy to occupy her and she spent at least one hour between midnight and dawn recalling every time she had gotten the brush. Every word that led to the brush. Every smirk or slamming door. The musty odor was stronger now. Water bugs jittered along the corners of the kitchen. The rusty ceiling fan would not stir the air. The apartment had a crooked feel, like Van Gogh's *Room at Arles*. It was a place she did not want to be any longer but she had to wait until daylight. It would be safe to leave when she saw the women squatting on the street, selling grass-green vegetables from baskets.

She was required to wait. It made her think of every waiting time: when Aunt Teensy had locked her in and when she waited for her parents' bodies to be sent home for burial and waiting for Johnny's phone call. She had been in Saigon for nearly three weeks before he called and she did not ask why. She had not asked for the details.

All the memory and anger funneled into this vessel: prayer. She prayed a child's prayer: Don't let it be this way. Don't.


Sue-Sue had cut her hair. She had prided herself on her long hair but now it was short and dark with yellow tips.

He didn't come.

Jill said, You waited all night?

I waited all day and all night.

Sue-Sue sighed, exasperated. She hauled her by the arm into their room. They had not gotten dressed and Ruth Anne felt disoriented seeing them in their robes. It did not feel like morning. The room smelled steamy, perfumy. Jill's hair was up in rollers. The radio was on: lowdown American music of some kind; she couldn't place it. Everything about seeing them felt unreal. She was supposed to meet them in the Bamboo Forest, holding Johnny's hand. She had imagined rushing up to their table, grinning, Johnny's arm around her waist.

Sue-Sue sat down in an armchair and her robe fell open to reveal her garter belt, her stockings. Her legs brown, a little plump. The smooth nylons new.

Jill had her wits about her. She said, We can find out. Whatever it is, we can find out. I know someone who'll find out for us. She's high up in the Red Cross. I've often thought that if I didn't hear from my brother—God forbid—that's who I'd turn to. She's the kind who can pull strings to find out anything.

You don't think he just didn't show?

Sue-Sue.

It happens, she shrugged. Guys disappear into Saigon alleys and you might never see them again. She went into the bathroom and shut the door.

Don't pay any attention to her. She's got some guy after her. A civilian. From D.C. She's going to meet him later.

Traffic bellowed down in the street. Wow-wow-wow-wow: police and ambulance sirens perpetually sounded. A chenille bedspread had been pulled hastily up to the pillows and there was a dry grayish stain on it. The air-conditioner gave off a moist stale smell. Wallpaper had peeled from the corners near the ceiling. It was another place she did not want to be.

Sue-Sue opened the door and said, Honey—

Don't honey me.

Ruthie—

Jill. I feel sick. I feel like I can't breathe.

You're anxious.

We're all anxious, Sue-Sue said, tapping a cigarette from a pack. She lit it, blew smoke toward the ceiling, and carefully positioned the cigarette on a black onyx ashtray from a hotel in Thailand. She took off her robe and began to dress: flats and a petticoat and a full striped skirt and matching blouse.

It was an outfit Ruth Anne recognized from home. She held her hand at her chest, taking shallow breaths. She shook her head. I have to go home.

Sue-Sue said, That's a pretty drastic measure.

Jill said gently, She means the convent, don't you?

He—might—call.

He might.

Jill said, They'd take a message, wouldn't they?

Of course. But I want to be there when he calls. She did not say, Sister Michelle. Or Vo. She was in relationship with them. They somehow mattered more than Sue-Sue or Jill but that thought perished the filmy moment it occurred to her. Sue-Sue and Jill were all she had to cling to. Friends. Old friends.

We'll go with you. We'll see where you live.

Then? This is our big town trip.

Jill said, I know that. I know that. She took Ruth Anne's hand in hers. But don't you see? She's upset.

What about your brother?

Jill glanced at her watch. That's hours yet. What do you want to do, Ruthie?

It might be some small thing. I just want to go back. I can't explain it. I just want to go back. I want to go to Mass.

Sue-Sue sighed, put out. She smoked her cigarette. Look. I didn't come to Saigon for that. I'm going down to get a Coke. She stubbed out the cigarette and ducked in front of the mirror, fingering out her hair. She opened her mouth and carefully rolled on lipstick.

When she had gone, Ruth Anne said, I'll go with you. Let's go somewhere. She pressed her temples with her fingers. She flung her hands open and shut as if to rid herself of something toxic. The hotel window looked smeared with dust and oil and made the sunshine gray. A helicopter vibrated over traffic, over the raw, sleepless rant inside her—where is he, where is he? I'll go. But I hate Sue-Sue. I hate her when she's like this.

Light fell into the museum's courtyard with the clarity of glass. Against the high yellow walls.

There was a dry fountain. A cactus grew tall in a pot shaped like an elephant. It was a small courtyard. Jill and Ruth Anne sat on a bench, Jill holding her hand. She had calmed down. She could breathe. It was quiet in the museum; voices echoed, but still, the racket—the backfiring motorbikes and trucks belching and chatter—was out there, beyond the museum. Jill had only one hour more. DDs they called themselves—sometimes with pride, sometimes derisively—and she traveled with another Donut Dolly who would meet her at the Continental. Her brother would be there and Ruth Anne had known him from a distance. Jill said, Come along, but Ruth Anne did not have the heart for it.

They could see into the next room where Sue-Sue in her striped outfit feigned interest in the statue of the female incarnation of the Buddha. Two Buddhist monks in yellowish robes whispered off to the side. Their scalps were smooth and hairless and shiny. She thought of the persistence of religion. She had wept at the Passion as Félicité had. These monks knew nothing of the Passion of Christ and she did not understand how so many had lived without the story of turning the water to wine or the Beatitudes. She knew little of other religions and yet here were the statues and the monks and everywhere she went joss sticks were offered and makeshift shrines in billiard halls and beauty shops were lit up for the Buddha or for ancestors. Tears came easily when she was a girl; she did not know if she would cry at the Passion now. She had crossed over some line; her emotions were caught up with other concerns. A man entered the room and glanced around: he was thin, with a pale American face, in a starched white shirt and slacks that draped loosely from pleats. His eyes lit on Sue-Sue and he walked over to her and embraced her. They had already slept together. They possessed each other.

Jilly—

I think he's in love with her.

Ruth Anne could not bear to watch. Do you think you're doing any good?

I think I am. Do you?

It's not the same. I'm on an assembly line.

I like these guys, Jill said. They're like the guys we went to high school with. We make hospital books—

What's a hospital book?

A book of games and cartoons. It's hard going to the hospitals. That's the hard part.

She slipped Jill's hand from hers and stared away, at the glassy light contained within the high courtyard walls, at a family noisily arriving, the father letting the mother shepherd the children.

Jill went on—Do you hear from your aunt?

No.

Nothing?

One letter.

Sue-Sue left the man standing beside the statue and she came to them and said goodbye. They went out to the street without her and took a cyclo to a lane of antique shops. Ruth Anne bought a blue willow butter dish. She did not know why. What would she do with a butter dish? But she wanted to buy something. Jill wanted to buy silver chopsticks but she thought they might get stolen or lost. She reiterated her philosophy: travel light. The lane of antique shops was narrow, cobbled, and only a Renault or cart and horse might get down the lane. People wandered, shopping. There was a feeling of frivolity, Sunday, and white women and officers carried reed bags of whatever they had purchased. A boy with stumps for arms planted himself in front of anyone who would glance his way. His wares he kept tucked close to one armpit. You want postcard Saigon? You want souvenir?

# 8

Johnny Bond had his preferences while she was gone.

On a good morning he would meet Tuck at the blacktop court behind the brick elementary school-turned-community center. He would have been awakened early by the coyotes yipping at the edge of the woods beyond the golf course. He rose alert, surprised at Ruth Anne's absence, even after two weeks. He missed her but he felt good; healthy; interested in the day. After a wake-up shower he would go up to the big kitchen and in the hard steel shadows start a sponge for rolls or bread. He would drink the blackest coffee. Songbirds flittered in aural calligraphy outside the kitchen window. He let Moxie roam alone among the birches where he could keep an eye on him. Everything was working toward that blacktop and the moment he dribbled the ball, the fine pebble of the ball like the touch of dawn, of first sunlight, that salubrious.

Two days before the Fourth he shot around a little before Tuck arrived. His best shot was always a jumper from the left side. He did that a few times and then he stood at the imaginary free-throw line and shot into the sunrise. The ball bounced off the rim once, twice. He had not stretched and he did not like to stretch beforehand. He told himself that the walk from his house to the blacktop was a stretch. He liked to walk down the lane and through the golf course when it was still too early for the golfers, the sky streaky with night colors. He carried the ball under his arm. It was bearable to be outdoors in the early morning, with sheens of humidity hovering over the college airport and the soccer field and the strip mall.

The college air jocks were still asleep and he did not have to listen to them revving their engines or taking off; that was a sound he never liked; he was not sorry he and Ruth Anne had chosen to live sixty miles from the nearest international airport. He'd been airborne—with his knees in the breeze, as they liked to say. When he thought about it—which was not often—Johnny realized that he had arranged his life so that he would be reminded as seldom as possible of what he did not want to recall.

Instead, he cooked. His mind was full to the brim with ingredients and processes and visions of the final ephemeral result. He understood that some men thought primarily about sports or war and some men thought primarily about sex and some men thought primarily about money, but for Johnny it was food. Cheeses. Flours. The difference walnut oil might make in a salad dressing. The best way to meld butter into a frosting of Chambord and egg whites and sugar. Olives in all their variety. Gaeta. Sevillano. Kalamata, with their deep-plum briny leatheriness. If he were to organize his solitary thoughts like the food pyramid, cooking would be the broad foundation. Fruit trees were edging in as a possible respite from cooking; he wanted to plant a few trees while Ruth Anne was away. She was opposed to more shade in the yard; shade kept the best flowers from thriving. He felt like a bully about it—she's not here, she'll live with it. When he mentioned the fruit trees to Tuck, Tuck said, They're a pain. Old La-di-da planted fruit trees and take it from me, they're a pain in the old kazoo. Old La-di-da—Tuck's number-two ex. AKA Joyce. Johnny had not known her well. She moved to Chicago; Tuck had quoted her: I want a life that's about more than junior-high basketball and watching thunderstorms. About the fruit trees Tuck had insisted, You have to go to war with the birds. But Johnny was not deterred. He wanted those blossoms in the spring almost as much as he wanted the fruit.

Then, he thought about Laurel. Laurel and her upcoming move. It had been so long since he and Ruth Anne had moved that he had forgotten how a move takes you over; all of your resources galvanize for it. He felt tender toward the girls, in spite of himself and his natural tendency—he was sure it was natural—to wish Laurel were not what she said she was. Still, he could not help getting involved in the delight they took in the appraisal and the best mulch for the flower bed and the heat pump and the abstract for the old house, which had been built in 1947. He had grown fond of Oceana. Prairie director. A job he had not known existed: perfect for her. She could tromp around the state park in her boots and sturdy clothes. He caught himself testing her knowledge, asking about a grass or sedge or flower. They had begun to tease each other and teasing her made teasing Laurel easy, as playful as it had been when she was a kid, and the teasing made talk come. They had had some good talks at Brambles after hours. He would tell Ruthie when she called but the sweetness and truth got lost. I wish your mother were here, he said one night. And Laurel said, It might be different if she were. The meditation seemed off-limits. As it should be—that was part of their private business: what they did when they were alone and what they did for religion. The idea of sitting still and thinking nothing or sitting still and counting his breaths made him want to jump up and jog or dance. He did not see the point in it. There was a lack of sensuality to it. He would rather swirl the juices of a good cut of beef with red wine and garlic; he would rather have his hands in yeast dough; he would rather play basketball or fool around with Ruth Anne or drive the back roads or plant fruit trees. Life was too short to sit still, ignoring it.

Patience was required with Ruthie. He did not know why Jill's monastery had a hold on her but he knew that she would sooner or later come back and slip into the stream of all they had. He imagined her watching soap operas with Teense, holding her hand, if Teense would allow it. She was a tough old bird and she might go down without comfort. Teense did not figure large in his life, even though she had liked him when he courted Ruth Anne. The stories of the beatings with the hairbrush turned that around—he could not respect her.

He knew this much although he had not said so to Ruthie: the girls should be getting married. The first time that thought reared up it broke his heart. For them. You could sense their union. I'm on your side, Oceana would say. That's all it took if you loved someone. He planned to do the move up right: the day they closed on their saltbox—their castle, they called it—he would have a bottle of champagne and flowers delivered. He would bake a cake.

Five more lay-ups from the left and Tuck's pickup eased into the gravel parking space. The pickup was equipped with what Tuck called skookum speakers and he rolled down the window and the classic rock station let loose with "Light My Fire." It qualified as classic, he supposed. If you ever heard the Doors on NPR the music itself would be brief, buffered by interviews of fans at Morrison's grave site. July 4 would be Louis Armstrong's birthday and they would play "What a Wonderful World," a song that would not bring up bad memories. He tended to skirt music that brought up bad memories. He could remember where he was the first time he heard "Light My Fire" and it was not a place he wanted to think about. Ft. Benning, in a sleazy bar. The night before. So everyone wanted to overdo it. It was mostly men in the bar. They did not know much about the summer of love or whatever it was out in San Francisco. It seemed like a circus and had nothing to do with what they were about. He had gone to a pay phone beside the men's room and telephoned Ruth Anne and she did not answer. She was at work in her English wench uniform and he had drunk enough that it was hard to figure out when she might be home. He could picture her sitting cross-legged in the hammock, in the yellow deck light, counting her tips, her skirt a bowl of coins and dollar bills. With the lake dark below the deck. He might have sat on the glider with a beer, watching her and not caring about another thing. Watching her was enough. It made her happy to count her tips. Watching her would be enough until she tossed the coins into a coffee tin and insinuated herself into his arms. He ached to think of that. The pay phone receiver felt greasy. The odor of old urine spilled into the corridor every time someone opened the door to the men's room. He felt sappy about it, but he wanted to ask her if she had planted the morning glory seeds yet. Back at the table the buddy he was with said, Nine weeks. This's been in the Top 40 for nine weeks. Some people kept track of the Top 40 and Johnny had nothing against that but Jim Morrison did not interest him then or now. Then the buddy said, The more Viet Cong we kill, the more beer we get. They were in the same high-speed unit. Comrades by necessity. Johnny was drunk enough to say, Right on. He had gone to the Bob Dylan concert with the girls and he had felt good about the young people singing the peace songs but that did not mean he thought peace was viable or imminent. If you were lucky, something like personal peace might be within your grasp. And that came from doing what you were supposed to do. An axiom he had not understood when he was young.

The court had buckled one bad winter; sprigs of volunteer chamomile sprouted in the cracks, the seeds of which he imagined floating from some senior citizen's garden. Johnny's thoughts pounced from chamomile to his own kitchen garden and the basil he planned to pick to Ruth Anne, what she had said on the telephone last night: They don't cook the way they used to. When they were kids the nuns had made homemade caramels every Christmas and they had prided themselves on their meals from scratch. Ruth Anne said, It's all in cellophane packages. She was doing what you do when you don't want to tell what you're thinking: Find some morsel to offer. Take the spotlight off you. He had done it himself. The distance between them expanded, took on the shape and proportion of the ancient moraine that lay between them. It was not what they wanted, but it had a will of its own. Olive you. Olive you.

Tuck was a man who never seemed quite dressed—his wrinkled tattersall shirt was unbuttoned almost to the waist, his shoes had not been tied—and he always juggled several things, as if he needed more hands: his Starbuck's mug and the front-page section of the paper and a bag of yellow squash, just picked.

First fruits, Tuck said. Then, You see the paper?

Not yet.

He set down his coffee and the squash and he opened the front page. FAG CHURCH in red paint dripped from the Episcopal Church garden gate, a carved stone gate Johnny had noticed hundreds of times because it was old, carved with birds and flowers and leaves, a thing of beauty.

That's too bad.

Yeah. Well. Maybe they'll find out who's doing it. He knelt down to tie his shoes. They've offered a reward.

Who?

The Episcopal Church.

Good for them.

Johnny knew Tuck. He knew him in a way he knew no one else. They were connected when they were not in each other's presence. With everyone else—sometimes even Ruth Anne and Laurel—Johnny had to shake himself to pay attention; he had to sort back through his recent conversations and think, ah, yes, and latch on to whatever was on Laurel's mind or Ruth Anne's mind. Even more difficult were his employees, who changed more frequently than he would have liked. The waitresses who quit to become stewardesses or to go to graduate school. The line cooks who lost their tempers and walked off the job. When they were right in front of him, he paid attention and he gave out big doses of empathy, and, in some cases, cash for new contacts or parking tickets or vet bills when their dog was sick. But then he would forget them. He got lost in the intricacies of cooking. He might spend two hours deciding to buy a new skillet online and human concerns faded. But with Tuck there was a kind of fraternal shorthand and they kept track of present situations. It was something to be thankful for, the give-and-take with Raymond Tucker, who had been in Vietnam but understood not talking about it, who drove a schoolbus, who coached a loser junior-high basketball team, and who still took communion at St. Joan's, in spite of being twice divorced. Their birthdays were a week apart in January. A gloomy time to be born, Tuck always said. Johnny said, If you were born here. Yeah. By here they meant the Midwest where January weather was cloudy right down to the barren ground. To commiserate they would buy a bottle of bourbon and drive to the round barns and drink it.

They played one-on-one, pushing themselves to get their heart rates up. Sweat staining their shirts and running down their faces. Johnny's white hair flopped this way and that when he dribbled and feigned a move hoopward.

At a lull, Tuck said, So when do they close?

Two weeks.

Later still, Tuck went to his pickup to fetch a quart of Gatorade. He returned to the court, wiping his face with the tail of his shirt. You're worried.

Johnny drank from the bottle, tipping it up, maintaining eye contact. The firefighters a half-block away opened their doors and began dragging out the hoses for their weekly washing of the trucks. Their dog—a lively springer spaniel—came trotting toward the basketball court. The firefighters called, Come 'ere, fella. One of them stepped out of the stationhouse and tossed a Day-Glo tennis ball against the building to coax him back.

Johnny said, I'm going to add some money to that reward. That's all.

Don't tell Ruth Anne, Tuck advised.

About the money?

About the front page.

⟶

The bunting lay in swags across porches and banks, the courthouse and the movie theater. If Ruth Anne had been driving, he would have averted his eyes the way some people do when a violent act comes on the screen. He kept a vigil against the violent acts the bunting precipitated: what he had not necessarily seen and what he had. If only Ruthie had been driving. He would have managed to turn away. Not so anyone would notice. He did not think Ruthie noticed. It was not unusual for them to traverse downtown on July the Fourth and meander out Tenth Street and along the river road into the countryside where the fiddlers' gathering was held. He had flipped the CLOSED sign on Brambles' front door. Near the courthouse he shut his eyes at a red light. NPR was on the truck radio, a story about saunas in Finland. Babies used to be born in saunas. The dead were washed in saunas. It was the second time the local station had run the story, and he switched off the radio, roughly, and the knob fell off and rolled under his seat.

He was sick of Ruthie being away. He needed her on the Fourth and she knew that. He churlishly expected her to know it without being told again. Or asked again. The bunting drove him crazy. The red and the white and the blue and the cheapness of it and the false optimism. The bunting represented what did not exist, to his way of thinking. If you were going to fight for something, it better not be represented by muslin bunting. Misanthropic—Laurel had taught him the word. Don't be like that, she said. Anyone could piss him off.

The light changed. The parade had ended hours before; a denuded float had been left in one alley, dragging fake flowers, hallucinogenic blooms that in the humidity bled into the white butcher paper taped to the float. The street was strewn with wads of fast-food trash and disposable American flags. His skin itched and his breath was a little short. Keep on, keep on—the girls were meeting him at the gathering and they would get him grounded. He would not want to wander. He would depend on the girls. He had prepared himself to face it and he thought that having plans and seeing the girls would occupy him. Later, Tuck would meet him at the big kitchen and he would barbecue steaks on the patio and he and Tuck would talk. They would watch the stars. On the stars there was no Fourth of July. They were far enough from the river that they would not have to watch the fireworks and if they turned some music up they could drown the crack and peal of the fireworks the town council had spent a fortune on.

Not far from the river the road narrowed, the wild roses and chest-high thistles growing in lush baffles on either side and the windrows from the first cutting of alfalfa lying in the fields. It was a sunny day, almost too hot. In a fallow plot sunlight bounced on the hoods and roofs of vehicles parked in tight rows. He rolled down the window and let the insects purr.

Bumper stickers brought him down. The veterans. The pet-lovers. The smartasses. The hotheads. A teenage kid in an orange vest waved him into a parking spot and without a word fanned a palmful of five dollar bills to let him know to pay. A woman with big blond hair stepped out of a sports car and said, I have to have half a cigarette. She patted her purse and her daughter climbed up on the hood and combed out the hair of a Barbie doll. He felt the pang of missing Ruthie. Of a story she might've told him about the woman when they sat down. She liked to make up stories about people they saw and knew they would never see again. She liked the details. That's her Barbie from when she was a little girl, she might say. Or, She's really waiting for her sweetheart who wears black cowboy boots. He wanted a bench and not the ground, but he took the quilt from out of the lockbox anyway and started watching for the girls. He moved invisibly through the crowd and, solitary, he found it simple to weave among the banjo players and fiddlers with their black instrument cases and the children and the women carrying baskets of provisions and the men in sweltering jeans and ball caps standing in line at the elephant-ear concession or the hot-dog concession where you could smell the meat and sizzle. The onions. The beer. A blacksmith in goggles hammered out a hunk of iron over coals so hot they left a shimmer in the air.

Bluegrass like spring water percolated from musicians gathered in knots beneath the trees and as he walked he sampled it. The banjos twanging. The mournful mandolin and dulcimers that collapsed time and made you feel a piece of another dreamy world, a time of screen doors instead of central air and sitting in the evening without television and long hours passed in visits. A car would've been a wondrous thing.

He had not lived through that time, not really. He thought of it as the early part of the twentieth century before World War II. He skipped over the Depression and all the terrible stories. He thought, Sentimental. Don't be sentimental. You don't know a damn thing about it. But still the music buoyed him up.

Daddy—

Laurel waved. She and Oceana had saved space on a bench about four rows from the front and he made his way there through the picnickers and strollers and lawn chairs and quilts. The stage of bright new plywood had been set amid a cluster of maples. No one was on the stage. Big black speakers flanked it and a little girl stood in the wing which was visible and tap-danced without any music but what floated nearby from the musicians gathered under the trees.

She did not usually call him Daddy. It surprised him and pleased him.

Into her ear he said, How you doing, baby? And Oceana smiled and said, Hi, Johnny. And he said, Hey, girl, for they had agreed that he could call them girls. Are you having a good time?

We are, they said, grinning. In love, Johnny saw.

He sat down next to Laurel and they had picked a shady spot and if a breeze should come up, Johnny thought, the maple leaves would ripple and fan and it was a good place from which to view the show. He began to relax.

You look sunburnt, he said. She wore a sleeveless blouse and her arms were pink. Her thighs were pink.

Oceana patted her thigh and said, Does it hurt?

He caught himself glancing to see if anyone else noticed that pat. The festivities had not been interrupted. Babies still squalled and a nursing mother picked one up and went off to the private place to nurse, behind a hedge. The little girl in the wing still tapped, her hair bouncing. Boys of seven or eight wove in and out of the trees in chase. A woman with snow-white hair napped in a wheelchair, a paper plate of chicken scraps about to slide from her hands. And the women chatting food and church and the men chatting baseball and weather kept on.

Not too much, Laurel said. Then, Don't worry, Dad.

We bought a table for the kitchen, Oceana said. It's oak. A round oak table.

Whereabouts?

We went to an auction, Laurel said.

In Belle Fleur.

What'd you give for it?

One hundred dollars. And we need your help to move it. Laurel said this sweetly, appealingly. Can you? Help us?

No problem. And Johnny was about to ask, When? And Johnny was about to ask, What else did you buy? But a clogging troupe came out onto the stage and the noise of their recorded fiddle and their feet upon the plywood stage made him think to give up talking.

Laurel leaned over and said, Look. There's Limbo.

Limbo lay on the ground not far from them, propped on his elbows, in baggy shorts and a T-shirt. Two other boys lay beside him and they drank beer from green bottles and they were older than Limbo. They were young men. Their sparse mustaches still grew in silky. A girl in a halter top passed by and one of the young men reached up and swatted her rear and Limbo laughed. The girl dodged them, casting back a glance that said, You are disgusting, and a glance that said, Let me alone.

They look like trouble, Laurel said, leaning toward Johnny to make herself heard.

He leaned in close to her and said, Limbo came to the restaurant a couple days ago.

He misses Mom.

He gets into things. He's a pain in the ass.

Laurel put her hand on his arm and said, Are you all right?

I'm all right. He sounded short-tempered to himself.

The dancing made him think, Jig. Irish jig. That's what they're doing. His mother in a white dress with blue flowers had danced for him or when he was a boy he had thought it was for him. She never forgot she was Irish. But being half-Irish was not that important to Johnny. He did not want to think about his mother and he found himself waiting for the dancing to stop, a frenzy like bees when they rise from an apiary went on inside him, and he felt like striking out and he felt gripped with the notion that he should not be out in public. A danger.

He put on a good front.

The dancers asked for volunteers to come up for a lesson and Laurel and Oceana without hesitation leaped up and went with others, children mostly, to the stage, and they were in the circle with the dancers and they stomped and laughed and the bees the feeling of the bees did not stop. He was sick with it. Limbo with his friends watched the young girls, the teenage girls who strutted through the crowd. Johnny could see their lust. He could see it plain as fucking day. Limbo bugged him and he always had, even when he was a boy. But Ruth Anne was a kind person and she put up with him and Johnny felt like a jerk objecting to it. Ruthie made him want to be kinder himself. He had given Limbo a wedge of pecan pie and Limbo had said, Thank you, Mr. Bond. And, When's she coming home? I miss her. And Johnny had said, Join the club, son. Join the goddamn club.

Without him noticing, the cloggers had ceased their stomping and bowed to the clapping with big smiles and Laurel and Oceana and the children had come down from the plywood stage and the sound system had erupted with a sweet rendition of "Tennessee Waltz." Laurel and Oceana were making their way back and were still in the grassy emptiness right in front of the stage when "Tennessee Waltz" took hold of them and they met spontaneously to waltz. They took a turn around the grass.

Those girls are queer, Limbo blurted.

Laurel and Oceana broke apart. They had not heard. They were only returning innocently to Johnny, all smiles.

Don't push your luck, Johnny said to Laurel.

You better go if you're going to be like this.

Like what?

Oceana started packing up their rucksacks—water bottles and snacks and sunscreen in a tube. She said, Maybe we better go.

Let's go, Dad.

He let himself be led back to the pickup and Laurel took the folded quilt from him and he opened the lockbox and she laid it in and she put out her hands for the keys. They got in, Laurel to drive.

It's all this shit.

What shit?

All this shit, Johnny shouted. You know.

Oceana came to the open driver's side window and with her hands on the edge of the glass said to Laurel, Will you be all right?

We'll be fine. It's the Fourth. The Fourth is hard.

# 9

Harvey's Bristol Cream bottles came to mind: cobalt blue.

And the feel of the sherry on her tongue, a velvet stain. She missed perfume. She missed hot soaks in the tub. She missed streaking her hair to keep the gray subdued. All that she missed paraded before her during the first sit of the day at four o'clock. In the pitch dark. Jill liked to say that the Dalai Lama's family rose at three in morning to meditate and rid them themselves of afflictive emotions before the day begins.

An ache like a splinter began in her hip. Is that how it started, she wanted to ask Aunt Teensy. An ache you ignored? She had chosen to sit on a zafu the first time and she had maintained that habit, although her hip ached every time. Others sat in chairs and on folded quilts and oak meditation benches, low to the floor. She wanted to switch to a bench but she was ashamed and saw it as somehow a lesser practice and during her sits she would get a grasp of that for what it was: her small self concerned with appearances. But she did not switch to the bench.

The meditation room was dimly lit. A candle burned on the table beside a vase of peonies. Candlelight flickered on the icons: Thomas Merton and Jesus and Teresa of Avila. Twenty minutes. Twenty minutes watching thoughts like whimsical boats on a current. Her hip ached and she had not showered yet and a sour odor arose from her body, her orifices, and with that she stepped onto the boat of grooming. She thought of showers, baths, bath salts, shaving cream, lotions, shampoo, conditioner, nail polish—she polished her toenails in jewel-tone colors, steely, industrial. Nail polish had been left behind and she wanted some.

Her sacred word was Sabbath and she silently said, Sabbath, Sabbath, Sabbath, Sabbath, Sabbath. In theory, the word was supposed to return her to the shore of watching, to the place of being the witness. Sabbath.

The phone call from Laurel kept on, like a leak in her mind that needed repairing. Just wanted you to know. We thought you should know. We. He's fine now. Deep in cookbooks. Tuck brought him back to earth. Tuck brought him back. If you'd been here—

It might've happened anyway—

He needs you—

Laurel, honey—

He does—

I'm beginning to understand why you meditate.

Right before the phone call ended, Laurel said, It just doesn't seem like you, Mom. Monastic life.

She worked her way backward through the phone calls. Laurel and she had talked after she called Johnny on the Fourth. Late that night, when Tuck had gone home.

Where are you?

She said, I'm at a pay phone outside the swimming pool. It's private.

I'm in bed, Johnny whispered. I'm in bed in the dark. Mox is right here on the floor, trying to stay cool.

How was your day?

Not so good, Ruthie.

What happened?

All this shit started coming up. Shit I don't want to get into.

We don't have to.

We don't. You're right. Then, How's Teensy? How is the old gal?

She's bedridden. It's a very big deal for her to get out of bed for anything. She has to be lifted out and put in a wheelchair. She used to dance and stand on her feet all day at the shop and now she's wasting away.

How's her mind?

She repeats herself. But mostly, she's lucid.

Is she glad you're there?

Reluctantly, she said, I can't tell.

That made him quiet. That made him feel bad. He didn't have to say so; she knew. If Aunt Teensy were glad, if some sort of rapprochement were cobbled together, if they had begun the soulful journey, Johnny would feel it had been worth it.

I wish I had my bicycle.

Why don't I bring it up there? I'd like that.

Would you?

We can have a conjugal visit.

Sabbath. Sabbath.

She kept hearing Johnny say, I'm in bed. If she were there with the catalpa leaves rustling outside the window, would she be comforted by Johnny? Her desires had engorged, swollen. She wanted to gather together all the people she had ever loved. She wanted them to love her so much they would love each other: a dream where rancor stopped. Where boundaries dissolved.

She had had a nightmare: Johnny hugging her, and she said, Get away from me. Leave me alone. She woke up crying: She loved Johnny and would never hurt him. But you did. Intentions don't matter; what matters is whether you hurt him or not. He doesn't know. She tried to imagine telling him. She could not form the words.

Sabbath.

Tin was the central thought, the obsession behind all other obsessions, which were merely whims, trivial, compared to the realization that Tin waited for her response. She had written one, but she had not sent it. She managed to keep from thinking about him. Sometimes.

Her response said, Yes, I do wonder.

I think of you. Thank you for writing to me. To know that you are alive and well and living not far from me—I am happy to know that you are well. The poem makes me think of the stories I read to your father before you were born.

She had gotten that far. Next, her heart sent out another sentence: Where are you? But she had not added that to the message.

She kept the hard copy of his message inside her pillowcase. At night she read it right before she went to sleep. No one sees clearly; I don't even see myself. Our voices rise like fish bubbles—

She would skip ahead to the end. It's the fishhook of dreams I've swallowed half my life. The fishhook—

➣

We didn't drink milk when I was a girl.

Aunt Teensy would say this nearly every day.

Sometimes Ruth Anne answered, Never? And sometimes she changed the subject.

We didn't have refrigeration.

People had iceboxes, didn't they?

Yes, Aunt Teensy would say cantankerously. But we lived on the farm out of Fennville. She squinted, her face a powdery mask. Mexicans hadn't come in yet.

Ruth Anne bit her tongue. They weren't all Mexicans, she wanted to say. Some of them were from Puerto Rico. Some of them were from Texas. She murmured, I wonder if my mother would've had osteoporosis.

We had electricity by the time she was born. She liked buttermilk. She was born when Mother was in her forties. Women didn't have much choice.

Do you regret not having children?

I don't know what would've happened to you if I'd had children of my own.

But do you regret it? She would have to raise her voice over the soap opera. There was a smell in the room, a smell she hoped was not getting into her clothes, the way smoke got into your clothes. It was the smell of getting old.

I never think about regret, Aunt Teensy said. That's what you think about. Isn't it?


Summer people invaded the lakeshore, in their big cars and vans, with all their children. Every day the beach adjacent to Our Lady of Holy Mysteries would be dotted with umbrellas and coolers and piles of floating devices. Dogs ran in and out of the surf, chasing Frisbees. The sun gripped the beach and the lake pulsed with its tide and the wind was high and regal. Sister Jill would wear her sandals—her one concession to the beach—and Ruth Anne would wear a frayed pair of walking shorts and a worn, thin corduroy shirt of Johnny's. After her visit with Aunt Teensy they would walk into the wind for what they gauged was two miles and then they would walk back, invisible women among the other women of the beach: the girls in their tight skin and tight swimsuits, the young mothers, or any woman with a man. Any woman with a man prepared herself to please him—with a scent, a filmy cover-up. Ruth Anne was taking a break from that but Johnny was coming. Her hair felt weighty, damp. She kept it in a single braid, out of the way.

Where do you go?

I just need to get out sometimes.

Sister Jill frowned. She picked up a stick and tossed it in the lake.

Ruth Anne said, I drive to all the little towns. There's something about them. I want to see what they're like. We grew up here and I want to see. It's all changed and I want to know how they've changed. And I eat Vietnamese food. I sit and eat my noodles and read. Just because I'm centering doesn't mean I can't read. Does it?

Reading might be something that keeps you from God. What you read.

Ruth Anne laughed but the wind carried her laugh away. Ah, the evil of the short story!

Seriously, Ruthie.

Talking might be something that keeps me from God.

That too.

Reading Scripture, as well.

No, not that.

We're so frail, aren't we? Humans are so frail. Language fails us. We don't know anything about anything.

Don't talk that way.

I'm sorry.

She was sorry. Sorry to have upset Jill.

They arrived back at the monastery, where the wizened sisters who still wore the black and white habits were seated on the lakeside porch under a blue awning, knitting or dozing or saying the rosary, framed by shrubby hydrangea. The hydrangea petals floated, zinged, on the wind. On the arbor over the breezeway the grapes had popped out in perfect embryonic clusters; so time had passed. She had been at the monastery for nearly three weeks and time had become a substance surrounding her rather than discreet units ticked off, just water, not waves. Is that what eternity was? She missed Laurel and their talks on the deck but she held fast to the notion that she would have things to share with Laurel when she returned and that Laurel would be proud of her. She might have Tin to share if she could only bring herself to be direct. Or brave. Instead she wandered. Every afternoon for three hours she drove to this town or that and asked at a gas station or a chamber of commerce, Is there a Vietnamese restaurant? And more often than not, there would be, and if she found it, she might find more, a nail salon or makeshift market or a bakery with French pastries with Vietnamese names. She might buy a persimmon from a Vietnamese woman who spoke English. Watching. She always watched for him. She would know him. She was sure of that. The afternoons would begin with hope and end with self-loathing. She would drive back to the monastery in time to sit on the zafu. In time to watch her self-loathing dance and leer: What did you expect? Just what?

She did not like to think that Vo was in on the message. She told herself that only she and Tin knew. Johnny needs to know but Johnny doesn't deserve to be betrayed. But Johnny was betrayed. He was. You can't move that rock from the middle of the road. I am connected to Tin by the knowing. There is a connection between us and he waits for me. He waits and I am a coward. Lower than that. I am a mother who abandoned her child. But it wasn't that. She made you. I didn't have to agree. She made you. The giving away haunted her. The moment when she placed him in his grandmother's arms. The moment when next he cried and she was walking away. The moment when her breasts prickled with the milk coming in at his cry. The way they rushed like a stream with milk. Her clothes had been stiff with dried milk. She made it sound like the right thing to do. She made it sound like he was theirs. He was Vo's. Vo needed him. I am a mother who abandoned her child. Madame Thuong in her rhinestone-studded spectacles would become the vehicle of her self-loathing. The twenty-minute sit expanded beyond her ability to count the seconds, to measure out her Sabbaths; it ballooned into a lifetime of deceit. The memories fluttered like transparencies in a textbook, a dissection of lies—so many memories but no one knew. No one knew her inside. The way she went crazy with the giving away every time she lived it. She cried silently during the sit; she did not want to disturb the woman next to her; she did not want to make trouble. He did not want to make trouble in her life. But the innocence was over; she was called to respond and all she could do was cry. Would she ever come to the end of tears? Her face was swollen from crying. Tender to the touch. The delicate whisper of the gong would break the spell. You're unloading something, Sister Jill said to her one night. Something you've held tight to for a long time. If you ever want to talk, I'm here. It's Teensy, isn't it?

Later she would think, That was the worst time. But you don't leave times like that. They become your psychic skin.

Later still, What was Madame Thuong's worst time?

Or Vo's?

Or Johnny's?

She had seldom asked those questions and asking made her feel she had leaped outside her own skin, what held her earthbound. The answers required imagination, for she did not think the freedom to ask was hers. In any case, Madame Thuong was buried on a terrace at her farm near Dalat. Where the mountain winds blew chilly. You could see your breath in the morning. You wore a woolen cap and you put a tiny woolen cap on your baby. Elfin face, rosy cheeks. A pine tree might grow over her grave; you might think it was all elephant grass, all jungle; but the pine trees whistled; they might grow over her grave. No one could ask Madame Thuong what moment was the worst. Being cast out by her father? Losing her French officer? Losing her photographer who made her see her own beauty in photograph after photograph? Returning from Paris with the money she had put aside? When Vo's eyes were burned? When Saigon fell? Some boundaries you cross only in your mind.

Ruth Anne hated her.

Hate is a very strong word, Laurel would say.


That night she was awakened around midnight by a voice telling her what to do. Not a dream, a voice. A resolute voice. Not male or female. She had never heard a voice in her sleep before and she could not tell anyone, not even Jill.

She went down to the computer room on the basement level. In the narrow hallway she could feel the women—the nuns—in their cells, breathing in sleep; they seemed like women who had no regrets; they had not squandered their sex and bodies. They were whole. She shivered at the thought of Tin, shivered with the phrases she had worked over, fussed over. An unseen hand was at her back, pushing her down the stairs. A snip of moon was visible out a narrow window at the end of the hallway. Moon and a silo. Moon and a silo and a curve of railroad track. A waxy smell—the hall just cleaned—rose all around her. At the next landing a felt banner hung from the ceiling. A canister light gave off a bronze glow. Someone had taken much care with the embroidered words on the banner. I have been trying to give birth to myself. Adrienne Rich. One should identify with the universe itself. Simone Weil. Blessedness is not promised, it is not tied to any condition: it is the only reality. Nietzsche. Blessedness. Blessedness. She kept the word rolling over and over in her body as she crept down the stairs. Blot out the other way. Blot out whatever doubts assail you. It *was* like giving birth. To change. To know you were changing—it's all uncertain. How.

The door to the computer room creaked open. She did not turn on the overhead. The computers in two rows of four seemed nearly alive, perky, with the same screensaver: a cottage garden in flower, hollyhocks and dahlias, stepping-stones leading to a pond. She sat down in the back row and clicked herself into Hotmail and she started a new account, a separate account that no one would know about. No one but Tin.

She wrote: Dear Tin, Yes, I am your mother.

There she stopped. How peculiar to claim that for the first time now. To him. All the lies pressed around her, spookish torment, they could not be left behind. At times she had forgotten she lied; it had become second nature. Mechanical. She accepted the condolences of other women when they learned she had only one child, that she had been unable to have more children. The dream of the children in bunny pajamas, sweet-smelling after baths, all in a row on a king-size bed, listening to a story—that dream hovered over the tale. Over coffee she had told this tale. Over wine. Walking with young mothers when Laurel was small. Pushing a stroller. There would be pregnant women all around her so many of those years. Women in their twenties and thirties, propagating. Comparing labors. Stretch marks and episiotomies. Sex after.

How they did not want to do it and what a shock that was. She could not avoid the tale of her sterility; if intimacy opened up, she had to tell the tale. She had fraudulently accepted their condolences.

I am your mother.

I am your mother.


Windfall, Michigan, was only forty minutes north of the monastery. On the way, she went through apple country. Vineyard country. Everything growing fatly, plaits and stratum of leaf, vine, bud, fruit.

Tastings at the wineries were held on Saturdays. She would not stop for a tasting, even if they were open; wine and leisure to shop for wine seemed like an indulgence. Not for her now. If she had been with Johnny, they might have come back for it, later in the day. Johnny knew how to relax; he knew how to live in the moment. He did not have to go to confession. She wondered if he ever would. If he were dying, would he want the last rites? If he were dying—What a strange phrase. We're all dying. She wanted last rites. She was sure of that. But not the words, just the anointing with oil. Was there a priest anywhere who would let her tell him how to do it? Who was she to tell him that? She did not miss Father Carroll; she felt she fit into the community of women at the monastery; she fit almost too well; she had become habituated. On the phone Johnny had finally said, What's going on up there, Ruthie?

When will we be close again? she wanted to say. When will we go to the round barns?

Tin's response had been brief: We live in Windfall. Do you want to correspond?

I need to think about it, she wrote back. During the first sit she understood that for what it was: power-garnering. And below that: fear. She wanted to see him before he saw her.

She told Sister Jill, she told Aunt Teensy: I need time to think. She showered and dressed and did not join the sisters for breakfast. The beach was empty, the sky lint-gray. She drove north in light traffic; on the radio the weather report warned of fog. It was a four-lane state road, with a fifty-mile-per-hour speed limit. She stopped at a bakery and bought two scones and a paper mug of hot tea. The woman at the counter said, Watch out for cops. They have their quotas.

A clump of trees eclipsed the road sign to Windfall. She nearly passed it by, but braked and backed up and took the curving blacktop down into the sleepy town, a lakeside resort, past its prime. The clapboard hotel needed painting. The town hall was brick; the library next door had been boarded up; a sign said that the bookmobile from Grand Rapids came every other Thursday.

Clouds and fog settled in the alleys and between the buildings. She stopped beside a gazebo. Across the street at a corner park were the women and a market: six elderly Vietnamese women in black pants and blouses squatted beside their baskets of fruits and vegetables. One had set up a wok on bricks; beneath it burned a Sterno fire. The fog obscured the women; their presence might have been a thought or memory, so ethereal was the image.

She drank her tea and ate a scone and watched while people came and bought a little bag of this or that. Coconut shavings. Dried pineapple. Squash. She was close enough to see them place the coins in the wrinkled hands of the women. No one looked familiar. Finally she got out, and pulling up her raincoat's hood, she decided to walk. She locked the Tercel. The downtown street was three blocks long.

A boardwalk led up to the beach and she took it, thinking, I'll see the lake and the lake will make sense to me, which is to say, she felt such ravelment at the women selling their goods at the park. She felt torn out of time. She did not think they would speak to her even if she might remember the greetings. She wanted to say, Does a blind man live here? Everyone would surely know the blind man.

At the lake's edge she spread her raincoat on the damp and creamy sand. She sat down and tried to still her confusion. She had taken a step; the voice had told her what to do and now she felt at the mercy of that, thinking, Where will it lead? And, What will be required of me? The fog did not seem gentle or benign. Driving back would be difficult. Often fog lifted midmorning but that was not about to happen. Rain began, a silvery mist. She shook the sand from the raincoat and put it on and stood at the lake's edge. Lacy waves curled against the shore. She would plant herself there. The weather would not separate her from the lake. No one else was on the beach and she wondered why not even children had come down, not even a dog-walker, not even a fast walker or jogger, and that brought to mind the doctor and the bone-density test—all that was on hold. She had left it behind. She did not want to become a fast walker in the mall. Johnny would hoist her bicycle into the bed of the pickup and he would come for his visit and then she would be free. She would bicycle along the lakeshore; she would take flight. The doctor had said that because of the osteoporosis Aunt Teensy was rotting from the inside, like a fruit. Bedridden, she had to be turned. The blood pooled in her lower body and secretions settled in her lungs. This is not the way I wanted to die, Aunt Teensy had told her. It's hard to hear the truth.

She thought these things and stood there, hands in her pockets, stiffly. Pointed against the wind like a masthead. She did not see him until he was nearly upon her, a man with a white cane with a red tip. He had come down off the boardwalk through the wet packed sand and before walking into the lake he turned south, as if he had counted the steps and knew exactly where to turn. Vo walked away. His gait was the same as it had been: a lanky, tall man's walk. But he was not so tall here; in Vietnam he had been taller than most men. They had been the same size. And might still be. The memory of his skin, his smell—the jasmine tea, the dusty books—assailed her. A room where plaster flaked from the wall beside the bed. A palm tree she saw over his shoulder. His knees on either side of her. His wiry, perfect body. He stroked her symmetrically, forehead, eyebrows, eyelids, cheekbones, shoulders, breasts. He lingered there in wonder at her breasts.

The cane floated before his step. He wore a navy blue beret. His hair was white in tufts above his neck. He wore a maroon windbreaker and cotton slacks. And court shoes.

He looked old.

She thought of herself in the mirror, free of lipstick. How gaunt her face, how fragile her skin. If he were to recognize her, it would be by voice or touch. She stumbled back to the boardwalk, the soles of her shoes gritty—squeaking—in the sand. She turned twice to watch him. A man not quite fifty. His beret at a jaunty angle.

Did someone read to him now?

The enormity of seeing him did not hit her until she was back on the main street: she felt the way she might if she had been in a minor car accident; no one had been hurt; it happened so fast. At times like that you

just keep going. Later it hits you: your heart pumps and you tremble un-
controllably. You might retch on the side of the road. You might need
to go home and stay in, with a pot of tea and a good book.

Her hands shook as she wiped at her eyes and unlocked the Tercel
and got in. She had forgotten this—they had walked along the lake in
Dalat. Lake of Sorrow, she thought it was called but that might not be
right. She remembered what she wore. She had begun to show; she al-
ternated the same two tops over stretch pants, a sweatshirt from Grin-
nell College and a big orange sweater. She did not know where the
clothes had come from and she did not know what had happened to
them after. Sometimes they were there alone and sometimes his mother
would come from Saigon and stay for weeks. She sent them out for
walks. She thought they spent too much time reading and talking on the
veranda facing the terraces.

She had held his arm, a formal, courtly gesture, but in truth she had
been in the lead. He did not have a white cane then.

What had they talked about? The books they read. *Madame Bovary.*
*The Quiet American. The Hunchback of Notre Dame.* They had brought a
dozen books to Dalat and they read them slowly, rationing pages,
mulling them over. They talked about the characters as if they were
their neighbors. They whispered what they could not say to anyone
else.

You know Martin Luther King?

I know of him. Of course. Aunt Teensy had told her never to mention his name. Aunt Teensy had pursed her lips at demonstrations on
television.

Your Martin Luther King has nominated a Vietnamese monk for the
Nobel Peace Prize.

There would be news—rumor—about the war that surrounded
them, the bombing of Hue. People warned of plastiques. At the market
she would see children who had been hurt. There would be news from
the States. Old news. It was an election year. She had never paid much
attention to elections; Vo thought that she should pay attention. The
letter from Johnny's father had come: Jill knew where she was. No one
knew where Johnny was; he had disappeared. When she tried to piece
it together, years later, she would have a difficult time remembering

which came first—learning that Johnny had disappeared or that first touch from Vo, the first time he said I want to see you. She had knelt where he could touch her face. He had read her face.

She remembered writing to Aunt Teensy, how hard it was to write the words—I'm going to have a baby. She remembered the post office with its bowls of paste, the flimsy airmail stationery. If only Aunt Teensy had written, Come home. Would she have gone home? You don't know how young you are when you're nineteen. If someone says, Come home, you might.

He would lean and whisper as they walked along the lake's edge. Dalat at dusk, an emerald's interior, the dark green lake, the forest. This monk—he has spoken to the pope.

She considered crossing to the park and buying a small bowl of broth from the woman with the wok. She was in America. Everything would be as it should be: the foggy day, the women in their black cotton pants. Flecks of green onion and tofu floating in the broth. She wanted the warmth of the broth.

She wanted to walk up to him and say, Vo. It's me. Do you remember me? But she was not free or whole; she did not have the right to seek her past. Her real life—Johnny, Aunt Teensy, Laurel, and yes, even Limbo and Daisy and Father Carroll—all of them rose up and frowned. She drove out of Windfall gripping the steering wheel. The fog frightened her; the visibility was poor; she was afraid she would not be able to stop in time to avoid hurting herself. Or someone she loved.

# 10

Quinsy was a word neither Vo nor Ruth Anne knew.

Félicité suffered from quinsy. She grew deaf. They rushed through "A Simple Heart" from that point onward, fearful of the outcome. Vo did not like to hear about the parrot. It made him tap the table with one fist—a tender hammering—to hear about the teasing with the parasol. He tilted his head, as if to avert his gaze. Terrible things happen to animals. Stay away from the animal markets. There are restaurants where people watch the monkeys being slaughtered before they cook them.

God, don't tell me.

He said, You are older but you are innocent.

I'm not.

She could not dispute him seriously. For he had seen what she had not. He had seen what she never wanted to see. A lack of feeling would settle around her down to her bones: she thought of it as the lassitude, an equatorial malaise grown personal. Not grief; she could not call it grieving. She knew from when her mother and father had died that a wound eventually becomes a scar. You cannot force it. But then she had known the worst. Their bodies had been dredged from the river and flown home from Boise and she had seen their faces in the back room of the funeral parlor in Grand Haven before they had been dressed up for the viewing. Her mother had hit her head on a river rock; the split had been sewn together with pink stitches. Her father appeared smaller, almost dainty. She and Aunt Teensy stood like strangers at the graveside in a light summer rain, mosquitoes aggravating all around. Aunt Teensy had looked puzzled; she had inherited a girl to care for.

There was nothing to know about Johnny but memories and at night she seized the lifeline of his voice whispering, Think of me at night and I'll think of you and we'll be together.

Are you all right? Vo would say.

I'm fine. It's the heat.

You don't seem yourself.

She picked up a book and began reading. C'était l'heure du thé avant l'entrée des lampes. Her voice quavered, but then it grew resolute—expressive—as she settled into "Happiness," one of their favorite stories.


The first time Sister Michelle returned to her room and knocked—surreptitiously, two slight raps—she went to the door and opened it a crack and said, I can't. I can't. I just can't.

The next night she came again. Please, she whispered. Please let me in. She offered the brass flashlight. This is for you. I want you to have it.

All right. She pursed her lips to indicate reluctance, when, in truth, all feelings have unutterable folds and pleats and within the pleat of that reluctance she was relieved. And she nearly knew it. If anyone had heard the door opening and closing, the sound might reveal every tawdry thing: a sweaty feverishness and secrecy, the scent of lavender. She did not want to want her.

The flashlight felt cool to the touch and useful; she laid it precisely on her desk beside a row of pens. Her impulse was to plunk the flashlight on the bed but the bed was not for them and she did not want to draw attention to the bed. She still wore the clothes she had put on that morning, a print skirt and a rayon blouse. The blouse stuck to her skin. Since the night in Connie's apartment, she would postpone until late, ten o'clock or later, getting undressed, confronting her body, feeling the slip and cool of a cotton nightgown. She tried to ignore the body. The mosquito netting over the bed grayed in the wind and weather. There were two chairs and she gestured with an open hand, as if to say, Whatever will happen between us will be formal. They sat down side by side, the chairs angled toward each other. Sister Michelle still wore her habit but she had exchanged her practical convent-issue shoes for red leather flats embossed with palm trees. The ceiling fan stirred long shadows across her face.

I'm sorry, she said. Sorry for what you're going through. She reached for Ruth Anne's hand.

Don't. Don't make me cry.

Sister Michelle tucked her hands beneath her thighs.

I just have to go through it.

I'm going home. I'm going home and I'm leaving the convent. My parents know. Life's too short—

When?

Whenever they find someone to teach my class. By the end of January. I hope.

I'll miss you.

I want to be someone's wife. I want to be a mother.

We all want that. We were taught to want it. In Sister Michelle's case she was not so sure. The memory of the kisses, the smooth cheek against hers, the petite lips and their hunger—there had been a seasoned feel to what they'd done. Sister Michelle might be adept at mysteries of the body Ruth Anne had not given much thought to. Mysteries of the body that bore exploration and might not be compatible with marriage. She had not thought about what you give up until she became engaged. The boy at the produce stand flickered through her thoughts. The night she might have met him at the beach. She felt his voice against her hair. She might have playfully shoved him over in the sand and arched above him, her eyes shut, her body in the glare of the summer moon. For the slightest moment she saw herself as he might have. She shook her head, shook away shame and cunning. She and I are capable of it. We're not so different. Want could be unleashed and what happened then might hurt you. It might be dangerous. She was nineteen and she did not understand want at all. Want was a current. Why were some girls wired with the current and others were not? Jill was kindhearted, but it was Sue-Sue she longed to please and imitate and that was why: Sue-Sue was wild. Slut, people whispered with derisive pleasure. She hated that.

She said, How's your brother?

He's already in California. He's going to be all right. As all right as you can be with just one hand.

Jesus—

My mother's just glad he's coming home. Then she whispered, I have to ask you.

She looked into her eyes and saw the tears welling there. What?

Do you think we did anything wrong? Her face was red.

The lacquered spoon slipped under the bathroom door. There was nothing to do but be still. She thought of the sister inside, brushing her teeth, staring at her loveless self in the mirror. A pair of sisters went by in the hallway, the rosary beads around their waists clacking, and what privacy they thought they had was an illusion, hoax of desire. Ruth Anne had thought to keep her at arm's length but at the sound of the sisters in the hallway she felt the loss of truth-telling or an embrace. She felt again the risk that they had taken. The humiliation inherent in being discovered, if it were to happen. The repulsion a nun might feel at finding them out. Johnny might return and she would be waiting and she wanted nothing transitory to get in the way. Nothing selfish. Nothing stupid. To make selfish mistakes you needed privacy. At home the boys and girls at the beach and she and Johnny and Jill and Sue-Sue had always sought the dark and freedom. It had been theirs for the seeking. She might never know that again exactly as she had—the tussles in the hammock and life lived in a car, when you could borrow a car. She thought about home nearly every day: Pier Cove and its environs and the familiarity of the roads and the beach and the dunes and the white pines. The ice barges in the winter. The high hard sun in the summer. Never having to worry if you might get sick from drinking the water. Never having to worry about the boys dying. But they die. Nonetheless—

The toilet flushed and the spoon was taken away. You had to trust that no one remained in the bathroom. That no one held an ear to the blue door.

Ruth Anne said, No one needs to know.

Sister Michelle let out her breath. I'm not so sure.

You'll find out more about that when you leave the convent.

Will you come and see me? I'm going to move to San Francisco.

I might, Ruth Anne said.

Someone knocked on the door; the knock vibrated, hung in the air.

After a moment's hesitation, she said, Come in.

Sister David opened the door and said, Girls. It's late.

Her face was puffy in the heat. Her habit askew from all the day's chores and effort. She appraised them suspiciously, her eyes lighting on the angle of their chairs, Sister Michelle's delicate feet in the red shoes. She frowned and her face was froggy, jowly.

Oui, Soeur.

Oui, Soeur.

You must restrict yourselves to social hour. You must remember why we are here. We are here to serve God and He expects us to serve Him early in the morning.

Sister Michelle stood up and her seductive scent seemed released from her clothing, released from the black serge skirt and the white blouse.

Until social hour.

Until then, Ruth Anne said.

She worked toward certain points: mail arriving and social hour. She thought of these as clearings in the day.

Anyone might write to her. Johnny himself might write a letter and all it would take is one thin sheet of paper, one stamp, one sentence— I'm all right, he would say, don't worry—and all that had been closing down would open up again. When she thought about this, she pictured the Street of Flowers. She would feel that much abundance. Gladiolas and lilies and roses. Stall after stall.

We must know everything about each other, Sister Michelle said at social hour. Pretend you are a character. Tell me everything.

They sat in French armchairs, with curving legs. The others gathered on the sofas, nesting close to each other. The French armchairs looked out on the street through a long window. Sister Michelle would arrive first and she would open the plantation shutters, secure them with a hook and eye. It would be evening, with a patch of black sky visible and a coconut palm and a taxi stand where two rusted-out Fiats dove in and out of traffic. On the wide sidewalk half-dressed boys kicked a soccer ball and shouted. The boys and the blat-blat of horns sheltered them. Mrs. Ha might bring them tea in a metal pot; she might bring too-dry cookies on a plate, but more often than not the tea would cool in the pot, the cookies would remain on the plate.

She spent a long time on the silver hairbrush. When she finished, Sister Michelle told her about her family's discipline and punishment: enduring her father's shouting, going to bed without supper. Once her mother had thrown two eggs at her brother—the one who had lost his hand—and when he ducked the eggs spattered on the kitchen wall. They did not hurry the stories; time was all they had.

Sister David had taken to stopping by her room around eleven o'clock. She would not knock but would stand in the hallway for just a minute, clearing her throat.

Ruth Anne would perch in her nightgown at the open window, smoking a cigarette, listening to her clear her throat. She had bought the cigarettes at the black market and she had never been a smoker but she had to have a vice. She had to have a secret that would distinguish her from the nuns. While she smoked she would read the letters Johnny had written before he disappeared. She had three letters. And she had the photo of him with *2 dumb cherries 1967* written on the back. She knew the letters by heart and she sought out certain phrases. Whatever had to do with her and his view of the future. How much he loved her eyebrows, toes, elbows, her neck beneath the long red hair. I want to take care of you and I want you to take care of me. I want to have the kind of home I never had. I want our kids to have some safety. Your aunt thinks we're too young. We're not too young. I can feel it. I just know it's right. She would smoke the cigarette down to the filter and when Sister David glided down the hallway, she would mouth, Bitch.

At social hour one night in mid-December, Sister Michelle said, Do you feel it?

I can't let myself.

I feel it.

I know you do.

I want to come back.

She's there every night.

I can come later.

Let's not—

Sister David appeared as if signaled. A telegram in hand. Her face wore a look of concern she had composed for just that moment, but she could not quite carry it off, for every time she noticed them together her eyes narrowed suspiciously.

Pour toi.

Ruth Anne took the telegram and went aside. She tried to erect a private space for reading the telegram behind a pillar. Across the salon the nuns laughed and chattered. An Advent candle flamed, danced upon their faces. Music came in snatches through the open window: classical music—floral, buoyant. She did not know classical music and at that moment she wanted to know it. She wanted the music to mean something to her. But it was simply classical music. She felt a muted roaring in her ears, the tide of her own heartbeat. She opened the telegram and looked to the end: Jill. Exhausted all avenues. On assignment with team. No one knows whereabouts. Will try again next month. Sorry. So sorry.

The sisters lit a Christmas candle in every window and gave each other glass-bead rosaries and holy cards. Presents arrived from France. Jam and cheese. Downy woolen things, useless things. The temperature was up in the nineties. Not as hot as it could be, everyone said.

Connie Mattingly invited her to a Christmas party and she went and drank three hand-squeezed daiquiris complete with curls of lime peel. By dark she had told them about Johnny. They stood in a circle—Connie's friends—drinks in hand, and she sat in a rattan chair and told the story, which was not much of a story. He had disappeared. Off the face of the earth. Even as she spoke, she thought, This cheapens it. She had fallen apart, drunk and maudlin, tearful; Connie had been sympathetic but embarrassed; she took her home and dropped her at the convent door with a pat on the arm. She said, I won't be around for Tet. If you want to use my place.

She would never go back there; when she thought of it she felt imprisoned. But she said, Where are you going?

The highlands, Connie said. You should go sometime. You feel above the fray. And Ruth Anne—

Yes?

Don't go home. You'll regret it. You'll never have another life like this one.

She turned away abruptly, thinking, Don't tell me what to do.

Sister David hovered at the gate to let her in, a brown-leafed shadow. She said, You're just in time for Vespers.

I have to lie down.

Sister David pinched her arm. You can't come back this way.

What way? She twisted free.

Like this.

It's Christmas Day.

Our Lord's birthday.

Oh, please—

You misrepresented yourself, Sister David hissed.

She shouted, This place changes you. Don't you see that?

Three sisters strolling toward the chapel halted in the deepest shadows—it was twilight, a delicate blue night—and she could feel them recoil.

Go to your room.

Oui, Soeur. She hung her head and ran to her room, thinking, I will be sorry for this, thinking, I've screwed up, thinking, She makes me sick. She vomited the bitter lime daiquiris and haunting her even as she hung over the toilet was the accusation: You misrepresented yourself. You lie.


A letter came from Johnny's father.

Never before had she seen his father's handwriting; it had been written with a fountain pen with a wide nib; she could hardly imagine the effort it had taken, or him in his trailer, a pile of cigarette butts in the ashtray, falling asleep in front of the television. We don't know nothing. No one can tell us nothing. He must have gotten her address from Aunt Teensy. In spite of the engagement, he and Aunt Teensy had not been introduced. He must have gone downtown to the candy shop, in the last busy time before the winter lull; customers would come in from the snow for slabs of fudge. The radio station would be playing nonstop Christmas music: "White Christmas" and "Blue Christmas" and "Rockin' around the Christmas Tree" and "Silent Night" and "I Saw Mommy Kissing Santa Claus." Aunt Teensy would glance up from the cash register and see him, see his hesitation, and she might not have been considerate. Ruth Anne knew her well enough to know that. A foreman at one of the farms, he would stink of cigarettes and diesel fuel, whatever work he'd done that day. My boy can't be found, he would say. I want to let your girl know. He might sound gruff. He had a way of sounding gruff but Johnny always said, He doesn't mean it. Would anyone in the shop overhear? Would what he said mean anything to them?

Aunt Teensy did not write or send a package. She could not help herself: She catalogued Christmas gifts Aunt Teensy had given her in years gone by. U.S. Savings Bonds. A charm bracelet. Plaid wool skirts. A circle pin. Can-can petticoats. Aunt Teensy had given her what girls wanted; she had not been stingy. When Ruth Anne would say thank you, thank you, Aunt Teensy would joke, I'll take it out of your hide. As if she hadn't. As if they did not share the brutal memories. As if a clean slate were there for the taking.

A kitten came slinking around the tea shop, a skinny tiger-striped cat with bulbous golden eyes. Madame Thuong would bat it with the broom. I have enough mouths to feed, she would say. But if she left to run an errand or see a friend, Ruth Anne would scoop the kitten up and comb out its fleas and Vo would tell her where to find the cream and the kitten would lick a dab of cream from a chipped saucer. Madame Thuong might have gone down to Le Loi Street with piasters in her dress pocket to buy menthol cigarettes. She would open up a pack and sell the cigarettes one by one to the domino players in the evening. She might stop at the meat market and that would give them time to baby the kitten.

You could go home, Vo said.

I have an agreement with the order. Sister David sets aside money for me each month. For college. Outside the open window a boy walked by tapping out with a metal rod the tune that reported fresh noodle soup for sale. You know I came for Johnny. She had told him; her story sounded clinical by now. My fiancé. The number of books she had bound.

You think he might return?

I have to think that.

Your friend will find out. He spoke deliberately, gently; he would wait for her response, listening; any sound she made, a pause in answer-

ing in which she swallowed or a catch in her breath or the merest of
sighs—any sound at all warranted interpretation.

Tell me about this man.

Eight months had passed since he had sat in the kitchen at Pier Cove
and nicked the morning glory seeds to help them sprout more readily.
His arms were long. On the deck above the lake he would slip behind
her and hold her; she would feel him hard and pressing against her buttocks. They had never taken their clothes off and now she wished they
had. She kept these recollections to herself while she said, He's twenty-
one years old. He's a good cook. He went to college for a year but
didn't like it. He could've gone to work where his father works. On a
farm. But he went into the Army instead.

Their hands would graze each other, petting the kitten. In the dim
brown light, the tepid interior, with ceiling fans paddling above them,
the murmur of the old men beyond the lotus screen.

Do you read to him?

She said, It's not what we do together. We have other things we like
to do together. But she thought, He doesn't read like we read. She smelt
the betrayal of Johnny in that.

My mother is going to her cousin's maison de campagne. Before Tet.
And you?

I do not want to go.

Mrs. Ha says Tet is for families.

She will return the last day of the holiday. And besides, the maison
de campagne depresses me. I prefer Saigon. I want to see the satin dragons of Saigon. You will be my eyes. We will sit at the window and you
will describe everything. Won't you? He spoke in a lighthearted man-
ner, as if her answer mattered little one way or the other.

I would like that.

My mother's cousin has the opportunity to sell vegetables to the Special Forces—the Americans—near Dalat. This is her big opportunity.
She wants my mother's advice. And my mother has the opportunity—

For what?

To be forgiven. At Tet, there is forgiveness. Her cousin's mother is
the family matriarch.

The kitten leaped to the floor. Nervously, he fingered her hands, like an instrument he did not know how to play. With his forefinger and thumb he circled her wrist. And will you come to read? And will you be my eyes?

She drew her wrist away and said, Oui. Of course. And what shall we read?

Vu Thu Hien has been arrested. I have a translation of his book about his childhood.

Why was he arrested?

The authorities fear writers.

The servant girl Mai slipped behind the lotus screen. She was younger than Vo, with thick black hair Madame forced her to wear short so that she would not always be late. She offered a bamboo tray of rolled cool washcloths. Ruth Anne took one and pressed it against her face, while Mai set the tray down and unfurled a cloth and patted Vo's face. Monsieur. Monsieur. She had been taught to call him Monsieur.

Merci, Mai. Merci. And where is my mother?

To the bank, Monsieur Vo.

Next she brought the meal, enough for two.

I should go, Ruth Anne said.

Please. Share my food.

Mai smiled perfunctorily and placed chopsticks on Ruth Anne's side of the little table. Platters of banh xeo were set before them, the mung sprouts steaming. Mint and lettuce in a basket. Tall glasses of lime drink. Mai stood behind Vo and stared out the window. She ran her hands—once, lightly—over his shoulders. Vo reached up and touched her fingers. Merci. Merci.

She wanted Mai to leave them alone.

When Mai had gone, he said, Mai is like a little sister to me. Sometimes we listen to music in the kitchen. We have the Beatles. We have Rubber Soul. And she tells me about the movies she sees.

Later she would think about his fingers around her wrist. She would feel again a fine electricity where he had touched her.

She imagined herself as Mai. Patting his face. Her hands on his shoulders. The books they would read. She thought that he would go to Dalat to the maison de campagne if she went along. It would be a good time and she was ashamed that she could consider anything a good time. She had seen photographs of Dalat. The princely villas and the deep lake. The pine trees and the Montagnards in their tribal clothing. She had plenty of time to think these thoughts. At Morning Praise and Eucharist, where she went through the motions. In the library every morning, her job rote by now. At night in bed, after Sister David walked by, after the cigarette at the window and reading the letters.

She was ashamed of herself on several fronts. She had not cared enough about the war effort to be of use. Sue-Sue cared enough to fly in helicopters where she might be killed and Jill's brother cared enough to join up and Jill cared enough to make her stupid hospital books and face the men who had been torn apart. The men whose blood and body parts fell into the blood buckets. Jill had seen a field hospital where they brought the wounded men and the blood buckets set up beneath the gurneys. Jill told her stories she did not want to hear the day they walked the curving paths in the botanical garden. And what were Johnny's sacrifices?

I don't want to be scary or weird. I want a life with you far away from here.

Sometimes she wished him dead, instead of suffering.

Then she would reel herself in, rescue herself, from such thoughts. She had gone out too far. She would think instead, He's resourceful. He'll get by. He's strong. She thought of times after a big meal he would say, I could go a month without eating. If I had to. I have great reserves.

Then she would wish him lost. Anything but captured.

As if her wishes mattered. As if wishes or prayers or incantations mattered.

She felt of use in the library and with Vo.

Reading to Vo. But reading was a selfish pleasure. The words and sentences gave shape to their hours. All literature is about hope, a professor had once said to her. Before Johnny asked her to marry him. Before she knew where Vietnam was.

Vo kept her informed. Your Army, he would say. Your president.

And, Did you know the Chinese invaded us two thousand years ago and we fought the same kind of war? Like phantoms in the countryside. Very substantial phantoms. Le fantôme. He liked the sound of the word and she had to smile to hear it. He loved language and would repeat a word several times—in English or in French—simply to feel the word roll from his mouth.

And, Do you know how many American dollars it takes to fly one B-52 raid?

And, Ho Chi Minh asked Woodrow Wilson for help. In Paris.

Whose side are you on?

Taking sides prolongs the war.

She escaped to the tea shop every other day, riding her bicycle along the edges of the streets, watchful among the motorbikes. The visits were no longer at Madame Thuong's request; they had made a list of books they wanted to read together. The dry hot season was upon them and Mrs. Ha had given her a conical straw hat to protect her from the sun, tied under her chin with a rag, a strip of a worn dress or shirt, but she let the hat fall back upon her shoulder blades while cycling and she would stop and buy dried strawberries and she would feel free now and again and the palm trees in the park would whisk her into an ebullient, violent joy—for she could not live up to the wretchedness of Saigon and the loss of Johnny every single minute. She did not wonder how she would tell him if they were reunited. She did not think about how she would look back on this time in her life; instead she swam in it, the moodiness and tears and the stories and the banh xeo and the lime drink and the joss sticks burning and the chanting at the temples when she passed by. She would walk her bicycle alongside the temples just to hear the strange baritone chants like whales calling.

What is religion for?

Vo said, The rituals make our joy ecstasy, our sorrows bearable.

Who told you that?

A teacher.

But you are not religious.

I go to Mass.

That's not your choice.

I go to Mass for my mother, oui. How did you know?

I can tell. I can tell. You're . . . disinterested.

I like the stories.

What religion would you be if you had your choice?

Maybe Buddhist. It might be in my blood. But did you know in Cao-daism Victor Hugo is a saint?

He was no saint.

That doesn't matter. What matters is the strength that people gain from reading his work. Someday, I will choose my religion. In Vietnam there are many choices. Or there have been. That might end. With the Communists.

I listen at the temples.

He swatted houseflies from his face. We should visit a temple. You will be my eyes.

When?

Why not now?

Madame Thuong presided behind a counter, counting piasters. She did not lift her gaze but said, Oui, oui, when Vo said, Mother, may we take a cyclo to the pagoda?

Ruth Anne said, May I bring my bicycle into the hallway?

Oui, Oui.

She went out to the street and with a key she kept on a long chain around her neck she unlocked the U-shaped lock and wheeled the clicking bicycle among the domino players and smokers, their talk desultory, past Madame in her bright dress, her hair like the oily feathers of a duck, and into the narrow hall where one yellowish bulb lit the flaking plaster. Vo waited at the front door in a shim of sunlight. She allowed herself a glimpse into the kitchen. Mai swabbed the tile floor with a rag mop. On a shelf the tea tins told the tales of sailing ships and Chinese men with mossy beards.

Women crouched on the sidewalk, doing each other's nails. The odor of polish remover rose up when they walked by.

Take my arm.

All right.

They'll see you.

He was right. Four cyclo drivers swerved to a stop in front of them. Cyclo? Cyclo?

She chose one. One is enough?

He laughed. Oui. We are skinny like the cat.

The driver was a man with a gold tooth, a wiry body, a thatch of graying hair. He took Vo's elbow and Vo reached out and deftly felt for the rim of the cyclo and with the slightest shrug he let the driver know he was fine, he could do it himself, and he swung himself up into the cy-clo and Ruth Anne followed. The leather bonnet was open and they fid-geted for a moment, settling in the meager shade of the bonnet.

Xa Loi Pagoda, Vo said.

They set off, the cyclo driver pedaling in wide, slow arcs into the flood of traffic. She closed her eyes to know what Vo knew: the jiggle of the ride and the backfiring and the horns and the wow-wow-wow of sirens and the whistle of police and the children, cries of children, mothers scolding. She could not bear to keep her eyes shut for long and when she opened them they had turned into a lesser street, a quiet street. Monochromatic, grayish or brown, with little sun. Here the beg-gars lived. A naked old man perched backward on the curb, shitting. Whatever buildings there were had been surrounded by cement walls topped with rolls of barbed wire.

What do you see?

Beggars.

Xa Loi, Xa Loi, ahead, the driver flung over his shoulder.

I see the bell tower.

Vo asked the driver to wait and they agreed, in Vietnamese, on a price for the waiting.

Take my arm.

She did and the women who squatted in the street—the vendors and the beggars—stared at them, at her. They reached toward her and be-seechingly placed their palms before her, a stylized begging that of-fended her somehow. Yet she knew it sprung from need.

Don't pay attention to them.

It's hard not to.

We're here to see the pagoda.

They took the wide stairs behind the wrought-iron lotus blossoms. A banyan tree too big for them to stretch their arms around lay shade and leafy respite on the stairs. Below, a white statue of the female Bud-dha reigned over the little mishmash courtyard: umbrellas and awnings this way and that, the naked children, candles and joss sticks for sale in half-barrels, bicycles in a row, and the fringe of palms.

She looks like the virgin.

Describe her to me.

It's smooth. I'm not sure what stone she's made of. She's glancing down. Or inward. Very gentle. She's like the virgin in front of the cathedral.

She is Kuan Yin, from China. The embodiment of compassion. She hears the cries of the world.

The chanting began, the voices of men.

Are we near the bench?

She led him to the bench on the veranda outside the meditation hall. He sat down and said, You go look. Go to the door.

When she returned he said, So?

He's huge. Made of bronze. They've made offerings. Eggs and bananas. Flowers and grapes.

You see the tower behind us.

Yes?

Sit down with me.

She sat. She fanned her face with her hand.

Monks were thrown from this tower. You can still hear their cries. This was after Thich Quang Duc set himself afire.

He what?

You must have heard of this?

No.

In 1963 a Buddhist monk died not far from here. I saw this with my own eyes. He set himself afire. A young nun stood beside me crying. Her gray sleeves were in shreds and she wiped her tears on them. I had never seen such agony on a woman's face.

And why?

Diem. They wanted to be rid of Diem. People are willing to die.

I'm not willing to die.

Nor I.

He leaned a little closer. Miss Ruth Anne.

Weeks before they had stopped calling each other Miss and Mister. She leaned in curiously to hear what he would say. Why had he returned to such formality? His collar was frayed and his dark glasses reflected her face. He's very young. She could forget that, talking. Or reading.

What are you wearing?

What am I wearing?

Yes. You are my eyes.

A skirt.

May I touch the fabric?

All right.

Vo tentatively reached out and she lifted a gather of her skirt into his hand. Cotton, he said.

Yes.

He politely folded his hands in his lap and tilted his head, to listen to the chanting.

A skirt and a blouse.

And the blouse?

It's blue.

Blue like the sea?

No. Blue like a sailor's uniform. Dark blue.

The chanting ceased and nuns and monks in gray and orange robes filtered purposefully out of the meditation hall. The odor of incense trailing.

Are flowers growing here?

No. Palms.

A clap of thunder shook the sky and the banyan tree. The tree shivered in the wind.

We'd better go.

She led him down the stairs and into the cyclo. Children squealed and ran crouching under awnings. Lightning lit the sky. The rain pelted them and the cyclo driver was not sorry to keep going. He braved the rain and the water that pooled in the pockmarked streets. They did not talk in traffic. They would have had to shout and she did not want to shout after the whispering. They had almost whispered into each other's ears. The man she had seen shitting now slept in the dirt under a tree. His skin—his back, his bony buttocks—like lacquer. A hard skin. How had he come to this? The thought lasted only a moment, less than the lightning. He was old and she had not paid much attention to old people. They were invisible to her. She could not imagine herself old if she had wanted to. Or Sue-Sue or Jill or Johnny or Vo or Sister Michelle.

At the tea shop Vo paid the driver and she waited, drenched, her clothes plastered against her skin. People huddled under trees and awnings and newspapers and ponchos.

Just inside the door she said, I thought this was the dry season.

Vo said, Nothing is as it seems.

How profound, she teased.

They came into the tea shop giggling. Madame Thuong flung back her head and smiled at them and it was the first time Ruth Anne had seen her smile and she understood her approval and she understood that Madame Thuong wanted happiness for Vo. In that moment for the first time Madame Thuong's motherhood, her love for Vo, was evident. Her smile was beautiful and Ruth Anne saw what men had seen in her.

Mai brought them towels and they wiped their faces. The Edith Piaf played on the turntable. Love lyrics. The rain stopped as suddenly as it had begun, as if some hand had gathered the rain and swept it elsewhere. The sound of it ceased and the people went back into the street.

I need to go.

Will you come again tomorrow?

I'll see. I'll see how much work I can get done. She went into the hallway to retrieve her bicycle.

She had propped Sister David's bicycle against the flaking plaster wall and now it was not there.

Where's my bike?

Madame Thuong and Mai came to the end of the hallway. The two of them—one tall and chic, one girlish, with perplexed looks—threw up their hands. Ruth Anne rushed to the opposite end of the hallway. The door was open into a yard covered with corrugated metal. Wet clothing hung on a clothesline under the metal roof. Tins and plastic buckets and household odds and ends filled an open shed.

Where is my bicycle!

Vo felt his way to her, his hands skimming the flaking plaster.

It's not my fault, Mai screamed.

You were here, Madame said.

You were here too, Madame.

Mai, you never speak like this to me!

I'm sorry, Miss Ruth Anne. I am sorry.

She leaned against the wall and touched her forehead to it, the clammy wall, the wall that had absorbed too many storms. It's not mine, it's not mine, she fretted. Sister David's face seemed to appear right before her. There would be trouble. I'll get in trouble, she said. You don't have any idea the trouble I'm in. She could feel tears in a knot in her throat.

Mai, you are finished for the day.

Madame, Madame, Mai wailed.

Vo leaned close to Ruth Anne. He took her hand in his. Let my mother speak to the nun.

You don't understand. She hates me. You just don't—

With that Ruth Anne yanked free and ran back the way she had come, back through the old men at the tables who peered up at her, out to the street. She would walk to the convent through the hagglers and the banter. Past the park where the palm trees could not reach into her heart. She groaned out loud. She had done nothing wrong. I have done nothing wrong. It's not my fault. I am only doing what you brought me here to do. I did not ask to be sent over there. She pounded in the direction of the convent, past the cathedral and the post office. She stepped into the Saigon traffic and let it river around her. Nothing could repair her upset: not sunlight or church bells, not the sight of silk dresses in the tailor's windows, not a GI grinning at her from a cyclo. It would be Sister David's straw, Aunt Teensy would've said, that broke the camel's back.

# 11

Johnny Bond resented the month of July. He always had. The humidity got a grip on the Midwest in July. Professors and administrators and lawyers and doctors who loved his menus and left fat tips to keep his help from mutiny all went out of town to Michigan or Oregon or, more recently, to the Alps or Alaska. Anywhere to cool off.

If Ruth Anne had been home he might have said to hell with it himself and put a CLOSED FOR 2 WEEKS sign on the door. He might have gotten out his maps with their calendar-art illustrations of obscure waterfalls and covered bridges. He might have packed up Ruthie and driven to the Smokies and on the way there they would have stopped at Cracker Barrels for lunch and dinner and he would've ordered sweet tea and butter beans and burgers, food of his childhood, and Ruthie would've wandered aimlessly through the shop and they would've made fun of all the country junk, the quilts and aprons and peppermint sticks and rocking chairs, the excess of nostalgia you could drown in. Still, for road food you could not beat it. On the road he and Ruthie would talk or be silent or get mentally soused on the twang of country stations, whatever suited them. Such road trips were a married time. Ruthie would slip her feet from her sandals and prop them on the dash. They would stop at an air-conditioned motel somewhere in Kentucky and she might take a bubble bath and he would turn on a baseball game, maybe the Braves would have a night game, and it might be the only baseball game he would watch all summer, a simple pleasure, in the chill of the A/C, and there might be kids in the sparkling pool outside the window, kids squealing in delight or cranky, kids in summer whose parents slumped relieved in chaise lounges beside the pool, the chlorine scalding their nostrils. After a while Ruthie would come out of the bathroom and she would be wrapped in a white towel and she would smell beautiful. He would turn off the TV. The kids outside would be taken in, their last protests trickling in an ideal world toward another wing of the motel. She might spread a clean towel on the cool white sheet and hand him a jar of body cream and he might rub the body cream into her skin in plumy strokes that to him were not about sex but for Ruthie might be square one. She might reach for him after. But even if she did not reach for him he liked to care for her. He liked to feel the lean muscle of her back and thighs. Later, he might get a Coke from the machine near the elevator and mix the Coke with rum in plastic glasses and to be cool and a bit abuzz with rum and to have Ruthie there and to know her—that was sufficient contentment. Ruthie would read a book of stories and he would read a cooking magazine. If she drifted off before he did, he would drape a towel over a lamp to dim the light and keep on reading.

But Ruthie was at Our Lady of Holy Mysteries.

July had not been a good month so far.

August would be the same, but then the burnt-out foliage, the droopy dahlias, would echo the wilt of the citizenry and if you drove along a back road for relief the insects crusted up your windshield. People would talk about fall and yearn for fall and only a severe thunderstorm would lift their spirits. A storm that might take down power lines or whip the gutters from a house would also cool the trees, soil, machinery, attics, cornfields, blacktop. Everything that held the heat and bounced it back at you.

He had placed an ad in the newspaper, looking for a cook who might be mature enough to leave in charge now and again. He was going up to the monastery to take Ruthie's bike to her. Beyond that, he wasn't sure. The idea that he might keep going pressed itself upon him. When he looked at the ad in the Sunday classified section, he did not recall using those words. Inventive. Mature. But he had. An unusual ad and he hoped to attract the unusual person. Someone who would not have to be taught every little thing. Monday afternoon, two people called while he was spreading weed-killer on a potential berm where he planned to plant three redbuds in the fall. Tuck had made him reconsider the fruit trees. He had prepared another spot for a magnolia. And another for a chorus of cedars. The treeless berms and holes gave the place a cratered, devastated feel, much less than tidy. He was going overboard with the trees. At first, planting more trees had been about beauty, about wanting to look out and see the blossoms or the sweep of the cedars. Later, it felt like the satiation of a desire to change what she would see when she came home. To astonish her. Every time he thought, She's not going to like this—about the trees—he stilled himself by saying, She's not here. The phone lay beside him on the grass and the first ring woke him from a reverie of motel times and rolling in the middle of the night toward Ruthie in her gown and whispering, Do you want to fool around? He dropped the sack of weed-killer and a pouf of poison came from the sack. Git, he said to Moxie. He felt a stab of planet guilt about the weed-killer and the phone went on ringing insistently and when he finally got to it the first caller said, I'm told I'm inventive. A woman with a sugary voice like a greeting card and he did not think she would fit in. The wait staff and the dishwashers were vulgar and he did not have time for anyone who might not like that. But he said, Give me a for instance. And she said, Black bean lasagna. A cockamamie idea if he'd ever heard one. I'll be in touch, he said, and he hoped he had not wasted the money on the ad.

He went inside and scrubbed his hands. Fed Moxie a handful of biscuits. Mox was bored without Ruthie. He lay around sleeping with his paws over his eyes. Brambles was closed until lunch Tuesday. He wished he had what it took to go for a walk with Mox but a lethargy had entered his body, dead ringer for a person he thought he had left behind: troubled by memory. You could talk about living in the present and everyone did. He had learned that lesson long before it became bar talk or golf talk. Just because you learn a lesson like that doesn't mean you put it into practice. Once, malaria had run around in his brain like cocaine and he had still been capable of making food lists, capable of envisioning a month hence or a year hence. His present then was not a time to enter fully into. When his friends at home were singing the song about cocaine, aspiring to a counterlife, he had been behind enemy lines with malaria. So far behind enemy lines, it was another country. Laos. He had never heard of Laos until he was sent there. He had cast a net into the future with his food lists. What he would cook if he were ever free. The food lists were linked with that girl. The one they had captured the day before. A Bible-thumping nurse from a cinder-block hospital. That might've been the closest he came to being saved, to converting to Protestantism. He had not thought her name in years. He wanted it to be hard to remember. If her name arose from the midden pile of names from that time, he turned away; her name had weight, visceral encumbrances. A bile would rise in his throat.

He came to when the phone rang.

Mairead. Rhymes with parade, she said.

He invited her over for an interview and he called Laurel and said, I think I've got a live one. She's Irish and her father apprenticed her to a cook at a Dublin hotel when she was fourteen.

How old is she now?

Hard to say. She's got another job. Teaching dance to girls in Indy.

How's she going to juggle that?

The other job's part-time.

Let us know if you need taste-testers, Laurel said. We're packing. We're taking a load to the Goodwill.

In the big kitchen Johnny waited and set out the ingredients for a blueberry pie. He had a good feeling about her. He would hire someone and then he would take a trip. He might see if Tuck wanted to go somewhere with a temperature low enough and a breeze so stiff that jackets would be required. Up north. To Sleeping Bear Dunes. Or he might go car-camping with Mox at the state parks. He might see Ruthie and then spend some time driving the Blue Star Highway. There was a summer feel he hankered for, a feel that might be conjured by a trip.

Mairead-Rhymes-with-Parade drove a humpbacked Volvo from the sixties, black and rusted out along the wheel wells. The muffler broke the silence as she lurched up the hill in first gear. She parked beside his pickup and twisted her rearview mirror and stretched to see herself and with three precise jots she applied lipstick and tossed the tube onto the passenger seat and got out. She was short and wore her gray hair to her chin and it curled like a silver-tinged cloud and he knew that some women permed their hair but this looked natural. She had a cowlick. And big tortoiseshell sunglasses. Johnny rarely noticed women's clothes but hers were impossible to ignore. A long wispy skirt and a red top that left her shoulders bare. A scarf to dress it up. She was a far cry from the girl who had been apprenticed at fourteen. The midwestern vulgarity of his help would seem tame to her. He was ready to hire her on the spot and he did not even know if she could cook or if she only thought she could.

Mairead O'Connor, Mr. Bond.

He welcomed her into the big kitchen and sat her down and gave her a glass of midday wine, a bright chilled chardonnay, and they talked. He was glad that it was Monday and Brambles was closed. He was glad to talk. She wanted to know the history of the place and she wanted to know how he had gotten interested in cooking—To be sure, most men don't have that interest, Mr. Bond—and when he said, Look, no one calls me Mr. Bond, I'm Johnny, it hit him that she was interviewing him.

So why don't we cook up some lunch? Johnny said. With his forefinger he pressed the butter he had left out on the counter to see if it had reached room temperature and he said, I'll go on with my blueberry pie.

I'll do the entrée and a salad, Mairead said, and when she smiled her dimples deepened and he saw the imp that had probably been inside her since the day she was born. She must have been around fifty. Around his age.

And what will you make?

Pasta?

All right. The pastas're all in bins beside the walk-in.

Do you have bow-ties?

Bow-ties, yes.

I need lemons and olives and garlic.

He told her where to find the things she needed and he gave her a fresh white apron and she took off her rings and scrubbed her hands and Johnny turned on NPR and a world music show was on and the music was from Africa. He cut up his butter into cubes and began. They cooked and Johnny asked her questions and found out that the type of dancing she taught was modern and that she had not been in town long and that she had come because her son was a sophomore at the college—taking summer classes—and he had been in a car accident.

He wanted to say, Where is his father? But he said, Is he all right?

He'll be all right. He lives in the dormitory. He has to go to physical therapy three times a week and I take him for that. I stay in a room downtown.

Whereabouts?

Above the brew pub.

When she slipped off her rings he had not seen the finger she had taken them from and she laid them in a fish-shaped ginger grater and he did not want to seek the answer to his question with a curiosity that would scare her and he finally decided that he did not want to know. He did not want to know if she were married. He wanted to assume she wasn't. He told himself, It's simpler that way. If she has a husband to contend with, every arrangement will be complicated. Why would she want a job like this if she has a husband? These thoughts lurked beneath the surface and he veered away from them, claiming, She'll be a good employee and that's all I care about. I want to get out my maps and go somewhere. But as the afternoon wore on and he watched her expertly wield a knife and chop the garlic and they sat down to the pasta and the spinach salad and a dressing she had concocted and they talked a little more and the berry pie baking smelt fatty and rich and she refused another glass of wine but she did not seem in a hurry, she did not leave when she might have, Johnny realized, I'll enjoy this. Training her. I'll call Ruthie and see if she minds if I wait until next week to bring her bicycle. And the ceiling of doom that had pressed and weighed upon him since the Fourth lifted. It just lifted.

Mairead, you're on, he said.

When do I start?

When do you take your boy to PT?

Monday, Wednesday, Friday. At eight in the morning.

Let's start tomorrow. Can you come early?

How early?

Say seven?

She grinned. I'll be here with bells on.

Later Laurel called and said, How was it?

She'll work out, Johnny said.

You don't sound too enthusiastic.

Oh, I am. I am.

# 12

Ruth Anne paused under the grape arbor, between meditation and Aunt Teensy. Between profound rest and agitation. Between the sunrise splintering among the trees and the confinement of Aunt Teensy's room. She could not picture the room without the omnipresent soaps on TV. They irritated her more every day.

Beyond the arbor lay the beach and the big lake. Even a glimpse of an empty beach, the damp and creamy sand, brought to mind Vo. His red-tipped cane bouncing along the shore. Vo had sent a message—a question—by way of Tin. Do you remember *The Tale of Kieu?* It was a story—a poem—he had recited and he had said, All Vietnamese know this story. Kieu and her sister have bodies like slim plum branches. Snow-pure souls. She remembered his voice when he recited the lines he knew by heart. The years compressed and at the very mention of *The Tale of Kieu* she felt again the needle of jealousy at his voice describing the two sisters in the poem. She felt the needle of jealousy even though she had lain with him in the loft where she would describe to him the flight of the moon across the terraces. Perhaps she felt it because she lay with him. Her belly like the moon. A dark brown line from her navel to her pubic bone. Like the line on a map. At night she would sit on the edge of the rough mattress and she would rub the royal jelly on her breasts and belly. A snaggle-toothed woman in the market had recommended it. What had she thought about Johnny then? He was sure to ask. And she held to a narrow truth that would need fleshing out. It was hard to remember. He had disappeared, just as her parents had disappeared.

She and Tin had exchanged three messages. Late at night in the computer room she had printed them all and except for the first message she kept them in a manila envelope. She had taken to carrying the first message with her everywhere. In a sweater pocket or in a pants pocket. She liked having it handy. She patted her pocket.

The morning was chilly. Later the sand would burn your feet and the beach people would stack themselves on blankets and the children would shriek in the water. She wrapped her thin sweater more snugly against her ribs. Beneath a wind-scoured pine, songbirds dashed and trilled near Aunt Teensy's birch-bark feeder. She heard the sisters singing in the chapel. Tendrils of a chant to morning.

Johnny was coming soon and she had made up her mind to tell. I've made up my mind, I've made up my mind. Sometimes she whispered such resolve. To the lake or the birds. She had begun rehearsing the phrases. They would go down to the water at sunset. The sunset would be the reason to go down there. There was a cove. There was a fire pit. They would build a fire of driftwood and they would sit on a log or in low beach chairs and she would say, I have something to tell you. It's hard to tell but I can't go on until I do—

She did not know what going on would mean. But this state— suspended, monastic—could not last forever. She was grateful for the practice. The dawn sits. The clear chime of the gong. The silence and the rest from thoughts. Even the ugly self-knowledge. Jill would not think she should call it ugly, but to herself she did. Jill said, Be patient with the way your thoughts keep you from God. Even that was conceptualization and centering was supposed to free you from thinking. About danishes, sex, money, parking tickets, dying, coffee, hot baths, old wounds you labor over, all the desire. God. Even God. There was something ironic in the talk about centering; they always went back to talking about God, but centering was supposed to teach you not to talk like that. Laurel would be pleased that she had come to this and she vowed to remember and to tell Laurel. But the place of no language frightened people, frightened her sometimes; we are forever striving, failing, striving, failing, to make meaning with language. All the Gospels and every holy book are evidence of that. Be patient, Ruthie. Jill liked to joke, patience is a virtue possessed by few women and no men. Johnny was patient. Johnny was a saint and that might not last forever. Her patience could extend to Laurel and to Father Carroll and to Limbo and even, yes, usually, to Aunt Teensy. But she had not extended patience like a peace offering to herself. Not quite.

Jill opened the door at the nursing-home end of the arbor. She waved. Did you forget? It's almost eight. She's having her hair done. She needs your help.

I did forget.

Ruth Anne let go of all the thoughts she wandered among and, slipping through the door that Jill held open, she said, Morning, and smiled. They hugged, as if to brace themselves. At this time of the morning the spasmodic waking up of all the men and women who had survived another night gave the hall the feel of unpredictability. Someone might cry out or fall or curse the Almighty or pray. Radio volume might be turned too loud. Memories might be shouted out. They weren't ready to face the staff and doctors and visitors.

With her back to Aunt Teensy's door, Jill said, We need to get her in a wheelchair and you can wheel her down to the beauty shop.

When's her appointment?

They don't have appointments. She swung the door wide. They wait in line. It's a social occasion. You'll see—

Aunt Teensy fretted, Jack up the bed, will you?

Ruth Anne pressed the button that made the bed fold up and with great effort Aunt Teensy inched into a sitting position. She rearranged her bed jacket, a quilted satiny yellow one with ribbons at the throat. Her hair had thinned and her rosy scalp shone through the white.

Did you forget me?

How could I forget you? I was watching the sunrise.

I'm worried about my birds. My dear birds.

Shall I feed them?

You know Rosa always feeds them. But she's late—

Let me, if it'll make you feel better.

Nothing makes me feel better.

All right.

But I have to get my hair done. Do you remember my hair? The way it used to be?

I do.

It was still pretty when you were a little girl. Wasn't it?

It was.

Jill wheeled in the chair and between the two of them they trundled her gently over the edge of the bed and into the chair. She was not heavy. Her shins beneath her gown were cloudy blue.

My spine feels mooshy.

You look pretty cheerful, Jill said. She handed Ruth Anne a pair of booties. I have to go, but here. You like to be completely covered up, don't you? Otherwise she'll get cold. She left the door ajar.

It's awful being old.

Ruth Anne said nothing. The booties did not go on easily.

Can't you help me?

I'm trying.

At last they were on and Aunt Teensy said, You see my cardinals out there?

I see them.

I've always loved cardinals.

Ruth Anne tucked the soft blanket around her lap and around her calves so that no skin was exposed.

You never were interested in birds.

Ruth Anne's shoulders slumped. She sighed. I like birds.

Oh, you've changed. You think you're the only one who's changed.

Ruth Anne thought, That's not true. She wasn't sure if she had changed. In so many ways she felt the same.

From the room next door a television burst into the news or weather. And then a commercial for Firmalift, a remedy for wrinkles. Guaranteed.

The telephone rang and Ruth Anne said, Where's the phone?

I don't know, I don't know.

Ruth Anne ran her hands among the bed sheets and discovered the phone and answered it.

Sweetheart—

Johnny—

I thought you might be there. My plans have changed.

Aunt Teensy sat staring out into the hall, her hands in her lap. Her hair smashed up on one side from sleep. Where is that Rosa?

Oh?

I need to train a new employee. Once she's trained, I can feel free. It won't take long—

How long?

A few days.

Ruth Anne lowered her voice. I was looking forward to seeing you. I need a break.

No one said anything. Then, Is Laurel all right?

She's fine. Thursday they close on the house and I can be here for that. I'm going to send champagne. From us.

That's nice of you.

How does Friday sound?

Can you stay?

There?

We could go somewhere. Remember Valentine Lodge? Let's try to get a room there.

Sure. That sounds good.

You don't sound like yourself.

It's been a while. I wasn't sure you wanted me to stay.

Oh, Johnny—

What?

I do.

I am going to be late. I am going to be late to have my hair done. I am eighty-six years old. Eighty-six.

How's she doing?

She's fine, Johnny. She's better than you might expect.

You tell her I'm coming up. I'll bring that chocolate sour-cream cake she likes.

*Where* is Rosa?

Ruth Anne hung up and said, Let's ask at the desk.

She wheeled her down the hall and stopped at the desk. A bowl of wooden lemons and a fake lipstick plant, ever in bloom, were the only ornament. A skinny black woman with brassy blond hair counted out pills into plastic cups on a tray.

Where's Rosa?

Rosa is sick.

What's wrong with her?

She sure don't tell me, Miss Teensy.

Who'll feed my birds?

I will, Ruth Anne said. I will. Now let me get you down there and I'll come back and feed the birds.

The skinny black woman shoved her glasses up her nose with her middle finger and harrumphed, not loudly, but to make her point: it was clear—Aunt Teensy was a royal pain.

Ruth Anne set the wheelchair rolling and glanced back apologetically. To no avail. The woman had turned back to her pill-counting.

They were alone in the coppery elevator and the low ceiling and the silence made for an intimacy. Ruth Anne did not know what to say. They had not set foot on the soulful journey. If her mother had not died she would not care. If her mother had not died Aunt Teensy would have been a postscript to her life. If her mother had not died she would never have known the silver brush. What would she have known? A pliancy? Safety? That was forever lost. Just as the years with Tin were lost. Time you skip with loved ones may never be retrieved. She was skipping time now, with Laurel, with Johnny, and she felt her heart zigzag at what she might be taking from herself.

My birds depend on me.

I'll go right back up there.

The food is in the closet. In a Tupperware container. Don't mess with anything.

What would I mess with?

Just feed the birds.

The elevator landed with a wheeze in the basement and she wheeled her around two dim corners into a daylit pentagon where a dozen white-haired women in wheelchairs were queued for service. Two stylists— young women in their twenties with jangling bracelets and platform shoes—leaned over shampoo bowls, suds up their wrists. A giddy chatter wafted over all. A coffeemaker perked on a chrome table on wheels, and mugs in a row beside the coffee and a sugar bowl and creamer completed the tableau. Teensy, Teensy, the others said. Ruth Anne left her there among the women. I'll come back after I feed the birds and take a shower. You should be done by then. She was glad to leave her there and ashamed to feel that way.

Upstairs the black woman passed her a grudging nod of complicit relief. I'll be in there to change her bed.

I'm feeding the birds.

Good girl.

Oh, I'm not, she thought, I'm not. If you only knew.

Aunt Teensy's room without her there felt larger, less oppressive.
The call from Johnny came back. He had seemed so willing before,
so eager to come, and now she sensed a trace of reluctance. But the
weekend—

They might have the entire weekend.

They would need it.

The closet was crammed full, smelling of mothballs and cedar. A
cedar-lined dresser from the cottage had been fitted inside and in the
dresser were nightgowns and bed jackets and underpants. Aunt Teensy
had instructed her to bring this one or that from the dresser. The peach
flannel or the granny gown with eyelet trim. Such were the choices she
had. Ruth Anne tugged the container of safflower seeds out of the
closet and down at that level she spied peripherally and to her left a see-
through box. The beaded bags. They glistened through the plastic. She
lifted the box out and knelt for a minute, deciding. She went to the door
and shut it and sudden silence buffered her.

She opened the box, recognized the bags. Red and midnight blue
with silk drawstrings. Black with a gold clasp. Black with a rhinestone
clasp. An opalescent clutch. And others. She clicked the well-made
clasp on one and inside she found a matchbook from a nightclub in
Chicago—Lakeland—with a saxophone flocked in red against gold. In
another, a silver compact. Inside, mousy beige powder lay cracked beneath a cotton puff. The scent of the beaded bags, part mint, part perfume, part cigarette smoke, transported her to the moments of purchase
at a flea market or antique shop. Aunt Teensy would always be in a good
mood after buying a beaded bag. She knelt on the floor and laid them
out on the hooked rug beside the bed. She did not hesitate. She did not
consider whether she had the right. In the bottom of the box lay the
largest one, a pink sequined envelope with a loop-and-button closure,
fat with whatever Teensy had stored there. It might have been antique
handkerchiefs or stockings or a frothy shawl. Ruth Anne reached into

the box and knew the second she laid hands on the pink bag: her letters from Vietnam were inside. She did not know how she knew. The silence ballooned into a muffled pounding in her skull. Her knees ached.

She undid the loop and the pink bag fell open. The thin airmail envelopes had been slit precisely with a letter-opener. At least she had read them. Or was her silence worse because she had read them? She had never given up watching for a letter from Aunt Teensy. Waddling up the hill in Dalat to the post office, eight months along. The smoky blue-green terraces alive with dew and fog and the ruffle of the vegetable gardens. She would stop to rest at the church partway there, holding her belly underneath, catching her breath. She rubbed one of the envelopes between her fingers. There was her girlish handwriting. It looked like the handwriting of a fourth-grader, carefully crafted, but not quite sure.

A clamor rose in the hall. You can't make me. It might have been the man in the next room: a codger, she had determined from the start that he had probably been a shouter all his life. The nurse's aide mollycoddled him, crooning like a blues singer, Now, Mister, now Mister, don't you go being low-down.

The songbirds perched on the pine's low boughs and darted to the rungs of the feeder and back. Aunt Teensy's voice haunted the room. My birds, my birds—

Jill knocked perfunctorily and stuck her head inside. Ruthie—

Yes?

What're you doing?

Feeding the birds.

Jill stepped into the room; she came curiously around the bed, her neck craned. Ruth Anne felt small, caught. She ran her hand over the beads, the rough sequins. They could cut you.

I just wanted to see them. I just wanted to touch them.

She's very private.

I know that.

They'll be yours eventually.

I don't care about that.

You don't?

She laid the bags into the box as she'd found them, saying, Johnny can't come until Friday, Jill. I wish he were here. I'm starting to lose my bearings without Johnny. She's not dying—

I never said she was—

I don't blame you—

Jill said, Let's feed the birds. They tucked the see-through box into the closet and each with a tall paper cup full of safflower seeds they went down the hall and out the double door, into the still-cool morning. A trail led around the corner of the building to the bird-feeder. Jill went first, her sandals dryly rasping in the pine duff, and the pines let out their scent for all to smell and the pine scent and the birdsong were a part of the suchness, whatever she was not supposed to think about but be: a woman feeding birds with her friend. But the letters were like a bone caught in her throat.

My father says that you wrote letters, Tin had written. I wonder what you wrote in the letters.

I wonder too, she had written back. You forget so much.

They dumped the seed into the feeder. They were on a slope, with the lake visible in shards between the upright trees. Jill said, Sit down. Let's talk.

They found a treeless bench of moss and settled with their heels planted down the slope for ballast. An interval of quiet passed: within it was the history of their affection and what stood between them now. A question or admission.

Finally, Ruth Anne said, I can't tell you what's going on.

You don't have to.

I know you must wonder.

I just—sense—something—

Hidden.

Yes.

It's been good to be here.

Has been?

Eventually I have to go.

Of course.

I have to tell you, though—it's raised more questions than it's answered.

About?

The spirit. She picked up a twig and stuck it over and over into a pad of moss between them. It'll be hard to go back to Father Carroll's homilies. I prefer the silence. And when you say that being attached to the experience of God is not God but thought—the word God has nearly lost its meaning to me. But when you instruct us you say God with such—

Such what?

Such certainty.

Closing her eyes, laying her head on her knees, softly Jill said, I don't know any other way to talk about it.

If we all became mystics, the churches would be empty. She had stolen that from Laurel and she thought she ought to say so but she didn't.

What's going on with you aside from this?

Tin has contacted me. She did not know why she finally told. She had wanted Johnny to be first and she had spoiled that.

At last, Ruthie—

He lives here now.

That's where you've gone.

Sort of.

Where does he live?

Windfall.

Have you met?

It's hard to make the leap.

And what about—his father?

He's married. They have a video store. It's what they do.

He—Tin—must be in his thirties.

He'll be thirty this fall. He teaches junior-high history.

Does Johnny know?

Not yet. She reached into her sweater pocket and brought out the first message. A wad of paper that had been folded and refolded countless times. Damp. The creases torn. She handed it to Jill.

The grandmother—you said she was—

A bitch—

Ruthie—

She was!

He wants to know you.

Yes.

It's the fishhook of dreams I've swallowed half my life, Jill read aloud.

The fishhook. Every time I read that part I feel like I can't swallow.

Jill said, You must meet him. Don't you want to? You have to, Ruthie—

Jill always argued that hearts should open to each other and that the truth would forge a link and that deception bogged you down and that forgiveness was inevitable. She had wanted Ruth Anne to write the letters from Vietnam and she had wanted her to tell Johnny years ago. She had wanted a reconciliation between Aunt Teensy and Ruth Anne. She had wanted Sue-Sue to have her baby. But Sue-Sue had been determined. She went home for the abortion and they never saw her again.

Nothing is as simple as you make it out to be.

Jill laid the open message between them on the moss. It fluttered there.

Ruth Anne snapped it up and folded it and put it away in her pocket. What's the worst thing that could happen?

Are you kidding?

Jill put her arms around her. You're trembling—

I feel the way—I felt—when I was pregnant. She wiped at her eyes.

A rap on the window startled them. They turned to see Rosa in Aunt Teensy's room, her big hair sprayed into a crown. You fed the birds! Gracias! Where is Miss Teensy?

With her forefingers Jill spiraled imaginary curls around her face. Let's go in, she said, patting Ruth Anne's hand. Let's get on with it.

Telling Jill unleashed a furious thrashing, a disturbance. Whatever she did, she tossed and turned inwardly with the question: when?

Even though she paid a modest sum for her keep at the monastery, she had taken to working in the kitchen for an hour a day and while she cut up carrots and sliced zucchini within the gab of the sisters, she argued with herself. While she retrieved Aunt Teensy and admired her white sausage curls. While she walked on the beach with Jill after lunch and Jill held her tongue and the wind rolling over the lake was a white noise sunbathers slept beneath. While she sat on the black zafu in the meditation room, unable to center, unable to come into the calm.

Phrases from the messages cut into her thoughts.

My father still loves stories. I am a teacher. I have not married. Not yet. Are you happy? Do I have sisters and brothers? My father keeps a photograph of you in a leather billfold in his dresser. He keeps it for me. His wife would not like it if she knew, but we protect her. In the photograph, you look like a child. When you were my age I was already ten years old. I have the feeling we will meet someday, Mrs. Ruth Anne. I move at your pace. Thank you for saying, Yes, you are my mother—

Even if we never meet—

When she remembered that—even if we never meet—she would avert her gaze. Don't say that. A natural protest answered back. But she was careful. She did not tell him. She was afraid and she was locked in one place and she knew she must move further into whatever was happening and every time she felt that urge she froze.

That night after dinner, after saying goodnight to Aunt Teensy, she slipped down the stairs past the banner with its declarations and admonitions every one of which she translated to Own Up and Stop Kidding Yourself. Slipping down the stairs, she dismantled boundaries. There was a new message.

Dear Mrs. Ruth Anne,

Today my father told his wife that you and I have been writing to each other. She did not take it well. She wants you to know that she is the jealous type. She hit him with his cane. Not hard, but just to let him know. Later she brought him tea on a tray and they forgave each other.

To answer your question, Why did I become a teacher. It's something I'm good at. I enjoy explaining things to children. Why did you become a librarian?

She was disappointed he did not mention meeting. But she did not want to bring it up. She wrote back:

I'm not technically a librarian, but I like working there because I like to know how to find the answers. I'm sorry she hit him with the cane.

She needed a question. She always posed a question, worrying that he might not respond otherwise. She typed: Are you teaching summer school?

In the corner of the computer room was an overstuffed chair beneath a reading lamp and she did not turn on the lamp but rested in the chair. Her bare feet out of her slippers and cool on the tile floor. Writing Tin exhausted her. Every word mattered. The blackness of the lake and dark outside weighed in against the window. She hoped for a swift reply but after twenty minutes she checked her INBOX and nothing had arrived. What might he be doing on a Tuesday night? Did he work in the video store? Did he have a girlfriend? While Vo and his wife finished supper, did he go into their bedroom and take the leather billfold from the drawer and was her picture in a plastic slip that had grown cloudy with age or was it in the fold usually reserved for cash?

She dozed. Pulled under into luxurious napping. She told herself, Get up and go to bed, but the lure of now, sleeping now, was irresistible. All was quiet save for the computers humming. Her sleep tangled with images of the beach at high noon. Sitting on Johnny's lap in the big kitchen. Laurel in a linen summer dress the color of eggplant.

With a start she awoke and went to the computer for one last check and yes, she had mail:

No summer school. I am free to meet with you.

Before she could think twice, she wrote:

I am free to meet with you too.

Are we ready?

I'm closer than you think. On the lake. Do you know the restaurant with the water puppets in Cortland?

Yes, of course. But first I want to know if you feel ready.

With what she felt as cruelty she closed the window to her mail. She could not say it. She wasn't ready and she did not think she ever would be. At the pay phone near her room she did not wait to catch her breath or gather her thoughts. She called Johnny in the big kitchen. Her grasp on the telephone nearly hurt her fingers. Be there, be there—

Johnny Bond.

It's me.

Ruthie—

It was after hours and she had imagined the darkened kitchen and Johnny planning a menu on a sheet of yellow legal-size paper, still in his stained whites. A beer at hand. But there was a gathering, people, music. Otis Redding. "The Dock of the Bay."

Who's there?

Laurel and Oceana. Tuck. Mairead and I cooked up a feast—

Who's Mairead?

The new cook I told you about.

Ruth Anne said nothing.

Are you okay, Ruthie?

I wanted to talk.

I can call you back. I'm sure they can manage without me.

You don't have to do that.

I want to. Talk to Laurel for a minute. I'll go up to the house and call you right back.

She gave him the number.

Laurel said, Hi, Mom—

Hi, sweetie. How're you doing? How's the house?

We don't close until Thursday.

Are you happy?

I am happy.

Give Oceana a hug from me.

That's nice. I will. How's Aunt Teensy?

She's about the same.

Are you glad you're with her?

Glad's not the word. No. But I feel like I'm doing my duty.

Laurel said nothing.

She could hear Tuck saying, Whoa, whoa— Listen, I better go. Dad's calling me back from the house.

Mom?

She had moved away from the revelry. Lowered her voice. Ruth Anne could picture her in the pantry, Moxie at her feet.

I'm here.

What's with you?

What do you mean? She strove for patience, begged herself to be that way.

Dad's going bonkers. He's digging all these holes. To plant trees. She lowered her voice even more. It looks like a graveyard around the house.

I'll let him tell me about it.

They hung up and Ruth Anne slapped the receiver too firmly, too loudly into its niche. A woman came out of the restroom, her brow furrowed at the noise. Her hair in curlers. The smell of disinfectant, that same waxy church smell, came down the hall in a wave from the restroom. She turned away from the woman and held her head in her hands. When the phone rang she jumped on it.

I'm in the bedroom, Ruthie. It's not so hot tonight.

Are you going back?

Eventually. But talking to you's more important.

She said, We have to talk. We have to talk about all the things we never talked about. From before.

Before what?

Before we were married. When we were separated. She did not want to say Vietnam. We have to be together and talk and I don't want to make life hard for us but I feel this pressing. This terrible pressing—

She inhaled sharply. I need you.

I need you too. I've missed you. What do we need to talk about? You're making me nervous. Tell me now.

No, not now. She had to soothe him. It had to be face-to-face. She struggled to speak in a lighter, quieter voice, a wifely voice intended to allay whatever fear she had engendered. It can wait. I didn't mean to alarm you.

Johnny matched her tone of voice. Olive you.

You do?

Of course.

They spoke of Laurel. The yellow the girls planned to paint their back porch. They wanted a dog. Oceana's parents had given them an iron bed with whimsical iron birds perched on the headboard.

So they know?

Everyone knows. Everyone's doing the best they can.

# 13

A warm wind blew up, contoured by the old trees and sounding like the ocean.

Johnny stood outside the back door surveying his holes and berms. The yellow utility flags glowed in a long arch. Moxie lay under the picnic table. Insects screeched. The skin of the turf had been turned inside out and the mounds of soil were dark, pillaged. His muscles ached from digging and he felt the direct connection between the holes and the hardening and quiver of his deltoids. She had not seemed surprised about the trees. It was something else. The trees were all he had to hide and now that was out in the open and she was upset but not about that.

It had to be one of her spells. Until they got together there was nothing he could do. The best you could do on the telephone was contain the fire. Keep a fear or anxiety from escalating. You could not stamp it out. Only touch did that. They had never been separated for so long. He did not like it but Ruthie did. He had come to that conclusion. If she did not like it, she would have come home now and again. He tried to recall the exact reasons she had gone, the exact words with which she told him. It was all vague to him. The meditation and Aunt Teensy. He was ashamed to admit that right on the tip of his tongue tonight had been the question, Is Teense dying or not? Her leaving had seemed matter-of-fact but now he thought about what Tuck called his own hard times: midlife crisis. Ruthie was having a midlife crisis and he had no choice but to go along for the ride. It was a catch-all for assorted dissatisfactions. It was a ride that could veer in directions no one had prepared for. He would not veer. He would hold a steady course. The trees would go in the ground and he would be there to see them mature. Up the hill the friendly lights of Brambles beamed in each direction. His domain. He had retreated to his domain after the incident on the Fourth. That's how he thought of it: the incident. And after, a gloom that seemed opaque. Until yesterday. Until Mairead. He liked having a woman to talk with. That was as far as it would go. Tuck had brought a packet of CDs and the music entered the night and made the night alive. The Dylan Bootleg Series. If not for you. Couldn't even find the door. Couldn't even see the floor. They had not had a party in a long time and a party was what he had needed.

The screen door at the big kitchen banged and Mairead came out and lit a cigarette. Her face a smudge. The light from the kitchen window polished her bare shoulders. She sat down at the table on the patio and he saw her face more clearly. Round inside her silvery hair. She crossed one knee over the other and she stretched and wiggled her toes and when she began to bounce her foot the sandal she wore slapped against her bare sole. Some women could bounce a foot and make it seem the most impatient movement. With others, Mairead among them, it was a sign of leisure or eagerness. Her arch was high and he had noticed her arches. All that Johnny saw was in shadow and dim light and he filled in for himself what was not truly visible.

Mairead had asked, And what about Mrs. Bond?

Ruthie.

Ruthie.

She's caring for her aunt. In a nursing home. In Michigan. He left out the part about the meditation. It seemed private, unmentionable. It was the first time he had thought that Ruthie preferred the company of nuns to him.

A rabbit hopped from beneath the Nova. Mox gave chase, barking.

Get back here, Johnny growled. He felt the red wine he had drunk and he set off up the hill with Mox at his heel. The party awash in his arms and legs. The music melding with her presence, her watching from the patio as he climbed the gravel drive. If not for you. He thought, Don't make a fool out of yourself.

It's a big night.

She reached down and put out the cigarette against the brick and laid the butt beside her on the bench to carry inside and dispose of. My first night.

I mean out here, he said, with a sweep of his arm.

It's lovely.

Moxie placed his muzzle on her lap and she scratched behind his ears.

Tuck came to the screen door. His tropical shirt partway open. His baseball cap in his hand. Behind him, Johnny saw the girls putting away leftovers. The music clicked off. Tuck stepped out and said, Nice night. Not so humid.

That it is.

So, Johnny—he tossed an imaginary basketball skyward—are we up for hoops in the morning?

Morning seems a long way off.

Hard to let go, I know.

I learned that from you.

Tuck's tuckered out.

Johnny sat down beside her on the bench. It was a subtle alignment: You don't have to go. He willed her not to leave. Just yet.

Johnny saw Tuck's curious appraisal but he did not think Mairead paid him any mind. Tuck went in and gathered up his CDs and a plastic pouch of lasagna he said he wanted to eat for breakfast. After his good-night to the girls he came out again and shook a pebble from one of his sandals and went whistling down the drive. At his pickup he shouted, If music be the food of love, play on.

Johnny might have shouted back, Go home, you son-of-a-bitch. On other nights when he and Tuck had stayed up half the night. But he said to her, We've been friends a long time.

I can tell, she said.

The girls came out and settled down in the lawn chairs. He saw that they planned to occupy the patio for a while. Oceana bummed a cigarette from Mairead. He was outnumbered and Tuck's taillights fading down the drive left him confused: either he wanted Tuck to stay or the girls to go. He and Mairead had been about to wade into something together. Confidences might be offered. Now the girls wanted to talk about the brew pub and music and she liked that. Johnny did not pay precise attention to what they said.

It was quiet. No air jocks split seams across the night sky. Johnny stood up to stretch his legs at the edge of the brick patio. A car stopped at the bottom of the hill and someone got out. You could hear the footsteps of whoever it was crunching up the cinder drive. He squinted, waiting. A man emerged from the darkness. He registered: a man. But then as he drew near, Johnny saw that it was Limbo.

Mr. Bond, I'm coming to visit you. I'm coming to visit.

I see that, Johnny said.

Can I visit you? Limbo stopped a few feet away, hesitant. His pack was unzipped. Comic books nearly fell out. Johnny could see the indentation of a loose CD in the front pocket of his jeans. He had gotten a tattoo: a rose on his forearm.

Hello, Limbo, Laurel said.

Hello. I know you. I've known you a long time.

Laurel smiled and said, That's true.

Johnny said, Come on in. I've got some pecan pie that has your name on it.

That's nice, Limbo said. It has my name on it. My name's not Henry. You know that. He walked obliquely toward the kitchen, unsure of how to communicate with Laurel and Oceana and Mairead. He was shy.

In the kitchen Limbo sat down and unloaded his pack and CD player. While Johnny cut the pie and doled out ice cream on top of it, Limbo talked. He said, I wonder when she's coming back? The library's not the same. I don't go there much. Daisy doesn't like me much. Daisy's all right but she doesn't like me. Not like Ruth Anne. Father Carroll says we're not going to Chicago this summer. I don't know why he doesn't want to go. I wonder, when will she be home?

You know, son, I wonder too.

It was easy to let Limbo talk and think your own thoughts. Johnny thought about Ruth Anne saying, I need you.

He had given a thousand dollars to the Episcopal Church reward fund.

He had hired a woman he wanted to get to know better.

He had dug up Ruthie's sunny yard to plant trees.

His present-day confessions paraded before his eyes. What would she confess? What did she consider hidden?

He was the one with secrets. Secrets almost never given heed and lodged so far in the past that he did not think he could tell them if he wanted to. And what did it matter? All that had happened back then did not exist. What did it matter what prisoners' names he had refused to list? What did it matter what small arms the techs had been denied? There was one nicknamed Jabber he had gotten to know. He did not like to think his name but it was the sort of name that came up in other contexts and each time it did he was forced to remember. Sometimes Tuck would say of a boy on the junior-high team, He's a jabber-mouth. Or Ruth Anne would say, I'm just jabbering. And when that happened Jabber would spring full-blown into his mind. A skinny guy in wire-rim spectacles. With his fake corporate ID in plastic clipped to his shirt pocket. The techs on the mountain in Laos were not supposed to fraternize with the rangers but they did. They were sent there to protect the techs in the event the equipment had to be destroyed and everyone evacuated and that was all they were supposed to do. In the inevitable event. It was ground-directed navigation equipment and it was a mission you thought you could feel proud of. They could bomb the hell of out of Hanoi in the fog or rain. He and Jabber told each other that they had not given much thought to the end result of all that bombing. Bombing was a word that cut off imagination unless you were forced to see it. Jabber had been from Grand Rapids and they had spent a few hours at the cliff, talking. With a view of the field of poppies undulating at the foot of the mountain. Jabber did not know what to make of his government sending him to the installation without even a pistol. He felt naked. He liked to be near Johnny because Johnny always had weapons, even if it wasn't his watch. At the cliff they could see plain as day the red dust rising from the road-building ten clicks away. And the road was for the men who wanted to capture the equipment and kill everyone on the mountain. That was their single-minded goal and everyone knew it. You had to believe that the brass knew it and ambassadors knew it and even the president. All the big boys. With their liquor cabinets and their servants and their hot showers and cars and women. Jabber had a girl in Grand Rapids and they talked about her and they talked about Ruthie. Jabber had slept with his girl. He was afraid he might lose her because he had accepted the assignment on the mountain. They had not been allowed to tell. Talking about Ruth Anne, Johnny could conjure a wisp of memory. Not much more. He had left her high and dry, waiting for him. That had not been his fault. She knew that much. He had told her that. He did not like to recall the last time he saw Jabber. His face chalk-white and his entrails shining and his fingers shot. Flesh is so destructible. How do so many of us survive? Oceana had said that humans are a weedy species and he saw the truth in that. In spite of wars and disasters, too many people survived. That's what he thought in his darkest moments.

He had been sworn to secrecy. By his captors and his superiors. That had suited him just fine. Secrecy like some cellar of the mind and heart. But he knew Ruthie down to the marrow. There was nothing that could happen up in Michigan to change that. Nothing.

# 14

The road to Windfall had not been paved in a long time. She swerved to avoid potholes. The trees along the road met overhead in the narrow curves, leafy arbors, where you might feel like stopping if you had all the time in the world. Among the trees there might be a picnic table in pine duff. Places she and Johnny might have taken as an invitation to lollygag. If she had been with Johnny there would have been treats in the car and a bottle of wine. Without him, she had neglected the Tercel. It smelled dusty and latte cups and candy wrappers littered the floor. Here I am, your mother: a mess.

She thought that but she did not feel bad.

She had taken care with her clothing and her hair. She wore pressed jeans and a red camp shirt. Her wedding rings. She had polished her toenails and put on lipstick. Her hair curled in the humidity.

She felt focused, in the extreme. Whatever would happen would happen only once in her life. Only once in Tin's life. People talked about once-in-a-lifetime experiences but this was it. Like giving birth. Or having sex for the first time. Or dying. Would Johnny have given his blessing to what she was about to do? That's what she wanted: his blessing. It might take a long time to move from her confessions to his blessing. Maybe forever. Meeting Tin had nothing to do with Johnny; that was hard to accept but true. She had to go alone. For nearly thirty years Johnny had taken care of her. He had fed her and held her hand through dark nights and he had poured her whiskey and he had cleaned out the car and changed the oil and he had supported them and said so many times how lucky he felt to have her in his life and he had made her laugh and he appreciated the ordinary—the walks with Moxie and the tulips blooming and the warped humor of his employees and stories he heard on NPR and the sweetness, the tenderness, of Laurel and Oceana, even though she knew that had been hard for him. His baby girl choosing a life like that. Or being chosen—Laurel would have said. Johnny appreciated cuddling with the catalpa in the breeze outside their bedroom window. He still wanted to make love at the round barns and he would still say, Listen to this, when he found a song he thought she might like and he still said, You're my home, Ruthie. I adore you.

She had awakened that morning knowing what had kept her from being ready. Not wanting to do it alone. But she had to be her own home now.

She had cut a swath—straight and hopeful—through the morning. Rising early enough for yoga in her loose black meditation pants and a T-shirt. The plough. The cobra. Homage to the sun. Her bones stiff. Her bones that might be eroding even as she worked them hard. Out on the monastery deck she watched the empty flat lake grow bright as the sun rose from behind her—the east—over the trees and the dunes. Then, sitting. Candles lit the meditation room, a light with weight, substance. Among the other women she had closed her eyes and breathed from deep in her belly and it was not long before the rest—the Sabbath—cradled her. Time disappeared. Or so it seemed. As soon as she would think, Time's disappearing, her knees might ache or an itch behind her ear would beg to be scratched and she would think impatiently, When will this end? When? Still, instead of thoughts like commuter trains her thoughts would lazily drift by, like birds with wide wings on a breeze, with rest in between. She craved the rest. But so long as she craved anything, Jill always reminded her, she could not rest. And then, Aunt Teensy: a morning visit—weak nursing-home coffee and a cup of yogurt while she cooed about her birds. Around nine o'clock she had gone to Jill's office and said, I might be away all day.

Knowledge had been there all along, all morning: she would go to Windfall.

She did not know when she knew. In the night while she slept, her subconscious might have decided for her. Her dream self who could see in the dark and who knew much more than the false self. She had awakened thinking of the quote from Thomas Merton: There is in all things an invisible fecundity, a dimmed light, a meek namelessness, a hidden wholeness. On days when she did two sits in a row she would walk in a circle with the other women in between the sits. Each loop around the room she would see the quote and she had committed it to memory without effort. She awoke with the words *hidden wholeness* in her heart. Jill had said that she would not be whole until she integrated everything that had ever happened to her. When you have babies you stop being whole. You just do. Jill said, You're at a different stage now, Ruthie. You have the chance to join with yourself. To stop hiding. I can't. You want to or you wouldn't be here. How do I know it'll be all right? You can't know if it'll be all right with others. You can't control what they think any more than you can control the weather. I'm afraid. What are you getting out of the fear? I know it. I know what that feels like. They had walked every day on the beach under the bright July sun and Jill had insisted. Jill was the voice of God.

You know what I wonder sometimes?

What?

What if I had gotten an abortion?

You can't know how you'd feel about that.

It wasn't that I was stronger than Sue-Sue.

I know that.

She had her mother on her side.

I know she did.

Ruth Anne thought of those white patent-leather boots. Her garter belt, the lace of it against her brown skin. The day in the museum watching Sue-Sue and her lover embrace near the statue of what Mrs. Ha called the female Buddha. With the Saigon sunlight lapping on the yellow walls. Johnny gone. That was the day Johnny had not shown up. Sue-Sue had been self-congratulatory with sex. It was what she wanted and she would have moved heaven and earth to get it. Ruth Anne had wanted it too. She had wanted to strut through the park. A carnal smile playing about her eyes and lips. The minute her period did not start Sue-Sue said, I'm getting rid of it. I'm going home. Ruth Anne could not say that she had not thought about an abortion. But thinking about it and rejecting it had happened in the same moment. Her decision had not been about the baby who did not seem real. She felt the lethargy of the start of pregnancy. As if she had been drugged. The lethargy and the wet Saigon heat and Sister David saying what she said about trust:

she had slept off these things under the tick-tick of a ceiling fan while others went about boarding up windows that had been broken. They braced for the war. Bodies had lain in the street. Fires had burned. Soldiers disguised as comrades coming home for the holiday had sent the city up in smoke and blood and dust. The lights had gone out at the American embassy. What home would she go to if she went home? And how did you find a doctor who would do it?

All this had passed through her mind as she stood at Jill's office door.

I don't know what kept me from it but I'm thankful I didn't.

I'm sure you are. Then, Jill put her finger in a large appointment calendar to hold her place. She turned up her face distractedly. Be careful. I'll see you at dinner?

I can't say when I'll be back.


Vietnam, c'est fini.

Sister David knelt before the safe, squinting at the lock as she turned it counterclockwise, then clockwise. I am from Le Folgoët in Brittany where we are famed for the grand pardon. Once a year everyone gathers to beg remission for sins. Would that Vietnam had the grand pardon. The bagpipes play. We eat bigorneaux with hatpins. There are many blessings to be had in France. With a grunt and her rosary beads rattling she stood up and handed Ruth Anne her dog-eared airline ticket and an envelope of cash. Her hand trembled. Take my advice and go home. We're going home. We're locking everything away and hiring a guard. Our mother superior has decided. She has called us home to Brittany. Vietnam, c'est fini.

When?

When, Soeur. Her face appeared thinner and sallow; she had not eaten out of worry. Her cap was crooked.

When are you returning to France, Soeur?

Within a few days.

What about the books?

That matters no longer. Our priests in Hue were taken from the Cathedral. No one has heard from them. Many people have been slaughtered or buried alive. She sat down stiffly in the chair behind her desk and folded her hands at the desk's edge. It was a gesture Ruth

Anne recalled from Catholic school: they had been forced when their work was finished to sit with their feet together and flat on the floor and their hands folded, staring straight ahead. With military precision. They had used a ruler for their arithmetic assignments, underlining each problem with firm No. 2 lines. They had stood in straight rows going out for recess.

I'll leave today.

And where will you go?

Two sisters burst into the office, chattering, their hands punctuating the problem. Anger burned in the air. Someone had broken a statue. Sister David scolded them in French, her forefinger before her face. She got up and swept them out of the office and barged down the corridor with the young sisters in tow.

Ruth Anne had been about to say, I'm not sure. They had rescued her from that admission. In the salon she went where she and Sister Michelle had talked those pent-up nights. At the window she opened both shutters and the streets were empty in the curfew save for the trash and the human excrement set upon by flies. The bodies that had lain there when she first came back to the convent had been removed. It had been weeks and she felt as though she had slept all those weeks. A chilly wind blew up and banged the shutters and she closed them securely. She could not get over the way it had turned cold. Domestic order was linked with civic order and it had collapsed; the lightbulbs of the dusty chandeliers were burnt out; piles of worn linen lay here and there outside the bedrooms. The doors were open and the sisters had hauled their trunks and suitcases out of closets and from underneath the beds and they were agitated with leaving. With anxiety. Ruth Anne slipped along the corridor, unnoticed. She had napped all morning and her body felt swollen as if she had soaked too long in a hot bath. She had not eaten. The night before, she had thrown up her supper. Slim with hunger, she resisted the moment she would throw up and she wanted to wait as long as possible to eat.

At the library door she looked both ways and when it was clear that no one was about she went inside and shut the door without a sound. A watercolor light shone into the library. A sepia wash. The books were stacked in the sentimental light. The books reinforced with the buckram boards lay piled on the work table and on the shelves. A wealth of books. She wanted them all but of course she must choose. She dropped her airline ticket into the bottom of a box. She filled the box with books, her skin feverish at the theft even though she did not think it was wrong. The books would go back to Vo. There was a rightness to that. They would read. They would keep on reading. No one could stop that. They would pretend they were beneath the Eiffel Tower. Without cares. Before he was blinded. Before she was pregnant. She filled a box: with Cheever and Katherine Anne Porter and Flannery O'Connor and Colette and Somerset Maugham and Graham Greene and Joyce and Woolf. She opened the French doors into the garden and she stepped across the garden to the window of her room and set the box beneath the window. Her face reflected in the windowpane was freckled and determined, older and foreign, not at all the way she pictured herself. She pictured herself as she had been when she arrived in Saigon. Pale. Unsure. The lavender had not been tended and it lay nearly flat like a crop in a field and she crushed the lavender. She walked upon it. The lavender scented her sandals and rose around her. She went back inside and out of the library for perhaps the last time. To her room. She lifted the box through the window into her room. The ceiling fan ticked. The sisters bustled in the hallway, their voluminous skirts switching. She lay exhausted and out of breath beneath the mosquito netting. She slept, the envelope of cash beneath her pillow.

Rumors filtered from Hue. From a secretary she met at the black market. But before Tet they had not heard rumors.

Madame Thuong had taken the train to see her sister in Dalat. Mai had gone home to Cholon to share Tet with her family. From Connie she had gotten the key to the apartment on Nguyen Du Street and that was her insurance. When she announced her intention to spend Tet with Vo, Sister David said, Don't leave the building.

I must.

You have turned out to be lacking in virtue. First you come home drunk, and then you steal my bicycle—

I didn't steal it.

I no longer have a bicycle and you were the last person to ride it.

Soeur, he's all alone.

She hired a cyclo driver. They were to have a midnight supper and she was the first person to cross the threshold of the tea shop and Vo said, You are the auspicious visitor. You will be important in our lives this year. The tea shop was closed for business and they opened shutters and sat near the glassless window and watched all that happened on the street. The flowers trucked in and arranged in buckets until the street was ablaze with flower stalls. The children with their red envelopes of good-luck money. Lee-see. Lee-see. The women in ao dais of shot silk or organdy. Some men in three-button suits. Some men in silk shirts and gold cuff links.

Tracers arced across the city sky. There was no despair, no bitterness. Only joy. Joy of peach blossoms. The voices of children gladdened the night, much later than usual. Two women carried a roasted pig on a silver platter, skinned and daubed bright red. Firecrackers popped on long strings. Lanterns hung in the trees and a wind from the wharf and the river gave breath to the lanterns and the light seemed alive. Vo told her the story of Kieu, who married a man she did not love. He knew short passages by heart. He recited in Vietnamese and line by line translated into English. By lamplight turn these scented leaves and read a tale of love recorded in old books.

For hours they sat beside each other on straight-back chairs. In the open window she had placed an iron teapot and Chinese cups. Spring buds of jasmine tea had steeped and she had poured the tea and refreshed the pot and taken some pleasure in doing what Mai did. He wore a rayon shirt and pleated slacks. His hair had not been cut in a long time and he ran his hand through it excitedly, and said, Smell the smell of the New Year. The firecrackers. The new clothes. Spring cheers up everyone.

Me too.

I have one wish.

What's that?

I want to see your face. I know your voice and will never forget your voice. But I wish to see your face.

She turned to him but, turning, knew he would not see. I see your face.

What do you see?

You look more like a man now than you did when we first met.

Four months ago—

Yes! You do.

His hand reached tentatively out. She took it.

May I touch your face? To remember?

Not in the window.

No.

She folded her shawl and knelt upon it. She guided one of his hands to her cheek and closed her eyes. Street noise receded. He placed his palms upon her cheeks and held them for a brief time—a warm brief touch—then with his thumbs he traced her jaw. He brought the first two fingers on each hand light as feathers to her nose and across her cheeks. As if to make a mask. And then the lips. She felt she had not thought about the shape of her lips until that moment. The kitten meowed and a sigh escaped them both; they had held in all sigh, all response. Tears welled up; she did not know where Johnny was and no one had contacted her since that first letter from his father. She wanted to be true to Johnny and she felt that slipping away. When Vo touched her face she felt her body press against the boundaries. But he was only touching her face and he was only caught up in the holiday. He was young. He did not know the effect touch might have on her.

He held her shoulders and said, Are you all right?

I'm fine.

I can tell that you are not fine.

I ought to go back.

It will be hard for you to find a ride back at this time of night.

They had read two stories. That was their usual limit. They felt they had to digest them and two was their limit. They had talked and eaten and watched the street. They had told stories of their own, stories of his life in France, jokes the schoolboys played on each other, and her stories of summer at the lake and her parents dancing cheek to cheek when her father would come home from tuning pianos.

There is a beautiful lake in Dalat, he said. I want you to see it.

An orange flash filled up the window. An impact shook the building. She huddled on the floor and pulled at him. It had not been their building, but a nearby building. Screams circled around them like ripples on water. She pulled him down, away from the window.

Close the shutters.

I will, I will. You stay down. She crawled to the window, crying out to herself. A prayer or curse. She could reach the shutter from the floor and she slammed first one, then the other, shut and she lurched up the wall on one side of the window and she latched the hooks. Vo lay prostrate on the floor.

We must hide. We have a place.

Where?

Upstairs.

They managed to crawl up the narrow stairwell. Gunfire crackled on the street.

Her knees shook crawling up the stairs. What is it?

At the top step he sat down and pulled her to him. It might be the end.

The end of what?

The war.

They held each other, shivering. She felt like a child and his ribs felt like a child's ribs beneath her hands. She had never been in their living quarters and it was dark and there were smells she recognized from threads that had always trailed into the tea shop. Potent odors. Madame Thuong's perfume: woody, viscous. Fennel. Jasmine tea.

We must not have a light.

I know.

The upstairs windows were glass and beyond the glass the sky was lit with an unnatural white light. Two more explosions shuddered some distance away.

It's the radio station. They want the radio station.

I want to look out.

He grabbed her arm. They will kill you. They will kill any American.

Let go—

She hid beneath the sill and stole glances down the alley: men and women in red armbands brandished rifles toward the flag. Take down the flag! Saigon is liberated—

The people fled, like spokes in a wheel. Into their homes. Lights were extinguished. A military jeep roared up to the alley and military police—Americans—

Vo, crouched and stumbling, found her at the window and pulled her to the floor. We will hide. Listen to me. We will go to a place they will not find. He held her hands. Their hot breath mingled with the dust. The unnatural light in the sky lit up the room in waves and he said, Take what you can find from the kitchen. We will need to eat.

She crawled to the L-shaped kitchen—a narrow galley—and she waited for the next wave of light and she shoveled bananas and mangos into a reed bag. She thought that they would need water and she marveled at the pace of her thoughts—clear and steady—but her hands shook almost beyond her control. They would come out for the water. It would have to be boiled. She could not drink water straight from the tap. Whatever was happening would be over soon and they would boil water and she would find a cyclo driver to return her to the convent.

They crawled into a closet in the back of the apartment. It had been a room at one time, perhaps a servant's quarter when the building had been a house for one family and there was no tea shop on the first floor. It was a small room without a window. Once inside they stood up; the gunfire bedeviling the street was muffled.

Is there a light?

There is a lamp. In the corner.

She felt her way to the corner and nearly knocked the small lamp over. She switched it on. It was a tiny-watt lamp with a beaded shade casting a gold and scarlet light. The room was lined with Madame Thuong's clothing. Dresses Ruth Anne had never seen her wear. Silk and imitation silk. Wool sheaths. Ao dais. And scarves of every color. A wire mannequin stood dashingly in another corner, wearing the uniform of her French officer. The white kepi, little round hat. A red sash. Ruth Anne saw no need for the light and she wanted to be in the same dark he was in and she said, I'll turn it off.

Find a place to sit before you turn it off.

She made them a nest of winter coats Madame had worn in Paris.

You see the trunk?

Yes.

If they come in, you get in the trunk.

What about you?

They have no reason to hurt me.

They settled into the nest of winter coats. She turned off the light. In the dark the odors gave shape and imaginary color to the room: she assigned the color yellow to Madame Thuong; saffron, straw, marigold, oil. It was the smell of Madame's body and her clothes. The smell of her old life.

We have no book.

I know.

We forgot the kitten.

She will hide.

He held her in his arms against the slippery taffeta lining of the winter coats. Their breathing slowed; she lay with her head on his shoulder, her palm on his chest. The darkness was complete. Dense. Relentless.

Ruth Anne?

Yes?

We may die here.

Don't say that.

She felt her spine against the floor. The winter coats were not so thick. He rolled on top of her. He was thin. She explored his back with both her hands. His ribs. His shoulder blades. His cheek brushed hers. The smell of him became the only smell: boy smell, the dried strawberries on his breath, his forehead a little sweaty. She felt his hands upon her face again. The buttons of their shirts were hard against her flesh. He kissed her mouth. Sister Michelle had kissed her last; the man at the party before that. This was different. He whispered from *The Tale of Kieu:* How strange the race of lovers! Try as you will you can't unsnarl their hearts' entangled threads. He touched her mouth, outlining it with a finger. She felt the wetness of her tongue against his finger. They were breathing hard again. She felt his hand beneath her skirt. Her full gathered skirt. The best she had. His fingers brushed her thigh. Inside.

I want to see you, he said.

I want to see you too.


Cortland was the halfway point. She drove down the street of renovated bungalows to the church, where she pulled to the curb. A circle of young mothers with babies in strollers stood in front of the church chatting, their sunglasses glinting with light. I was a stranger and you welcomed me. She imagined that the verse from Matthew had been on the pillar for so long that no one noticed it anymore. She wanted to see it; she wanted to go to the pillar and run her fingers over the carving, over the sheaves of wheat. But the women were standing there and she did not want to interrupt their talk and she did not want to feel conspicuous. Farther down the street there was a Coca-Cola sign, the sign of commerce, and she drove on down and saw that, yes, there was a pay phone. She turned to the thin white sections of the telephone book that contained the numbers for the small towns not far from Cortland: Inlet, Briarville, and Windfall. It was a toll call. She punched in the numbers—her credit card number and their number—and then she hung up, her fingers on the chrome hook that broke the connection. The air was close inside the phone booth. The phone felt grimy. An enormous man in a white shirt and bolo tie pulled his low-slung vintage Buick into the gas station and got out to fill the tank and music blurted from his car, country music, hard-done-by music, and he bobbed on his feet while he pumped the gas. He was happy-go-lucky. Did he have anything he was ashamed of? Did the mothers in front of the church? Was she the only shameful person on the blistering street? What would he think of her? When they finally met would he hurl accusations at her? Would he let out whatever resentment he had carried like a coal since he was old enough to realize what she'd done?

A line of sweat broke out along her hairline. She hung up the receiver and went inside the gas station where she asked for the restroom key.

The woman at the counter said, Key's for customers only, hon.

I'll be a customer. She bought a small orange juice and a bag of peanuts.

The woman slapped the wooden key paddle into her palm. She jerked her head to indicate that the restrooms were entered from the side of the building. Out in the sunlight, out into the world, Ruth Anne prayed a prayer she had thought she never would again: God help me. God help me do the right thing.

The restroom was filthy. She squatted above the toilet without touching the rim.

God help me. God help me. God help me. What if Vo or his wife answered the phone? She could hang up. Chickenshit, Johnny would say.

Her hands rinsed and wiped on the shins of her jeans, the key deposited inside, she took her orange juice and peanuts to the car and set them carefully on the passenger seat. The fat man was gone. A pile of real estate guides in a wire rack fluttered in the lake wind. A lawn mower sputtered into action not far away: the summerness evident in the light, the sounds, the air: she would always remember it. She went to the phone and punched in the numbers and squeezed the phone, gripped it, her fingers aching and her heartbeat pulsing in her ears.

Hello.

She could not speak.

Hello?

May I speak to Tin?

Speaking.

It's—it's Ruth Anne. Ruth Anne Porter.

A silence seemed to expand. Later she would think, It was only ten seconds. But the silence expanded and did not sound like anything she could name. Surprise or perplexity. If she had been talking to Laurel she could have guessed what the silence meant.

So you are ready? His voice was kind. Before that she had not been able to tell.

She took a big breath. An audible breath. I think I am.

I am ready. But—I'm actually standing here in what I went to sleep in. I'm taking advantage of the summer—no school—to sleep late. Are you an early riser?

Yes.

I'm a night owl.

Is this a bad time? How ludicrous to even offer that. As if they were longtime friends who could get together anytime.

He laughed. He sounded like Vo. Where are you, Mrs. Ruth Anne?

Call me Ruth Anne.

Please—my father and grandmother drilled Vietnamese manners into me.

I'm in Cortland. She glanced around. Not far from the church—the one where they have the Mass in Vietnamese.

I know where you mean. Do you want to meet for lunch?

That sounds good.

You won't change your mind?

I hope not.

How well do you know Cortland?

I sort of know it. I used to work here. I've been driving here for the last month. Thinking—that I—might see you.

Oh—so you have been ready for a while?

She thought of saying, For years. I've been ready for years. And didn't know it. But she said, It's been hard to make the leap. Not because of you. Not that.

I can imagine.

I wasn't—ready—to change things—

He waited, as if he expected more. More truth. She wanted to tell the truth.

Find your way to Dune Beach. There is a hot-dog stand at the south end of the beach. I will meet you there in less than an hour. We can go together from there. You like Mexican food?

Sure.

Dune Beach. And Mrs. Ruth Anne?

Yes?

Don't be afraid.

How will I know you?

By the dragon on my motorcycle. The dragon is the sign of prosperity and happiness to Vietnamese. You know this, of course.


Oh my God. Oh my God.

She stood paralyzed beside her car. The woman in the gas station stared out the window, her squint a bad sign. She didn't want any trouble and had no way of knowing that Ruth Anne was not a woman to cause trouble. While she had listened to his voice all perceptions had ceased; her senses rushed to his voice. But now the day returned in layers: the lawn mower grinding, a jet exhaust trail overhead in the blue sky, someone playing a cello, the church bells—fake bells—ringing. Two children across the street busily chalked in hopscotch on the sidewalk. Girls. One of them sang out: Down in the valley where the green grass grows. There sat Mandy as sweet as a rose.

She went inside and in a polite, firm voice said, Could you tell me the way to Dune Beach? She had to get her bearings. Tears swam in her eyes and it might be hard to keep her foot on the gas. Hard to shift gears. She had broken through. The word caul came to mind. She had been nearly suffocated by a caul of silence.

Are you all right?

I'm all right.

You're ten minutes from Dune Beach. It's a hangout.

She worked at getting there. Aware of every turn signal, every red light. Nagged by the thought that something stupid might keep her from the moment. She had to be careful. The water was big, blue, and ever there. Paradoxically the lake brought her into the present, yet memories rode on every wave. Times with Sue-Sue and Jill when they did not have a care in the world and they didn't even know it. The fires with Johnny. Storms she had watched from Aunt Teensy's deck. The winter ice. Times she would clatter down the long wooden steps to the lake after the brush. Her rear end stinging, tears stinging, her heart a snarl of hurt. Aunt Teensy always let her go. She needed to be alone as well, to come back to her senses. There had been a rotten dinghy at the foot of the steps and she would sit in the dinghy and cry until she had cried herself out. Sometimes the neighbors would come out on the deck of their screened-in boathouse. Far enough away that they could not see her face. They would wave. She had not known those neighbors. Aunt Teensy had not been neighborly. It did not feel painful to think about those times. She had been through the pain of remembering and she had come out on the other side and she had not realized how far she had come until seeing the lake that sunny day. Waiting for Tin. Was this what wholeness felt like? She thought that she had come to Michigan to make the soulful journey with Aunt Teensy, but she had come to make it with herself. The unloading Jill said would happen had happened: her burdens had lifted, weightless, like vapor—what's done is done.

She found a concrete bench under a sycamore tree above the beach. Not far from the hot-dog stand. A volleyball court where brown young people played in neon swim trunks and bathing suits. She drank her orange juice and waited. She could see the road and she did not know what direction he would come from. The cars did not register; the motor homes did not register. She watched for the motorcycle with the dragon. The sign of happiness and prosperity.

Once she and Vo had gone down to the China Sea. A friend of Mad-

ame Thuong's had driven them there—a detour of a few hours—on
the way from Saigon to Dalat. She had been seven months pregnant
and she put on a pair of loose shorts and a halter top. She had been
huge. Americans were there, drinking beer and shoving each other in
the water. She had led Vo away from the Americans. She was nervous
about them. You could rent a cotton shelter for protection from the
tropical sun: faded red or blue, expertly tied to poles. The sky was dusty
blue; the wind blew hard and hot and filled the cotton shelter like a sail.
A woman in a conical hat had sold them soup for one P, little more than
a penny. She carried the soup in tin baskets hung from a yoke she wore
across her shoulders. She and Vo spoke to each other in Vietnamese and
Ruth Anne thought that they spoke about the Americans and that they
disapproved of them. She did not want to know. She only wanted to
feel the China Sea wind on her flesh and she only wanted to step into the
salty sea. Thank God they were free from Madame for a little while.
How happy she was to be alone with Vo who was her lover and her
brother and her friend. Her pregnancy was like a protracted dream;
she had given up thinking she could change her life or make decisions.
The baby swam across her body as she tried to sleep in the humid
nights. One tiny foot hammering her bladder. Her back ached. Her
breasts ached. There is a big mirror at the house in Dalat, Vo said. I remember this big mirror. You will see yourself. You will see how beautiful you are. On the way back to the main road they stopped at a pagoda
to see the twelve-meter-long reclining Buddha. Niet Ban Tinh Xa. She
dredged that name from God knows where. The entrance to the pagoda
was guarded by a good deity and an evil deity. Good and evil, Vo had
said, guard the entrance to Nirvana.

What would he want?

Would they meet and see each other and ask a few questions and drift
back to their realms?

What would be required? That was always the question, with all of
them. Except Johnny. Until now.

She saw him from a distance before he saw her. His motorcycle
zipped into the parking lot and he stopped in a narrow slot. His helmet
red. In a white T-shirt. She could not see his face at first. He unsnapped
his helmet and carried it under his arm and looked around. Someone at
the volleyball court yelled, Mr. Tran! He waved but turned in her direc-

tion. He was a man. He was tall and that seemed right. He wore his hair in a ponytail. She took off her sunglasses. Her eyes swam again with the tears. But she did not cry. The time for that felt over. A clear path lay between them and she stood and stepped into the sunlight. Someone from the volleyball court called, Hey, Mr. Tran! He did not respond, but ducked almost imperceptibly, watching her, assessing her. He had the lithe body of a dancer or gymnast.

Hello, at last. He took her hand.

Hello.

I am American through and through, he said, smiling. I know Americans like to embrace. May I embrace you?

He hugged her, lifting her from the grass, and when he let her go they went without a word to the concrete bench and sat down.

Those are my students, he said.

They want your attention.

They get plenty of attention. He studied her face. I recognize you. From the photo.

That was a long time ago.

Do you see your face in me?

She studied him in return. I think so. You have the cleft in your chin that Vo had.

He still has that.

But around the eyes you look like Laurel.

Laurel?

Your half-sister.

How old is she?

Twenty-four.

And does she have children?

No children.

Does she live with you?

She did. Until recently. She did not know where to begin and she understood that news of his life and news of her life would not be shared in any coherent way; they would ask each other questions and each answer would elicit another question. Each answer like a one-inch ceramic square in a skywide mosaic.

And your father, she said, does he know about this?

Not today. Not right now. He's at the store.

You said he isn't well.

His heart isn't strong. He turned to say, And your family? Do they know?

Ruth Anne slipped her sunglasses on. The riffles on the lake shifted color. The cries of the volleyball players flew on the wind. Finally she said, They don't.

They don't need to know.

Why do you say that?

Well. You might give me the answers to my questions and then we may never meet again.

What questions?

I am about to marry. I will have children. I want to know my ancestry. My family medical history.

We could have done that by e-mail.

We could have. But I was curious. And I believe you were curious too.

She was of two minds. She wanted to say, Is that all? Is this all? After the brutal arguments I have had with myself? But another voice prevailed and she began the story. She said, My parents died quite young in a boating accident. But of course, your father knew that.

He said as much.

I don't know what their ailments might have been as they aged. My mother's sister is my only living relative. She's dying of osteoporosis.

And you?

I'm healthy so far. She thought about the bone-density test.

How old were you when you lost your parents?

Thirteen. We lived not far from here. In Saugatuck. My aunt owned a fudge shop there.

I know that shop.

She wanted to listen to him speak. He had a teacherly voice, kind but firm, as if he were accustomed to people answering his questions. She was afraid to ask about what happened when he was a boy before they came to the States. But she wanted to know.

It's amazing. You sitting here beside me.

I know, he said. I have spent my life wondering.

That poem—

Did you like it?

Yes.

My father told me about the stories you would read to him. He told me about the bicycle being stolen. He told me about the nuns and their library. But there are things he won't talk about.

For instance?

What it was like when you left. What happened. Or how he felt.

I can't say myself. I've blocked it out.

I've wondered about that more than anything. Maybe you'll remember.

Maybe.

Let's go find that Mexican place. Follow me.

Later she would think, Can it be this easy? The dread of thirty years had washed away. They ordered beers and a baseball game from Puerto Rico was on the big screen TV and a waitress in a pink uniform was all business and did not keep checking back once she had delivered their platters. Ruth Anne left hers nearly untouched; no appetite could compete with his presence, his stories.

There are many con lai—people of mixed blood—in Vietnam. Americans first came to Vietnam in 1950. Some con lai may be almost your age. And then the French—

He shrugged.

What happened to you?

I had my father. I was an exception. Vietnamese believe in citizenship by blood.

But what was it like for you there?

Everyone suffered after 1975. We suffered along with everyone else. But Vietnam is a country at peace, whatever the suffering. My grandmother—she was a very strong woman. In Dalat there is a statue in the center of town in honor of the women. Whenever I would go to the market or to my school I would see the concrete statue and in my child's mind, she was my grandmother. She did not want to leave her beloved Dalat. But we heard about the Orderly Departure Program. And we kept it on hold. When she died—

What happened to her?

She just died. We found her among the camellias.

But she wasn't old.

No. The doctor thought it might have been a blood clot. In her brain.

She ruled your father.

Yes, and we could not consider leaving. We honored her. But then, we applied to the ODP. It took a long time. Red tape—he waved away the red tape, grinning—you would not believe it. I was angry at the time.

And now you're not?

This is America. We have prospered. We came with nothing and now we own the video store and I am a teacher.

He drank from his beer. The waitress stood in front of the jukebox, one ankle hooked behind the other, the lace of her petticoat crookedly showing. On purpose, Ruth Anne realized. She dropped in four quarters. A rap beat took over the small dining room.

He said, Kids—

I like you, she said.

I like you too.

# 15

Wednesday night Mairead was still there at eleven, nibbling at a slice of banana cake, when the dishwasher—a pimply fifth-year senior—shoved the mop and bucket into the corner and said, G'night. All was quiet. She had wheedled Johnny about a tofu special; her dimples got a workout; she had ideas. He had watched her cooking and trusted her instincts. Her deft hand and judicious eye. Whenever the plan to travel arose, he thought: No problem. And: She can handle it. But the urge, the wanderlust, had gone the way an illness goes. He wanted to take Ruthie her bike but the small towns along the lake had lost their appeal. An adventure with Tuck had lost its appeal.

He had a crush on her.

Simple as that.

Not the first time. But Ruthie had always been there and the crushes had been on young women and having a daughter had made him incapable of thinking for long about them. He and Ruth Anne had been true to each other. Or true to themselves. He would never want to hurt anyone and that kept him true since the day they were married. It was not a grand ideal; it was a habit that let him live in his life without feeling fraudulent.

Mairead perched on a stool, her shirt dusty with flour. Steam and the night's labor had flushed her cheeks and curled her hair. She had energy, he had to give her that. After cooking since five she was still keen: she might never tire of talking technique and admiring the glossy photos in cookbooks.

He tuned the radio to a station out of Bloomington that played Irish music until midnight. A harp guitar. Songs of pilgrimage to sacred places. He might prefer the Dylan CDs but he wanted to please her. He wanted to keep her there. Her sandal dangling from one foot. Her toenails polished brick-red. With Moxie taking his ease just outside the door; Mox was glad to have her around.

He set out the ingredients for the cake for the girls. Ever since Laurel was able to say so, she had loved a spice cake. This one would be dense with currants and coriander. With a Grand Marnier frosting. They would close on the house at noon and he planned to have the cake and a bottle of chilled champagne at the new house when they took possession. It was to be a big day. Their first house and a declaration of who they were together. And he was beginning to be fine with that. He wished that Ruthie could be there and he thought that Ruthie might understand the girls if she had been there over the summer. They were in love and they wanted what lovers wanted: to live together and nurture each other. They had stopped by for dinner after meditation. He gave them full plates to take out to the patio and he went out and sat with them, a beer in hand, with the sound of the mourning doves linty among the trees. All the kitchen clatter far enough away that he could let go for ten minutes. We can't sleep, Laurel had said. We're too excited.

In a nighttime voice as smooth and dark as a good roux, the radio announcer quoted from the CD case: Jeremiah: Stand at the crossroads and look. Ask for the ancient paths. Ask where the good way is and walk in it and you will find rest for your soul.

The good way, she said.

Whatever that means to you.

Dance is where I find it.

That opened the gate. They talked until after one, while he baked and while the cake cooled and while he frosted it. They talked about the church and they talked about politics. She had opinions about the Internet. And NAFTA. And Bill Clinton. She told him about her father, a streetcar conductor in Dublin who carried the poems of Yeats in his rear pocket. He had wanted his daughters to get an education, but there had not been money for that. And the first husband, that story too. He didn't mind listening at all, for Mairead had a generous take on her failed marriages. He was a good man, she said, and he wanted me to walk the straight and narrow with him. And I tried, I did, Johnny. She smiled sheepishly. She had been too wild, too unpredictable, too given to singing in the pubs, even though she had the boy. She would take him along and strap him into a kid seat and he would fall asleep in the smoke and the shenanigans on stage and off. The boy had not been harmed, she said. Look at him now—on his way to being an engineer. She had gotten her green card by marrying number two, a mandolin player who left her for a rich girl half his age. Well, he hurt me, sure. But I got over it, she said. A life without a broken heart—how would you ever learn anything? Finally, when he had frosted the cake and declared it a beauty, they drank shots of tequila and talked about tequila, its virtues and its evils.

Mox whimpered.

He's hurting to get out, he said. Johnny felt like trotting alongside him, loving the night and his body in it. The golf course would be empty and the moon would be overhead. Mallards on the golf course pond would glisten greenly.

Where do you go?

Out to the course. It's quite a sight without the golfers. Would you want to come along?

That sounds like a good way to end the night.

So the night would end. He felt relief and regret. But the walk first would clear their heads. They set off across the lawn, threading their way between the holes he had dug and into the woods, with the moonlight trickling through the trees, the humus spongy underfoot, and the odor of the honeysuckle radiating from the wire fence behind Brambles. She stumbled once and he reached to save her and the touch—his fingers inside her arm—burnt it felt so good.

That burn made him pull back. He had to go that far to know he was in deep. They did not speak except to say, It's nice out here, and Yes, it is. Mox wandered on ahead, poking under brush and into a sand trap. He returned panting and shivering with joy at Johnny's call. Johnny cut short the walk; he'd been shaken by that touch and he thought that she had too. They went a distance that would not seem unusual; he did not want to alarm her by turning back but he wanted to be by himself and he wanted to figure out what was happening. It was a walk he often took with Ruthie and he wanted her there and he didn't.

Back at Brambles he waited on the patio while she fetched her purse.

The stars winked above and Mox sighed contentedly. It had been a good night. No denying that.

Your machine's blinking, she said.

Whatever it is can wait.

He walked her to the Volvo and opened her door. She got in and said, Think about that tofu recipe.

I will.

And are you still planning to go away?

I'd like to leave on Friday and return Saturday. Before the dinner rush.

I can handle it.

I'm certain of that, Mairead. Her name in his mouth tasted unfamiliar and pleasing.

Her tires crisp in the cinders, the wind in the birches, the echo in his mind of the harp guitar, the mournful music—it was a quiet that he did not seek. A quiet that would force him to look at something he wasn't ready for. He was sick of Ruthie being gone but he did not know what to do about it.

At the house he gave Mox a treat. Turned off the A/C and opened the windows. He wanted to make the house his own but the kitchen felt abandoned. Food rotted in the fridge. The windows were streaked with dust. He had run out of laundry detergent and had substituted dish detergent instead of making a trip to the grocery for basics. He was about to run out of toilet paper. Catalogs and bills were piled on the kitchen counter helter-skelter. And every time he knelt to spoon out wet food for Moxie, his bowl was a-crawl with ants, industrious day and night. It was no way to live.

The answering machine blinked, orange as a lit cigarette in the dark. He pressed the message button. Ruth Anne's voice came haltingly. It's me, sweetheart. I know—it's late—it's after one. I only wanted—to hear your voice—I hope you haven't changed your mind about Friday. I've been thinking about those fires we used to build at the cove. Do you remember that? Her voice grew soft, almost inaudible. I guess I was hoping you would pick up. There was a stretch of silence. A wait. Okay. You're not there. Okay—maybe we can talk tomorrow. I know they close on the house tomorrow. Hugs to Laurel and to Oceana, too. And you. Olive you.

His watch read 2:08. Too late to call the pay phone near her room. Definitely too late. And the monastery office would be closed and he would get their machine and their recorded message would bless him—for what that was worth—but he would not get one whit closer to Ruthie.

On the ragged side of the tequila, he wasn't sleepy. Upstairs he got out the garden catalogs and his potential tree list. He opened the window and got into bed in boxers and a T-shirt. The sheets needed washing and he knew how much better clean sheets would feel but he did not want to change them. Flowers drooped in slimy water on the dresser. He would have to take a day—Monday, maybe—to nuke the house. He couldn't go on living depressed. He wasn't depressed and he didn't want to live like that. Other things had been on his mind. The new trees and the berms. Training Mairead. The girls and their move. He could be excused for letting the house go but that had to change. The lamp cast an amber circle in which he opened his catalog. He added hawthorn to his tree list. For the fall color. Ruthie would make an arrangement of leaves on a slender branch in a vase. Surely she would be home by fall. Some people thought it was bad luck to bring a hawthorn branch indoors but he was not superstitious and was not about to become so. Moxie slept on the landing. Thank God for Mox's company. The counterpane lay crumpled at the foot of the bed and Johnny had flung back the top sheet and he was cool and a new mood like a new ingredient—a flavor—folded into his consciousness. He wanted to take charge of the life he lived alone instead of waiting for her to come home.

The phone ringing tore open the silence. That has to be her.

Hello, sweetheart.

Mr. Bond?

Yeah?

Lieutenant Travaglini. Tarkington Police. I've got some unfortunate news. Your daughter's been injured.

*Je*sus—

She's alive and she's going to be all right. She's been transported to the hospital. And her friend—you wouldn't know how to contact—

Jesus God—

Mr. Bond—

I'm coming—

Your daughter and her friend were attacked. I'm not sure what they were doing. It was after one, so far as we can tell. We got an anonymous tip. We haven't been able to get the full story. Your daughter—she's still in Emergency—

I said I'm coming. He gripped the phone between his shoulder and his ear and jerked on a pair of khakis.

You wouldn't know—

Ten minutes. Tops.

He slammed down the phone. His head felt like it might explode. Fucking bastards. I'll kill them myself.

Later he would not remember leaving the house. The slam of the screen reverberating or Moxie at the door whining and wagging his tail. He ran two red lights. Not another soul was on the street and it was a clear shot through campus, past St. Joan's, across the bridge and up a hill from downtown to the hospital. He could not think straight. But he was sober. Sobered immediately.

A nurse in green scrubs came out of Emergency into the waiting room. She looked tired, with gray sacs beneath her eyes. Hair clipped close. Pokémon shoelaces in her white runners. Mr. Bond, she's going to be all right. They'll both be all right.

He wished they would stop saying that. What was all right? What was all right about it?

Your daughter has a skull injury, but the doctor believes it's minor. She has assorted fractures. Her clavicle. Her elbow.

Do you know what happened?

She sat down in the end chair of a curved row. The television was on: the Weather Channel. The dotted lines and colored segments of the country made no sense. He thought, They don't know shit. She said, Please. He sat down next to her.

She lowered her voice. Doctor's with another patient, but you can see him later.

You tell me. Can't you tell me?

Someone—a gang—attacked them. Attacked them with baseball bats. The other one—Oceana Carpenter—talked a blue streak when the EMTs brought them in. She said they were holding hands. In front of their house.

Their new house. They're buying their first house.

I'm sorry.

What else—

You'll have to talk to them. They won't be able to really talk until morning. But you can see Laurel. She's sedated right now. But you can see her. I'll take you in and then we'll move her upstairs after we get some information from you. Doctor wants to keep them overnight to keep an eye on them. You can spend the night if you want.

I will, yeah—

She leaned in close and brought a sandwich bag out of her tunic pocket. I'm obligated to give this to the police, Mr. Bond. But I wanted you to know. I found this stuck in the sleeve of your daughter's blouse when I cut it away. It's a shock to see this sort of thing in Tark—

It's not a shock to me. He took the bag. Inside was a small metal pin, like a campaign button: KQ: KILL QUEERS.

I handled it as little as possible and I'll give it to the police officer. But I wanted you to know.

He amazed himself with calm pretense. Thanking her. Following her into Laurel's section of a curtained emergency bay, the lights ablaze. Laurel slept. Bandages cutting him out of getting close. Rendering him helpless. Her face was bruised: a violent red. And swollen. Her arm was in a sling. Layers of white sheets and layers of bandages swaddled her. A patch of hair had been shaved and stitches lay in a precise row on her scalp above her left eye.

Jesus God. Laurel of the perennial skinned knees. Of lipslides and every conceivable flip known to skateboarders. Of lucky pennies stashed in cedar drawers. Laurel who cried at romantic comedies. Lover of maps. And dogs. And Chinese food. And elegant sentences. She had told him once that she liked teaching composition because of the sentences. Laurel of the look of love that brought him close to tears at the most ordinary times. Laurel who took charge of him on the Fourth. Laurel who called him Papa Bear when she teased him. His Laurel. His only. Laurel who always said, Hate is a very strong word.

Mr. Bond?

Yes?

Did you want to see her friend?

Of course. Of course.

They'll find her parents through the college.

Why didn't she give you their number?

The nurse turned to a table and gathered instruments, discordant clanks into a stainless steel tub. Over her shoulder she said, She—didn't want them to know. I guess.

They live in Colorado.

He took Laurel's limp hand. He whispered, Laurel, honey—

She'll be waking up around four and we'll medicate her again. The nurse faced him, hugging the steel tub to her stomach. But you might be able to say hello. There might be that little window. If you spend the night.

Where's Oceana?

They took her upstairs. She has a broken ankle. And cuts and bruises. They'll be in the same room.

He sat unnerved at the admissions desk and a robust woman took down all that he could tell her of Laurel's medical history. She had a common history, but some answers did not come readily. Dates of childhood diseases. Allergies. He recalled that she had been in Emergency once before—when she had broken a wrist skateboarding. The woman kept pausing to nibble at a Butterfingers bar as she typed his answers. Laurel had no insurance. She was too old to be covered under Johnny's policy and the college did not provide health benefits for adjunct employees. All of this came out.

You're responsible then?

Yes, I am. He signed the papers.

Orderlies—men with gym-developed arms and chests—wheeled her on a gurney out into the hall and into an elevator.

Wait, he called. I'll go along. He grabbed the elevator door a second before it closed and he pushed it open and slipped inside.

In the whoosh of rising, one orderly said, Bless her heart.

The other said, She'll be all right.

He thought about the fundamentalist pamphlet under the magnet on the fridge; it had been there for months: If you are one of those fools who goes around parroting that God loves everyone, this world's condition is your fault.

I'll kill whoever did this, Johnny said. I mean it.

✒

Ruth Anne had not slept long. After calling home around two she longed to sleep and knew she needed to sleep but Tin—his voice, his presence, his kindness, his stories—filled her. She had gotten a crash course and given one.

After the Mexican place they had returned to the lake and walked for miles. He had shown her a wallet-size photo of the woman he planned to marry. She was Vietnamese. A manicurist. I worry, he said, about the chemicals she inhales every day. Many Vietnamese are in this business. I want to send her to college. She is a smart woman. Very good with numbers. Her name is Le. Her American name is Lee Ann.

Why did she change her name?

Obvious reasons, he shrugged. She wants her life to be easy.

Later he said, My father loves the store. He loves listening to Jackie Chan movies.

He waited, thinking, she imagined, that she might have questions about Vo. But none emerged in clear language. When she thought of Vo, half-felt curiosities arose, unfinished inquiries. She surrendered instead to what Tin wanted.

He had questions and he was direct. Why did you come to Vietnam? How long were we together? What did you think of me when you knew me? What illnesses did your grandparents have? What was your labor like? Tell me about Laurel. And your husband, what happened to him in the American War? Why are you living at the monastery? Did you ever think of finding me? Tell me what you thought when you first received my message. Who knows about me? Will it be hard to tell? Will you tell? Will you?

Until the western sun slipped away, until the cool of the evening chased the sunbathers back to their cars and motels—they talked. Her throat felt sore from talking.

They sat on the bench under the sycamore, Tin with his helmet on his lap. She worried her wedding band around and around her ring finger. Her knuckle was swollen and ached. She had noticed a voice of late: the Witness of Aches and Pains and Physical Malfunctions. This voice prompted, Arthritis, but she did not want to think about her bones and joints.

Do you want to go for a ride on my motorcycle?

Not tonight. I don't know—motorcycles make me nervous.

He stood up. Let me walk you to your car.

Her sandals scuffed against the sidewalk. The hot-dog stand was closed. The volleyball net hung loosely between aluminum posts and footprints pocked the sand beneath it. Waves curled against the shoreline, reminiscent of musical notation.

At the Tercel she said, I'd like to meet again. If you would.

My stepmother is jealous. That makes it difficult.

Must she know?

He shrugged. We live in the same house. We don't have big secrets.

Do you go to the Vietnamese Mass?

Sometimes.

Maybe we could meet there. On Sunday.

Sunday is soon.

Yes.

Mrs. Ruth Anne—please do not be offended. But I need to take in all that you have told me. I need to think. Do you understand?

She said, Yes. I do. Not sure if she meant it.

I'll e-mail about Sunday. You will be checking e-mail?

Of course.

He pressed her hand with his. He let go, reluctantly it seemed. It brought to mind that letting go she never wanted to relive: handing him to his grandmother. His cry. Her breasts brimming hotly with milk he would never taste.

He walked away.

Tin!

He bridged the few steps he had taken and came back patiently and waited.

My aunt has the letters I wrote. If I can get those letters—

Those letters are history.

You might say that. I'd have to read them first. I just don't know—

You're sorry you thought of them.

I don't know what I wrote.

If you can get them and you want me to see them, I would be grateful for any news of that time. Very grateful. He set his helmet on the ground. With his hands together at his chest he nodded, an abbreviated bow. His T-shirt looked blue in the dusky light. I need to tell you. I don't think I can call you Mother. Please forgive me. But it does not come naturally.

Gooseflesh rose on her arms. They were contained in a pocket of cool ascending a sandy draw. The lake had flattened out dully. That doesn't matter. It just—doesn't.

Let me know if you tell. I would like to know how it goes.

I'll ask Aunt Teensy about her parents. About their ailments.

May I embrace you again?

She lay in bed and his voice returned, May I embrace you again?

She had not been able to answer all of his questions. I love history! he had said. Give me my history! I want my students to know that history did not begin on the day of their births. She imagined him in front of a class of seventh-graders: energetic, lecturing, correcting, praising. He had told her about his classroom. His bulletin board of twentieth-century heroes: his students added heroes every week. We tell the stories over and over, he said. I have future heroes in that classroom.

Blessedness is not promised. It is not tied to any condition: it is the only reality. What did that mean? How was it possible that the conditions under which you live—the choices you make and fate—had nothing to do with blessedness?

We don't know where we'll go from here.

We just don't know.

She got up and opened her louvered windows. It was before dawn: gray, cloudy. The breeze filled her robe that hung on a hook on the door. The robe was old, a favorite, printed with watering cans and flowers, belling out like a skirt in the breeze. We just don't know. At the sink she looked into the mirror and said, We just don't know. She had wanted to commit his face to memory but she could not keep it there. She had to see him again. He looked like Laurel around the eyes. Where will we go from here? She practiced what she would say to Johnny. The dread of meeting Tin had become entirely the dread of telling. The dread of owning up to her betrayal. She had a lifetime supply of dread and like money it might be applied to this debt or that.

The pay phone rang in the hall. At first she hesitated, thinking, That can't be for me. It's only a little after four. Whoever it was insisted. There were two other women on her hall and she did not want to take the chance that the phone call was for her and might awaken them. She pulled on the robe and tied the belt slapdash, slipping into sandals. She scurried.

Ruthie—

Johnny!

Look. We need you. Something terrible's happened.

What is it?

Laurel, honey. She's been hurt. The doctor says she's going to be all right, but she's been hurt pretty bad.

She could feel the knock of her heartbeat to the tips of her fingers. She cried out his name.

I'm not sure exactly what happened. But someone beat them up. The cops're investigating.

She bit her lip; she squeezed back tears. I'll leave—

Now. Leave now.


She parked next to Johnny's truck in the visitor lot and felt a tender rush toward him upon seeing his truck. She thought of the night at the round barn. His unwavering attention. But that memory did not end with sex and it did not end with frozen custard in Delphi. It ended with Laurel clattering down the stairs and leaving the house and beginning her separation from the house and from her childhood. She might have let them spend the night together. What if she had? What if she had helped them keep their secret? She thought of the next morning. The newspaper photo of the Unitarian Church. Those concrete flower tubs of geraniums. The brick wall. That red spray paint. She thought of them kissing at the long window. Anyone might have seen. Anyone might have let that image fester. You walk around naïve, ignorant of what misery accretes in the hearts of your neighbors. The hospital doors fanned open and closed, open and closed, busy with employees in uniform and visitors. A mind-melting heat already rose from the pavement. The sun was high at eight o'clock.

Her legs felt unsteady; she had driven all the way with only one stop for gas and a coffee. Her stomach ached. Laurel, she had breathed, over and over. Laurel, baby. She was their baby. The desire to be there, to hold her, had driven the car. There was a pressure to hurry into the hospital, but she needed strength and she needed to be ready for what she could not foresee. Let it be not so bad. Let her be whole, she had petitioned. She rummaged in the glove box and found an energy bar and it was soft with the heat and sticky and she ate it greedily.

Inside, she stopped in a restroom. She splashed her face with cool water and brushed her hair. A shift was occurring. She wondered if she would bring the monastery home with her. And Tin. Was there room wherever she went? Aunt Teensy had awakened to say goodbye; she had told her simply that Laurel needed her and Aunt Teensy had said, I didn't expect you'd be here this long anyway. I'll be back, she said. I hope you will. That would whisper at her as she drove. I hope you will. She had gone to Jill's room and Jill had opened the door sleepily, wearing baggy striped pajamas. Her face free of age. She was taken aback. She said, How can so much cruelty exist? They talked on the foot of her single bed. Ruth Anne said, We met. We spent the afternoon together yesterday. Jill asked, Was it good? Very. Then she said, Be careful, and, We'll pray for her. And for you. Don't think too much. Call me, will you?

Was it good? Very. On the highway, in the sway and buffet of the big trucks, she kept telling herself, I am the mother of two children. She had never owned up to that. It felt luxurious and weighty.

Johnny had given her the room number: 305. She took the elevator and wandered on the third floor. Past murals and stainless steel racks of breakfast trays. There he was. Asleep in a recliner in a family waiting room. An AM talk show muted on the television. His khakis rumpled. Stubble gray on his cheeks. His hands across his belly. She went to him and took his hand. His eyes flew open. She knelt at eye level. He gently cupped her head in one hand, tugged her to his shoulder.

God, I'm glad to see you.

Ruth Anne kissed his forehead. He smelled garlicky, buttery, and it was a good smell. She associated it with the big kitchen at Brambles and after hours there with him.

Let's see if she's awake.

They went into the room across the hall, with exaggerated quiet, nearly tiptoeing. Oceana's bed was near the door; the ice-green curtain between the beds hung gathered at the wall.

They didn't want the curtain closed, Johnny said.

The opaque window blinds let in a fuzzy morning light. Oceana was asleep, her face turned toward Laurel. One eyelid was swollen the size of a plum. Her arms lay outside the blanket and her hands lay palm-up and they were scraped and raw.

They had been beautiful young women, flawless and confident. The damage would go deep. It would be interior damage. What you carry for a lifetime. The soul of a spitfire entered Ruth Anne: temper like she'd never felt before. But sham was called for. She did not want to alarm them any more than they were. She felt the urge to bolt the door.

Who would do this? Who?

Johnny cut his eyes away from her. He sat down in a chair and rubbed his forehead with the heel of one hand. We might never know.

The police'll find out.

He hissed, They don't give a rat's ass.

That was the first indication that he might be difficult or volatile. Of course the police would do their job; she hoped that they would do their best. They'd better. She searched his eyes.

Don't look at me that way. I don't have confidence in them.

Ruth Anne took Laurel's hand and held it. The back of her hand was scratched and the delicate scratches had begun to dry up and heal. Laurel murmured, rising from sleep, from sedation.

She opened her eyes and said, Mom.

Her voice was not durable. As if the sound—Mom—had diminished in meaning. She had reservations about her. She did not trust her. A dream from years ago rose up in Ruth Anne's memory. She had been a child in the passenger seat of Aunt Teensy's cavernous car. Trees were a spring green canopy over the road to Pier Cove. Aunt Teensy turned to her in the dream and said, Your mother will never be well.

I'm here, sweetie.

I wanted you.

I'm right here.

She cried out, Oh—a singular, almost operatic sound. She winced. Everything hurts. It hurts.

Oceana said, Good morning. If it is a good morning. As if she had stones in her mouth.

Johnny went to her bed. How're you doing?

I've been better.

Just rest.

I want to get out of here.

Laurel locked eyes with her.

Voices pattered in the hall. A booming voice said, May I come in? Bond family, are you in there?

Johnny said, Yeah?

Lieutenant Travaglini, he said, his big head poking inside. He was a young man, in his thirties, and out of uniform, in slacks and a white dress shirt, the cuffs rolled on his meaty forearms. He had a thick, shiny mustache. I have a few questions. If you don't mind.

Johnny waved him in and circled around to the door side of Oceana's bed, to protect her. Them. Ruth Anne felt protected; she had almost forgotten Johnny's proclivity to taking care.

Lieutenent Travaglini stood between the two beds, his arms folded. He said, Can we get a lucid story? A mutually agreed-upon story? I'm here to tell you the reporter'll be here soon and I want to warn you. Don't muddy the water by telling her what happened. You'll come down and press charges as soon as you're capable. That's what you say—

We're not pressing charges, Oceana said.

Don't give me that.

We're not. Oceana puckered her face bitterly. We'd have to stay here to press charges and I'm not staying here a minute longer than I have to. We're—

She raised her head and from the way she let it fall Ruth Anne imagined that it hurt and that it felt heavy. In that brief nod upward she met Laurel's eyes asking for support.

She said, We can't live here.

Laurel said, I'm with you.

Johnny said, What about—

I don't care about the job. Or the house.

Lieutenent Travaglini said, The guys who did this can't get off. Only you can prosecute. He glanced at Ruth Anne as if to say, You know I'm right. Chime in.

Ruth Anne averted her eyes.

Laurel said, We want to leave. Her voice not so clear or sure as Oceana's.

Ruth Anne said, Where will you go?

Johnny said, I left to take a nap and you decided this already?

We have to go.

I can't let you leave. Like this. Who'll take care of you?

We'll go where we won't need to be taken care of.

Where, for Christ's sake?

New Orleans, Oceana said. People like us can hold hands on the street there.

That's a hell of a reason.

Ruth Anne thought he was about to be unreasonable himself. She reached out to touch him, but he was far away. Johnny—

Oceana peered up at him with her good eye and said, I thought you were on our side.

I am on your side—

Lieutenant Travaglini said, You girls better give this a good think. You want my advice, getting these guys behind bars should be at the top of your list. This investigation is tied to the other—the churches—

Lieutenant, Johnny said, a hand on his shoulder. Ruth Anne thought that Johnny would never have touched him had he been in uniform. Or if he had been older. But it seemed natural. Could we have the morning? They'll be released this morning and they'll be less sedated later and your questions can wait that long, don't you think? He ushered him out the door, patting his shoulder. Lieutenant Travaglini handed him a business card. He said, I told you so.

A slim young woman under the weight of a huge shoulder bag peeked into the room. The reporter. Her face like a mouse. A gnawing look, Ruth Anne thought. She would go to any lengths to get her story.

I'm from the *Chronicle,* she said hastily, her words butting up against each other. We want to tie this to the desecration of the churches and we'd like to run it tomorrow morning—

No questions, Johnny said. He shut the door with a crack.

Thank you, Dad.

Johnny said that they would discuss New Orleans. He wanted them to be sure they knew what they were getting into. He'd heard it was dangerous. Oceana laughed, curtly, cynically. Ruth Anne had not heard it quite that way before. It hurts to laugh, Oceana said, but you have to realize, Johnny.

What?

New Orleans is the yin of this yang. We—cannot—stay—here. We just can't. Like you said—we pushed our luck. It's better now than later on.

The police want to contact your parents.

I'll take care of that.

Leave her alone, Dad—

Sweetie, I'm only—

No one can stop us.

I don't want to stop you. I want you to do what's right. I want you to prosecute the bastards who did this. Don't you understand? It'll happen again and that'll be on your hands.

Laurel cast a silent plea at Ruth Anne.

Just tell me this. Did you recognize anything about them?

Dad—

Let's go out, Ruth Anne said. Let's go out a few minutes. I need to talk to you.

He scowled. But he allowed himself to be led into the hall and to the family waiting room where they could shut the glass door. The reporter waited a not-so-discreet distance away near the elevator, her bright blue cell phone at her ear.

And what're you doing, he said, shaking her hand from his arm. Coming in here like you know what's going on and you've been gone for six weeks. You've been gone all summer. You don't have a clue—

Could we just sit down?

Okay. I'm sitting.

We can't stop them from going.

What is it with all of you? Isn't this place good enough anymore?

Calm down.

I—am—fucking—calm.

I don't blame them for wanting to go. Think what it would be like for them if this goes to trial. If they can catch whoever did it. It'll be awful—what they'll be dragged through. As if they're—

To blame.

Yes. As if the way they live is immoral. They won't have any privacy.

They should've thought of that.

Johnny—

I'll tell you one thing: I don't like the idea of them being in New Orleans.

What if I went down to help them get settled?

I don't understand you, Ruthie. This doesn't seem like you.

It's me all right. I feel more myself than ever.

A volunteer in a flowered smock opened the door and rolled in a cart of coffee and doughnuts. She sang a hymn under her breath: "This World Is Not My Home." The coffee smelled good but the doughnuts looked stiff with grease.

Now you know what Critical Mass means—

Ruth Anne put her hand on his arm. She mouthed, Could we wait?

Coffee this morning? the volunteer asked.

No thanks.

No thanks.

She smiled falsely, miffed. She rolled her cart back into the hall and the reporter hovered over the cart and said, May I?

The door closed with a satisfying click. Through the window they could see all the action in the hallway. A young priest walking by, a bouquet of flowers in hand. Two nurse's aides gossiping. Johnny hung his head. Ruth Anne wondered if he had given a thought to what she said on the phone about talking over all they had kept hidden. They would have to talk and she did not want to admit that the emergency would make talking more likely but it did. The old order was shaken. And that instability would open cracks, avenues to discuss what had never been said before.

Her motherly self had a range of feeling she had never thought possible. She said, I didn't think this through. When they said New Orleans, I just thought, I'll drive them down. I'll help them get settled. They're going to need some help. I want to be supportive. I—I feel like I wasn't before, but I want to be.

I don't like the idea of *you* in New Orleans.

She had to smile at that.

I *don't*.

Do you have any idea who did this?

It's that element. The kids who painted the churches.

I'll talk to Father Carroll. He needs to speak out.

Good luck.

Father Carroll will speak out about it.

Wake up, Ruthie. He's a candy-ass.

Johnny—

He's not your friend. He won't even join in the reward.

What reward?

We've collected five thousand. But Father Carroll said that St. Joan's has no business getting involved. He didn't even give us that love-the-sinner-hate-the-sin crap.

I'll talk to him.

You do that. Meanwhile, I have to get back to work. And I have to call the goddamn realtor. They were supposed to close at noon. Do you want to stay here until they're released? Is that all right?

Of course.

This is a hell of a homecoming. I wanted to—

I'm afraid for them.

Johnny took her hand. He held her hand and it was the touch of a husband. Who knew her. Who knew that hand. The familiarity of it opened her heart. She started to say, I love you— To reach into his softness. Beyond his gruffness.

But Johnny brought her back to the seat of dread. He looked into her eyes and whispered, I know you want to talk. And we will.

# 16

Someone had painted a tree of life—replete with childlike apples—on the Volkswagen bus in front of Oceana's apartment house. She parked behind it. Oceana had given her the key to the back door. The yard was a jungle, the shrubs overgrown. She thought of burglars. Intruders. The black cat with the white ring around its hind leg crouched on top of the heat pump, meowing plaintively.

Inside, the house was quiet. Creepily so. She had a mission: to bring clothes to the girls. They needed clothes to leave the hospital in. She wanted to make haste and she did not want to be there. The stairs were dull with dust and mounds of cat hair. The door to the apartment creaked open; one long screw was about to fall out of the hinge. She left the door ajar. Their belongings were packed in liquor boxes. On the kitchen table Laurel had left her grade book. They had abandoned a packet of crackers and a sandwich bag of cheddar cheese cubes. An open bottle of five-dollar wine. Two wineglasses, with the dried blackish residue of the wine in the bowls. What was left of a celebratory moment before they had walked around to the new house and stood on the sidewalk holding hands.

Blue duffel. Red duffel. They had given her instructions for finding underpants, T-shirts, and soft pastel workout shorts. Oceana said to look for a rucksack hanging on the back of the door. Bring what you can in that. She did not take the time to fold the clothes but rolled each garment hastily and stuffed the rucksack.

Five messages blinked on the machine. Five. They had not said a word about messages and they had not said a word about retrieving another thing. Clothes were all they needed at the moment. Just as surely as she had wanted to leave the door ajar, she decided to shut and lock it. She went to the window. The same long Italianate window where she had seen them embrace. Snowflake decals from Christmas past were coming unstuck from the windowpane. The park across the street had a straggly look about it, the grass deep along the chain link fence. Trash overflowed its striped receptacle. No children played there. It was too hot. The air in the apartment was stuffy; a line of sweat ran down her back. She turned to the telephone. Pressed the message button.

Oceana's mother said, Honey, did you get the check for the bed? Please let us know. Sky has decided to move to Eugene. You girls are far-flung. So far apart. But we'll come see you later this year. Your father sends his love. Let us know about the check.

She had never heard her mother's voice before and it sounded much like her own. A woman in her fifties. Someone who named her daughters Sky and Oceana. And what did that mean? Would they meet? Would they take a mutual parental interest in the success of the relationship?

There were two hang-ups.

And then, a man said, This is a message for Oceana Carpenter. You need to fill out a tax form if you want to receive your first paycheck on time. Stop by the business office.

And then, a clumsy rattle, as if someone had fumbled the phone. A gravelly voice said, We almost—

The voice was muffled, the words spoken through a scarf or mask. The hair on her head prickled. Her heart raced.

We almost got you. Better watch out. Sluts.

She felt watched.

Someone knew where they lived. Had the phone number.

Someone knew their private lives. Imagined God knows what about them.

She pressed the ERASE button. That was wrong. That was the wrong thing to do but she could not think straight. She sweated and her face and neck flushed hotly. A dizzy moment almost made her sit down. But she felt watched and she wanted out and she pounded down the stairs as if in warning to whomever might be watching.

She did not feel up to driving. She stashed the rucksack in the Tercel and locked its doors. She jammed on sunglasses and walked the two blocks to the library where she slipped past the circ desk and a long line of patrons. No one looked up and recognized her. She took the computer booth farthest from the circ desk and she logged on and checked her e-mail. In spite of everything she kept a portion of her mind on Tin. On seeing his face once more. On being open to what he would decide. Johnny must know soon and she practiced telling. But it was only practice and she thought that when the time came words might fail her. She could not foresee what she would say. Let me know if you tell. He wanted to know. Jill would say she was not living in the present. She had never done that. All of her life had been about regret or sorrow or anticipation. Maybe there had been times—sex brought her into the present and the first ten minutes of a glass of wine or childish moments with Laurel when Laurel was small—but those were flames soon doused by her inner chatter. That gravelly voice brought her into the present. Threats brought her into the present. Sluts. You know you are. We almost—

We.

NO NEW MESSAGES.

The walk back to the car in the heat felt grueling. Waves of heat rose from the sidewalks. Her hair hung heavy in the heat and irritated her. At the car she pulled it into a hurried braid. A woman hustled—all business—out of the Red Cross building a few doors down. In lime-colored slacks and a linen blouse. Her hair was white and cut short in what had once been called a pixie. She looked ice-cool, lime-cool, and Ruth Anne impetuously decided: I'll cut my hair. She drove to a walk-in hair salon near the campus and with the students gone, four stylists filed their nails and read magazines. They flipped a coin to see who would do the job.

She walked out shorn. Unburdened. It had taken twenty minutes. The stylist had cut off all the tinted hair and now she was an honest woman. In a cut that left no place to hide.


St. Joan's looked shabbier than she remembered.

On the sunny side of the building curly dock and dandelions sprouted through the old mulch. A pebbled basement window was cracked. Inside, she blessed herself with tepid holy water. The church was empty and she had not intended to but she went into the side chapel to center. It was cool, shadowy. A place for a little time out. She knelt. It was humbling to kneel and admit all that you did not know. But too much rankled; she could not quell her thoughts and she could not simply witness them.

Once Laurel had made her first communion at the filigreed communion rail.

Once the name of God came easily to her and she did not question the existence of God the Father.

Once she had thought eternity happened after you die.

A butterfly bobbled in through an open transom, its forewing bright yellow. From not far away she heard the rattle of a mop bucket and the slop of water on the concrete floor. Then the shuffle of CDs. Limbo.

He gasped. I thought you was a ghost. With no hair.

How are you, Limbo? She waited while he slipped a CD into his player and clipped it to his belt. He adjusted his headphones.

Aw, I don't know how I am. He grabbed the rag mop and leaned on it.

You don't?

I never go to the library. Without you.

You should.

Aw, I don't read much anymore.

Is Father Carroll here?

We're not going to Chicago. Not this summer.

How come?

Nothing stays the same. My mother says.

That's true enough. Is Father Carroll all right?

He's all right. Are you all right?

Someone hurt Laurel. You remember Laurel, don't you?

He nodded. The start of keeping time to a song that only he could hear. I know Laurel. I saw Laurel at the Fiddlers'. Laurel was dancing. Laurel's a good dancer.

She thought of the muffins and danishes she had brought him. The way he had waited all those years every Saturday on the library steps. The soft packets of fingernail clippings.

Daisy doesn't work at the library anymore.

She doesn't?

That's a good thing.

How do you know she doesn't?

I look for you. Sometimes I look for you.

Father Carroll stepped out of the sacristy. Over his shoulder he carried a Kelly-green liturgical garment on a hanger under a filmy dry cleaner's bag. His voice echoed against the domed vault above the altar. Well. Well. Well.

Father Carroll. Ruth Anne took a step toward him.

Limbo's mop hushed, hushed, wetly; he had gone back to work when Father Carroll pursed his lips.

He waved her toward the sacristy. She followed. Fluid light filtered through a stained-glass window. Maple cupboards gleamed in the light. A sack of unconsecrated hosts lay on the counter.

He had his back to her and he put away the garment and fiddled with another hanger, stalling. When finally he turned to her he said, I don't think it would do for you to come back to work. Under the circumstances.

Under what circumstances?

I'm well aware. Ruth Anne, I tried to warn you.

I'm—not—even interested in coming back. Not right now.

Have a seat, my dear—

I will, Father. I came to talk to you.

They sat down in magisterial chairs with claw feet and worn arms of gold leaf. Ruth Anne rubbed the arms.

It's a terrible thing that's happened to Laurel.

Laurel was a sweet child.

I mean what happened last night.

I'm well aware. People have already come calling.

She's not the only one who's been a victim. Under these circumstances.

As long as they persist they'll get hurt.

St. Joan's needs to take a stand against this.

There may well be parishes that would. We don't have to. This isn't Ann Arbor. Hell will freeze over before St. Joan's or this diocese will take a stand.

Jesus would not hurt these girls.

This is God's way of calling them back to Him.

I can't believe that.

You've been gone all summer. You've been listening to some wrong-headed people. They mean well. But they're wrong-headed and—

If you're silent, it means something.

God gives me the strength to harden my heart.

Listen to what you're saying.

He looked at his watch. I have an appointment soon, my dear. Do you want me to bless you? You might need God's blessing.

No. She stood up and said again, No. I don't need God's blessing, Father. Blessedness is not something you can give me.

Don't say that, Ruth Anne. You're distraught.

Jesus would not say fag, Father. I heard you say it.

You'd better go.

I belong to this parish. I've been here longer than you. I have a right to be here. I have a right to tell you what I think.

He walked her to the back door of the sacristy, his hand pinching her elbow. It was a metal door with a brass bar across it. He pressed the bar and swung the door open and said, It's a beautiful day. An apron of sunlight fanned out from the steps. The neighbor next door had planted a citrusy bed of flowers.

He had the weight of millennia behind him. Laurel would say, Spirit's bigger than you think. It's not conceivable. We're in the cosmos. It's not something out there.

Adrenaline rushing, she rounded the building to the lot where she had parked her bicycle and there was the reporter, dressed in slacks and practical shoes that would allow her to track her story on foot, if necessary. She spotted Ruth Anne and barked into her cell phone, Catch you later.

Ruth Anne's hands felt like rusty mechanisms, cramped, as she unlocked her bicycle and hooked the lock through the frame. She was on the verge of tears.

Mrs. Bond. I know you're her mother and you want to protect her but justice must be served, Mrs. Bond.

And I know you're doing your job, but leave us alone. She wheeled the bicycle from the parking lot to the alley, dogged by the reporter.

What did your priest have to say? You might as well talk to me. I'll be fair to you.

Did you hear me?

Did it come as a shock to you? I could do a human interest story, Mrs. Bond.

Get away from me.

Are they going to press charges? Are they?

She turned a cold back to the reporter. Chanting inwardly, We have to go. We have to. She took off flying down the alley.

Tin, there will be time. She wanted to believe it.

# 17

Friday morning she said to Laurel, You come to the lake with me and I'll go to New Orleans with you. She told herself, Keep quiet. Stay calm. Don't let on. It might do you good to be at the beach. I have to say goodbye to Aunt Teensy and I have to pick up my things at the monastery.

You're serious about helping us move?

I'm serious.

A reporter from the Indy *Star* had already come to the door—a shy man in his forties with the whiff of Altoids on his breath through the screen—and she refused him. Before giving up he had parked at the entrance to the golf course for an hour, drinking coffee from a thermos. He had watched the house through binoculars and she had watched him back, all the while sifting through the mental rubble of the day before. What she would never say to the girls.

The sun burned the corn in the fields, it was that hot. The girls had slept together on the sofa bed and she had been afraid of that before but not now. She was relieved to be able to look into the living room and see them lying there, holding hands.

Laurel said, How many days should we pack for?

We'll come back Sunday. I want to go to the Vietnamese Mass in Cortland.

Why?

I'm working through some things. Some things that happened a long time ago.

That was sufficient for Laurel. Her sling kept her from hugging but she got up and scooted around the table to Ruth Anne and awkwardly patted her head with her good hand. I love your haircut.

I'm glad you do. Dad doesn't.

Ruth Anne held her coffee mug in both hands and sat still for the head-patting. She could smell Laurel's skin. A good smell, part soap, part cotton. We make the skin of our children. We revel in it. We touch them day and night. Then they wander and seek that mother love from others. Was that, finally, at the root of their attraction? A return to mother love? A dissolution of female boundary, skin to skin? Was that what she and Sister Michelle had wanted from each other, with the insects beating against the windowpane? Would they tell her if she asked?

Oceana loped into the kitchen, her crutches preceding her. She said, My mother cried. It made me feel awful.

Laurel said, It's not your fault.

Those were the most loving words Ruth Anne could imagine.

Laurel went to her and rubbed her head and kissed her cheek and when she did Oceana glanced at Ruth Anne to test, to discern, her reaction. She smiled.

I told her not to come. There's nothing she could do. She's glad to know you're going with us, down South. She might give you a call. Whenever you decide to plug in the phone full-time. You need to feel up to it. She's not easy.

The girls talked and she could not concentrate. Johnny was out in the yard, his boot on a shovel, about to pitch himself into work, digging deeper a hole already there. His back sweaty.

The night before, he had gone to their apartment and retrieved the duffels and meditation cushions. When he returned, Ruth Anne awakened, groggily, and said, Was everything all right?

I guess so, Johnny said. It's a dump and it shows when it's empty like that. I'll send a couple guys over there. To move everything to a storage unit. I don't mind telling you again—I hope they change their minds. Not about the house. I understand that. How could they go back? But New Orleans, Ruthie, I hope they change their minds about New Orleans.

I know you do. And, What happened with the realtor?

That's going to be a royal pain in the ass. It's up to the sellers. They can be benevolent. Or they can make it hard on them. On me, is what it comes down to. Either way, it's going to cost.

Her throat felt parched. She said, Would you bring me a glass of water? Please?

He did and after she drank the water she lay down on her stomach. In the artificial cool and patina of moonlight he sat beside her on the bed and made gentle clockwise circles on her back. He said, I miss you already.

I know.

He ran his hand urgently up the nape of her neck. With his knuckles he drubbed her new haircut and she thought he might say, I'm sorry you cut your hair, for she could feel that he was sorry, but he didn't. He kissed her shoulder. The distance to go to take him in her arms was sizable, a voyage. Sex could be a panacea for much that ailed them. But she said, I'm worn out. I need to sleep.

He had come to bed and in the sticky heat he turned to spoon. Ordinarily Johnny would curl his arm over her and cup one breast and she would rest easy. But now she felt the pressure of his hand upon her shoulder, as if to stop her, warn her.

Listen.

She turned over and in the moonlight he made a small circle with his forefinger jiggling.

They found a pin on Laurel's shirt. Like a button. He stared at the ceiling and said, KILL QUEERS. That's what it said.

Ruth Anne inhaled sharply. He took her hand in the secret soft folds of the bedclothes between them. He said, I'm going to find them. I will.

His white mustache gleamed in the dark but his eyes disappeared into shadow. Kill queers and sluts. Her thoughts, any of her own thoughts, were plowed under by that. Finally she squeezed his hand so hard it hurt her bones. She said, We need you—to take care of—

What?

Our lives here. Can't you see how frightened she is? I want to help them do whatever they're drawn to doing. Then I'll be home. Please—

As if she were promising that nothing would change. As if decades would unfurl as before.

This is what I mean by Critical Mass, Ruthie. This is fucking Critical Mass.

Johnny.

Don't worry—

I love you. I do—

When she woke up, whatever scent or concavity his body might have left was gone.

She had not turned on the kitchen lights. It felt cooler that way. The girls sat down and she toasted their bagels and was heartened by their presence, by the three of them together. As long as they were right with her she would not worry. She would fly in the face of danger for them. They wanted the beach, the wind. The road and all that it implied. Escape and possibility. She described the photos of the Dalai Lama at Our Lady of Holy Mysteries and they agreed to stay there. To sit meditation with the nuns. To visit Aunt Teensy.

They went to gather their belongings. She started the Tercel and set the A/C on high. Upstairs, she flicked on lipstick and surveyed what she was leaving behind. She flung the counterpane up to the pillows, a halfhearted effort to establish order. She scribbled a note and left it on Johnny's pillow. You're my dear, it read. What had been seducing her surreptitiously all morning finally could not be ignored: she pulled down the attic stairs and went up to find the cinnabar basket. The attic was like an oven. A diffused light bled through dirty pentagonal windows at either end. She knew exactly where it was. Everything else in the attic seemed to fall away in its glow. Red as a burning coal, carved with dragons. She lifted the lid.

Vo looked askance. He wore a suit with a silk handkerchief dangling from the jacket pocket. His hair was glossy, dark. She looked like a child. Diminutive in a flowered shirt that was too big for her. She thought of how young Laurel seemed and when Tin was born she had been four years younger than Laurel. Compassion washed over her. Not pity. Compassion for the girl in the flowered shirt. What had she felt during those spells? When Johnny would pour her a whiskey to alleviate all she could not articulate? Was it guilt? Or loss? The word loss could not fully describe the want she had for him. The rack of it. She had ached inside and out. For Tin. She saw that now. But at the time she was only aware of the evil of giving up her child and feeling relieved about it. That feeling had overwhelmed her. Like a flood that makes you forget the weather elsewhere. Tin was wrapped snugly in a receiving blanket, asleep. Vo had one arm around her waist, one hand upon the baby's head. Her heart went out to him. They did not know much but thought they did from reading all those stories. You couldn't learn everything from books. No one tells you the truth about what to expect. Vo's touch could keep her steady or his touch could leave her quaking and confused. Each time, afterward, they would lie entangled and not knowing where one skin began and the other ended. She noticed the shadow in the corner of the photograph: another person—Mai. Then it came back to her. Bad luck would come if three people were in a photo. Three was an unlucky number. Mai had been asked to hover on the edge. What else had she forgotten?

She did not take the cinnabar basket from the attic but carried the photograph by one corner down the stairs to the bedroom where she found an envelope for the photograph and slipped it into her purse.

When the girls emerged from the house she was ready, at the wheel. Johnny pulled on his T-shirt and came over to say goodbye. He hugged the girls. He leaned into the car and kissed her on the mouth, his hand on her cheek. He said, I thought you wanted to check your mail? As if to keep her there a few more minutes. She said, I'll do it later. We'll only be gone a couple days. At the end of the cinder drive she tooted her horn and in the rearview mirror she saw him. Waving. A quizzical look on his face. Mox beside him. The pitted ground like a graveyard. And up the hill a red slash—a lipstick-red blouse—and a gesture, someone on the patio behind the big kitchen lighting a cigarette. Her.

Still, she let it go. She had appointments with her own fate.

She thought of Aunt Teensy giving her an allowance and saying, That money just burns a hole in your pocket, doesn't it? A word burned a hole in her mouth: brother. He looks like you around the eyes.

# 18

They listened to local radio until south of Gary. Country and classic rock. Plenty of Bob Seeger. The Beatles.

You could listen to the Beatles for a long time and not get tired of them. She had not learned to like the Beatles until the seventies. When she first came home from Saigon she did not listen to music. Music did not lift her up; it only made her cry. At the library in Cortland she had been hired to work the circulation desk but after a year she was transferred to fine arts and required to spend long hours in the stacks cataloging sheet music. Boogie-woogie. Ragtime. Torch songs. She was stationed in the grim stacks at a metal desk and the song titles and the very feel and odor of the yellowing paper would tie her up in knots of sorrow. "Someone to Watch Over Me." "Cry Me A River." She could hear the music in her mind and that was more music than she wanted. Her life was small, a hard-edged box. She would spend the evenings alone in the studio apartment over the flower shop. It's killing me, killing me, she would lament to no one but herself. She had been afraid to make a friend, to reach out to people she had known before. No one wanted to hear about Vietnam and that made keeping secrets not so difficult. She did not go back to Aunt Teensy. She did not go back there until after Laurel was born. She waited for Johnny or news of Johnny. Somehow when she came back to the States she shifted her attention to Johnny. Eventually she bought a car and drove the back roads, and the lake and the mint fields dispersing mint oil into air brought Johnny to the forefront of her imagination. She did not know how it was possible to do what she had done but after a while what she had done began to seem like events in another life. Not her life. During that waiting time her dreams were bad: Tin would be a boy who fought with other boys; he banged his chin against another boy's head and split his lip; there was blood everywhere. She knew that Madame Thuong would do the best she could. The dreams were not about that. Finally, Johnny's father tracked her down. He stood at the open door smoking while she read the letter. The letter said, I'm all right. But she did not believe that. She wished that she could feel pure-hearted in her love for him. In her prayer for his return. But she had wronged him and wronged herself. Music only made it worse.

Now if she heard *Abbey Road* she thought of moving to Tarkington after they were married. The trailer they lived in while they both worked two jobs to save for Brambles. Johnny would take her to work at the library and he would do a shift at Wabash National, riveting semis together. On the weekend she had waited tables at a now defunct Italian place and Johnny worked in the kitchen. Johnny had brought his turntable from his father's trailer and when they did manage to be awake and together at home he would lift the hi-fi needle and set it down time after time on "Something." Something in the way she moves. Attracts me like no other lover. The trailer they lived in was on the prairie and it rocked in the storms. He had shown her the food list he had kept. Everything he would cook if he were ever released. That was all she knew of that time.

What're you thinking about, Mom?

Your dad. This song. The way he was when he came home. She thought, Not the babies that fell into the China Sea when a helicopter crashed. She would not think about that. No, not that.

Laurel said, She means when he came home from the war.

Oceana talked then. Her father had been 4-F. She was not sure why. Her parents had met and fallen in love at a Buddhist retreat in Boulder. I'm second-generation American Buddhist, she said. She went on about the Transcendentalists, who were, she said, the first Americans to take an interest in religions of the East. As a child she had gone to Buddhist family camp and she had done walking meditation. She had memorized the five precepts and a poem by Han-shan when she was only six years old.

Laurel said, Recite the poem!

Oceana leaned forward from the back seat, grinning. Ruth Anne could see her in the rearview mirror from the nose up: the swelling of her eyelid had gone down.

> *Yes, there are stingy people,*
> *But I'm not one of the stingy kind.*
> *The robe I wear is flimsy? The better to dance in.*
> *Wine gone? It went with a toast and a song.*
> *Just so you keep your belly full—*
> *Never let those two legs go weary.*
> *When the weeds are poking through your skull,*
> *That's the day you'll have regrets!*

My father thought it was funny. A child saying, When the weeds are poking through your skull—

In a whisper, Laurel said, Now the precepts. Listen, Mom—

Ruth Anne said, I have to stop for gas, honey.

You still have a quarter tank.

It makes me nervous. Just humor me.

They stopped at a Shell station. Ruth Anne went into the restroom and she did not want to hear any precepts. She wanted to be a good Catholic. But she had never been: the lie had kept her from it. She did not want to know another thing about Buddhism. All this time when they had gone to meditation she had thought it might be a phase or a whim and that Laurel might come home. Home to St. Joan's. She did not want to admit that she had imagined Oceana joining the church. It was a mother's wishful thinking. You stray from reality. Wanting to gather all your loved ones under the same roof. Kindness drained away; she called Father Carroll spiteful names. After meditating at the monastery up in Michigan all those weeks she had thought—hoped—that her reservoir of kindness might hold out indefinitely. But no. That was a pitfall, thinking that. Oceana's family was Buddhist. American Buddhist. Whatever that meant. There was something else that fed the panic and she could not touch it. One of the worst memories. Don't tell me the precepts. She wanted to say to Laurel, We're Catholic! Don't you know what that means? Don't you remember, Once a Catholic, always a Catholic? What about Dad, Laurel had said more than once. Dad's troubled about authority. He might come back someday. She had heard that New Orleans was a Catholic city and maybe Laurel would come back to the Church there. She was dependent on her and she would be for a little while and when Ruth Anne went to Mass, Laurel would go too. The worst memories hung about. She washed her hands with liquid pink soap; she scrubbed them hard. There was a metal machine you could put two quarters in to buy a vial of fake perfume. Fake Opium. Fake White Shoulders. The mirror was cracked. She put on lipstick and she rubbed in hand lotion. Her knuckle hurt. It had to be arthritis, intoned the Witness of Aches and Pains and Physical Malfunctions. She was hurt and she did not want to say so. She was rising to the occasion. It was the occasion of a hate crime.

By the time they arrived at the monastery Aunt Teensy was asleep and Jill led them to their rooms and all was quiet. Or Ruth Anne imagined all was quiet for others, the girls and the nuns and any centering students who might have moved in during her absence. Women who had come to the monastery for the deep silence. They would not speak and that suited Ruth Anne fine. She did not need to be known by them or to know them.

She lay in bed and it was as if she had never left, so familiar was the monastery. The louvered windows letting in the lake breeze. The rusty basin. She almost fell asleep but in the chink between wakefulness and sleep the memory came alive.

A woman selling green onions on the street.

Connie Mattingly.

Her skirts made into curtains.

Vo's blind face open with wonder and desire.

His kiss.

The walks they took.

Connie Mattingly had quit her job in March.

Wild horses couldn't keep me here, she said. But my rent's paid until the end of the month. It was evening and the trees had been painted halfway up their trunks with lime to ward off insects and they were bright in the evening. At the corner, women who had been selling greens all day packed up their leftovers in shallow baskets. Boys in torn T-shirts kicked a soccer ball about. One boy had no arm below the elbow. Another gaped at them with one wild eye; his other eye was an infected hole. On Nguyen Du Street, Ruth Anne followed Connie upstairs. You'll have to be out by the end of the month. Leave the key with the neighbor.

Where're you going?

Hong Kong. I met a man in the rug business. He collects Chinese wedding chests.

An American?

A Brit.

Are you in love with him?

I don't know exactly what that means anymore. Connie laughed at herself. Her eyes dripped with black mascara and eyeliner. It made her look like a sad clown, but she was happy. Laughing. Switching her skirt. Glancing at herself in the mirror.

She helped Connie pack. Connie sorted through her clothes and left almost everything behind. She took what she could pack in one hard-shell suitcase. She had three white tennis outfits; she packed two and left one behind.

You can have this stuff. She was thrilled about leaving. She said, Why do I think you're going to be here for a long time?

Ruth Anne sat down on the vanity stool. She stared at her damp face in the mirror. The overhead lightbulb cut harsh shadows and behind her the shiny clothes gleamed on the bed. The traffic sounded far away.

Staunchly she said, I'm going to have a baby.

Oh my God. Connie stopped in mid-fold and flung a garment on the bed. She knelt beside Ruth Anne. What're you going to do?

Have it.

Honey, you need to go home. She took Ruth Anne's hands in hers. Don't you want to go home to your family?

I can't.

What about your mother? A mother would want to know about this.

She would. I think she would.

Have you told her?

Not yet. I will. I'll be all right.

Whose is it? Who's the father?

He knows. He knows and his mother knows.

Will she help you?

Oh yes. She wants the baby.

Then the story came out. Connie perched on the bed and smoked a cigarette. She offered her one and Ruth Anne said no. She described the toothless seer who came and said, Yes, it's a boy. Her pendulous breasts. Her metal earrings brushing her shoulders. She had been shot in her village and left for dead and she did not have one of her feet. Now she made a living in the city divining the future. Madame Thuong sat Ruth Anne down in the kitchen at the tea shop and said, Eat. She placed a steaming bowl of noodles and shrimp in front of her. Squatting near the door, peeling papaya, Mai looked petulant. Madame Thuong said, Ne t'inquiète pas, je vais bien prendre soin de toi. I will take care of you. This baby will take care of Vo. When I die he will need someone to care for him and that is a son's responsibility. You must know this. It does not matter that I have been to Paris. It does not matter that I loved the Frenchmen. I have the same wish as all Vietnamese. To have at least one son and to die in his presence. Vo has this wish as well.

Madame Thuong had never said so much before. All of who she was seemed compressed into that time at the kitchen table. Ruth Anne thought, Yes. Take care of me. But this is my baby. You can't have my baby.

It's none of my business, Connie said, but how could you? How could you sleep with him?

He loves me.

Connie blew smoke toward the ceiling where the fan circled and vibrated. She said, Pardon me for living, honey, but I don't think they know what love is. They're not like us.

They're not like us.

She stayed in Connie's place until Mai was sent home to Cholon. Then she moved to Mai's room, a closet behind the tea shop. She washed the tea glasses three times a day but they remained permanently stained with tea—a topaz glaze. She did what Mai had done, serving the old men, running errands for Madame.

During the indolent afternoon—when the tea shop was shuttered and Madame went to play mah-jongg with her friend near the black market—Vo came to her room. She had made it her own. A window looked out on the inner yard where chickens roosted and rain pinged on the corrugated roof of the shed. She had made a curtain for the window from Connie's skirts shot through with gold threads. Those afternoons the light might be sharply gold if the sun were shining or it might be cottony, cloudy. Light did not matter to Vo. She would welcome him into the little room and he would lie down on her cot under mosquito netting. They did not undress. She would read to him. She would whisper the French stories or the American stories into his ear as he lay there, his hand on her breast. Her breasts had swollen. After the story he knelt over her; he unbuttoned her shirt. She never closed her eyes. She wanted to see the wonder on his face. His hair would fall over his eyes. He slipped her black pants down and laid them at the foot of the bed. He had to see her first and that meant touching her as if to shape her flesh. Breasts, stomach, flanks, knees, toes. He always returned to her face. The kiss. The kiss that trailed all over her body.

Afterward they would doze, their arms around each other. Sweating in the heat. Slick with sweat.

Later when Madame presided at the counter, selling cigarettes to the evening crowd, they might walk to the pagoda. They might buy a bag of dried strawberries or a slice of melon. She guided him across the streets. The smell of garlic and lemon grass and cabbage and fish sauce mingled in the night. The smell of charcoal fires. Life was lived on the sidewalk. Women cooking. A man with a motorcycle engine torn apart on a cloth tarp, his wrenches greasy. Children, children everywhere.

On such a night in April they came upon a crowd near the pagoda. She did not see it coming and she was afraid and she put her hand on his arm and said, Stop.

What is it?

I can't tell.

Let's see.

She put out her arm and he placed his hand on it. He bobbed his head as if he might be able to see if he strained. About the crowd there was an audible hush, an expectancy. They wormed their way up a staircase at the pagoda. Below, the crowd was one. A circle. The circle parted for a car. A gray Buick. She could see the plush gray seats—they were that close. A Buddhist nun dressed in gray cotton robes emerged from the Buick. She was young. With a shaved head and smooth skin. Resolutely she walked to the sidewalk in the center of the circle. Two nuns accompanied her, older women. They were crying. One of them went back to the Buick and opened the trunk with a key and took out a plastic jug. It was quiet; you could hear the trunk pop open. She left the trunk lid up. A singular wail cut into the evening. Then another.

What is it? Vo said. What is it?

She squeezed his hand. She told him what she saw.

I've heard of her. She is a poet. She feeds the poor.

The nun seized the plastic jug and poured the gasoline over her head. She kept her eyes closed but she poured it over her head and Vo sniffed and said, Petrol, and Ruth Anne said, Oui. She could not pour out all of the gasoline. She needed help and one of the older nuns helped. She tipped the jug nearly upside down and poured the gasoline on her back. A stain spread charcoal dark against her light gray robe. People wept. She sat down and assumed the lotus position. She pulled a paper book of matches from her pocket. She lit one match and flames jerked into being.

Ruth Anne clung to Vo. She felt her stomach like a fist. Her throat ached. She whimpered. She cried out. She did not want to see but Vo said, Tell me. I have to know. A human being burns very fast, she said. Can you smell it? Can you?

Later he came to her room and said, I wanted to cry. But a blind man cannot cry.

They did not make love for weeks after that. All desire went the way of clouds. Thinning into atmosphere.

She was afraid the baby might be scarred by what they had seen. She had heard of such things. But Vo said, That is superstition. I expect you to be beyond superstition.

Vo came to her room and wanted to teach her what little he had learned about the new Buddhism. In 1966, on the full-moon day in February, the Order of Interbeing was established. The ancient precepts were rewritten for their time. He had committed them to memory.

Do not be idolatrous about or bound to any doctrine, theory, or ideology, even Buddhist ones. Buddhist systems of thought are guides, not absolute truths.

Do not avoid contact with suffering or close your eyes before suffering. Do not lose awareness of the existence of suffering in the life of the world. Find ways to be with those who are suffering, including personal contact, images, and sound. By such means, awaken yourself—

I can't listen to this, she said, pacing three steps, bed to window.

Why not?

I am Catholic, Vo. Catholic. You are Catholic!

I go to Mass for my mother. You say this yourself. She has been unduly influenced by the French.

Stop! She put her hands over her ears. I just can't hear about other religions.

Crestfallen, he said, I hoped we could talk about it.

No! Please go! Please let me alone for a little while.

Don't you see? That nun sacrificed herself to end the war.

I am sorry about it. Believe me. But that moment will harm the baby. I can't think about that nun. I want to erase that. I never want to think about her again.

There are more precepts. Someday you'll want to know.

I never will. Never.

# 19

Remembering the burning nun rendered her weak, leaden, the next morning.

She met the girls at breakfast and guided them to the meditation room, grateful that they had agreed not to speak until after the sit. Thank God for small favors, her mother used to say. Not without irony.

Fifteen women sat in an oval. Some on cushions, some in chairs, some against the wall nesting in blankets. The twenty minutes crept along. By the time Jill tapped the gong to signal the end, she was ashamed of all the thoughts she could not resist. Three hours on a paved highway, back and forth, the lake to Tarkington. The driving that stayed in her bones. The trucks that even in sleep swerved beside her. The voice on the answering machine. Each question or worry or transparency of memory was inspected thoroughly, greedily. Jill would have said she was too mental.

Afterward they made their way to Aunt Teensy's room where she lay in a delicate twisted heap, her hair flattened against her skull. Laurel went to her bedside and took her hand and kissed her cheek.

This is my friend, Oceana.

Hello, there, Aunt Teensy said. She patted Laurel's hand and said, It's good to have a friend. And, Tell me what happened to you. You're all banged up.

An accident, Laurel said.

They stood around her bed and talked. Of Johnny. Of weather. Of the cardinals at the feeder. Oceana knew something about cardinals and she told about the soft lining of their nests. Made of fine rootlets. Dog hair. Human hair. Aunt Teensy perked up for that. But after a while they did not have much to say. Ruth Anne snatched at graceful exit lines—she had not gotten used to ending the visits—but before she could speak, Rosa stepped in and said, Time for a bath.

Rosa, I need a few minutes with my great-niece. Laurel. You stay. Now go, you two, I need to speak with Laurel.

In the hall, Oceana said, She's a handful.

You said it.

Laurel slipped into the hallway and said, I need your help, Mom— What's up?

She's giving me this box. A box of beaded bags. She says I admired them once. She had them hanging in her bedroom. I don't—really—remember—

Ruth Anne went into the closet. Into the bitter of the mothballs. The sweet cedar. As if she had never been so deep into the closet before. She tugged the storage box from its depths.

Rosa poked her head in. Ready?

Don't open them now, Aunt Teensy said, waving them out. They're yours.

Laurel kissed her cheek again and said, Thank you. Incredulously.

Ruth Anne had come into brief and astonishing possession of the letters and she wanted to read them and in her thoughts she tripped ahead to a midnight raid on the box. She plotted to be the first to read the letters. They're my letters, her heart pounded. At the hatch of the Tercel they opened the box. The beaded bags seemed anachronistic: in sharp contrast to Laurel in her workout clothes and the natural setting, cypresses and sunlight.

She gave me something, Laurel said.

Those'll come in handy in New Orleans, Oceana said. Maybe we'll get into vintage clothes. You know. Little black hats with veils.

They laughed.

It's nice of her. It really is.

Ruefully, Ruth Anne said, Maybe she's turning over a new leaf.

You know what she said, Mom?

What, sweetheart?

She said she always wanted to buy a blue tugboat and be a nomad on the lake. She said, Do whatever you really want. Whatever makes you happy. No matter what—

~

That night she did not know where the day had gone.

There was no message from Tin. Her heart called his name but there was no message.

They had driven to Pier Cove and walked down the steep stairs to the beach. Oceana struggled with her cast and crutches but she insisted she wanted to be there. Clouds built up in ominous sheets across the lake toward Chicago. Big winds blew in. They had walked first against the wind and then with it, as far as they could go, southerly. The wind kept them from talking and they walked as if they were strangers, meandering near the surf and then away, with gulls riding the wind above them. Ruth Anne could not imagine Aunt Teensy on that blue tugboat and it was a new piece of the puzzle and it made her wonder what else she might not know. What dreams lay unexpressed. What wishes withered. Then, they had lunch at a café in South Haven, with talk of jobs they might pursue in New Orleans. She told them about working at the library. How she might within one hour look up the tools of a painter's trade and the history of World War I and the way rivers work. They stopped at a junk shop near Ganges where wrought-iron fence sections lay like headstones propped on truck engines. Salvaged church doors weathered against a barn wall. The girls wanted to buy something. Anything. They decided on a rusted section of wrought-iron fence for Johnny. Laurel said, He'll plant a vine on it. Ruth Anne willed there to be a message upon their return to the monastery; in the next breath, she thought, That might have been all. That day on the beach. At the Mexican place. The end of it. The beginning and the end. She imagined keeping Tin a secret until she was very old. What would it all matter when they were old?

In her room alone, after a nearly silent supper among the demure nuns, the rain began. She thought that the rain would let up and she did not undress. She did not get into bed as she might have any other night. She waited. For this she was patient. For a message from Tin and the news of herself the letters would bring. She tingled with deception. She was sorry to be deceiving Laurel but Laurel might not discover those letters for years. She might sell the beaded bags to a dealer in New Orleans and the letters might become anonymous history. Years hence, someone might come across them in a mildewy junk shop. They would be a curiosity. She drifted, imagining this. Time did not pass as usual; she was not that aware of time.

A knock at the door startled her. Laurel said, Mom?

She opened the door. She whispered, Are you all right?

Laurel fell into her arms. They shut the door and she did not know why they whispered, but they did.

Laurel was dressed in her PJs and she had taken a shower and Oceana had helped her tie up a fresh sling.

She said, I want Dad.

Why don't you give him a call?

I want to go home.

We will. We will.

In the morning?

Ruth Anne hesitated. The Vietnamese Mass where Tin might or might not be—that's all that kept her from saying yes.

I want to see Dad.

Ruth Anne kicked off her sandals and said, Come and sit down with me. They settled upon the bed cross-legged. The rain hit the window in metallic rushes. A freight train passed by, whistling.

Laurel said, I'm sorry. I'm sorry to be so much trouble.

You're not—

This is trouble, Mom. If there ever was.

All right.

Laurel hung her head. With her good hand she reached for Ruth Anne. Her hand was small and the nails squared. She knew that hand. Laurel glanced up teary-eyed. She said, It was so—so—scary. She rocked as she talked, her face contorted. They had on these stupid masks. I don't even know how many there were. It happened so fast. They were laughing, Mom. Laughing. But they were afraid. Oh, you could tell, you could tell they were afraid of what they were doing. The way they sounded. Nervous, like. They smelled awful. Like motor oil and stale beer. I thought we were going to die. I really thought we were going to die. It didn't hurt at first. There was just—just the impact. They said terrible things. The worst things.

The voice on the machine whispered into Ruth Anne's ear.

What's wrong with people? What's wrong with them? Why would

anyone want to hurt us? We would never hurt anyone. You know we wouldn't—

Ruth Anne squeezed her hand. Come here. Come here, she said. She took her in her arms and Laurel shivered and wheezed.

I was afraid they might—you know—rape us. She nearly choked, crying. Her face grew red, membranous, as if she were turned inside out. Wounded. She did not look like herself, her downy beautiful Laurel. And there were so many, Mom, so many—

# 20

A fine drizzle came down all Sunday morning, like a mild headache. At lunch Laurel said, Maybe the rain'll stop later. After your Mass in Cortland.

That one remark tipped the scale: she would go, after all. In spite of her fatigue and Laurel's wish to see Johnny. Maybe it will, she said. As if not much mattered; as if she did not stand to gain or lose by going to Mass in Cortland. They packed up everything and said goodbye to Aunt Teensy. To Jill. To Rosa.

Down the block from the church in Cortland, Ruth Anne said, Sure you don't want to go?

I'm sure, Laurel said. They stood out on the sidewalk in the drizzle under umbrellas. See that library?

I used to work there a long time ago. Before you were born.

The lights are on. We'll go over there and chill out. We'll meet you back here in—an hour?

An hour. Yes. Here's the key to the car, in case you want to come back. She wanted to show them the limestone pillar carved with wheat sheaves. But after, when the rain had stopped. She had not been to Mass for a week and she wanted to lose herself in its joy.

She was almost late. Recessed lighting cast bright shining splotches on the mosaic of the foyer. The pews were not filled but she had not expected that they would be. The priest and two children—a boy and a girl—waited at the rear of the church for the procession to the altar. The girl carried the metal cross and wore a sports T-shirt that said A GIRL'S PLACE IS ON THE FIELD. She had wanted to be an altar girl when she was a child but the very phrase—altar girl—was unheard of.

What one generation is forbidden, another can disdain; Laurel had no interest in it. She took a seat near the back on the left-hand side, her habitual side. She knelt and crossed herself and thought, Be here. Please—

She scanned the pews and did not see him but she did not know if she would recognize him from behind. Then he turned around. In the first row. He turned around and smiled. Candles flickered at the altar. It was too late to change seats and she was not sure she would have if there were time. She felt shy. He touched the shoulder of the woman beside him and leaned and whispered to her. It was enough to know that they were here and they would experience Mass together. And after—what would happen after?

Tin spoke to the man beside him and then she knew: she recognized that tuft of white hair. The maroon windbreaker. I am Catholic but my father is Buddhist.

The Mass felt out of time. She remembered an essay by a man who had come back to church after twenty years away. He had written that the Mass was the longest-running performance art in history. Everywhere on the planet at any given moment there was a Mass celebrated. Jill would say, And everywhere on earth at any given moment there are people practicing meditation. People of many traditions. The peace greeting went on for a long time; people from the next row over came to her to shake her hand. To peer into her eyes. Did she imagine forgiveness like a current? Was forgiveness a human need? The naked girl in the famous photo running from napalm had forgiven the pilot who dropped the napalm. She gave a speech on Veteran's Day in Washington and the pilot went up and said, I am that man who hurt you, and she opened her arms to him. Ruth Anne went to communion thinking of the girl running naked on the road and the children beside her, all of them with open mouths, terror-riven. Laurel's face had been like the faces of those children when she said, Why would someone want to hurt us? She walked back from communion with the host melting in the quick warm taste of wine on her tongue, with the song, the music what she wanted to hear even if she did not understand the Vietnamese, and she felt his eyes on her.

Then it was over. With a blessing and instructions in Vietnamese to serve the Lord and one another. It was over. The rain had stopped and

wafers of sunlight shone here and there on the maple pews and hardwood floor.

She stood alone at the back of the church beside a bank of lit votive
candles in red glass cups. They came from the front row, after everyone
else had funneled out into the sunlight. She remembered that first time.
In the foyer of the Cathedral in Saigon. Vo tall and slim, still boyish, not
quite seventeen. With his black hair in an unkempt wave across his forehead. His chin squared. His skin lustrous against his white rayon shirt.
How do you like Saigon? I haven't seen much of Saigon. That will have
to change. She waited. His white cane like a compass before him. The
woman Tin would marry—Lee Ann—wore white high heels and a
sleeveless polka-dot dress. She greeted Ruth Anne encouragingly, with
a womanly rapport. She did not wonder but a moment why he had not
e-mailed. Even as the question arose she answered it: he had not wanted
the meeting to be planned. He wanted to chance it. And he wanted the
visit controlled, an after-Mass chat. Her intuition said, He's unsure too.
About what's next.

We meet again, Tin said, happily. He took her hand.

Miss Ruth Anne, Vo said. He offered his free hand and she cleaved
to it.

Vo.

We are meeting just as we did. The first time.

Yes, I thought of that.

He said, I had to come to church to meet you. It was his joke and
everyone smiled.

I have many memories, Vo said, hearing your voice. He carried a
leather pouch over his shoulder and he reached into the pouch and
brought out a paperback book. This is for you.

She turned the book over. *The Tale of Kieu.*

This is a new translation, Vo said. My son has read it to me. I want
you to have it. I always wanted you to know the entire story of Kieu.

Thank you.

Let's go outside, Tin said. It's a sunny day now.

They made their way through the foyer where the churchgoers lingered, talking. In ruffled dresses and bow ties, small children toddled
and threaded among the grown-ups. Outside, the rain evaporated from

the puddles, steaming. They stood beside the pillar carved with wheat sheaves.

Vo said, My wife—

Ruth Anne said, Yes?

She would not understand. I will not meet you again.

I understand. She said that but she thought, They have their own rules of engagement. Their tussles I will never know about. I don't need to know about that.

Looking up to him, puzzled, Lee Ann said, But the wedding. She'll come to the wedding, of course.

Ruth Anne said, If you want me to.

Tin said, Oh—we'll see about that. My father's wife—she is the boss of our family.

Vo said, The wedding—that might not be possible.

Ruth Anne said to Tin, I have the letters. Looking into his eyes made her nearly dizzy.

Ah, the letters!

Half a block away she saw Laurel getting into the car. Oceana shunted her crutches into the back seat.

Tin checked his watch. We have to go now. You will e-mail me, won't you? About the letters?

She clutched the book, *The Tale of Kieu*. Of course I will. I'll e-mail you. Laurel's moving to New Orleans and I'll be in New Orleans for a while. Maybe a few weeks.

Go to Pho Tau Bay while you're there. They have the best Vietnamese food. The very best.

Banh xeo, Vo said. Have banh xeo. You made banh xeo for me. Do you remember that?

I do.

Vo handed his white cane to Tin. He reached for her. They held each other's hands. Miss Ruth Anne—

Yes?

He let go of her hands and brought his together and shook his head. Too many things crowd together when I think of what I would like to say.

She said, I feel the same.

They parted. She walked to the Tercel, a startled charge throughout her body. Pangs of wanting to go back. Pangs of wanting to say more. To know more.

She slipped into the driver's seat, tucked the paperback book under the seat.

Laurel dangled the keys and said, Who was that you were talking to?

Children played a game of chase or tag in front of the church. They had not tarried. They were gone. Clouds sped over and blue sky was revealed again; the lake would be deep blue. She took the keys and stuck the ignition key in and sighed. She closed her eyes. Her heart beat hard.

Your brother, Ruth Anne said. That's your brother.

# 21

Johnny cleaned like a madman.

He went room to room and threw out clutter and scrubbed down baseboards and swiped the cobwebs from the corners with a broom. He swept and ran the vacuum and mopped on his hands and knees with rags he found neatly folded in the basement. Moxie wisely slept through it. The scouring powder flew. Windows shined, inside and out. That was the first step.

Every once in a while he would telephone Mairead in the big kitchen. He'd say, How's it going? And she always said, So far, so good. He had given her free rein for the day and she liked that. Bossy as she was. He did not know how long Mairead would be there and that did not matter to him. She no longer agitated him. That night they walked on the golf course in the moonlight had perplexed him. That burn when he touched her. But now he could think, Sweet bottom. Or, She sure smells good. Or, I like the way she fillets a fish. But that was as far as it went. Other things were on his mind.

Once the house was clean he showered and felt the satisfaction of grime going down the drain. The mustache would come off later and keeping it off would be SOP until he caught them. He had worn a mustache for a long time and Ruth Anne loved his mustache but he had seen for himself in mirrors how it gleamed in the dark.

The day before, he had gone to the hole-in-the-wall storefront where they sold police gear. He did not need much. Fiberglass handcuffs and a window punch. At a farm store he bought a compact cattle prod the size of a cell phone. He would exercise control. Oh, he wanted to kill them. Every time he thought of Laurel lying there in the hospital bed with fresh stitches on her shaved head, he wanted to kill them. But he knew he would not. He did not want to suffer the consequences. He might settle for hurting them. He thought of toe-poppers. Designed to maim, not kill. As a civilian he did not own a gun and he never would. He had a special knife, a K-Bar, and he had to sharpen it later if he could lay hands on his whetstone. They had all had special knives on the mountain. Gerber daggers. Bowie knives. Even the techs at the site who had been sanitized carried knives. One tech carried a secret pistol for a while but it had been taken away from him. Near the end the techs were issued M-16s but only a couple knew what to do with an M-16. Someone bent the rules. That's what rules were for so far as Johnny had been concerned. Bend them until they break. He had given Jabber a knife. And Jabber had died with that knife in his hand. He opened a drawer in his dresser and made sure the handcuffs and the window punch and the cattle prod were still there. He picked up the cattle prod and thought about how handy it seemed. He had heard a story on the radio about torture and the big business of the accoutrements of torture. He took the K-Bar with its blood gutter downstairs and laid it on the kitchen table.

He opened a beer. Mox lay down in the doorway. It was a quiet afternoon, Sunday. It suited him to have a day he could count on to be slow. Mairead intended to entice the vegetarians in. She wouldn't be there in the long run. She had never stayed anywhere more than six months or so; she wore out a place pretty fast. You could look at it that way. Her stories were entertaining, but would you want to end up as one of her stories? He wanted constancy and Ruth Anne had given him that and he thought she might again.

He drank the beer and got out Ruth Anne's cycling map of the county, printed on water-resistant paper that felt almost as durable as plastic. His Area of Operations. The ice-cream stands and frozen custards were marked on the map with waffle cones. He opened the yellow pages to Churches. It was not hard to guess which churches would never be targeted. You had to have lived under a rock not to know. He made a guess at which ones might be next. He marked them with a ballpoint pen. The Quaker Meeting House. Another Episcopal church in a town called Riley. The Presbyterians. But there were two kinds of Presbyterian and he did not know which one took the hard line. He marked both Presbyterian churches.

About six o'clock he whistled for Moxie and they went for a walk in the band of woods on the edge of campus, through the hardwood trees on a curving path mulched with sugar-brown bark. Moxie ran ahead, sniffing out whatever he dreamed of, barking now and again as if to urge Johnny onward. They walked the perimeter of the campus. He remembered rules he had not thought about in years and years. Don't ever return home the same way you came. Don't cross a river by a regular ford. Don't stand up when the enemy's coming at you. Let the enemy come until he's almost close enough to touch. He conjured up involuntarily the times he had sat on the cliff with Jabber and talked about their girls and home. They had talked about what they missed the most. The red poppies flowed in the valley below. There was disagreement about whether they were supposed to be in Laos. Ambassadors and the brass and the CIA disagreed. But no one really cared about what would happen to the men. They said they were not expendable, but that was just talk. He could still remember that startled look on Jabber's face. I'm going to die, that look said. How could I die so soon? Jabber's name was probably not on the wall. All of the techs had been issued civilian papers and fake corporate IDs. They were not really military anymore. Johnny had not been to the wall and he had no intention of going. History was not where he wanted to be. He wanted to plant his trees and catch whoever hurt Laurel and shoot some hoops with Tuck and get through the summer without Ruthie. He had the feeling that fall would bring a kind of peace. Fall was a good season, with the hardwoods in glory. The students coming back with the best of intentions. And the stagnant summer air would dissipate.

When he and Mox came to the end of the trail not far from the river they cut across the campus, across quads of red-brick pavers where fountains were dry in summer, across grassy knolls with commemorative stones attesting to one class or another's having been there. He did not know what went on in college. It might be a little like listening to NPR. There was not much traffic on the town streets once they left the campus. He and Mox passed by St. Joan's and Father Carroll was out in the rectory yard, barbecuing a chicken. Johnny did not wave when Father Carroll did. You prick.

He said, That felt good, didn't it, Mox, when they approached the cinder drive. The Tercel was parked near the house at the edge of the red cannas and Moxie recognized the car and went bounding up. From that angle, Johnny could see how much Moxie favored his right hind leg and he felt for him.

So they were home. He would not sharpen the K-Bar. He would come into the kitchen and casually slip the knife into a drawer and he would not get it out again until after they left for New Orleans.

Ruth Anne must have been looking out the window. She came down the cinder drive. She looked good to him in spite of the haircut. She had on cigarette pants with a sharp crease and a blouse he had always liked on her. As she drew near he was able to see the pinched look on her face. A worried look. He never wanted to worry Ruth Anne. He said, Hey, hon. And he opened his arms and she slipped in there, where she fit.

She said, Johnny, we have to talk. Could we go out somewhere?

It's not about the knife on the table, is it?

No, it's not.

What about the girls?

Just us, Johnny. Please.

Let's go to Panos', he said. I could use a gyro.


You have to tell Dad.

Laurel had said that over and over driving home from Michigan. Ruth Anne had recounted the story of Vo and Tin from beginning to end. They ran into rain again on I-94 and she gripped the steering wheel tightly to keep from blowing into semis. The wipers banged against the windshield. Dense waves of rain scuttled across the highway and once they had to pull into a truck stop and wait inside among the truckers, drinking coffee.

You have to tell Dad. I can't believe he doesn't know. I can't believe I didn't know. How could you? She was not accusing her; she was genuinely curious.

I can understand why, Oceana said. The people you love are the hardest to tell the truth to. You have to ask, Why would you? Is it going to do some good?

About those beaded bags—there's one in the bottom where she put my letters from then. Technically—I know they're yours.

She probably forgot the letters were in there—

I'm not so sure about that. By that she meant that she did not trust Aunt Teensy and wasn't sure she ever would. She might have been feeling generous or she might have been trying to upset Ruth Anne by way of Laurel.

You can *have* the letters. But I have to know what's in them. If *he* can know, I want to know. Laurel had not said Tin's name. The rain slapped against the window of their truck stop booth. She said, What's going to happen with you two? Where do you go from here?

I don't know. I don't want to push. I don't want to. It comes down to whether we like each other, doesn't it? We have nothing to go on but that.

Laurel leaned across the table, confidentially. Her eyes rapt. I have to meet him. Even if that's all we do. What if I'd met him some other way and didn't know?

And, You have to tell Dad.

Johnny did not cook Greek and Panos did. Panos owned the entire careworn brownstone across from the courthouse. From the bar you could see the courthouse out a picture window. At night it was lit up and limestone-white, a Neoclassic confection with Corinthian capitals, turrets, and Tecumseh himself emerging from the pediment above the twelve-foot walnut doors. The same courthouse where they had gone arm in arm to buy a marriage license.

They waited for a table at the bar and Johnny ordered a gin-and-tonic but Ruth Anne said no. She wanted to have a clear head and she did not want whatever she felt or said to be distorted. She sipped a virgin margarita.

They talked about Lieutenant Travaglini. He had called Brambles twice. If they caught whoever desecrated the churches the girls might be required to come back and identify them. Johnny wasn't sure. She told him about the towns they stopped in and the tavern where they had pea soup and Scottish ale and the meditation among the sisters at Our Lady of Holy Mysteries. He had taken care with his clothes—ironed khakis and a white polo shirt—and Ruth Anne saw that it was a special occasion for him and she was unstrung with gentle urges, secretive urges. She wanted to go for a walk and slip her hand in his rear pocket and forget telling the truth.

Laurel's afraid, Ruth Anne said.

Hell, yes.

She never used to be afraid of anything.

That's one reason why this happened.

They watched a couple in love at a nearby table, holding hands. Candlelight like something spilled.

I've missed you, she said.

Me, too. He met her eyes and said, Has Teense been difficult?

She's been herself.

You're all she's got.

I'll be relieved when she goes.

Ruthie.

That's the truth. You don't think I'm a bad person to think that, do you?

I don't think you're a bad person. I think you're the best person. I never want to be that alone, he said.

I hope you never are.

You'll never be. He took her hand and brought it to his mouth and kissed her palm.

You're a sweetheart. She understood that she was about to give up power. The truth pressed against her back. Shoving her about.

Finally Johnny said, So what's on your mind? He patted her thigh.

This'll be hard, she said.

What's that?

I have to tell you a story that's hard to tell.

Tell me.

During the war I fell in love with someone.

When during the war?

While I was in Saigon.

Wait a minute, Ruthie.

I have to tell.

You're getting into something I don't want to get into.

At the courthouse an Indian couple sat beside a fountain, watching their baby walk his way around the fountain's outer rim. His mother wore a red sari. Barefooted, he was learning to walk and still needed to hang on. Every third step or so he would pat the concrete and laugh. Ruth Anne wanted to be down on the street, in the summer dusk. She wanted to be anywhere but at Panos' telling her story.

It's not easy, saying what I have to say.

All right. All right. Why didn't you ever tell me?

As if she would. As if whatever happened then could be discussed.

Was it someone I knew?

No, not that.

Don't tell me he's contacted you.

In a way.

Johnny drank from his gin-and-tonic. His glance tracked over the bar, the television tuned to a baseball game. Panos himself swaggered out of the kitchen, wiping his hands on a blue towel. He waved to Johnny and Johnny waved back but not demonstratively, as if to say, Not now, Panos. Don't come over here now. He said, Tell me. Go on, tell me. He sounded grim. He ducked his head and she regretted coming out with it in public.

This part's hard to say. I've struggled with it day and night.

Spit it out.

I had a child there—

He closed his eyes and pressed his fingers to his temples. Wait, wait—

He's thirty years old. And he has contacted me.

The bones of her story were laid bare. He swung his head and that motion took forever—it was agony and her heart quickened—and she knew his head would turn over and over again in memory and he faced her squarely and above his right shoulder hovered a tray of salads being presented lavishly to a table and music wafted from the kitchen—Latin rhythms—and in his eyes and in the ashen way his face fell she could tell that he fleshed out everything in a moment—years, sex, the disconsolate longing for a second baby, lies, sins of omission, her spells when he would hold her hand and pour the whiskey they reserved for grief or emergencies.

What're you telling me?

I've lied, she whispered. All this time, I've lied.

Let's get out of here. He jerked out his wallet and flattened three five-dollar bills on the bar.

Out on the street that was cobbled and dappled with lamplight Johnny charged ahead of her. It was not full dark yet. He turned at the corner and said, Let's walk. They set foot in the direction of the pedestrian bridge. A delicate tube of neon light ran the length of the girder and it zipped from one color to the next, red and blue and yellow and purple, and it was festive and the bridge was an outpost for young people who had no place else to go. They skateboarded wildly above the river. The river looked black and oily. A summer wind from two directions crosshatched above the river.

Wait up, she called.

He turned abruptly and grabbed her arm. Don't ever tell me what to do.

He let go with a twist and pushed on to mid-bridge and peered over and when she got to him he said, You're not who I thought you were. That's what it comes down to.

That might be true.

I can't believe what you're telling me, he said. And he began to weep.

# 22

You get out, Johnny said. I'm not coming back to the house until you're gone.

Where will you be?

He nodded up the hill. It won't be the first time I've slept up there.

Johnny—

Just get out. He leaned across her and opened the truck door and thrust it open. Go on.

She got out of the pickup and stood in the cinder drive, watching him go. A vibration as given as breath surrounded her: cicadas and crickets and katydids. Brambles' big kitchen was lit up. Some song scalloped in the trees like party lights. It took her a minute to make it out: "If Not for You." Mairead's Volvo was the only car left in the lot. Johnny parked right next to it. The sky was midnight blue, still not quite dark. A rare pink moon had risen while they talked on the pedestrian bridge and she knew that they both had seen it but neither had the heart to say, Look at the moon. Moxie's collar and tags jingled and he slipped into place beside her. She reached down and petted him and said, I'm sick it hurts so bad. I'm sick.

Inside, she found the girls in the kitchen, drinking V8 juice, a string of commercials on TV.

Laurel punched the remote to mute the TV and said, What happened?

It's pretty bad.

What did he say?

He says he's not coming back to the house until we're gone. Until I'm gone.

I'll go talk to him.

Don't.

I want to.

You can't imagine how bad it was.

Oceana limped over to the counter and opened a drawer and took out a clean tea towel and wet it at the tap with cool water. She handed it to Ruth Anne and said, Put this on your eyes. Your eyes are puffy.

Ruth Anne said, I don't blame him. I don't blame him. She tipped up her face and closed her eyes and laid the folded tea towel over them. She said, We have to go. Would you want to drive a little tonight? In the cool?

We can't drive.

I can drive.

Are you sure?

I'm sure.

It did not take a half-hour for them to prepare to leave. Laurel went up to say goodbye to Johnny while Ruth Anne waited in the Tercel. Oceana hunched over one crutch beside Ruth Anne's open window, smoking a cigarette. Mairead's Volvo was still there, a black lump against the birch trees. Lump of coal. What you get if you're not good. People did not tell those stories to children anymore, did they? She had heard them. She had always been told she might not be considered good enough. By God. Or Aunt Teensy, who was a branch of God. The high-and-mighty hand of God. And she had not been good. Definitely not. She had earned the highest grades in religion when she was a girl. Why was I born? To know, love, and serve God. What that meant when you were ten had to mean something different when you're fifty. Evolution creates more complex structures from less complex ones.

The screen door at the big kitchen banged. The moon lit up Laurel in her pastel T-shirt and workout shorts and when she settled into the passenger seat and strapped on the seat belt, she said, They were baking. She held up a produce bag of kiwis. They were baking kiwi tarts. That's all. He said be careful. Oceana stubbed out her cigarette on a garden stone and chucked her crutches into the back seat.

They entered the southerly tunnel of the trip. Driving purposefully felt good. They drove into the night with the windows rolled down, listening to talk radio until it pushed them into talking out the issues themselves, more sensibly than the wrathful callers. The girls were sensible and smart. Laurel would reach over and pat Ruth Anne's hand on the wheel and say, Are you all right? I'm not but that's okay, she'd say. Or, We'll be all right. She meant they, the girls. She did not think that she and Johnny would ever be all right. Second guesses wavered before her as she pressed on. Why did she have to tell? Did they have the sort of marriage where you had to tell? Johnny did not think so; that was clear. He held in abeyance all that had happened to him from the moment he nicked those morning glory seeds and left her to plant them in the spring of 1967. And she did not want to know. They had conspired to keep their secrets. You keep yours and I'll keep mine.

Second guesses drove her through rain showers and mountain passes in Kentucky. Finally she could not go another mile and she pulled into a motel with a blue neon VACANCY sign. The town was small. Even though it was the middle of the night there was no tight security, no Plexiglas window under which she had to slide her credit card. Just a fat, balding man, sleepy-eyed, in a tuxedo shirt. He offered to haul in their luggage and she let him.

In the fuzz of the motel-room darkness, as they lay in bed, she said, Saint Euphrasia lived around 400 A.D. She was a wealthy heiress. She was betrothed at the age of five, but as the wedding date grew near she decided to enter the convent and give all her money to the poor. She was stricken with the intense desire to know what the life she'd given up would've been like.

Oceana said, So what happened?

She went to work moving heavy rocks in a quarry.

So what's the lesson?

Laurel said, Hard labor suppresses second guesses?

Ruth Anne said, I wish it were that simple.

They slept past ten o'clock. She awakened feeling gritty with the road. What had happened with Johnny came back to her and she did not want to remember him weeping on the bridge. The girls needed her and she had to rally around them. She could not take back what she'd said. Even if she wanted to.

The second day was hot. Storm clouds gathered over the foothills to the east, but the sky above I-65 was blue-white and hard with sun. She would have welcomed rain at that point. Even with the A/C on she wanted a wet towel over her shoulders and drinking water handy. They got out what she called her documentation. *The Tale of Kieu.* The six letters. The photograph in front of the lotus screen.

You both look so young, Laurel said.

I guess we were. I was nineteen when we met. He was not quite seventeen.

From the back seat Oceana said, Did you ever think about an abortion?

Briefly. But it was illegal and you heard all the scary stories. And you had to know somebody who knew somebody. Having a baby felt natural. Although that was scary too. You do get scared as the time draws near. You do.

Did it hurt like you thought it would?

God—don't get me started on that.

But you got pregnant again—

Your dad and I wanted babies in the worst way.

I still don't get it—why you didn't come home.

A kind of passivity just—came over me. I had no one to come home to.

How can you visit Aunt Teensy? How can you forget all that?

I don't exactly forget. I just look at how helpless she is and I want to do the right thing. I think I do it for me, not her. She thought, Abandonment runs in families. What she did to me, I did to Tin. But she could not say that out loud. She could not use that word. Listen. Read to me from *The Tale of Kieu.*

She did not believe that she could answer questions all the way to New Orleans. Laurel had a strong reading voice. She opened the paperback book and started at the beginning.

> *A hundred years—in this life span on earth*
> *Talent and destiny are apt to feud.*
> *You must go through a play of ebb and flow*
> *And watch such things as make you sick at heart.*
> *Is it so strange that losses balance gains?*
> *Blue Heaven's wont to strike a rose from spite.*
> *By lamplight turn these scented leaves and read*
> *A tale of love recorded in old books.*

No one mentioned the letters. Ruth Anne wanted desperately to see the letters before anyone else, before she laid the story open. She did not remember what she had written.

Laurel did not mind reading. They had read most of the poem by nightfall. The story of the beauty Kieu. How she fell in love with the young scholar. In spite of her love for the scholar she placed chastity above all else. They struggled with their passion. Love nearly turns to shame but they are separated by fate—a death in his family. They swear an oath to love forever. Meanwhile, false charges are brought against Kieu's family and she is forced to barter herself to free them. She's matched and married to a pimp. They take a long journey and she is faced with his wife who runs the brothel. She calls her strumpet. You merest chit, she says, do you already rut? She teaches her the craft of prostitution. She's forced to give herself to all the men who crave her.

Oceana said, Why do you think he gave you this?

It's a story he told me parts of. But he didn't know it all. It's a popular story to Vietnamese.

It's a very sad story, Laurel said.

I think it has a happy ending.

They were crossing the Tennessee–Alabama state line. Magnolias on a billboard welcomed them. She said again, I think it has a happy ending. But she kept hearing Johnny's voice. Get out. Go on. Johnny's weeping. She said, I'm not sure what it cost her. I'm not sure about that.

# 23

Johnny was drunk, atop the red caboose at the River County Living History Museum.

With the moon like a clamp above the woods. The moon keeps the sky from falling. He had stopped at the Monon Tavern, across the county line, an establishment far enough from home that he figured he would not run into anyone he knew. He did not want to be a menace to society driving home; after two bourbons he decided to buy a liter and drink in his truck in a place he thought it wouldn't matter if he spent the night. In the pickup's lockbox he kept a sleeping bag that smelled like Moxie and wood smoke. He had his wits about him.

The windmill creaked discordantly, though it was not a working windmill and the cord attaching the mill to the iron water pump beneath it had long ago been severed. The blades rotated in the wind for the hell of it. The living history village of Loyal was spread out below the caboose. The jail. A print shop. The doctor's house. On the ground beside the caboose was a school bell the size of a blue-ribbon pumpkin. Its splintered wooden yoke had been carved with the name Lee Porter and Johnny wondered, Was that a recent carving or from the 1800s? And why did it bother him if some antisocial kid had carved his name recently? If it had been carved in, say, 1875, by a boy who had climbed to the top of the schoolhouse and risked life and limb to carve his name— that seemed all right, a moment in history. A moment in history he could stomach. Not connected to him at all.

Porter, Porter. That had been Ruth Anne's name so long ago that he never thought about it. There were plenty of Porters. He had peered into the window of the round brood house by the light of a farmyard safety lamp. There in the nesting bins were calico chicken dolls. That had sent him into a fit of laughter. Laughter that felt as if it traveled acres, across State Highway 33 and over lush cornfields. A laugh that seemed to travel all the way to the Tippecanoe River. Or beyond. So far as he knew, there was nothing to stop a laugh or wind between here and Hudson Bay. He did not know he had a laugh in him, but there it was. He pictured Ontario to the north as watery, porous with lakes, and he could conjure the dishwasher he had learned that from: a kid who wanted to study infrared mapping. He had learned a few things here and there from them. Mairead arose like a sprite in the mental wreck that the bourbon had merely decelerated. There had to be a reason he liked her so much. A reason why he had been susceptible to her charms. But now he thought he had been crude and self-serving. He was the only one who knew; she didn't know. It was all in his mind. He did not care if he ever saw her again. Or any of them. He said that but did not entirely believe it. He wished he could run a restaurant by himself. Devoid of personalities and the need to get along. A person gets tired of cooperating. It seems like a bright idea when you're young but it wears on you. That dishwasher had been a good kid, though, and now he was a professor in Arkansas. He sent a Christmas card every year. Hudson Bay and even Ontario were places Johnny thought he'd never see, and that was all right. The white round barn glowed. No evil spirits there.

He was long past making sense.

Semis lunged on the highway. But there weren't many cars. It was a night that might have made you glad to be alive. Under other circumstances.

Then he would remember. Tin Tran. Vo Tran.

All the years they had been married felt like items he could handle, cards he could shuffle; he had seen only one side of each card; there was another side, another design that changed the game.

Headlights brushed across the museum proper, a low-slung building with a steel roof. Johnny stretched out flat atop the caboose, his head on his arms. He did not think there was a night watchman but he might have been wrong about that. No doubt he was breaking the law to be atop the caboose but man to man he thought anyone would cut him some slack, if the truth were told. The pickup came to a stop beside the Trail of Death Monument, granite stones honoring the Potawatomis who had been forced to march from there to Kansas in 1838. Whoever it was rolled down his window. Opened his door. Every sound came to Johnny clear and precise.

He recognized Tuck. His squat silhouette.

Tucker. Tucker. You asshole. He flailed his arms sitting up and the bottle of bourbon tumbled off the caboose. As if in slo-mo. Crashing against the school bell.

Fuck, Tuck. He felt the loss of the bourbon, the end of something: a decision would have to be made sooner than he wanted to make it. The wind had stopped, the windmill with it.

Tuck waddled over to the caboose. You're pissed. I can tell from here.

You smell that? See what you made me do.

I'm coming up.

Tuck climbed the ladder at the end of the caboose, whistling some patriotic song Johnny could not remember the words to. He was American but not a good American. He was Catholic but not a good Catholic. What had Stockdale said to them? You are Americans. With faith in God. Trust in one another. Devotion to your country. You will overcome. Stockdale would butt his head against the wall of his cell to keep from being used by the North Vietnamese. His face bruised and battered, he would not make a good example of humane treatment.

Johnny had not felt one of them. They would tumble into their cells bloody. But not broken. There was a tool of torture called a bridle bit. A one-inch metal tube wrapped in a bloody rag. That never happened to him. He ate sewer grass. He had a busted cheek was all and malaria. He had waited that out. By the time they put him near the officers he had already made up his mind to do whatever they wanted, sign whatever they wanted, say whatever they wanted. The Red Cross bus was waiting and the Americans escorted him. They were sorry now. He had heard Jane Fonda say she was sorry. Who would believe that?

Don't be so goddamn cheerful.

Tuck sat down and hung his stubby legs off the edge. Good view, he said.

How'd you find me?

It wasn't easy.

Then Johnny told him. He wished he had the bottle of bourbon during the telling. There were points where he could have shut up and taken a swig. But no. He just kept talking and his voice hoarse and bewildered over the farm implements sounded like an old man's. He was not quite telling it right; he sounded injured, innocent, and that was not all there was to it. He thought about a secretary at Ft. Benning he had formed a sweet weekend alliance with. The shape of her breasts. The pink indentation her bra made on her back. He could still remember that. The smell of her, part Jean Naté, part baby powder.

You were in prison.

We were all in prison. After he'd been captured he was not sorry he had done that; he was still not sorry.

Not Ruthie, sounds like.

She had talked too long about the books and reading to him. The urgency between them after a story. How young they were. She had talked too long and it might not have seemed too long to her, but to Johnny it was. He had asked too many questions, like picking at a scab.

After a little while, he had told Tuck all there was to say. In the sponge of quiet and sky and fields, he felt like an inconsequential being, a speck, and he thought that Tuck probably felt the same. There were noises but they sounded like a part of the quiet. Frogs in a pond. Dogs a half-mile away. Or wolves. They weren't too far from the wolf research station. A train somewhere.

I'm going to catch whoever hurt the girls.

And how are you going to do that?

I wasn't trained for nothing.

Johnny, man—

You don't think I should.

You're not a dangerous guy.

You have no idea. But he thought, You're right, I'm not. It was drunken bravado that made him say, You have no idea.

Don't do anything stupid.

Forget I said anything.

Tuck said, Change of subject. I've got news for you. I've got a problem.

What kind of problem?

I've been—pissing blood.

What the fuck?

I saw a uro yesterday. He's not sure what it is.

Jesus, Tuck.

I'm fifty-nine, Johnny.

Johnny didn't say anything. It didn't compute: blood and piss.

He wanted to be there for Tuck but it was hard to concentrate. Ruthie kept rearing up. She might be sleeping the sleep of the relieved, the unburdened. They had talked on the pedestrian bridge. The skateboarders careening not far away from their concrete bench. Her haircut made her look like someone else. Now he wondered about those years she waited. Plenty can happen to a woman alone. Especially those years with all the crap going on. Communes and other assorted wildness. They had exchanged three letters. Once they allowed that. His history required revision and he was not up to the task. He thought about arriving home. Hanoi to Lebanon to London. Then to the States. His old man coming for him. He was skinny, malnourished, with blisters on his skin, and his old man cried when he saw him. It was the only time he had seen his father cry. Driving to Michigan, his father had said, I've kept an eye on her. She's waited for you. And at the trailer he shoved off. He said, I have to see her. He left his father sitting in a recliner, his schipperke Midnight on his lap. Cigar smoke stale in the room. Winter howling outside. He borrowed the car and drove to Cortland where she lived above a flower shop. She was waiting: in her five-year-old shantung silk graduation dress. They set foot into their future together. What was done was done. Now he thought about her body even though this was not about the body. He had treated her like the virgin she had been before. A woman always deserves tenderness no matter what went before. But that was the start of it. Her lie.

Would you consider driving to Indy with me? There's an outpatient procedure I need. But I don't know about driving back after.

Whatever it takes, Tuck. Whatever.

Tuck extracted a rumpled joint from his shirt pocket. See this?

Where'd you get that?

I've been saving it for a special occasion.

# 24

In the *Gambit Weekly* they found a sublet over Nance's Beauty Bar on Magazine Street, an artist's flat. The tenant—a painter and sculptor with a swampy lilt in her voice—greeted them at the top of the stairs in leopard skin pants, a Bloody Mary in one hand, a hunk of celery in the other. The art was bad art, Ruth Anne determined. Droopy androgynous figures. But southern light poured through a bank of windows into a cheerful kitchen nook with a gingerbread-trimmed screen door. There were two double beds, one behind a velour drape, and she thought that the girls could have that one and she knew that impulse for what it was: a need to keep them out of sight if and when they were skin to skin. And Oceana could smoke her vile cigarettes on the balcony overlooking Magazine Street. The tenant planned to meet her parents at their cottage in Vermont and she only wanted someone who would keep the neighborhood riffraff out. It was not about the money. Moving in was easy. Red duffel, blue duffel. Ruth Anne's suitcase. The box of beaded bags. Groceries they purchased at a corner market near Tulane.

She thought, I'll stay two weeks, no more. They might be done with me before that. Or me with them. She cast a line of motherly want into the future: maybe it won't work out and they'll come back. The summer before flashed vividly in memory: the blue-green sky and Laurel going up the hill and sitting on the patio with Oceana and falling in love. That pink grid on her thighs. She wanted to go back there. To be different. To say, even reluctantly, if only for safekeeping, Yes, she can spend the night. No one had mentioned the Buddhist precepts and they had not taken their meditation cushions out of the hatchback. Ruth

Anne deep down thought that maybe a change of venue would disrupt their practice and she berated herself for it but she could not help it either. It was a thought she was willing to watch go by—ramshackle boat—without getting on board. She did not want to be mean-spirited and thinking that way might make her so.

She wanted more of Tin. All the way down the continent that subterranean wish eddied in her heart: to know him. And to be known. Being mean-spirited to anyone might interfere with that. You reap what you sow: what the girls called karma.

The first night she read the letters aloud. With the girls together on a brocade loveseat. Oceana's leg and cast outstretched. A candle giving off the odor of pralines. Traffic sizzling on the street below. She had wanted to be the first to read them and she had wanted to be alone, but curiosity won out. She opened the beaded envelope and laid the letters on the coffee table, according to date, starting with November 3, 1967. Her handwriting was loopy, girlish. The first one was an account of her travels and arriving at the French convent. The next mentioned Sister Michelle. Now she could read between the lines: she wanted Aunt Teensy to know that she was not the only one who had come to Vietnam to be near a loved one. She wrote about reading to a blind boy.

That's all you said?

That's all.

There was a pause of months between the letters. Then came the hardest one to write.

I don't know where Johnny is. You might hear before I do. You always told me I'd get in trouble. You always warned me. I'm going to have a baby. It's hard to write and tell you. I need your help and don't know what to do.

Did she answer?

She never answered.

The letter went on:

You're going to hate this part, but I have to let you know. I have to let you know what you'll be in for. He's Vietnamese. His mother's taking care of me. The same thing happened to her. She got in trouble and her father banished her. She's never seen her father since. But I don't have a father. My father wouldn't have banished me, would he? He wouldn't have wanted that. Please don't tell anyone. Please.

It sounds like you were upset when you wrote that.

I guess I was. I don't remember being upset.

Why not?

Ruth Anne carefully folded the letter and put it back in its onionskin airmail envelope. She laid her hands in her lap, her palms upturned. She felt the weight of secrets, how she had been permanently damaged by them. As if she'd carried a load of secrets all her life and the tumpline across her forehead had left a scar.

Mom?

You know what? I remember the light. I remember the look on Vo's face when we made love—

Here she paused. Made love. She felt through with being clinical. The way parents are. I'll be different, she implied; come home with me and I'll be honest through and through.

I remember that nun. The gasoline on her robe. But I can't honestly say what I felt then. It seems so long ago.

You must have been upset about Dad. Laurel encouraged her with her eyes. She wanted that to be true.

I must have been. But he had disappeared and he might have been dead and I was alive. I wanted Vo. He wanted me. That seemed to be the crucial thing. We waited all day for his mother to leave. It took forever for her to leave.

You didn't think it was a sin?

Oceana frowned, as if to say, *You* don't think it was a sin, do you?

*I* don't think that, Laurel was quick to say.

Ruth Anne said, That's all I'd ever been taught. But what we felt was powerful. That force won out. Oh, we still went to church. For Madame. I worked for her and cared for Vo while she went back and forth to Dalat to help her sister with the vegetable farm. Her sister had contracts with both sides. The VC and the Special Forces. They grew the biggest cabbages.

She took up the next letter and then the next and the next. There was nothing new in them. They struck her as superficial, the missives of a girl who had not begun to make meaning or tell the truth. The letters of an unfinished girl. Until the final letter. She read the first lines.

What you taught me wasn't right. I had to leave to find that out.

And then, I'm afraid. I'm afraid she'll take my baby. I'm afraid I'll give him to her.

The Internet café in the back of a newsstand around the corner opened at seven in the morning. Time in New Orleans was a jam, a sap, a butter. The night was slow to end and the day was slow to start. The empty cobblestone streets were wet with dew and the garbage had not been picked up yet. She might hear a tugboat horn on the river, almost like an animal call. At the Internet café she bought a card that would give her the best rates and she made the café home. Her seven-in-the-morning home. The boy at the counter said he believed in being gentle before noon; he slipped in a CD of New Age music while she settled into her booth with a latte in a mug. It would always be a harp she remembered from that time. Harp and the espresso and an expectancy like the rush of wings: what the girls expected from moving to New Orleans and what she hoped for as she wrote to Tin.

Tell me about growing up. Why did you become Catholic? What did your grandmother tell you about me?

I could've gotten into a lot of trouble growing up if not for my father. I was expected to care for him and I did. My grandmother made me wear a secret scapular even when it was not safe to go to church. It was not always safe. She remained uncommitted as long as she could. This is the story I am told. Of course I did not understand politics or history. I only wanted my lee-see at the new year. I only wanted my tamarind candy. Mrs. Ruth Anne, I did not think about you much. I had my grandmother and my father. We worked hard to survive. Many did not survive, as I'm sure you know.

What kind of trouble?

Some boys became thieves or beggars. I don't judge them. They did what they did to survive. Some took drugs. Many Amerasians have no fixed address. They are homeless. But you know, Mrs. Ruth Anne, children of mixed blood were not only an American problem. The French before you airlifted forty thousand children and their family members to France in the 1950s. All métis. All mixed-blood. French and Vietnamese.

The questions were hers. Hers alone. He did not write anything that would require a response from her. Each morning she had to take the initiative. To start anew. She wrote to him every morning. Some days he responded and some days he did not and when that happened she held her breath, thinking, Is that all? Is that all?

One day not far from Tulane they saw two young women strolling hand in hand in front of a Laundromat.

See, Oceana said. See.

Laurel quoted Gertrude Stein on Paris: It's not what France gives you that is important. It's what it doesn't take away. I feel like that here, she said. The Midwest takes too much away from me.

That night they went to a blues bar. A converted sugar mill with serpentine paths between the tables. A mahogany stage with an ornate portico. A twelve-string neon guitar blazed behind the musicians. Cigarette smoke hung like a low ceiling. Ruth Anne resented the price of her gin-and-tonic and she was not sure it was a place she wanted to be. But the girls seemed happy. The voice on the message machine faded day by day, little by little.

Look, Laurel said.

I can't believe it, Oceana said.

A perspiring trumpeter aimed his trumpet in the direction of a swaying monk in a saffron robe. His head was shaved and the blue stage lights shone on it, enameled it. Another man was by his side, a companion, but he was no monk. His shirt cuffs glittered with gold cuff links. He had slung an expensive briefcase over a chair and Ruth Anne thought, Politician. Or lawyer. The monk bobbed like a child discovering the blues. He laughed. Ruth Anne asked, What's he saying? Oceana said, He says it's good. The music's good. I'm going over there. I want to find out where we can connect with people who sit.

Laurel rang out, Yes, go!

Oceana took up her crutches.

Laurel leaned toward Ruth Anne and spoke over the music or into the music as if it were a strong wind. You'd never see that at home.

Chagrined, Ruth Anne said, I guess not. Defense of herself or the Midwest was lost. A half-formed spiral of mind. She eavesdropped on two women elbow-to-elbow at the next table. I'm on my barstool, I said to him, and I'm not getting off.

The singer was a brown-skinned woman with crooked teeth and when she sang it looked as if she chewed them. She wore a flowered dress. She would put down her microphone and laugh and with both hands she'd toss her hem, an abbreviated can-can.

Oceana waved a business card triumphantly.

Later, above Nance's Beauty Bar, in a rest that contained the ghostly beat of the blues, they shared a bottle of fizzy water and talked. She finally said, What does your meditation teacher say about your relationship?

When she was a little girl in India she heard stories about them cutting gay people open and filling their stomachs with stones and throwing them in the river.

Ruth Anne could not speak; she closed her eyes to ward off the image.

But now it's different. The precept is to refrain from sexual misconduct—

Oceana went to her duffel bag and found a dog-eared copy of *The Mind of Clover. Essays in Zen Buddhist Ethics.* She thumbed through the book and said, Read this chapter. This is a good chapter. She folded down the corner of the page and Ruth Anne handled the book as if it might conduct electricity. As if reading the book might be an unsettling from which she could not recuperate. The precepts were determined to find her. The book fit in her purse. She might or might not read it.

In the days to follow, the girls ventured out holding hands or kissing—a woo light, feminine—while waiting in line at a bakery or wishing each other luck at the interviews. Sister Michelle came back to her as she never had before—the soft smallness of her lips. Did she ever find a love who suited her?

She had not expected life to be different in New Orleans but it was. Tarkington was austere, an upright college town surrounded by soybean fields and cornfields and all the straight gravel roads that bisect the acreage. Ornament might be considered vain or trashy. In New Orleans she found herself drawn to the courtyards and the shops, the mirrors and bejeweled lamps and velvet pillows. The colors of the plantation shutters: years of paint over paint. The statue of Saint Joan, blindingly gilded. Banana blossoms. The wobbly moan of a bottle-blond woman in her sixties plunking at a keyboard for dollar bills the tourists grudgingly tossed in her keyboard case. Sometimes it made her feel old to be there with the girls; her bones ached; she wanted all the change to go away. To rewind the summer. She had learned more about herself in two months than she really wanted to know. Other times she let herself go into the fringe and glitter and effusive flowers. She had not planned to begin long-distance walking. But the city seemed to coax her street by street.

Four-in-the-morning fears about Johnny would awaken her. She might get up and start the day that soon, but not productively, just waiting for the Internet café to open. Remembering the last time she saw Johnny. Getting out of his pickup beside the black Volvo. The resigned sag of his shoulders. His loving voice turned to stone.

Did loss always accompany gain? Did it have to?

After the Internet café she made breakfast for them, coffee and juice and bagels or waffles. Oceana would drink her coffee and smoke on the balcony. In the morning sun that splashed into the kitchen nook, she and Laurel searched the newspapers for jobs or apartments or events they might want to take in: a private time. She wondered, Is this what it feels like to have two daughters and will I somewhere down the road see Oceana as a daughter? Daughter-in-law. She did not think that in her lifetime they would be legal. They had packed the postcard of the woman carrying the BRIDES OF SATAN poster at the lesbian wedding and they had stuck it on the fridge under a Boomtown Casino magnet. Her scowl got a bead on Ruth Anne whenever she went to the fridge.

By ten they were usually ready to face the day. She drove them to put in job applications and after a week, to job interviews, ranging from Audubon Park to the quiet end of the Vieux Carré. She might sit in Jackson Square among the street people and street musicians. She might park herself on a bench within sight of the statue of Joan of Arc. Her statues were all over the world. A woman warrior. There were contradictions inherent in the sainthood of a warrior. What did Oceana like to say? In the coming change of consciousness, contradictions will resolve themselves. Oceana wanted to eliminate boundaries. She was a proponent of what she called perennial philosophy. Aldous Huxley was one of her heroes. She said, Find the common threads in the mystical traditions. That sounded simple enough. Until you went to Mass and heard the teachings that shore up exclusivity. Who's in and who's out was always a religious question. The divorced, the homosexual, the unmarried living in sin, women who wanted to be priests instead of priests' handmaidens. Tribal people had no trouble finding scapegoats. When the nation of Judah was rebuilt, Jewish men and women were required to divorce and banish non-Jewish spouses from the land. Half-breed children were sent out with them. To die the death of aliens. It goes way back. Didn't Christ say, Come to me, all? All? When she could not abide her own arguments anymore, she read *The Tale of Kieu*. Or she might wander through antique shops if there were shops nearby. Window-shopping seemed to shut down some of what nagged at her. She furnished imaginary homes. She spent imaginary cash. Other voices—Johnny's and Madame Thuong's and Father Carroll's, and yes, even Laurel's and Oceana's and Tin's—could almost dwindle. After hours of interviews they might meet in a pastry shop and reconstitute the interviews. If they needed to prepare answers to questions, they practiced with each other. She dispensed advice and encouragement.

Late afternoons were hers alone. She went to the public library. A library was a whole entity. Everything—from the anatomy of the universe to a wing nut on the most superfluous human invention—under the same roof, in the same place. All knowledge organized and available. She wandered among the reference books. Could I work here? I might end up working here. She was disoriented at the thought. She contemplated the mural of old Antoine's with its gas chandeliers and

New Orleans was not a place she ever thought she would end up. It had never occurred to her that she would leave Indiana. Or proximity to the lake and Jill.

Centering prayer had fallen away. She could picture being there, at the monastery on Lake Michigan, with the sisters singing the psalms in the chapel and the long felt banner proclaiming good news that once had given her impetus. I have been trying to give birth to myself. Blessedness is not promised, it is not tied to any condition: it is the only reality. Even that language—a word like blessedness—seemed to belong to a territory from which it was now possible to defect. Aren't you going to Mass, Laurel had said, their first Sunday in New Orleans. I don't feel up to it, she said.

At night it seemed a long time until she could go back to the Internet café. She felt homesick. For Mox outside the bedroom door, his tail thumping. For Limbo waiting at the library steps. For the familiar riverine bottomland where birdfoot violets grew under the old oaks. And napping in Johnny's recliner. Or going to the round barns. Late at night she would call the house. She would wait until she knew he would be done in the big kitchen and she would use her calling card and hear the muffled click of the machine and her own voice saying, You know what to do. We'll get back to you ASAP. She would say, Things are going surprisingly well. Or, We're safe. Don't worry about us. They have job leads. It's hot as hell, but we knew that. In the afternoons I go to the library. I would love to talk to you. She would start to say, out of habit, Olive you, but that seemed too flip, too intimate. She would make a point of clearly enunciating, I love you.

When she made these calls the flat would be still except for the drone of the A/C. The girls would hardly breathe or stir behind their velour drape. She knew they overheard and she did not know what they made of it, her calls. She did not care. She had to keep trying.

On such a night Laurel came to her and took her hand. A reddish light shone into the flat from a music club across the street. Laurel's sling was a red triangle in the light. She said, I just remembered when you used to come in my room and sleep on the rug on the floor beside my bed. I'd forgotten that. It's connected in my mind with you being upset.

I had spells.

What do you want to do? What do *you* want?

I want everyone to be together.

I'll never go back. I never will.

They could not escape the history of having spent their lives together. Dwarf moments they had forgotten, moments that hardly registered in them as separate—touches and glances and corrections and encouragement and decisions and questions and defiance—made up what they were and what they could not escape being. Mother and daughter. Mother and child. It was different with Tin. He looked like Laurel around the eyes and Ruth Anne had given birth to him and breast-fed him. A biologist might confirm that there were still fetal cells from Tin floating in her body. But his history had little to do with her. She wanted to begin with now, but he might not.

You know how you always say, I feel it in my bones? Well, I feel it in my bones. I won't go back there.

Ruth Anne said, Why would you?

The light across the street laid down red like cellophane in the flat. Red books. Red linoleum. Laurel sat down beside her and whispered what was really on her mind. I just keep thinking—I can't get used to it—I could've been his sister. I'll never be. A sister.

# 25

Mairead said, Did you know that the word restaurant means to restore? It's from French and Latin.

It was a game they played. Outdoing each other.

Johnny said, Did you know that rhubarb originated in northern Asia? It was introduced in Europe in the fourteenth century. He dumped a freezer bag of thawed rhubarb chunks into a bowl of mashed strawberries.

That's a good one. I'll remember that one. When I've long forgotten what brought me here to begin with.

He'd been quit so many times. He knew what that felt like. The way they eased up on it. He wasn't going to pave the way. He was making his rounds of the churches and he needed her at night until his mission was complete.

He had shaved his mustache and was shocked every time he looked in the mirror. His face felt chubby and naked. And less expressive. He caught himself fifty times a day reaching up to tweak the ends of his mustache. Just as he caught himself fifty times a day looking up to imagine Ruthie or Laurel, and yes, even sometimes Oceana, at the door to the big kitchen. But their absence meant that he could do whatever he wanted late at night with no alibis. He thought about it that way: They were gone so that he could get on with his plan. What he was doing was separate from them. A personal act he could never get away with if they were around. Women were put on earth to stop such things.

He always had plenty of gas. And checked the air pressure on the tires. He wore a black T-shirt with long sleeves and loose black slacks. Black socks and black bowling shoes. A dark fleece cap that covered his hair. He kept the K-Bar in a leather sheath on his belt. His tools he laid out in the front seat of the pickup, handy. Like tools of a trade. The window punch. The cattle prod. The fiberglass handcuffs with which you could link troublemaker to troublemaker.

He had driven by during daylight hours to scope out hide sites and surveillance sites. He had walked around the neighborhoods and given dog biscuits to dogs that might bark overzealously at night. His truck was not a vehicle to draw attention to itself. It was nondescript, a truck to make you feel secure sneaking up on someone.

When the pies were ready to go in the oven, Johnny said, You don't mind taking over?

It was after eleven. The wait staff and kitchen help had gone. The lights were off in the dining room. Moxie was at the house and he needed a few minutes among the birch trees to do his business and then Johnny could enter the night. He would change his clothes while Mox was out and then he would be free.

Mr. Bond, if I minded I'd say so.

He felt a slight tug at the teasing way she said, Mr. Bond. She was a flirt and Johnny had been a flirt a long time ago. He knew those pleasures, that jeopardy. Mairead was a woman for whom flirting had ceased to be a deliberate act. Instead her flirtatiousness reflected like sunlight off her skin and teeth, muscle and lashes and bone. But nothing appealed to him quite like getting in the pickup and cruising for the troublemakers.

You'll lock up?

Not to worry, she said. See you tomorrow.

She came around the steel table and tucked her arm in his and walked him to the door. That close he could smell the cologne she used, a scent like rosemary. The pressure on his arm did not mean she wanted more than a walk to the door. He had gotten used to her.

Fifteen minutes later he slipped behind the wheel. He never used the same route. This particular night he drove out past the golf course and the college airport in the opposite direction of his intended destination. A single-engine prop plane flew not far above the trees, red and white lights winking, about to land. In a week or so he had gotten to know the county better than he ever had before. The roads were cut in straight lines across the prairie and you could get lost out there without a good sense of direction. Corn grew up on both sides of the gravel roads, leather green and tall. If he stopped anywhere to take in the night he might hear frogs in raucous uproar and not much more. Dark bundles—baby raccoons with no fear of cars—might mosey across the road. The night was pitchy, the moon not up.

He did not have to drive so far out of town as he did. Ruthie's messages had a way of needling him and he wanted to think them through before he had to be alert. He wanted to go over what she had said and answer what she had said. They had taken so long talking on the pedestrian bridge. I have to bear witness to my own life. To everything I've done. And, My guilt came alive, Johnny. It moved me. I couldn't sit still with it any longer. Almost everything they had talked about was cemented in place for him. It had not lost its power. But finally he would wind down and then head into town. To the Quaker Meeting House.

The Quakers met in a brick house across from a machine shop. The houses on either side were empty and FOR SALE BY OWNER signs were stuck in the unkempt yards. A block away there were one-story bungalows with splintery porches all within range of the rank odors coming from the plant down by the river that recycled paper into cardboard boxes. He did not know that neighborhood well but he had now and again carted boxes of used checks and bank statements to dump in the vat that the box company kept open twenty-four/seven. You drove up to the foot of a steep concrete apron and inside the rubber flaps at the top that served as gates you entered a hellish room where men in overalls with pitchforks monitored the soupy vat of acid and papers. All those important papers mashed into oblivion. He thought that he could park down that street and no one would take notice. It was a dark street: his hide site. A hide site should be established one terrain feature away from the objective. The Meeting House was situated on the other side of the animal shelter, which is what he could see from the hide site. A low-to-the-ground stucco building with opaque windows. To his benefit. He knew about the lilacs behind the Meeting House. Lilacs at least forty years old: his surveillance site. He rolled down his window and he heard the river slogging along on the other side of the box company. He heard the men who worked the vat laughing. That seemed like a lonely job and a filthy job and he thanked his lucky stars that he loved to cook.

He slipped the cattle prod into his hip pocket, the handcuffs in his front pocket. He did not latch the truck door. Catlike steps in the bowling shoes led him noiselessly to the lilacs, where he waited.

He was patient, watching for a dart or slip. A man who crouched to keep from being detected. He had gotten on one of their Web sites—the hatemongers—and on the Web site there were messages from all over the country. If the girls thought that they were safe in New Orleans they better think again. Human beings were only beginning to rise up out of the mire. He said that to Tuck and Tuck said, Three hundred years of recorded history is all we have in Indiana. Not much. Oh, you think it's a lot when you're in grade four, but I'm fifty-nine, Johnny, and I'm here to tell you, we don't know much. Tuck might have cancer and it was what every man dreaded and he kept reminding himself—and Johnny—that he was fifty-nine years old. Too young to die.

Traffic thumped on the river bridge a block to the north. It must be past midnight, he thought, and, Half-assed, this approach is half-assed. He could not stay out all night. He could not be in four places at once. The voice of reason said, You're kidding yourself. Still, the ritual gave order to his anger. He decided to make his way to the other churches and loop back later to the Quaker Meeting House. For some reason, he thought they were next. But intuition could not be relied upon; he had been led astray before by intuition. He had taken his rest on the rock ledge above the poppy fields and that had been a mistake and he had not known it until he saw the green enemy tracers in the sky and men right down the trail shooting and Jabber coming to warn him and Jabber shot. His fingers shot off and spurting blood like faucets. Intuition was not entirely reliable and that's why he had a system and he revolved around town and the county to this church and then that one, waiting and watching. He knew the look of a man being stealthy and he watched for that.

Until nearly four in the morning.

The birds were singing when he quit. The birds trilled and the gray-orange sky unfurled into what would become another hot day. Without Ruthie.

# 26

I think I'm having a spiritual crisis.

That might be good, Mom.

They waited for Oceana to step off the streetcar, icy drinks before them at a patio café on St. Charles Street where they could watch for her. She had begun her new job at the zoo. Laurel was not working yet. She wanted to teach again; she might apply to a Ph.D. program. Or talk to someone at an ad agency. That did not sound like her but she tried on this or that job in her imagination and Ruth Anne tried them on with her. Like playing dress-up when she was a child. Wearing a lace curtain for a shawl. Or pointy shoes they would not look twice at now. Ruth Anne did not want to be an impediment. She remained of good cheer, for the most part. We've only been here two weeks, Laurel would say. I'm still not myself.

That's what they had taken to saying about the attack. I'm not myself. It had started simply, honestly. Laurel had said it one night in the flat after they had shared much of a bottle of wine in front of a Steve Martin video, wanting to laugh. I'm not myself and I don't know when I will be. But the next time it was spoken with rueful glances and they used it to explain any divergence from former habits. Laurel smoked on the balcony with Oceana and when she came inside if Ruth Anne cast a questioning glance in her direction Laurel would say, I'm not myself.

It's *not* good. Ruth Anne stirred her limeade with a straw. I want to be strong for you and I want to see you settled and then I want to go home and have whatever collapses might be. Whatever. I need to go home.

Please don't go yet.

I won't if you don't want me to.

Laurel, sweet Laurel, leaned across the table and said, Why don't you come to meditation with us?

I might. Then she said, I want everyone in the same place: all my loved ones.

Mom.

What?

Love what is.

It was early evening, almost six. Women commuters stood with tired shoulders at the streetcar stop and tourists unfolded and folded maps and glared west up the tracks. A gang of girls went snaking pell-mell among the people waiting at the tracks. Loud, in tie-dyed halter tops and cutoffs, their toenails painted black or blue, they might have been twelve or thirteen. The tourists blanched and sucked in their collective breath but the commuters only sighed and held tight to their pocketbooks. Laurel watched for Oceana over Ruth Anne's shoulder and Ruth Anne was tired of that. Laurel was anxious anytime Oceana was out of sight.

The waitress came by, in a T-shirt printed with Sai Baba's words: TREAT JOY AND GRIEF, GAIN AND LOSS, WITH EQUAL FORTITUDE. Whatever happened to T-shirts that advertised Pearl Jam or certain brands of liquor? Everywhere she looked young people were declaring their spiritual bents, reminding her of arguments she had with herself. Chaff and wheat. Wild and tame. Good and evil. Calm and stormy. Dark and light. Heaven and hell. False and true. Fake and genuine. These were real differences, were they not? She did not understand what Laurel or Oceana or Jill or Thomas Merton meant by duality and getting beyond duality. The idea of getting beyond a state of mind implied the opposite of that state. If she brought this up, Laurel was quick to tangentially say, Even the pope went public about hell. He told some tourists at the Vatican that hell is not a geographical location. There's a news flash, Oceana said.

How does my scar look? Laurel raised a tad the scarf she wore to hide the scar.

It's healing.

When my hair grows back a wee bit more and I can get rid of this sling, I'm going to tend bar.

Laurel—

I need—to make—some money.

You have a master's degree.

That's like having a driver's license. And with a driver's license you can deliver pizza. If you have a good driving record.

Sweetie—

You know—

What?

Do you think she misunderstood the plan? I thought she'd be here an hour ago.

Are you getting hungry?

It's not that—

Is everything all right between you two?

Laurel clammed up. She popped on her sunglasses.

Well?

I don't know. Everything's out of kilter. That's what Dad would say, isn't it?

It's hard having me here.

Laurel shifted in the bistro chair; she straightened her spine and squared her shoulders and made a delicately disapproving face, a tight smile. Something in the way she shifted said, Oceana's coming.

The mood ebbed. Oceana had much to tell them about the job. With her injury they were keeping her at a computer for a while but after that she'd be outdoors with her hands in the soil. She liked that. Assistant landscape designer. It was not as idealistic as reclamation of the prairie but it was a good job.

Ruth Anne thought, I should go. It's time. But she ventured timidly, I want to try your meditation group. If it's all right.

All right, they said. Sounds good.

That night the redheaded artist called. She was staying in Vermont until October. Did they want the flat another month?

Everything's falling into place, Oceana said. She grabbed her cigarettes and stepped out on the balcony among the potted fiddlehead ferns and strings of beads that had been tossed there during Mardi Gras and left to weather. I like it here, she said over her shoulder. Come on.

Laurel gave her simple instructions before they went in.

Keep your eyes open. Use a meditation bench if you think your knees will hurt. Pay attention to your breaths and count them up to ten. Just pay attention. That's what you do when you center, isn't it? Jack Kornfield says that teaching yourself to meditate is like training a puppy. Just keep bringing the puppy back to the newspaper.

The group met in a one-room guest house with brand-new wall-to-wall carpeting the color of oysters. It was empty except for benches and zafus in ascetic rows against the blank walls. She felt apprehensive but the girls were reassuring. It'll be all right. If you don't feel comfortable with your eyes open just close them.

An hour is a long time.

She wanted to scratch her scalp and she wanted to stretch and she wanted to roll her shoulders and she wanted to be rid of her self: what she was thinking. Pride kept her from moving a centimeter. After a while she would've been not exactly satisfied but relieved if she had moved a finger's breadth. She did not think pride was the appropriate motivation but it was there nonetheless, staring at her every three minutes or so. An hour is a long time. My bones are killing me. My bones might be like hers. Like my mother's might have been. She might have been laughing when she was tossed like a stick out of the raft. She might have been soaked and shivering, her foot nudged under a baffle of the raft. They might have made love the night before. They might have been in love. It seemed so. When they danced. Cheek to cheek. How much it embarrassed me. A kiss would make me want to steal away. How I wish I'd been able to see them kissing later on. How I wish. How I wish. How I'd lie abed after the brush. My rear end stinging or my arms stinging or my head bruised. Or I'd make a world in the dinghy. Sail out to sea. To the St. Lawrence Seaway. That blue tugboat story. That story. I'm not sure I believe that story. What she wished for. Her heart hateful. Slut and stupid and fat and nigger. Nigger and wop. Wop and spic girls. I'm selling the candy store to queers. Perverts. Johnny's dad works on the farm with spics. He's no better than they are. Jews killed Christ. There's a reason for their suffering. Martin Luther King is too big for his own britches. Never mention his name. Never. If you ever. If you. Stupid and lazy. Lazy and lying. You're lying. I'll teach you to lie. I'll teach you. I'll teach you to drive. I'll teach you table manners. I'll teach you to boil an egg. I'll teach you to shave your legs. I'll teach you to pluck your eyebrows. I'll teach you to hem a skirt. I'll teach you to balance a checkbook. I'll teach you to sit still in church. I'll teach you to be polite. I'll teach you to cross me. I'll teach you to talk back. Don't look at me that way. I'm not mean. I'm not mean. Whatever my faults I'm not mean. I never want to be. Like her. I never want. I never want.

Sabbath. She reverted to saying Sabbath. Counting breaths did not work for her.

Oceana looked stuck on herself this morning and Laurel looked scared beside her. Laurel is not a baby anymore. She's not a baby. She's in love. And Oceana is not in love with her. You don't know that. You can see it in the little gestures. A look she has. How do we fall in love? It's chemical. Do they fall in love the way we do? Sister Michelle was on the verge of falling in love with me. I felt it. A breakdown of boundary. We broke down. She broke down more than I did. I had Johnny. Johnny was a figment of my imagination long before that. I wanted that boy at the fruit stand. He hadn't been drafted and he was available. We were callous about the boys who had gone. An engagement ring wasn't enough. The memory wasn't enough. Jill says self-recrimination is a version of pride. Still, stupid. Birth control pills would've left me free. Or a diaphragm. Birth control didn't help Sue-Sue. She had a diaphragm and it slipped out of her hands when she tried to put it in. It slipped out like something alive. But I wouldn't have Tin. It's all up to him. It has been a week a week a week a week since his last message and it might end like that. Just like that. Don't push. It won't do any good to push. I and my desire were one. One. I couldn't step out of desire. I can rest now. But that's hormonal. Then I couldn't rest. I was propelled by desire. Fueled by desire. Enslaved by it. I wanted me, enslaved by desire. That moonlight on my nakedness. In the loft with Vo. In the hammock with Johnny. And everyone says it causes all the suffering. Greed and lust are big ones. Christians know that. Buddhists don't understand how suffering is redemptive. That doesn't make sense. It's twisted. We talk about redemption too much. Easter is not the best feast. It could be. It could be. If only. These girls think they can do anything. She feminized the psalm and now I cannot think it the old way: Blessed is the woman, not the man. Blessed is the woman who walks not in the counsel of the wicked. Wrongheaded, Father Carroll said. He understood their cause. But no. You start with a fag decal and where will it end? Where will it end? I can never read that psalm without changing the words. The woman walks not. The woman meditates day and night. The woman is planted by streams of water. Father Carroll wanted to get rid of me and he has gotten rid of me. For now. If only they talked about metaphor from the pulpit. How many people think in metaphor? We focus on redemption. Redemption of the body that has failed you. So much water, so much mineral. We shore up whatever makes us unique. Me. Mine. And the damage. We cherish the damage. What they did to us. What they did to us makes us what we are. My damage is different from your damage. It's special damage. The body is the vessel for our damage and desire. Why would we want to come back in that? In what drags us down and makes life hard? I can't believe in the glory of the body's redemption. The rising again. I can't believe in the redemption of my body I have never been able to believe in that I've read too much to have that simple faith that simple heart like Félicité had.

Counting breaths did not work. The din kept on.

Sabbath, Sabbath.

Afterward Laurel said, How was it?

Hard, she said. It was hard.

# 27

Lightning blotted the Indianapolis sky. They watched it from the pickup and tried to decide what to do: drive the sixty miles home to Tarkington or wait it out.

Tuck said, Let's eat. Eat, drink, be merry.

Do you want to talk about it?

Not yet. He screwed up his mouth and mocked the doctor: This might not be pleasant. Might not be. Under-fucking-statement of the year.

Rain fell in slots at first. They slammed shut the doors of the pickup and dashed to the city market. It was the only city market left but Johnny remembered when there had been others. This one was the size of a high school basketball court, a cavernous brick building, lined inside with chest-high display cases. Dried fruit. Candies. Sausages and salamis, spiced and aged and greasy-white with fat. Coffee in glass bins and loose tea in open odoriferous cans. Cheeses. Johnny liked to check out the cheeses in their creamy and blue-veined variety. Ruth Anne loved a Welsh cheese made with ale and mustard seeds and any other time he would've bought a quarter pound for her. They got in line at a sandwich stand and studied the menu board.

The storm brewed darkly. They watched it through the big plate-glass windows. Market Square Arena was across the street and people streamed into the arena, shutting their umbrellas behind them. Chorus line after chorus line.

Remember when——?

Johnny said, Yeah. He knew that Tuck was thinking of a year when they had season tickets to the Pacers' games. They had discovered that pro ball didn't interest them as much as junior high and high school ball.

They ordered sandwiches and Kettle chips and beer. The boy at the counter wore latex gloves and a retrohippie headband woven with peace signs. He had a smooth, bland face and he danced and jived while he made the sandwiches. Johnny was glad the boy didn't work for him; his kind drove him nuts.

The arena looked busy for a weekday. There were black and gray cars, not quite limousines, but uniform enough to make Johnny think that someone famous had arrived, someone with an entourage.

Wonder what's up?

The sandwich boy said, It's the Dalai Lama himself.

Tuck said, Oh, yeah?

Johnny watched the boy slapping the honey mustard on rye and gently padding the bread with feathered sheets of ham and he was hungry to the bone, watching. Tuck's problem made him want to eat. It made him sick to think that Tuck might have cancer and thoughts of cancer naturally led to thoughts of dying and the best antidote to thoughts of dying, to Johnny, was good food.

The boy cut the sandwiches in half diagonally and into each half he rammed a toothpick tricked out with a black and white Indy 500 flag. He said, For your info. In the year 2327 an evil conqueror will arrive. The Dalai Lama's here to give, like, a Kalachakra. He brought out the beer from a fridge and he covered his hand with his apron and twisted off the caps. A teaching, he said, that will generate positive karma and allow whoever takes the teaching to be, like, reborn at the right time to fight the evil conqueror. He took a deep breath. Got to stop those evil conquerors.

Right on, Johnny said, offering a twenty-dollar bill. Keep the change.

At the table by the plate-glass window, Tuck peered at the arena across the street. He said, The Dalai Lama himself. How about that.

Outside the window was a trash can on which someone had painted MAY ALL BEINGS EXPERIENCE PROFOUND BLISS.

I wish Laurel knew about this, Johnny said.

Have you talked to her?

She called. Yeah, she called.

And?

They love it there.

What about Ruthie?

What about her?

When's she coming home?

Johnny enjoyed his ham sandwich and he enjoyed the beer. He chewed and swallowed and did not know what to say about Ruthie. He shrugged and went on eating. The storm got nasty and whatever was going on at the arena had probably begun. There were no more stragglers going in. Just inside the doors were men in suits, not his followers but men who protected him, Johnny surmised. He would need bodyguards. Johnny did not know much about the Dalai Lama. He'd heard a story or two on NPR, that was all. He would tell Laurel though. He wanted her to know that such things happened in Indiana. She could come home and receive a teaching from the Dalai Lama.

Tuck said, I called ex number two last night.

Johnny said, What in God's name for?

I wanted someone to know. Someone I'd been close to.

How'd it go?

She was nice. Real nice. We talked a long time. It might've been over an hour. Her husband was out of town and I think she felt comfortable talking. It almost felt like it used to. I guess you have to be on your last legs before they'll let their guard down.

Johnny had been through both of Tuck's breakups. Each time he had thought, This will never happen to me. He remembered a barbecue when ex number two had gone over the edge after too many highballs. I feel like a cave-dweller living here, she screamed. It's like all we do is watch the campfire. Tuck made excuses for her—she's got the novelty-seeking gene. When Tuck had come to him with a bottle of bourbon and tears in his eyes, Johnny had thought, This will never happen to me. He and Ruth Anne had been constant. But what had she said about that on the ped bridge? I haven't been constant for myself. I've been stuck. That was an exaggeration and they both knew it.

Maybe so, Tuckster, Johnny said. But don't put yourself in a position where they can hurt you.

Nothing can hurt me now. I might be dying.

⟿

Later that night he sat alone on the patio, debating. He'd had four hours' sleep the night before and it had been a long day on only four hours' sleep. Mairead was in Indy teaching little girls in leotards and he missed her but he didn't want to miss her. A slow night, he had sent everyone home by ten. He was tempted to forego his rounds. He had already put off baking for tomorrow and wanted to let Mox out on his own and spend the night, what was left of it, in bed with a stack of cooking magazines. He would have to unplug the phone. He didn't want to hear Ruthie's nightly message. It might be hard not to pick up and he did not want to talk to Ruthie. Not yet.

Autumn red licked the maple leaves already. The rain down south had been isolated and the holes he had dug were dry and crumbling. The new trees would go in; he needed a bit of free time was all. Mairead would quit soon and the week before the students and professors came back would be a quiet time and he planned to close up shop. He planned to sweat in the sun. There was an order he was making of his own design. The house was kept neat: a tight ship. He wouldn't let the sloth of the early summer take him over again. The swine of it. No. He was figuring out what made him feel right with the world. He missed the girls. He missed their affection. Laurel had called and said, We love it here, Dad. Will you come to visit us? I'll think about it. I will. Mom doesn't know I'm calling you. It's all right if she does. You should call her. I can't, sweetheart. Not yet.

The volley of thunder in the river valley made him decide to go. And the memory of adrenaline. It seemed unlikely he would get a clue, let alone catch someone, but if he woke up the next morning, having been lazy, and the front page sported another FAG CHURCH photo—well, he'd be sorely pissed at himself.

He dressed in black and he loved up Mox and he made sure he had plenty of fuel time and headed out toward the Episcopal church in Riley, a crossroads town that had become the hub of a new subdivision to the east of Tarkington. It was late. There wasn't much traffic. The radio had warned of severe thunderstorms—a false alarm so far. Not an unusual situation. Thunder and lightning had a way of hanging in the river valley for days and the farmers and the gardeners would watch the sky and pray for rain—he had the notion that most of them prayed for rain, not formally, but wishing, hoping, and finally, begging for intercession even if they did not deep down believe there was a power that could intercede. When pushed, people prayed. He imagined that the churches were sending out streams of prayer weekly about the troublemakers. He was the only one willing to go the distance.

Riley was dead. Lights were low in a couple houses; not a neon sign lit up the gas station or taverns. People probably left their doors unlocked at night. Not a wise decision. Riley was not what it used to be before the subdivision came in. Strangers had moved in and the people in Riley proper had not caught up with the danger of the times. He looped around the block and then another: a figure eight. At a speed that kept him in first gear. It was too quiet. He decided to park at the edge of town in a turnout beside the railroad tracks. Pine trees hid the truck from anyone passing by on the road. He took his gear and he took an empty gas can out of the pickup and he started walking the quarter mile back to town, thinking that if anyone stopped him he would say he hoped to find gas. He could lie with a straight face. He did not even think of it as lying. It was simply the necessary subterfuge.

The Episcopal church was at the other end of Riley on a side street, its white steeple twilight blue. He knew two possible surveillance sites. Riley brought to mind the town where he and his father had lived in the trailer and he did not want to think about his father or that trailer. He did not want to but a smell or a noise—the odor of late August, whatever it was, vegetables left too long in the garden and rotting or the fur cats had shed to deal with the heat or the slam of a screen door—the slightest thing might make him remember. That trailer with his father had been lonely. Without her. He never got used to it. He swore that he would have a home life that eliminated the possibility of that. A woman leaving. And yet here he was—

He tripped on the sidewalk that had been heaved up by winter frost and the gas can rattled against a tree whose roots came busting through the concrete. He caught himself and stood stock still. In shadow.

A woman opened the screen door of the rectory, her hair long and wavy like a girl in a fairy tale. His heart fluttered. More than anything he did not want to scare someone like her. He knew she was the pastor, a single woman in her thirties. They had met at a meeting of the reward committee. She wore a long T-shirt and what used to be called pedal pushers. She leaned out the screen door and said, What's going on? She could not see him. A white cat sat on the porch rail. The pastor said, Sugar, come on. I'm tired. She made a smoochy noise, a noise Johnny thought most folks reserved for calling in dogs. Like a white handkerchief the cat dove down off the rail and into the house. That spoiled it for him. He did not like knowing she was awake and he did not want to take the chance she'd see him and call the police.

He took cover in the park across the street, his second-best hide site. In an outhouse where he set the gas can down so quietly it did not make a sound. A half-moon cutout on the outhouse door allowed him a view of the church and the rectory. Upstairs at the rectory, her lights went out. The street lay quiet in shades and sediments of gray and blue. An owl hooted from somewhere west of him, deeper in the park. He waited, watching, his hand on the cattle prod in the pocket of his slacks. The woman at the screen door, her hair loose, brought up Ruthie and how she'd cut her hair. He had not given in to what he felt when he saw her with the short hair, but now he mourned the loss. He did not want to be the kind of man who wanted a woman to stay the same as she had been when they first met—but her hair! Her beauty. It had been longest when they lived in the trailer. He would wrap his hands in her hair. On TV they watched the Hanoi Taxi, the plane that brought the first forty POWs home from Gia Lam Airport to Travis Air Force Base. They would lounge on the plaid sofa that had come with the trailer and watch the news. He wrapped his hands in her long hair and said, You're all that's real to me. She had cut it a few inches when Laurel was a baby. She worked part-time at the library and she would pump her breast milk into a bottle and bring Laurel up to Brambles where Johnny would feed her the bottle when it was time. To keep Laurel from missing her too much Ruthie would line the baby seat with a shirt she'd worn—a T-shirt or an old chamois shirt of his, sky-blue—and her scent on the shirt would be like a pacifier to Laurel. What was the scent? Baby lotion and her own skin. Maybe garlic or orange juice. Homey. He could remember that like it was yesterday, but it wasn't. He did not understand time, the way it compressed and stretched, depending. What would time be like for Tuck if the doctor gave him the bad news? He felt helpless thinking that he should be there for Tuck. What could you do?

Within minutes he had to take a leak. The outhouse must have triggered the urge. He thought about Tuck, pissing blood. On the way home he had talked about Dioxin. Eighteen million gallons of Agent Orange were used in South Vietnam. President Kennedy gave the go-ahead, Tuck said in the pickup on the way home. Whatever you might think of him, he did plenty of stupid things. Just as he zipped his fly back up he heard footsteps, then whistling.

At the other outhouse whoever it was said, Knock, knock? And banged on the door. The whistling began again: "Amazing Grace." Johnny held his breath. Then it was his turn: Whoever it was knocked hard on his outhouse door, shaking the wood slats it was built of. The door opened, creaking.

He faced a security guard. He looked like a retired cop. In a cheap green uniform the color of canned peas. He wore a pistol in a holster. His round face shivered as he absorbed Johnny's presence.

What are you doin' in the ladies', man?

I didn't know it was the ladies', Johnny said.

Get out here.

Johnny stepped out, his gas can in hand.

What're you up to?

I needed some gas.

I know you, don't I?

You might. Can I show you my ID?

The security guard slipped his pistol out of its sheath. He waved it. Show me your ID.

Johnny set the gas can down and tugged his wallet from his hip pocket. He flipped it open and stuck his driver's license out where the guard could see it.

John R. Bond. Johnny Bond. I know. I know. My boy worked for you. He worked for you while he was in college. Dave Watson. You remember him? Isn't that right?

Johnny flipped his wallet shut and offered his hand. The man stared at his pistol quizzically and struggled to get it back in his holster. He pumped Johnny's hand.

That restaurant's yours. Out by the college airport.

So how's Dave?

Dave's fine. He's in Louisville. He got his degree in sociology. But he works for an outfit that tutors kids who can't learn to multiply. They began walking toward the street and the guard said, It's a quiet job out here. Spooky, even though you wouldn't think it would be. This is my second night. I'm here to guard the church and the environs. Cops're shared with Romney and they don't get over here but once in the middle of the night and not then if they've had any trouble in Romney.

I'm sorry if I gave you a start.

Aw, you didn't.

Give my best to Dave.

Will do.

Johnny walked the buckled sidewalk and then the grassy shoulder of the road and he got in the pickup, thinking, What a tinhorn, a bungler, Dave's dad would be if ever he had the chance to catch the troublemakers. It was after midnight. He rolled down the windows and heard the tall corn shaking and the insects hurled themselves against the windshield and crusted up. He could not see well out the windshield and decided that yes, going home was the best idea. He was tired. The security guard waving the pistol had shaken him. Ruthie's message of the night before rattled around in his brain. Laurel doesn't want me to leave just yet. They're out at a movie so I can say this: It makes me sad to see her feel afraid. I'm not sure what's going on with them. She says they might not stay together. People don't stay together, he thought, upshifting to gain speed, to get away from Riley and the guard. If you started looking around, that became a fact of life. He was one county road north of the airstrip where they held the Vietnam Vets gathering. That was not for him nor would it ever be.

At the foot of the cinder drive he saw a car at the house, its taillights on: Mairead's Volvo. The driver's-side door flung open. He did not want to see her. She might be leaving a note for him, quitting. A chickenshit way to do it. So let her. He swung the pickup back out into the road, as if he were some stranger turning around, someone who'd lost his way. He went back into town, past the campus. They had begun turning on the fountains, for the students who might come back early. A fountain splashed and gurgled: he heard it while he stopped at a fourway. He passed St. Joan's and the rectory there. Father Carroll's light was still on, a cold fluorescent reading lamp. Now there was a lonely life: never to have known love. Or maybe he had. Maybe he had his own secrets. Johnny did not know where he was headed but he crossed the river and then it seemed obvious: the Quaker Meeting House. His hide site there was his favorite. He enjoyed sitting in the darkened truck next to the box factory. He took some odd and surprising pleasure from the breeze blowing the flaps and allowing him a glimpse into the vat room. Seeing the men in coveralls working late at night. Thinking of what their industrial lives were like. A snack van pulling around to the door at five in the morning to sell them bad coffee and pastries. How glad they'd be to see the snack van. He wanted Tuck to see the place late at night. It was like the post office murals from the WPA days.

He stopped in the dark street and he got out a few dog treats and put them in his shirt pocket. He waited a while. The lilacs were not in bloom but he knew they were lilacs and he knew that they were dense enough to conceal him. Now that an hour had passed, the scrimmage with the security guard gave him courage. That was probably the worst moment he would have all night. A semi hauled itself over the river bridge and screeched to a stop at a red light not far away. Downtown. This neighborhood was close to downtown but it did not have the ambience of downtown. Downtown was what everyone called charming. This neighborhood was utilitarian. People here let their license plates expire. There were too many dogs and he thought there ought to be a law about how many dogs could live on a block. The dogs had gotten used to him. He pulled on his cap and got out and shut the door with a controlled shove.

He walked soundlessly to the alley and ducked into the old lilacs that grew in the ten feet of useless yard between the shelter and the Meeting House. In his black clothes he disappeared into the shadow and he could see the back wall of the Meeting House. He could see the swing set in the side yard. Cars and trucks were parked along the street in front of the Meeting House and no one was about. He would give Mairead time to drive away. She might smoke a cigarette there before she'd leave. He felt for the K-Bar on his belt. He felt for the cattle prod in one pocket, the handcuffs in the other. This was an exercise but he should do everything for real. In case he should get lucky. No sense thinking he would get lucky but you never knew. His luck might change. When he looked where he had come from the vat men were on break and the snack van had arrived. Its tube light was inviting; a Mexican man had opened the window and he handed out ice cream bars and burritos wrapped in silver paper. And what if he did see someone? Who's to say they were connected in any way to what had happened to Laurel and Oceana? He tried not to give in to feeling silly, dressed in black, hiding in the old lilacs. He watched the vat men for a moment.

Peripherally, a sudden movement caught his eye: somebody darting between the parked cars in front of the Meeting House. Adrenaline set him up; it felt as if it poured from him the way sweat does. Had he imagined it? He did not want to give up his surveillance site. A likely place for a paint job would be the side wall he could not see. It had no windows. On a street that got more traffic. That very fact had made it hard to find a place of concealment around that side. He had to go there. He knew how to rustle out of the lilacs without the sound a rustle makes. The sound he made seemed to mingle with the sound the trees made. The leaves of summer in a breeze you could hardly feel. Shrub roses grew haywire between him and the side wall.

The man—it was a loner—came in a hoodlum's minuet around the west side of the building, his shape clearly visible. He crouched and came up on the side wall and he did not even take a cursory look around before he got out his spray paint and began.

Johnny let him get into it. He let him get out FAG.

He crept around the roses and at an obtuse angle came within a few yards. Pleased at the tightness and deliberateness of his body. What he could count on. He lunged and grabbed the man, grabbed him good. The can of paint flew on a bold trajectory across the roses. Together they rolled to the ground.

You *cock*sucker, Johnny grunted. His arm locked around his neck.

The man scrambled beneath him and cried out, unintelligibly. He was young and strong but scared. Johnny was scared and overjoyed. Breathing hard. Yes, yes, yes, yes, yes. You cocksucker. He yelled it that time and he knew that the vat men heard and might be curious and that soon his secret would not be secret anymore and neither would the troublemaker's.

He flung him over and saw what made perfect sense, even though he was taken aback: Limbo. His enemy. He pinned him down, his fists on his shoulders. Breathing hard. They both breathed hard. Limbo's head bounced side to side. Limbo whimpered, Don't hurt me, don't hurt me, don't. I'm the one what called the police. Mister Bond. Mister Bond. I called them. Don't kill me. Don't. Those guys said so. I want to be in a band with them. Mister Bond, Mister Bond—

You shithead, Limbo. Whatever strength that Limbo had seeped out of him in fear. Johnny sat on him. He jerked the handcuffs from his pocket and they were fiberglass and like fish bones in the little light there was from the industrial sky.

Put out your hands.

Limbo did so.

Johnny managed to snap the handcuffs on him. Don't get up. You've got a story to tell. He reached into Limbo's pocket and fished out his cell phone and called 911. Limbo knelt before him; Johnny gripped the back of his shirt. With one hand he tossed his own cap into the roses. He wanted to look presentable, like the upstanding citizen he was.

Mister Bond, I'm sorry. I'm sorry, Limbo cried.

I understand that, Limbo.

I called the police.

You can tell it when they get here.

A squad car poked down the alley, with no special effects. It might have been any other car but Johnny could see the town seal on the side and the unlit red, white, and blue bar on the roof. Two officers got out, alert.

Over here, Johnny said.

Well, well, the older cop said. His black uniform was starched and pleated. He looked like he'd shaved within the hour.

Johnny reached out to shake his hand and said, Johnny Bond. The cop wrote something in a pocket notebook, ignoring him.

The younger one—a skinny kid with his badge about to fall off—took Limbo's arm and stood him upright and said, Looks like you earned yourself a reward—

The older cop said, Are you responsible for those handcuffs?

You betcha, Johnny said.

You put them on him?

Yes, sir.

I'm going to have to take you in. Unless you're deputized. False im-
prisonment's the charge. You don't have a right to slap handcuffs on
anyone. No matter what.


Johnny's cell was in the old wing of the town jail.

The tile in the hallway had rotted in spots. Graffiti wove in banners
and circles on the cell wall. Obscenities and declarations. Bars covered
the high transom window that might open into an alley. He tried to figure where he was in relation to the town layout but they had made two
turns down short corridors and his sense of direction was screwed up.
No one else was on his wing. He had called Tuck and he had been told
he would be released in the morning on his own recognizance. He was
Johnny Bond and, given his life, he could be construed to be a pillar of
the community. He could be construed to be trustworthy. He did not
deserve to be in jail and he did not harken back to when he had been in
prison. It crossed his mind but this was not the same and he knew that.
He knew the difference between then and now. The jail was an extension of the street and the town and just another place a body might end
up for a little while. This is America, he told himself. I can be released
on my own recognizance. He lay on a top bunk that was covered with a
mushroom-colored blanket. He brushed a spider web from the ceiling
just above his face.

It was worth it.

That moment when he lunged at Limbo. When he encircled his
wrists with the handcuffs like bones.

He heard an echo of himself saying, Cocksucker, and he knew that
Laurel would not approve of that. It was a moment when you don't
give much thought to what you're saying. He would leave that out.

He was sorry for Limbo but it had been worth it. Whoever they
were, they had promised Limbo the moon to do what he was about to
do. They had promised the moon to a kid who couldn't read at a sixth-
grade level. A kid who missed Ruth Anne. They had that in common
but that was all. She made me want to be kind to him and I was. He sure
liked that pecan pie. He would be all right. Limbo would be all right if
he would tell the truth. He knew the difference. Ruth Anne would be

shocked and unbelieving and he wanted to be the one to tell her and he thought that if they would not come home he would go down there. This was not a story to tell on the phone. He wanted to see their faces when he told them.

Ruth Anne, you'll see. It was kids. They were over seventeen but they were kids. I was right about that. But kids have to be stopped. They have to be curtailed and taught what's right. Jail was where they belonged to start with and he wanted them prosecuted to the fullest extent. Ruthie. I did it for you. I did. Tuck talks about his funeral. What he wants. What music. The casket closed. He wants to look back on certain things. The boys he coached and not the games they won but how they stretched themselves for him. He wants to know he's been a good friend. He's got no kids. No kids to care. He wants to look back knowing people trusted him. You can't help but wonder what you'll want yourself when he talks about it. What I want. What I want is what I've always wanted. A reliable life. I want to know I never did a thing to make you anxious or unhappy. Until that night. I'll take that back. I'll take it back. I keep secrets that might hurt you. That's my way and it's what I want to be remembered for. It'll be my life I'm responsible for, not yours. What you've done will be yours to consider and make sense of. When I'm dying I doubt I'll think about how hard I worked or the money I made and spent. Or the secrets I take with me. What he never wanted to recall. How hard it was. His secrets were about how hard it was. The long walk with the Bible girl. She wasn't pretty. She wasn't anything outstanding in what they called the real world beyond southeast Asia, but she achieved a sharp focus, a clarity, every day they slogged between their captors. She had grown up a preacher's daughter at a mission near Madras and she had been bribed with candy to memorize Bible verses and that talent kept her sane during the long walk from the first camp to the second and it kept him sane too. He never told her about his food lists. He did not think he had been wicked, not then or ever. He considered this partly luck. Some men are placed in wicked circumstances. He had wanted to discuss that with the girl but rifle butts against their kidneys discouraged them from talking. At the second camp she did not have the strength to recite. She was skin and bones and he would lift her from the hammock when she had to shit. It had come to that. He had wanted her to die. To get it over with. That was one se-cret and it occurred to him that if he thought about it now he might not have to think about it on his deathbed.

Not secrets.

What we make together, Ruthie: whatever it is: I'll think about that.

I'll think that it's been worth it.

# 28

Pearly white moths clung to the back screen door like tiny envelopes. The girls were at the kitchen table. Laurel flung up her arms and sculled air with her hands. Dad's been calling you.

Ruth Anne said, When? She dropped her purse—frowning—and handed Laurel bagels in a waxed paper sack. When?

Now! A few minutes ago.

Her hands trembled at the phone. She punched in all the numbers and gazed at her strange self in the mirror over the mantel. Her hair was its natural dove gray. She did not wear lipstick anymore and wondered if she ever would again. Her fingers did not ache. Her bones seemed to like the southern weather, the ease with which she could walk out the door and know that even if she stayed until the winter no gale would freeze the flesh or make her joints resist. She walked miles every day, in spite of the tropical heat. Was it a phase she was going through? Did you still go through phases at her age?

The machine picked up and she said, I'm sorry I missed your call. I'll wait for you to call me back.

Oceana set before her what they called Vietnam coffee in a glass swirling with sweetened condensed milk. Ruth Anne could only watch the swirl; she did not drink.

What took you so long?

I printed out Tin's messages.

Laurel brightened at that.

He wants to meet you.

He's coming here?

Yes. He is. If you're ready.

I *am* ready.

He and Lee Ann are going to Houston to visit family. They'll stop here for a day or two. He's made up his mind. She stirred the sugary milk into the coffee. And I stopped in a church. She hesitated. I sort of surprised myself. The doors were open and I heard the singing and went in. It was a song I remember well. You might remember it too.

What song?

"O Taste and See."

I think I remember it.

It's from Psalm 34. God is close to the brokenhearted. Near to those crushed in spirit. She could not speak the words they waited to hear— why the song meant so much to her. Now she knew that brokenhearted was where she went in meditation. Call it centering prayer or call it meditation. Call it what you will. It broke you. It left you free. You finally face your wounds. Where God is. Where God is merciful. How frail we are in church, even though sometimes the language sounds boastful. We get confused: some stories confuse us. Language fails us. Language is the shadow of the mystery. She had gone to communion and the familiar wafer and the nip of red wine nearly spoke: Stop sequestering yourself. Jill always warns, You can only have one practice. That might be true. She might be right. Like having one lover. There is only so much time for practice. But you can listen to Buddha and Jesus and their conversation that might river for all time. Brothers, Thich Nhat Hanh calls them. She could not bring herself to speak a word of this. But she would, she would. This was what they shared: to be able to talk of all that is seen and unseen. From blues bars to the Holy Spirit. The soulful journey had been theirs and she would never regret the weeks she'd spent with them in the flat above Nance's Beauty Bar.

He says I'll receive a wedding invitation. Lee Ann wants her children to have all the grandmothers possible.

So you'll go?

They made an agreement with Vo's wife. I'm not allowed to sit with the family.

Laurel made a sad face.

It's all right. I'm not—really—a part of their family. I'm fine to move slowly.

The telephone rang and for a fraction of a moment—astonished fraction, as if the phone had never rung before—they stared at it. Ruth Anne lifted the receiver and said, Hello. Then, Johnny—

Oceana and Laurel gathered their fanny packs and the crutches and umbrellas and lunch bags. The pearly white moths on the screen door were not the least bit disturbed by their gracious departure. Laurel blew her a kiss as she backed out the door.

Johnny was talking. I feel like I never get enough sleep when you're gone. Do you sleep all right?

Sometimes.

The girls tapped down the back wooden steps—Laurel lightly, Oceana deliberately, her cast thudding—and Ruth Anne paced to the back windows and watched them petting the butterscotch cocker spaniel kept by Nance down below where sunflowers nodded at the bottom step.

I've got some big news.

What's your big news?

I have to see you to tell you.

Tell me now.

It's my secret. It's the best secret. I want to see the girls and you and I want to tell you when I see you.

What're you up to?

I'm coming down there. I love you.

So there would be reconciliation. She felt naked, with no place to hide and she had come to New Orleans to hide from Johnny. That had become clear to her: how much she had needed the security of hiding.

When'll that be, Johnny?

Soon. It'll be soon.

She didn't say anything. She heard the clang of pot against sink, pot against burner, knife against sharpener, and voices, kitchen voices.

I thought about what you said.

She said, What part?

About bearing witness to your life.

I still have to.

Maybe you do.

I know whatever I decide is for me. No one else has to do what I do.

That's fine. That's fine for now. We'll see how it goes. Then he lowered his voice. He said, Tuck's not too well.

What's wrong with Tuck?

Prostate cancer.

Oh, Johnny. I'm sorry. He's so young.

I took him to the doctor. He won't be able to coach this fall. He's in a bad way.

I'm really sorry.

Do you want to come home?

Oceana was fond of quoting the Dalai Lama: A place initially becomes holy by the power of the individual spiritual practitioner who lives there. That power charges a place. The place in turn can charge the individuals who visit. New Orleans, the seat of hedonism, had become the one seat of meditation. But home, she thought, home. Home is charged, home is electric, magnetic, live, hot. It's where she had the most to learn.

I want to. Yes. I want to come home.

Ruthie—

Yes?

She waited to see what he might say. She was curious and she thought that whatever he said, it would make a difference. All the declarations Johnny made had weight and substance. He spoke his truth.

Our life together—that saves me.


She needed a special box for her documents.

At the antique store on the corner she bought an oval paper box printed with palm trees and brought it back to the flat. She put on music; she had not felt like listening to music in a long time, but now she felt the leaning toward joy, and music would underpin that leaning. She wanted wordless music—a CD she found in the tenant's CD player, the London Symphony, a Brahms concerto, the questioning violins and their tender answers—so that all the words of her documentation would glister and sing without interference. She read her letters to Aunt Teensy again and tied them with a white hair ribbon and placed them in the bottom of the box. Aunt Teensy would have to be tended to but now she knew what to expect. She was being given the chance to help another human being make passage from this world. That was enough. Aunt Teensy would be Aunt Teensy, no matter what. Then, the photograph went on top of the letters. Eventually she wanted it framed and out on her desk in the sunroom. She wanted a copy for Tin and a copy for Laurel. And *The Tale of Kieu* would go in the box. She opened it and read near the ending once again.

> *Our karma we must carry as our lot—*
> *Let's stop decrying Heaven's whims and quirks.*

At the balcony window she watched the rain ring down. Shoppers ran from shop to shop. She made a pot of tea—Earl Grey—and every pot of tea she might make for at least a while would lift the memory of Vo from memory's vault. She could contain that too. Without secrets she had more room for whatever might happen and whatever had happened. Secrets with their regret and melancholy required too much psychic room. She unfolded the e-mail messages and thumbed through to the brand-new one, which brought her news she had never expected to receive.

Dear Ruth Anne,

My father says you cried for days before you left. He says that you were not consolable. My grandmother tried to find a broker to extend your visa but buying and selling visas and other official papers had become next to impossible for people of our income. You were a danger to the family. My grandmother was required to declare herself. Later on we had the right residency permits but if you had been there we might have been killed. Many people were dragged into the street and shot. My grandmother had to burn her dresses and the Frenchman's uniform. She had to dress in peasant clothes. She had to trim her long red nails. I was six years old and I remember those nails. And the books were burned. I am sorry to have to tell you that. I know you both held the books in high esteem. "White Christmas" was playing on the radio when Saigon fell. I cannot hear this song today. We hid in the closet. You remember my grandmother's closet. In many cities refugees fled the Communists. But there was nowhere to flee. Military uniforms and carts and radios were abandoned on the roads. When the Communists marched into Saigon the bridge was strewn like carpet with the uniforms of the South Vietnamese soldiers. Neighbors set upon neighbors, spying, but my father taught

English clandestinely to make a little money. He might have been imprisoned for that, but we were lucky. I learned to paint van Gogh's *Starry Night* when I was not in school. I sold them on the street to Russians. Her land she shared with her sister near Dalat was confiscated and we were required to grow only peppers for export. She gave the authorities gold jewelry she brought from Paris and they left us the house and a small plot. For a long time we ate nothing but rice. Rice is not enough to keep you from feeling hungry. You ask why I decided to look for you. That day on the beach I told you that I wanted to know my medical history. Lee Ann and I will have children and we need to know such things. But time goes on. Over these months I have realized that there is another reason. I fell in love with Lee Ann. And knowing love the way I do I wanted to know you. My father said he loved you.

She put the messages away in the oval box. Imagining Laurel years from now owning the box. The New Orleans box. She and Tin might sit down and read through it together. They will know their mother. What is left to say to children when they're grown if not the truth?

Laurel telephoned and said, What did he want?

He won't say. But he's coming down here for a visit. He's got something he wants to tell us.

What's the big secret?

I don't have a clue. But he was in good spirits. Then, How are you, sweetie?

I'm all right. I'm going to start that job tonight. Look: Don't stay for me. Dad needs you.

He does need me. And I need him. Or the person I am with him.

Tin and Dad might be here at the same time.

Are you ready for that?

It's what you wanted. You know what they say: Be careful what you wish for.

She imagined the wedding. The return to the church in Cortland. She would be the stranger in the back pew. Would they hang the red pennants she remembered from Vietnamese weddings? She had seen brides in Vietnam in golden dresses. The men in Western suits. There had still been weddings and babies born and lovers in the parks and alleys. In spite of the raw cruelty. The grisly life that words could do no justice to. In spite of that. She would be curious about Vo and his wife and even a glimpse might round out her thoughts of them. Would she hold his arm the way she had? Would their fingers entwine with the sentimentality of the wedding? Maybe Johnny would drive up to Michigan with her. She could ask; no harm in asking. He might visit Aunt Teensy while she attended the wedding. Later they might cruise along the Blue Star Highway and watch the sunset. They might return to Pier Cove and even though the beach had eroded and residents had laid out rubber-tire riprap to shore it up, the lake would be there, big and blue. You could count on it. They were not finished with weeping, she knew that. You're my home, Ruthie. You're all that's real to me. Our life together—that saves me. They loved September at home. The copper-red moon. Black walnuts falling from the trees. A trip to the round barns. Where will we go from here?

What she used to think of as the past dissolved into the present. The past was no longer a weapon poised at her perimeter. She lived it, becoming. Evolving. Those fetal cells of Tin and Laurel were inside her body. As she was in them. Tin had found her and they had come this far: far enough to share a wedding.

She went to check the mailbox. Blessed is the woman, she thought, who walks not in the counsel of the wicked, nor stands in the way of sinners, nor sits in the seat of scoffers, but her delight is in the law of the Lord, the law of mystery, she corrected, adding her own two cents worth to Scripture, and on that law she meditates day and night. She is like a tree planted by streams of water, that yields its fruit in its season, and its leaf does not wither. In all that she does, she prospers. She felt content, as if she were about to embark on the grand pardon. Where forgiveness is the coin of the realm.

She spoke out loud to her own reflection in the mirror above the mantel: May I embrace you?

Down on the street the invitation was in the mailbox. She tucked it under her shirt. A stylist from Nance's Beauty Bar swept rainwater toward the curb with a straw broom. It gone to take us, she said. Take us right in the flood.

Ruth Anne laughed. I'm on the second floor and glad of it.

In the flat she boiled more water. She opened the vellum envelope and the envelope inside of that. Tin Tran. Who might not have been born, given a degree's change of course.

The wedding would be a story to remember. She thought of all the stories she had read to Vo. "Araby." "Sonny's Blues." "Happiness." "Barn Burning." And the novels. *The Hunchback of Notre Dame. The Heart Is a Lonely Hunter.* How they had longed for stories. Stories had been their proving ground. They measured and tasted love in stories. Hate stood a test. And grief. Compassion came of that enchantment. Stories bridged the differences between them. More than lying tipsy under the Eiffel Tower might have. She opened *The Tale of Kieu* from the nineteenth century and read the last lines. May these crude words, culled one by one and strung, beguile an hour or two of your long night.

# ACKNOWLEDGMENTS

I owe a debt to the authors and editors of many books about what the Vietnamese call the American War, particularly the collections of first-person narratives. I'm grateful to the people who gave me telephone interviews and corresponded by e-mail. Special thanks to Rik Nelson, Mike Benge, Patricia Bowen, Dan Leaty, George Turner, Murray Shugars, John Barnes, and Doug Van Dang. Any errors I have made are my own, not theirs, for they were thorough and willing respondents.

I could not have written *In the River Sweet* without the friendship of Diem Tuan, my guide while I traveled in Vietnam. Together we sat in his university library in Ho Chi Minh City and looked at the terrible photos of the war. We took the soulful journey.

Part of this book was written while I was a fellow in the Center for Creative Endeavor at Purdue University. I'm grateful for the support I have always been afforded by the School of Liberal Arts at Purdue University. Thanks go, as well, to Faye Bender, LuAnn Walther, and my former department head, Tom Adler. And for his unflagging sustenance, I'm grateful to my husband, S. K. Robisch.

# ABOUT THE AUTHOR

Patricia Henley's first novel, *Hummingbird House,* was a finalist for the 1999 National Book Award and *The New Yorker* Best Fiction Book Award. Henley has also written two books of poetry, *Learning to Die* and *Back Roads,* and three story collections: *Friday Night at Silver Star,* which won the 1985 Montana Arts Council First Book Award; *The Secret of Cartwheels;* and *Worship of the Common Heart: New and Selected Stories.* Her stories have been published in such magazines as *The Atlantic Monthly, Ploughshares, The Missouri Review, The Boston Globe Sunday Magazine,* and *Northwest Review,* and anthologized in *The Best American Short Stories* and *The Pushcart Prize* anthology. Henley lives in West Lafayette, Indiana, where she teaches in the M.F.A. Creative Writing Program at Purdue University.